What others are saying

"The Unwilling is a great new take on vampires that comes as a breath of fresh air among many such stories. The characters are immediately likable and the story grand, stretching over the centuries though still managing to feel relevant to today. The action and the emotions feel real and the journey that the two main characters make towards redemption and towards each other was an exhilarating ride. A satisfying reading experience that made me thirsty for another installment."
—Michael Young, author of *The Last Archangel* and *The Canticle Kingdom*

"The Unwilling is a fresh approach to a well-traveled theme. The excellent character development melded well with an engaging plot, drawing me in immediately. Loved it!"
—Loretta Julander, Hooper, UT

"An LDS vampire story: what a concept! This is an interesting page turner that has all the twists and turns of a mystery novel, with a perspective that makes Church members sit and pay attention. A great read!"
—Rick Steadman, Salt Lake City, UT

"In a world awash with vampire stories, this one was really unique. With the main character doing his best to do what is right."
—Suzanne Sharp, Layton, UT

"It was a fun read with twists I never expected."
—Craig Foster, Layton, UT

"Ever read a book that's so gripping from chapter to chapter that you can't put it down? You're holding one now!"
—John Abercrombie, Bountiful, UT

"The Unwilling is a very interesting and engrossing read. A fresh take on old tale, with a touch of new elements. Truly an enjoyable and thoughtful book."
—Nina Doxey, Roy, UT

"Vampires as they should be and yet different than what I had expected! Thought-provoking and gripping plot. I loved it!"
—Olya Polazhynets, Khust, Ukraine

The Unwilling

The Children of Lilith
Volume I

The Unwilling

C. David Belt

ISBN: 978-1-4276-9521-5

Cover design: Ben Savage

PARABLES
PO Box 58
Woodsboro, MD 21798
http://www.parablespub.com
parables@parablespub.com

*For Cindy, who is both
my Sharon and my Moira.*

I am Death.
I am Hell.
I am Damnation.
I am Corruption Incarnate.
I am a Daughter of Lilith.
Look into my eyes and see the hellfire that awaits ye.

Moira MacDonald

To each there comes in their lifetime a special moment when they are figuratively tapped on the shoulder and offered the chance to do a very special thing, unique to them and fitted to their talents. What a tragedy if that moment finds them unprepared or unqualified for that which could have been their finest hour.

Sir Winston S. Churchill

Chapter 1

Six Months Ago

C arl! I'm in trouble!" It was Julie's voice on the answering machine. I was mildly surprised there was room left on the machine to record anything. I hadn't answered the phone in days. Not since the funeral. What did *not* surprise me was that she was in trouble.

She communicated with me only when she was in trouble.

I should have cared. I should have felt *something*.

But I felt nothing.

At least not for Julie. Not then.

Sharon was gone.

Lucy was gone.

April was gone.

Joseph was gone.

They were run down by a stoned teenager on a joyride as they had gone for one of Sharon's "walks."

Trouble? What did any of it matter anymore? When had *any* of it mattered? Ever?

"Please pick up! Please, *please* be there!" She sounded panicked.

No, more than panicked: she sounded *terrified*.

"Carl! Pick up! . . . going to *kill* me!"

Yep. I'd heard *that* before. Julie had the *worst* taste in men. She had an unerring talent for picking monsters. They would beat her. Then I would plead with her to leave them. But she always defended the creeps. She'd tell me that *I* was being a bully, that I didn't *trust* her, that I didn't *understand* her, that I was just *judging* her, that I didn't approve of her lifestyle . . . that I had *never* approved of her. Then she'd hang up and not return my calls for a while. Eventually she'd call back. The cycle would repeat with increasing intensity until, eventually, it would escalate to the point where she would tell me that Andy, Rob, Joe, or

1

insert-name-here was going to *kill* her. Then I would go and help her move out.

It didn't matter. She always went back to them. Oh, she had married and divorced a couple of them. Lived with a few more. I'd taught a few of them the *wisdom* to be found in never touching her again. Didn't matter. She always found a *new* creep. Or a new one found *her.* They could see it in her eyes, her body language. Here was a lamb *willing* for the slaughter, a punching bag so desperate to have a man in her life that she would put up with anything.

It'd been months since I'd heard from her. That meant she had a new man in her life and things hadn't escalated . . . yet.

Well, I guessed they finally had.

I was just not in the mood to deal with it. I couldn't. Not then. Maybe never again.

"She's going to kill me!"

She? OK . . . *that* was new. Had Julie given up on men and found a *woman* to beat her up and then tell her she was sorry and beg her to stay?

"Carl! Pick up! If she finds me, she'll *kill* me!"

I didn't *want* to care. I wanted to just sit there in the darkness of my empty family room and feel nothing.

But old habits and all that.

Ah, crap.

I picked up. "Hi, Jules."

"Carl! Thank God! I need help! She's . . ."

"Where are you?"

"Some bar."

Big surprise. When she decided to call, it was always from "some bar." I could hear music playing in the background. It sounded like something loud with lots of bass, lots of screaming, and not much of a tune.

"I don't know the name," she said quickly. "It's on Fifth or Sixth South and State, I think. You gotta come and get me!"

"OK."

"Carl, hurry! She's *hunting* me!"

Hunting? That was an odd word.

"Jules," I said, "get me the name of the bar."

"I don't know it!"

"Look on a napkin."

"I don't have one. I don't have a drink. Carl! Hurry!"

No drink? That *was* a first. Usually, by the time she called, she was already well into it. And, usually, by the time I got to "some bar," Julie was hammered.

"Look at a window. Ask the bartender."

"I can't! Carl! I'm *scared*! Please come get me!"

"OK, Jules. I'm on my way. I'll have my cell."

I picked myself up off the couch, pulled on my pants, shoved my feet into my tennis shoes, and headed to the garage. I squeezed past the gray minivan. Why was that still there? Why hadn't I sold it? Or abandoned it? What did I need a minivan for? I got into my car and pulled out of the garage. I pushed the button and closed the garage out of habit. Why bother?

I'd been on the road for thirty minutes or so, driving by reflex, not thinking about anything, not *wanting* to think about anything, when my sister called again.

Good thing she called. I would have missed the exit at that rate.

"*She's here!*" It was a hiss. "Carl, she's just sitting there staring at me."

"Don't stare back."

"I won't! That's how she'll get me! If she catches my eye, I won't be able to look away! She can make me do *anything*!"

Yuck! I did not want to hear that!

"Stay in the open. Stay with *people*."

"That won't stop Rebecca! She can make you do anything she wants if she catches your eye . . . or speaks your name."

I wanted to gag. "Then don't look at her. Don't talk to her."

"Not just me. *Anyone!*"

"Jules, I'm on my way. I'll be there in ten minutes."

"I don't have ten minutes! I'll be *dead*!"

This wasn't her usual melodrama. She sounded genuinely frightened.

"Jules," I said, "she's not going to kill you in the middle of a crowd of people."

"She can make them do anything she wants."

"Jules, I get it. You're attracted to this woman, but nobody . . ."

"*Rebecca?* No! Not Rebecca! *Michael!*"

"Michael? Who's Michael?"

"My lover." Her voice took on a different tone. "My *Master.*" I could *hear* the capitalization, the awe. That word had special meaning for her.

But me? I was completely lost. "Who's Rebecca?"

"Michael's wife."

Oh, crap. This was a first.

"His wife?" I said.

"One of them."

Polygamy? An image popped into my head of Julie wearing a long pioneer dress with her hair flipped up in the front like those Texas women I'd seen on the news. When it came to men, Jules could really pick them.

"A cult?" I asked. At this point, I really didn't want to know, but if I could keep her talking, I might keep her calm . . . keep her from bolting.

"Yes. That's what we call it."

I drove on in stunned silence. I didn't have any idea what to say.

It was time to start looking for the bar.

"Jules, stay put. Stay in plain sight. I'm almost there." I hung up.

I turned onto State Street and right away saw a bar that looked promising. I even found a parking space.

A parking space in downtown Salt Lake? A modern-day miracle.

I hated going into these places, not just because I don't *drink* myself and I find the atmosphere repugnant, but mainly because, since my years in the Air Force with its mandatory beer calls (even for non-drinkers like me), *every single time* I'd been in a bar, I had gone there for one and only one reason: to pick up my sister. This place was no different than all the rest. It was about as generic as they came. Neon beer signs provided most of the decor. It had the usual low lighting, the acrid, choking stench of cigarettes, the rotten smell of beer, and, of course, some horrible heavy metal playing on a juke box. *At least it wasn't country or rap.* It didn't even have the usually obligatory pool table or dart board. This was no pub; this was a *bar:* a place to get drunk or to try to pick up a one-night stand . . . or both. Nothing more.

I looked around for Julie. No sign of her. *Must be the wrong bar,* I thought. I turned to leave.

No. Wait.

That woman all in black, wearing leather or vinyl.

Julie?

She was sitting at a table staring *intently* at something. Since when did Julie die her hair black? And that horrible makeup! Her face was painted a very pale shade, and her lips and eyes were painted black. She looked like some pathetic Goth punk rocker. At least she hadn't shaved her head or spiked her hair.

And no pioneer dress. That was a plus.

OK. Found her. It was time to get this over with.

I started toward her, but she didn't see me. She just stared fixedly at . . . what? What was she looking at? There! A woman, dressed *mostly* in black, but far more stylishly, far more attractively. Sitting alone at her table, the woman looked out of place in that dive . . . too classy. She had long blonde hair that fell in waves down her back. She stared at Julie with a fierce intensity, and then she arose from her table and walked with a grace that was almost feline toward my sister, all without ever breaking her intense stare. Julie followed the woman with her eyes as the blonde approached her. Julie raised her head as the woman glided up to the table.

Their eyes remained locked on each other.

The woman (Rebecca?) paused in front of Julie and extended her hand toward her. Julie reached out and took Rebecca's hand. Julie stood and, never taking her eyes off the other woman's, laced her fingers through the hand of the blonde. They turned and walked together, staring into each other's eyes, toward the door, looking like nothing so much as *lovers.*

They walked right past me, neither taking any notice of my presence.

It wasn't until they'd actually left the bar that I realized I'd stopped dead in my tracks. I was just standing there staring out the door after them. This was nothing like I expected. In my astonishment, I was just frozen in place.

I started toward the door.

By the time I got outside, I couldn't see Julie or blondie anywhere.

"OK," I thought. "Think, Morgan! There are only so many places they could go."

That was, unless they got into a car.

Pushing that thought away, because, if they had, I was out of luck, I decided to check the side streets.

I saw what looked like matching alleys on either side of the street. I chose the left one. I darted to the entrance and found no sign of them. I ran across the street to the other alley.

And there, in the shadows, I saw them.

They were locked in an embrace as if they were lovers. I couldn't have told them apart, where one woman ended and the other began. Then they separated, and one figure fell to the ground like a broken doll. I shouted out my sister's name and ran toward her. The other woman, the one still standing, turned and walked farther into the darkness, black fading into blackest night. I caught just a gleam from her golden hair, and then she was gone. I shouted after her to stop, but it was as if she'd vanished into the stygian depths of the night. The alley was a dead end, so I knew she had to still be in there with us. I knelt beside Julie, but I tried to keep an eye out for the blonde. My sister was lying in a crumpled heap like a discarded pile of garbage. I knelt beside her still, dark form. I tried to pick her up. She was totally limp. A dead weight.

And cold.

I called her name. I shook her, but there was no response. She just lay there in my arms.

So cold.

I heard a rustling from the depths of the alley. I started, looked up . . . and there she was. The black figure walked toward us slowly. *Glided* toward us. The moonlight caught her golden hair and then her eyes.

Her eyes. I could see nothing but her eyes, shining in the darkness. At that moment, I couldn't remember ever seeing anything so *beautiful* in all my life as those eyes . . . shining and blue in the moonlight.

I tried to speak, but I couldn't say anything. Nothing would come out. I could only stare as she loomed over us.

I could only stare into her eyes.

Everything else faded into shadow. Then she seemed to grow, to expand, to fill the night. She was like some huge bird.

And I heard the sound of rustling wings.

Funerals are supposed to be on dreary or stormy days, not on sunny days under a brilliant blue sky.

Sharon and Lucy and April and Joseph had been buried during a downpour. I always listed them that way in my mind. *Separately*. I didn't want to lump them all together. I wanted to remember each of them individually. And I was *terrified* I'd forget their faces, their voices.

My family, Sharon and Lucy and April and Joseph, had been laid to rest with very few people in attendance, partly because of the rain and partly because most of my wife's friends and family had written her off the day she got baptized.

"YOU killed her! You *murdered* my baby!" Sharon's mother was the only member of her family present at the funeral. She stood there in the pouring rain, screaming at me as I dedicated the graves. I could hear her profanity-laced shrieks over the sound of the rain. Her rant drowned out my own voice as I bowed my head and said the prayer of dedication.

"You killed her the day she joined your damned cult in this Godforsaken state."

She was *right* to blame me, but not for the reasons she thought.

Sharon and Lucy and April and Joseph died because I was late on the night of the church social. Sharon had wanted to go, and I was late because I was trying to fix a bug at work. It was a low-priority bug in a video game that nobody would remember in a few years, but I absolutely hated leaving the office with something not working.

So Sharon got mad.

And when Sharon got mad, she went for a "walk." And since I wasn't home, she took the kids (Lucy and April and Joseph) along on her cooling-off walk.

And while they were out, some self-absorbed little monster from Ogden decided to get stoned and "borrow" his mother's car. He plowed into them from behind. I wish I could say they died instantly, but, no, they *lingered* for some time. Meanwhile the little teenage jerk drove off in a panic.

No one saw my family lying there.

I went looking for them as soon as I got home and realized Sharon had left. I actually drove right past them the first few times I took Sharon's normal route. It was dim twilight, and I was looking for a woman *walking* with three small children, not a woman lying dead on the sidewalk, her three small children dead beside her.

By the time I found them, they'd been dead for nearly an hour. They were so mangled . . . so twisted and distorted. There was blood everywhere. There were tire tracks in the blood, leading away down the sidewalk and into a twisting line down the street.

The police caught the little monster. In his panic, he'd managed to go off the road into a ditch a mile or so away. *He* walked away from that accident completely unhurt, and the police found him sitting at the side of the road smoking a joint.

I went to his hearing in family court. When I was asked if I had anything to say before his sentencing, I just shook my head.

I wanted to hate him for what he'd done, but I just didn't have it in me. He'd be in juvenile detention until he turned twenty-one. He'd go through rehab. And then he'd get a clean slate. Maybe he'd straighten himself out. Maybe he wouldn't. Man's justice had dealt with him according to the law, and, if that wasn't enough, God's justice would catch up with him eventually.

Either way, he was out of my hands.

Yes, he decided to get high, and he decided to steal a car, and those decisions caused him to be careening down that street at that time. But Sharon's mother was right. I *had* killed them. If I'd just come home on time, Sharon would never have left the house like that. They would never have been there on that sidewalk . . . at that moment.

". . . till that day when we shall be reunited beyond the veil and we will be together for all eternity," I said as I finished dedicating Sharon's grave. The rain washed my tears away as if they'd never been there. In a short time, their bodies would be covered over. Life would have to go on somehow without them. But I clung to the hope that I'd see them again, that Sharon and I would be man and wife for all eternity, that I'd hold Lucy and April and Joseph in my arms again.

"Burn in hell!" Sharon's mother screamed.

I turned and walked away into the storm as she screamed obscenities after me.

I hadn't seen or heard from her since.

Julie's funeral couldn't have been more different.

The day was beautiful: sunny, yet cool. The trees were in glorious colors without too many leaves on the ground. The grass was a deep green, newly mown (probably the last mowing of the season), and there were flowers everywhere. There were several people in attendance: mostly old church members who'd known Jules in her youth. Once again, I dedicated the grave. I was all that was left of Julie's family.

I'm all alone now, I thought.

The Unwilling

"Julie was such a bright, talented young woman," Bishop Pike said to me after the service. He'd been our bishop when we were teenagers. "So much *potential*."

The unspoken tragedy of *wasted* potential hung in the air between us like some dark family secret everybody knew, but nobody talked about.

"She was such a pleasure to have in my Laurels class," said Sister Williams, a sweet woman in her fifties. "She was the first in our ward to earn her Young Women's medallion, as I recall."

There is a plaque in the foyer of our old meetinghouse with the names of all the young women who'd earned that award. I remember my mother's pride when she first saw Julie's name on that plaque with all the empty spaces below it. Of course, that was before Julie went off to college and dated the wrong guy. Before we realized how bad an influence he was, she had dropped out of school and . . . fallen away. Afterward, that plaque had served as a stark reminder of just how far Julie had fallen.

It haunted Mom till the day she died.

Nobody at the funeral had known Julie in recent years.

Nobody . . . but me.

And nobody talked about *how* she died.

I regained consciousness in the early morning, lying in the alley near Julie. She was long dead. I dug in my pocket to get my cell so I could call nine-one-one, but my pockets were empty. I'd been robbed.

Jules was cold and ghostly pale. She looked like a broken and abandoned doll dressed in Goth style. I have a co-worker who has a collection of "Living Dead" dolls, done in a creepy Goth fashion. They're all displayed in his cubicle, neatly and proudly, in their clear, coffin-shaped boxes. Julie reminded me of one of those dolls. That's what a "Living Dead" doll would have looked like if it had been torn out of its coffin box and cast aside. Seeing Julie that way struck me as profoundly sad and pathetic.

I yelled for help, but nobody came. I got to my feet, my joints stiff from lying on the cold pavement of the alley for what must have been hours. I stumbled into the bar (which appeared to be open twenty-four/seven). The lights were still low, but they were painfully bright to me. I covered my eyes with my hand and yelled for someone to call nine-one-one.

I heard a few gasps.

Somebody screamed.

Others swore.

I guess I looked pretty scary. There was blood on my hand and on my shirt. I remember thinking that there should have been more. *I should have been covered in the stuff.*

When the police arrived, they questioned me and inspected the alley, but in the end they concluded that Julie had been mugged. Her throat had apparently been slit, I was told, though with a ragged knife. She had bled to death, but there wasn't much blood to be found since she'd been lying next to a storm drain. The police took my statement, wrote down my description of "Rebecca" . . . but that was it. There were no arrests, no leads, and no suspects.

The police disregarded the more unusual *details of my account.*

I guess I should have been grateful I was never treated like a suspect.

I made some inquiries on my own to try to identify and find Rebecca, but she was a nonentity. Nobody knew who she was. Nobody had seen her before. She was a cipher. I found no leads on Michael either, the one Julie called her lover and "Master." As for Julie, she had stopped paying rent on her apartment a while earlier. She'd just abandoned it months before her death, leaving most of her worldly possessions behind. Nobody knew where she'd gone. I had little to go on and everything I did know *led nowhere.*

After Julie's casket was lowered into the grave and people began to stream away, I noticed a young woman dressed in black hanging back in the trees. Her black hoodie cast her face in shadow, but her *pale makeup* made her face visible.

She turned to walk away. I started after her. I walked quickly, but tried not to run. I didn't want to scare her. She might be my only connection to Julie and her killer.

I caught up with her deep in the copse of trees. I called after her, "Did you know my sister?" That was stupid. Of course she knew Julie. Why else would she be here? She paused momentarily, glanced at me, and resumed walking. She moved faster.

"Please, if you *know* anything . . . ," I pleaded. "I need to know . . . to *understand* what happened." She pulled her hood closer around her face, trying to ignore me as she kept on walking.

"Tell me how to find Rebecca!" I was desperate. This woman was my only link to Julie. That name, Rebecca, brought her up short.

"Please. You don't know what you're dealing with," she said quietly, her eyes fixed on the ground, still not facing me. "Let it go. You'll be *safer* that way."

I stepped around in front of her. "I can't let it go," I said.

"You don't *want* to find Rebecca. Pray. Pray *hard* that *she* never finds you. Pray that she doesn't ever realize you *exist*." She lifted her head and looked at me. From the shadows of the hood only half-concealed a pale face and dark-painted eyes that fixed me with an intense stare. Without the makeup, she would be pretty. As it was, she looked haunted, like someone who was bearing more guilt and remorse than anyone ever should or ever could. "Julie never told anyone she even *had* a brother. If Rebecca finds out, you're a *dead* man."

"My name is Carl. What's your name?" I needed to change tactics. Make it personal, harder to ignore.

She looked down. "Angel . . . Angela."

"Angela. That's a nice name." That sounded so lame! "Angela, I need to find out what happened to my sister . . . to Julie. Rebecca killed her. The police can't find Rebecca. They've stopped looking. I need to find her."

She looked up at me, impaling my gaze with eyes that seemed to have seen too much pain for one so young. "That's *good*," she said. "Good for them . . . and good for *you*. Leave this alone, mister. You can't stop her. If she finds out about you, she'll kill you and your whole family."

The mention of my family was like a knife twisting in my gut. "I don't have any family," It was almost a whisper. "They're all dead."

Awkwardly, but gently, I laid my hands on her shoulders. "I have no one left." Her eyes began to shift back and forth as she looked deeper into each of mine.

"Listen to me, Carl." She spoke each word distinctly. "Rebecca . . . will . . . *kill* . . . you. She'll drain the life out of you and you'll *love* every minute of it, but it won't matter, because you'll be *dead*. Leave it alone and go home and remember Julie. Keep her memory alive."

"*Please*, Angela." I gave her shoulders a gentle shake. "You're my only link to her. I have *nothing* else left. I *need* to find Rebecca."

"And do *what*?" She was angry. "You can't *stop* her. You can't *kill* her. And if she finds out I talked to anyone about her or about any of the Teachers, she'll kill *me* too. Then she'll hunt down my mom and my brother and my nephew. She'll kill my whole family."

"She'll never find out from *me*," I said. "Please, give me *something!*" Her eyes looked hesitant. I thought I had an opening. "Julie deserves justice. Angela, *please* help me."

"You have no idea what she was into, do you?"

That was a shift.

"Some kind of cult, she said."

"It's not that simple. It's not like she joined the Hare Krishnas."

"Then *tell* me what she was into, Angela. Tell me what she *died* for."

Her face twisted into a sneer, and she gave a little, mirthless laugh. "Julie didn't die for *anything*. She died because some crazy psycho wanted her dead. Julie died because Rebecca thinks she really *is* a vampire."

I blinked. "A *vampire?*" What? What kind of crap is this?

"Yeah, it's a *vampire* Cult. Some of us just like the *vibe*, you know, the *power* of the lifestyle. It's very *empowering*, especially for women. I think Rebecca really believes it. I think all the Teachers do."

I could focus on only one word: "*Vampire?*"

"Not *real* vampires. No Dracula or *The Lost Boys* or crap like that. Just a lifestyle, ya know . . . a way of thinking, a way of drinking in *life*. We embrace the *darkness* and the *emptiness* of our souls. We let go of *conventional* morality and feed off the essence of others."

"You drink . . . *blood?*" *This is nuts. Julie was nuts to be a part of it. Face it, Morgan,* I thought to myself, *Julie has really gone off the deep end this time.*

"Only a little." She shrugged her shoulders. "Blood is just the symbol of life. It's just part of the Ritual. Mostly we feed off the *energy* of others."

"Others? Do you . . ." *What was the word Julie had used?* ". . . *hunt* others?"

"No way! We only take from others in the Cult. Nobody *forces* anybody. You *embrace* the power. You *embrace* your sensuality. You embrace the power you can exert over others. You embrace the Great Secret. You embrace the Gift."

"What about AIDS?" I asked in disbelief. "Aren't you worried about *disease?*"

Angela smirked. "We're all screened regularly and we take an oath to stay within the Cult."

"You *know* this is nuts, don't you, Angela?"

"I know how it *sounds*. It sounds stupid in the light of day. I *loved* it, but now . . . it all seems so stupid. Julie died for nothing. Just a stupid game."

"Where does Rebecca fit in all this?"

"Carl," she said, her voice stern as if she were talking to a stubborn child, "just go. Just *let* it go. I'm outta this crap-hole town, this crap-hole state. I want nothing to do with Rebecca and the others. I'm gonna go home. It's safer that way."

"Where does Rebecca fit in this Cult?" I persisted. "You called her a 'Teacher'?"

Angela gave a sigh of resignation. "You won't quit, will you?"

"I have to *know*."

"Teachers are the leaders in the Cult. They're the Circle of the Master, the inner circle. There are three circles: the Circle of the Novitiates (that's where I am), the Circle of the Chosen, and the Circle of the Master. Julie was one of the Chosen. Michael was grooming her to be a Teacher. He took her as a lover, and Rebecca got jealous. That's it. Now, let me go."

"Where can I find Rebecca?" I pressed. "Tell me that, and I'll let you go." I searched her eyes, pleading with mine for her to give me that last link, the link that could eventually lead me to justice for Julie, even if I had to worm my way into a pack of vampire wannabes.

She named an address in a Salt Lake neighborhood above the state capitol. The address meant little to me, except that it was most likely in a pricey section of town. I thanked her sincerely and let her go. Her parting shot, fired from over her shoulder as she fled through the trees was, "If you go there, you're a *dead* man!"

And then she was gone. Only a few swirling brown leaves marked her passage.

I stood there alone in that grove of beautiful trees, resplendent with their fall colors, on that glorious sunny day with its clear blue sky, wondering what I should do next. I had no plan, but I *did* have a lead.

Finally.

I knew where to locate my sister's murderer. I could track her down and get enough evidence to go to the authorities. In my mind, I pictured myself accompanying the police as they took her away in handcuffs, envisioned myself testifying at her trial . . .

And, also, in my mind, I saw two impossibly beautiful blue eyes shining at me out of the darkness. And I heard a sound like the rustling of wings.

Chapter 2

Now

D rink this."
The voice is lilting, gentle, quintessentially feminine, but urgent. It has an accent that I can't immediately place.

Where am I?

My eyes are closed. I know I should open them, but I'm so *desperately* tired. I feel dead. I just want to sleep . . . to sleep forever.

Something is pressed to my lips. It's cold. A liquid spills from it, onto and past my lips, onto my tongue.

Sweet. Salty. *Delicious.*

I remember eating pretzels covered in white chocolate. Sharon and I ate them at the movies. That's a *good* memory. I haven't indulged in a good memory in a very long time.

I open my mouth to drink. I reach up and grab the unseen glass. I drain it greedily. I'm so *thirsty*! I've never been so *thirsty* in all my life!

My eyes flutter open and I'm looking upon the face of a woman, a beautiful woman with long red hair, flawlessly fair skin, and bright, enchanting green eyes. I feel as if I should *know* her, but I can't remember . . .

"There now," she says in that lilting voice. "That's better."

"More," I croak. So thirsty. "Please. *More.*"

She takes the glass from me. It's a wine glass with the remains of something red in it.

Was that wine? Oh, I *hope* not! I don't drink! I've never had a drink in my entire life!

"I'll get some more," she says. She eases me down onto the couch I'm lying on. She must have been supporting me as I drank. She gets up and walks away from me. There is a grace that I can appreciate to her walk. And the sway of her hips in her dark knee-length skirt is . . . very nice to watch.

She leaves the room, heading into what looks like a kitchen. I hear her opening a refrigerator somewhere. It sounds so distinct and clear that I briefly wonder how I'm able to hear it all the way from the next room. I hear the sound of pouring liquid. I smell a salty, sweet aroma that is *maddening. I must have it!* I hear her walking back. She returns bearing both the wine glass with the red liquid and a large bottle apparently containing more of the same.

I can smell it from here. It smells so utterly delicious, not like any *alcoholic* beverage I've ever smelled. I *despise* the rotten, sour smell of beer or wine.

Another memory: cleaning up a smashed bottle of cheap wine at Safeway where I worked as a teenager. The stench was overwhelming. I remember thinking, *How can anyone* drink *this stuff?*

I reach greedily for the glass and drain it. Please, God, don't let this be wine! I hand the glass back to her, hoping for more. She fills it from the bottle. I take it and drain it again. We repeat this cycle until I've consumed the entire bottle.

I must have drunk half a gallon. I feel full, sloshy, but I could still drink *more.* I still crave *more.*

I stare at the empty glass. I've drained every drop. My eyes follow the empty bottle as she places it on a coffee table.

She kneels in front of me and smiles. Her face is breathtaking, her smile dazzling, her eyes mesmerizing. A man could lose himself in those eyes. If I had to make a guess as to her age . . . from her face, I'd say she was in her early twenties . . . *very* early twenties . . . but she carries herself with the confidence of maturity.

"I'm Moira," she says in that delicious, accented voice. It sounds . . . Irish or Scottish. She extends a delicate hand to me. "Moira Mac-Donald."

Scottish it is.

I sit up, all the fatigue suddenly gone, and take her hand, shaking it. "Carl," I say. "Carl Morgan."

I look sheepishly into her lovely green eyes. "Thank you. I can't ever remember being so thirsty." I'm ashamed to ask about the drink, but it's too important. "I don't want to seem ungrateful or anything, but what *was* that? Please tell me it didn't have *alcohol* in it."

She looks confused and a bit taken aback. She starts to say something, stops herself, and I can see in her expression that she's changing what she intended to say. "Ye must be jokin'. Surely, ye are havin' a wee joke with me."

Wariness is written plain on her face. And then suspicion.

"I'm sorry," I say. "It's just that I don't *drink*. I've never tasted anything alcoholic, well, except for a brandied peach my mom stuck in my mouth once when I was a kid. That tasted *disgusting.*" She looks dubious. "No! Not that!" I say quickly, pointing at the empty bottle. "That was the most *delicious* stuff I've ever tasted. It's just that I . . . can't drink alcohol. Mormon. You know what I mean?"

I watch as suspicion is replaced by disbelief and then by caution on Moira's face. I look at her expectantly. Even as I ask her about the alcoholic content of the red drink, I want *more* of it.

"Carl," she says slowly, "are ye mockin' me?" She doesn't seem angry. She just seems oddly perplexed.

Now it's my turn to be confused. "No," I say slowly. I can't think of what to say now. "I don't understand."

She stares into my eyes. I have never seen eyes so green. Or so lovely. "Carl, do ye know where ye are?"

With a shock, I realize that I don't. "No." I glance around the room. It's a small living room, tastefully furnished. The house looks older, but in good shape. It looks very clean, almost as if nobody lives here, but there are other indications that this is a *home*. Artificial flowers are arranged in a vase on an end table. An exquisite crystal model of the Salt Lake Temple sits on the mantle of the fireplace. I see an antique curio cabinet filled with other crystal models. They are all renderings of LDS temples from around the world.

"Where am I?" I ask.

She hesitates a moment and then replies, "Ye are in my home. Do ye know how ye got here?"

Now I'm getting worried. "My memory's a bit fuzzy. Sorry."

"Ye carried a young woman into the emergency room at the LDS Hospital. She was unconscious and covered in blood. Ye were staggerin' about and yellin' incoherently. Ye frightened everyone. We took the young woman and attended to her, but ye collapsed. I thought it best nae to let the staff examine ye. So, I brought ye here and tended to ye myself."

The girl. Yes, I remember the girl. "Is she OK?" I ask.

Moira nods slowly. "Aye, she's fine. Some blood loss, but she'll live. Ye did nae kill her."

Kill her? What?

"W ... why would I kill her?" I stammer. "What're you talking about?"

She stares at me again. She seems to be holding some kind of internal debate. Her eyes narrow as she comes to a decision.

"Blood," she says simply.

"What?"

"Blood. Human blood."

I look at her without understanding, blinking stupidly.

"The drink," she says. "'Twas human blood."

In an instant, it all comes back to me.

Michael. Rebecca. Chikah. Benjamin. The Cult. The Ritual. Everything.

I think I'm going to throw up.

I lurch to my feet and look around frantically for a bathroom, a sink.

Moira is at my side in an instant. She pulls me toward the kitchen. "Dinnae ruin my carpet, laddie!"

Wow! Her grip is strong!

By the time I reach the sink, the nausea has passed. I lean against the sink all the same. The room is still spinning.

Moira gave me *blood* to drink. I drank *human blood*.

And I *liked* it.

I crave it still. No, "crave" is too weak a word. A pathetic word. *Need*. I *need* it.

Moira eases her grip and lays one hand on my back. She begins to rub my shoulder. It's a comforting gesture.

A huge sob wracks my whole body. I'm crying. I haven't cried since I lost Sharon and Lucy and April and Joseph. *What is happening to me?*

"Please tell me this is some sick joke," I say, but I *know* it isn't. "This cannot be real." But I *know* that it is. "I never believed any of it. They were just a bunch of sick, morbid fanatics led by egomaniacs." I still don't look at Moira, but I plead with her. "Please tell me this isn't *real*!"

"How could ye nae know?" I can hear the wonder in her voice. "Ye must *choose*. Ye must accept it *willin'ly*." She pauses a moment. "Ye *had* to know. In six thousand years there has nae ever been an *unwillin'* Child of Lilith. Ye *had* to know what ye were about."

The tears are gone and my breathing speeds up. Rage fills me, nearly consuming me.

Only the thirst is stronger than the rage.

"It was all a sick *joke*," I say bitterly. "Michael and his 'wives' leading those pathetic people around, feeding them full of that vampire crap so they'd worship him like a god. *None* of it was real. *It can't be!*"

"Carl-laddie, ye *had* to know."

"No." I shake in vehement denial.

"The Teacher tasted of yer blood."

"Yes, but she'd done that many times before."

"Ye drank the blood of the Teacher."

"I tasted it."

"That's all it takes. And ye swore the Oath."

"I repeated some meaningless mumbo-jumbo words. They were just *stupid words!*"

"Ye submitted to the Ritual."

"It was a stupid ceremony. It meant *nothing!*" I'm trembling.

"Ye did nae *believe?*" Her voice is incredulous.

"No, I was just trying to get enough evidence to catch Julie's killer."

"Who is . . . I mean, who *was* Julie?"

"My sister. Rebecca killed her. I was just trying to infiltrate their stupid cult. Undercover, you know? The police didn't believe me. I had to gather evidence to prove to them that Rebecca is a killer."

"Oh, aye, she *is* that."

"None of it was *real!*" I insist. "Just Michael and his pathetic little cult."

"And ye did nae believe any of it?"

"It can't be real. *It can't!*"

"Carl-laddie," she says, wonder infusing her voice even as it takes on a soothing tone. "'Tis all *too* real. Ye are a *vampire*, a Child of Lilith. As am *I*."

She gently turns me around and fixes me with her green eyes. "I am like ye. I was Converted two and a half centuries ago. I did it will-in'ly as has *every other* vampire in the entire history of the family of Adam."

Please, God, don't let this be real! "I did *not* do it willingly," I say through gritted teeth. "I was just playing along . . . gathering evidence."

"If that be true, Carl, ye are the *first* unwilling vampire. *Ever.* Although, 'twould explain why ye did nae kill the girl."

"The girl?"

"The one ye brought to the hospital, lad."

A scene comes to my mind, like something out of a lurid dream or a low-budget horror movie:

I woke from a deep sleep to find Rebecca bending over me. "Awake, my Son. Awake and Feed." She took me by the hand and raised me from the bed.

I felt weak ... so weak. And hungry. I'd never been so hungry! I was in Michael's Sanctuary, his "Unholiest of Unholies." It looked like a cave ... or at least a cave in a Hollywood movie. The walls and ceiling were of rough stone, but the floor was smooth. Symbols and runes covered the floor, and tapestries covered the walls. I saw two braziers at either end of the room, their fires providing the only light. There were two passages leading out.

Rebecca escorted me to a table. It looked like it was made of stones, like an altar. There was a young woman lying there. She was dressed in jeans and a T-shirt. She had short black hair. She was asleep or drugged ... or something. Her breathing was slow, but steady.

Rebecca took an ancient-looking knife in her hand. It seemed to be made of black glass. "Obsidian," my fuzzy mind supplied. She sliced the girl's throat a little, and a stream of blood ran down the side of her neck onto the table, pooling there.

"Feed," she urged.

I wanted to. I wanted to drink the precious fluid. I could smell it. I could almost taste it. I could hear the girl's heart as it pumped the life through her body, through each artery, each vein, each capillary, carrying the oxygen and nutrients to each cell. I could think of little else but the hunger, the lust that consumed me, but my mind was no longer fuzzy.

In a moment of clarity, I knew what I needed to do. With a cry of strangled rage, I wheeled on Rebecca and slammed my fist into her jaw. I didn't wait to see what happened to her. I just scooped the bleeding girl up into my arms.

She felt so light.

She smelled so good. So delicious. I'd never wanted anything so badly in my life.

And then I ran.

I ran out of the Sanctuary. Up the stairs, out of Michael's "temple" and out into the night. I ran and I ran and I could think of nothing but the blood and the need. And the need to find a doctor for the girl.

"Ye brought her to the emergency room." Moira's voice wrenches me out of the memory and back into the present. "I knew at once what ye were, but I knew nae why ye'd brought her there. And I did nae ken why ye had nae killed her. But 'twas obvious ye had nae intention of killin' her."

She pauses for a moment. "So I took her and got her seen to, but, when I returned, ye were nae there anymore. Ye had collapsed and been taken to an examination room yerself. I took ye with me. I brought ye home."

She looks at the floor for a moment. "I dared to hope . . ." Her voice trails off, and then she looks deep into my eyes.

"Hope?" *I'm so confused. And it isn't helping that her eyes are so . . . hypnotic.* "Hope what?"

"That ye were . . . like me." I do see doubtful, hesitant hope in her eyes.

"Like you? You mean . . . a vampire?"

"Ach, I know that! I can *see* that." She hesitates. "I mean, I hoped ye might be . . . a Penitent."

"A Penitent?"

"Ye *are* new at this, are ye nae?" There is a wry smile. "When were ye Converted?"

"Converted?"

"When did ye become a bloody vampire, ye wee bairn! When was the Ritual?"

"Oh. That." Now I feel confused *and* stupid. "What day is it?"

She blinks at me. "Sunday. Monday now."

"Three days ago. On Thursday."

She stares at me with her lovely mouth hanging open. "Thursday? Then ye Awoke only last night? And ye did nae kill her?"

"Why would I kill her? Why would I *want* to?" *But that's not honest, is it? I had wanted to kill her.* At the time I wanted nothing more than to kill her and drain her life from her. I shudder with horror at that admission. "I *did* want to kill her," I say out loud. "But I don't want to kill *anyone*." Except Rebecca. I want to kill *her.*

"Carl, the girl was yer Offerin'. When a new vampire Awakes, the Teacher gives ye an Offerin' to be yer first kill, to crown yer damnation."

"Please, dear Father in Heaven . . . ," I begin.

"And ye did nae kill her? Ye carried her to safety? With her bleedin' like that? I have nae ever *heard* of such a thin'!" She begins to walk around the room animatedly. "There have been other Penitents like me, sure, but in all the histories, in all the legends, there has nae ever been one who *refused* the Offerin'! My own Offerin' was . . . but nae mind. And an *unwilling* vampire? Never! I mean, ye partook of the Ritual, but ye did nae ever *believe*!" She stops abruptly and looks to me for confirmation.

I nod my head.

She resumes her pacing. "Ye *consented* (Persuasion will nae work), but ye did nae *believe*! Do ye know what that means?"

I shake my head.

"Well, *I* dinnae know what it means!" she declares. "But it has to mean *somethin'*! Ye are a *Child*: ye have the Seed and ye have the Essence. I can feel it! Ye dinnae *smell* mortal. But ye did nae kill! I dinnae know what it means, but it has to mean *somethin'*!"

Abruptly she stops and, taking me by the shoulders, kisses me hard on the lips. She pulls back and holds me at arm's length. The wild joy on her face is unmistakable. And something else. Hope?

She takes me by the hand and quickly leads me out of the kitchen and back into the living room where she pushes me onto the sofa. She pulls up a chair right in front of me and sits herself down. She looks at me with an eagerness and an intensity and a *hunger* that should frighten me, but doesn't. She takes both of my hands in hers.

"Now, Carl-laddie, tell me all about yerself."

Chapter 3

The whole story comes spilling out of me.

I've been lying to everyone for so long. Well, not *lying* exactly, just not telling anybody the *truth*. I haven't told anybody anything truly *real* in a long time. All the grief and all the rage have been bottled up as I've focused all my soul on infiltrating Michael's Cult so I could gather my precious evidence. I haven't had anyone to talk to since I talked with Angela at Julie's funeral.

And Moira's a good listener. I don't hold back with her. It feels so good to just tell someone everything.

I talk about Sharon and Lucy and April and Joseph. I tell her about Julie. I tell her about Angela. I start to talk about the Cult, but Moira interrupts me.

"Carl, laddie, tell me about yerself. I need to understand what kind of man ye are."

"You mean what kind of man I *was*," I reply bitterly. She looks at me quizzically, so I add, "I'm no longer a *man*."

"Nae, Carl, ye are a man. Ye have a soul."

"But, you said I was a . . ." I can't say the word. I still can't wrap my head around the fact that my whole life, everything I've ever loved, everything I've ever worked for, is . . . gone.

"Oh, aye. Ye are a vampire as well. Vampires are human and we have souls, but our souls are damned."

"Damned." The word is so final.

"I'm nae so certain about *yer* soul. Ye have nae *killed*. Ye *did* swear the Oaths, but ye did nae believe they were *real*."

"I *have* killed. I flew B-52s during the First Gulf War."

"Ye have killed in *combat*, in wartime, in the service of yer country. My Donald, my betrothed, did as much in the service of Bonny Prince Charlie before I became a vampire."

She sees my astonished look.

"Aye," she continues, "I am more than two hundred and seventy years old." My jaw drops. "*Ye* are immortal as well."

"Your be . . . your fiancé?"

"Aye, my Donald. He was captured and executed by the English long ago."

Donald Mac*Donald?* Even in my present state of mind, the name strikes me as funny, but I leave it alone. "But, your name is *also* Mac-Donald?"

"Aye. We were both from Clan MacDonald. Distant cousins, as ye would say."

"When you say, 'immortal,' you mean . . . living forever? Like *this*?"

"There are very few truly *old* vampires. We call them the Ancient Ones. I'm nae ancient, by our standards, but I'm older than most."

"Why are there so few? What happens to them?"

"That is a question for another time," she says.

"Now, as to yer soul," she continues, "ye have nae murdered. Ye have nae *killed* another person to drink their blood. So I dinnae know what that means for ye. Ye are a vampire. That much is certain. Ye have drunk human blood and it has revived ye. I can feel the Seed and the Essence in ye. But ye have nae *murdered.*"

She nods. "Ye are *unique.* I, myself, have taken human lives, but we'll speak of me later. Tell me about yerself."

"Wait!" I've found a tiny thread of hope, and I try to seize it like a drowning man grasping at a lifeline. "Maybe I'm not really a vampire, then!" She sadly shakes her head, but I'm desperately pushing on anyway. "You said I was unique! I haven't killed!" *It can't be! It just can't!*

"Ach, nae, Carl, my poor, wee bairn. Murder is nae *necessary.* Only the *Ritual.* Ye have done that, whether ye believed or nae. Ye are most definitely a vampire." She looks genuinely sad.

"No! I'm different. You said so." I *won't* give this up. I *can't.*

"Carl," she says, fixing me with her eyes, now brimming with tears, "I shall prove it to ye." Still holding both my hands in hers, she stands and pulls me to my feet. Then, releasing one hand, she leads me to the heavily draped picture window. She releases my other hand and grasps my forearm. Once again I marvel at the strength in her grip, and this time she's holding my arm *very* firmly.

Standing to one side, Moira pulls me until I'm standing in front of her. With her free hand, she takes hold of the curtain several inches short of the edge and pulls the curtain back an inch or so until a thin shaft of sunlight enters the room.

I didn't realize it was daytime.

"Forgive me, laddie," she says sadly, and she deliberately pulls my arm forward and quickly thrusts it into the beam of sunlight. My hand is illuminated by the shaft of light, and instantly I feel the warmth of the sun.

And then I feel heat.

And suddenly there is searing pain!

I cry out and try to pull my hand back, but Moira holds it steady.

My exposed, illuminated flesh bubbles and smolders for a second. Then it bursts into bright flame. Suddenly Moira releases both my wrist and the curtain, cutting off the burning light of the sun. The flame vanishes immediately, but the pain and the smoke remain. The stench of burning hair and meat fills the room, and I look down at the blackened and still smoldering flesh on the back of my hand.

But the pain is already dropping off sharply.

I'm dimly aware of a smoke alarm screaming somewhere.

Now the pain is gone.

It's replaced by a horrible *itch* as the blackened flesh immediately begins to heal. Within seconds, my hand looks almost whole. I can even see and feel the hairs rapidly growing back.

"I'm so sorry, Carl, my poor, wee bairn," Moira croons to me like a mother comforting her child, "but ye had to *see*. Ye had to *know*. Ye *are* a vampire. And there is no escapin' that."

I stare at my hand in shocked disbelief. There's no pain at all. The smell of burning flesh and hair still lingers in the air, as does the smoke. The itching fades away to nothing as my hand looks completely unscathed. Even the hairs on the back of my hand are back and they look exactly the same length as they did before.

The smoke alarm behind me is abruptly silenced, and I turn in that direction.

What I see takes my breath away.

Moira is *floating* in the air! Spread out and flapping behind and above her are huge white-feathered wings. Her red hair floats around her face, framing it. She's dazzling in the artificial light in the room.

She looks like an angel.

She must have silenced the smoke alarm on the ceiling. As she touches down, the wings fold in behind her. And then they are gone.

Her hair settles around her shoulders as if it had never been disturbed. A part of my mind, the part that still looks at the world in a *sane* and *analytical* way, notes that while I *saw* the wings and I heard them flapping, the smoke seems undisturbed, as if the wings had never been there at all.

"Ye have nae ever seen the *wings*?" Moira looks stunned as I shake my head slowly. "Surely ye were Chosen, were ye nae?"

Chosen. That's what the middle Circle of the Cult is called. "Yeah, Rebecca told me that I was Chosen. I was shocked, because I'd heard it's unusual for someone to become Chosen after so short a time as a Novitiate. She took an unusual interest in me, in elevating me. I *assumed* it was because I took an interest in learning about her. Of course, *my* interest was in bringing her to justice."

"How long were ye Novitiate?"

"Almost four months." What is she driving at?

"How long Chosen?"

"A week or so. Why?"

Moira hesitates a moment. "'Tis most unusual, especially in Michael's Cult or in most modern-day Cults, for that matter, to advance someone so quickly. The Circle of the Novitiates is the primary food source for the Teachers and the Master. Moving someone to the Circle of the Chosen is reserved for those candidates that the Master is considering for Conversion. Very few are Chosen. It would nae do to have a large increase in the vampire population. Once Chosen, there is customarily a long period of testing and indoctrination before Conversion is attempted, so the Master can be certain the new vampire will serve him or her faithfully. If they will nae serve, they will be killed."

"The Master? You mean Michael?"

She nods in response.

"Michael wasn't there. Only Rebecca."

Moira's eyes widen. "The Master was nae there? Rebecca did this herself? *Alone?*"

I nod.

"That means Rebecca had another motive," she continues. "I wonder why she would do that, especially so soon . . ."

"Moira, tell me about the *wings*."

She considers for a moment. "'Tis actually a wee bit complicated. There is much ye must understand first, but, for now, I'll say nae more than that they're a visual manifestation of the Essence that exists within ye, that's a part of ye. They are nae real. And," she goes on when she sees the question written on my face, "aye, ye have them as well, but we'll get to that in good time."

Wings? I can fly? I mean, I flew jet aircraft when I was in the Air Force, but to really fly! Now that would be something!

"How fast can I go? How high?" I haven't flown, except for a couple of times in a Cessna, since I got out of the service.

She takes me by the shoulders. "Listen, laddie. Ye need to *pay attention*. We'll get to that all in good time. Besides, ye cannae go flyin' in the sunlight, now can ye?" I start to interrupt, but she puts a finger to my lips, stopping me. She guides me back to the couch and gently pushes me onto it. "Excuse me just a moment while I deal with the smoke and the smell." She pivots and quickly, gracefully walks down a hallway I haven't noticed before.

There's a lot I haven't noticed. I've been blind to so many things lately.

I hear the sound of a bathroom fan. Not just the fan! I heard the sound of the *switch* too! A few seconds pass and she returns with a large electric box fan which she plugs in and turns on. She positions it so as to draw the smoke down the hallway toward the bathroom. The smoke and smell begin to dissipate perceptibly.

She settles back onto the couch, bypassing the chair, and turns to face me. "Go on, Carl. Tell me about yerself."

"What do you want to know?" The need to talk about my problems has diminished in direct proportion to the increase in my curiosity about my current condition, particularly the *wings. Most* especially *the wings.*

I can fly!

"Oh, start with the usual thing men like to talk about," she says. "What do ye do for a living?"

"You mean, what *did* I do?"

"No, I mean what *do* ye do? Since we do nae live in a Cult, we must have *jobs*. We dinnae need to buy groceries, but we need someplace to *be* during the day. Nowadays, nobody wants to live in a crypt. We need electricity. We need water to bathe in. We use phones and cell phones and computers. We drive cars. (We cannae fly *everywhere*.) We need *money*. So, unless ye want to attract unwanted attention from the neighbors or the IRS, ye need a job."

"So, you mean a night job?"

"A night job certainly makes it easier, but there are ways to deal with the Sun."

The memory of the pain of my burning hand comes vividly to my mind. "How do you 'deal with the Sun'?"

Her lovely face twists into a smirk. "I can see that ye need yer questions answered, but I've been waiting for well over *two centuries* to find some hope . . . So, *please*, Carl, answer a *few* of *my* questions and then I will answer *all* of yers. I promise. OK?" She looks at me with an expression that can only be described as an amused pout.

It's a very *attractive* amused pout. I bet people have a hard time saying no to this woman.

"OK," I say. "Shoot. Ask me your questions."

"What do ye do for a living?"

"I'm a software engineer. Currently I develop video games."

"D'ye *like* yer job?"

"Sure." *Where is she going with this?*

"Are ye good at it?"

"Yeah, I am." I don't want to come across as *bragging*, but I am good at what I do.

"Ye said that ye are Mormon. Are ye active?"

"Very." I hesitate a second and then continue, "Well . . . lately it's been harder to make it to church because I've been infiltrating the Cult . . . to get closer to Rebecca, but I make it there most Sundays." With a sheepish grin, I add, "I haven't been a very good home teacher lately."

A disturbing question comes suddenly to my mind. "Can I eat and drink? What about the sacrament?"

She gives me a playfully stern look. "*My* questions, remember? Very well, yer turn . . . for now.

"Ye cannae ingest mortal food and drink, except in very small amounts; otherwise ye will be violently ill until yer body expels all of the foreign matter . . . unless ye mix it with blood, of course. For example, I learned to tolerate mixing blood with grape juice or tomato juice or wine, but I gave *wine* up long ago. This makes it easier for me to consume blood in front of mortals. Ye see, I bring a thermos full of tomato juice mixed with blood to work. But adding anything to the blood spoils the taste. Ye may find it difficult at first.

"As for the sacrament, ye might tolerate a wee sip of water, but nae even the whole wee cup. As for the bread, ye could just pinch off a wee amount of bread, just the corner of a piece. Just a piece of a piece of a piece, ye see. But frankly, ye have bigger problems than that with the sacrament. There's the whole eternal damnation thing, ye know?"

I start to follow up, but she stops me. "*My* turn, now, laddie."

I reluctantly nod to get her to proceed.

"Do ye have any family at all now and, please, dinnae be angry with me for asking."

"No one. Julie was it."

"Are ye a good man?"

"I try to be. I want to be. I want to be for Sharon so we can be together . . ." I trail off as it hits home. I look Moira right in the eyes. "I'll never make it there. I'm barred from heaven, aren't I? I'm immortal, damned to remain on this Earth. Damned to never see Sharon or Lucy or April or Joseph ever again. Where they are, I cannot go. I can *never* go."

Oh, please, God, have mercy *on me!*

"Do ye seek vengeance for yer sister?"

That brings me up short. Is it *revenge* I want? Or is it justice? It's not like I haven't considered this question many times before. Every time I come up with the same answer, but each time I search my soul to see if anything has changed.

Well, something certainly has changed now.

So, do I seek vengeance or justice? This is usually a debate I hold in the private depths of my soul, not in front of anyone else.

But, it's easier with Moira. I don't understand why, but it is.

"Do I *want* to kill Rebecca?" I say. "Of course I do. *Would* I kill her if I had the chance? Until today, I don't think I would have. I *want* revenge, but it's *justice* I'm after. And now, I'm not sure *mortal* justice would accomplish anything. So I don't know what to do. I may have to kill Rebecca to get justice for Julie. I haven't considered that until now. *Is* there any justice in vampire . . . community?"

Moira stares at me intently, but her voice is gentle, belying the intensity in her eyes. "Justice? Nae as *ye* mean it. Individual Cults impose their own brands of justice for offenses against the Law of the Master. He or she rules the Cult with a fist of iron and blood. His punishments can be deadly. Disputes between vampires from different Cults are resolved by combat or by assassination or even war. But there's only one crime which is universally recognized and lethally punished the world over: Betrayal of the Great Secret. The Great Secret must nae ever be revealed to anyone who is nae a Child of Lilith. Nae to a victim, nae to a Novitiate, nae to a Chosen . . . until that Chosen is ready for Conversion. 'Tis only revealed to the Immortals. A vampire who does this must be put to death by any Child of Lilith who can. Ye *know* this. 'Twas part of the Oath ye swore."

"I barely remember that part," I say. "I don't remember *what* I said that night. I just repeated what Rebecca *told* me to say."

"Ah, well," she says with a dismissive wave of her hand, "we'll go over that in more detail in the by-and-by, but, for now, I need ye to answer the question: Do ye seek *vengeance*?"

"Whatever has been forced on me. I won't betray who I am, who I promised God I would be. Even if I *am* damned, I will *not* become a murderer. Even if I must kill Rebecca, if it comes to that . . . and I don't see how it can't now . . . I will do it for justice. I will not do it to seek my own revenge. Revenge will not bring Julie back or give her peace."

"Aye, laddie, but neither will justice."

"No, it won't, but justice must not be denied. What does the scripture say? My sister's 'blood cries up from the ground,' right?"

"'Twill nae make ye feel any better. 'Twill nae give ye comfort. I know this from *experience*."

I can see the truth of that in her eyes. Such grief . . . enough to drown the whole world in tears . . . grief without end. Even when Sharon and Lucy and April and Joseph died, my grief didn't compare to Moira's.

I don't know what to say. Tears well up in my eyes and in hers and, without thinking about it, I find myself holding her in my arms. She's sobbing into my chest.

We sit like that, holding each other, for a long time. There's nothing sexual about it. I just hold her and she sobs. No other sound intrudes except for the quiet droning of the two fans and the beating of our two hearts.

As I'm holding her to me, I ask myself, as I have so many times before, why I'm seeking justice for Julie and not for Sharon and Lucy and April and Joseph. Why am I so *driven* to bring Julie's killer to justice, but at the sentencing hearing, I couldn't say a *word* against that teenage monster who took my family away from me? Did I *forgive* him? Maybe I did. I know he didn't kill them on purpose, even if he *did* choose to get high and drive a stolen car. Was it because part of it was my fault, because I didn't come home when Sharon needed me? I'm sure that has something to do with it. Had I thrown myself into catching Julie's killer because it was all I had left . . . because I had nothing left to live for except to wait till God called me home and I could be with them again?

Only, now, I could *never* be with them again.

My own grief wells up in me like a flood, and soon I'm sobbing too. That's when her arms wrap around me, and she starts comforting me.

I've lost so much.

I've lost Sharon.

I've lost Lucy.

I've lost April.

I've lost Joseph.

I've lost them in *this* life, and now I've lost them for *eternity*.

I don't *care* about heaven for myself. Without Sharon and Lucy and April and Joseph, there *is* no heaven. There is only hell. I could endure the loss if it only lasted for a handful of decades more, for one lifetime, but I've lost them for all time and eternity.

There is no hope. There is only eternal damnation. Forever in a world of endless night and blood.

Eventually, my tears are spent and my sobbing ceases. Moira's hold on me eases, and she looks up, into my eyes.

And she waits.

And I know what she's waiting for.

"Justice. I seek only justice."

She lays her head on my chest and hugs me once more. This time the hug is long and tender. After a while, she breaks the embrace.

"I will *help* ye to seek justice."

"Moira," I ask softly, "was it vengeance for you?"

Her head bows and she says quietly but distinctly, "Aye. 'Twas vengeance for my Donald and my parents . . . and for *me* as well."

"Did you find it?"

"Oh, aye. That I did." She looks at me again. She squares her shoulders. "Forty-six men for me and my parents and twenty-seven for my Donald. I killed them all . . . all save one. I *had* him. I *would* have killed him. I had him by the throat. I would have slaughtered him like a chicken in front of his wife and children and gloried in his blood." She pauses for a long time. "But, that is a tale for another day. I cannae tell it now."

The Unwilling

Her eyes smolder with a fierce light, sending a chill down my spine.

"I will nae help ye to take revenge. Vengeance will destroy ye. 'Twas for *vengeance*," she continues fiercely, "that I sought out the Ancient One who haunted the kirkyard. 'Twas for *vengeance* that I let her taste of my blood and I tasted hers and I swore the Oath and I received the Ritual under her hand. And 'twas for the sake of *vengeance* that she consented to Convert me rather than to take my life. 'Twas for *vengeance* that I begged of the Ancient One that she would make my Offerin' any English soldier from a specific garrison. 'Twas for *vengeance* that I slaughtered seventy-two men and nearly murdered a true innocent. 'Twas for *vengeance* that I *willin'ly* damned my own soul. I'll nae help ye destroy yerself. But I will help ye obtain justice."

The chilling light fades from her eyes, and they soften to a wistful, lovely green.

"Then, Carl-laddie, perhaps when ye have justice, ye can help me in my penance. I have nae ever met another Penitent, although there exist stories of other Penitents throughout the ages. I'm nae in touch with the vampire 'community,' so-to-speak, but I know of nae *living* Penitents. Ye are nae *precisely* a Penitent, mind ye, but ye wish to be reconciled to God as much as I do."

She drops her head and whispers, "And 'twould be *grand* to have a real *friend*, someone I could speak with honestly, without the half-truths and the secrecy, a real friend in this world to which I'm eternally bound. I've been *alone* for so long. There are and have been a very few who know my secret, know what I am. But I've nae ever had someone who could truly understand."

She pauses a moment and adds softly, "I've been so alone."

I nod slightly in answer, and we hold each other for a long time in silence. Again, there's nothing physical about it. We're just two lost souls, two *truly* lost souls, who have no one else in the world.

Eventually, with a sigh, she releases me and gently pushes me back onto the couch.

"Carl, 'tis time to begin yer education in yer new existence."

Chapter 4

The first thing ye must know is that ye need human blood to survive," Moira says.

"I figured that, but . . ."

"Listen to me carefully, laddie: *human* blood," Moira continues. "Ye cannae drink *animal* blood. Aye, ye can drink it, but ye will *starve* to death." Seeing the question in my eyes, she goes on, "Oh, aye. 'Twill take a long time, years or perhaps decades, but ye can starve to death. And it will be a lingering, wasting, agonizing death. Ye would be in agony after the first couple of weeks."

By the look in her eyes, I would bet money that she has some experience with such agony.

"But how . . . ," I say

"That takes nae thought at all. When ye are Hunting prey, yer canine teeth will extend. I hate the word 'fangs,' but 'tis accurate enough. When ye have Fed, they will retract. Ye could use a knife to . . ."

"No, I mean, how do I get human blood without killing people?"

She blinks at me for a second.

And then she laughs. It's a long, hearty, and musical laugh. *I could listen to that laugh for hours.*

"First of all, laddie, ye dinnae need to *kill* to Feed!" She laughs a bit more. "I myself have nae taken a human life in over two and half centuries." She suddenly looks mockingly serious. "I dinnae know about ye, lad, but the human body holds more than six quarts of blood and I cannae drink more than two or three at one Feeding. One quart is enough to sustain ye for several days, even a week, if need be. Nae need to be greedy, laddie!"

The mounting horror and disgust in my face stills her mirth.

"If ye take more than two quarts, the prey will probably die without medical attention. If ye take three, the prey will *certainly* die. Ye can easily take one quart and do nae more than simply leave a man feelin' weak for a few days.

"I dinnae Hunt all that often and, if I do, I Hunt *violent criminals* and then I leave them too afraid to ever lift a finger against another soul for fear of my return," she continues. "But I dinnae Hunt all that much. I get my food at work."

I stare at her stupidly. I don't understand. She . . . bites co-workers?

"I work in a hospital, ye ninny!" She's grinning widely. In spite of the sickening subject matter, her smile strikes me as beautiful. "I take the blood from the lab and the blood bank once it has expired and must be disposed of anyway. I have *conveniently* volunteered for that duty. The blood is good enough for me for several days after that with care. I can also take contaminated blood, blood that's infected with HIV or some other virus. Ye can *taste* the virus, but it cannae harm ye. The Seed makes ye immune to all disease."

I vaguely remember Rebecca mentioning "the Seed and the Essence" as part of the Oath, but I really didn't understand it at the time. I don't think I was paying much attention to that part. "What is the Seed, exactly?"

"Ach, now that will take some tellin'. So let me come back to that. But, for now, the Seed and the Essence are the two components of what makes ye a vampire. One is biological and one is demonic. I've spent more than a century studying it, and I still dinnae understand it all. But we need to focus on more *practical* matters, such as how ye are going to *survive*. There's much ye will nae understand at first."

She looks at me for a second. "Ye must *trust* me. D'ye trust me, Carl?"

I have known this woman for only a few hours, but it's true: I trust her. "Yeah," I say, "I do."

"As I told ye, ye must consume human blood to survive. If ye do nae Feed, you will become weaker and weaker until ye collapse into a coma. The smell of prey will awaken ye, but if ye do nae Feed, the *Seed* will eventually feed upon yer body and consume ye. It can take years or even decades, but eventually ye *will* die."

I shudder at the image in my mind of my body slowly wasting away. That image dissolves and is replaced by one of Moira lying asleep, beautiful, but deathlike. In my mind's eye, her body becomes emaciated, dries up, and then collapses in on itself.

I shudder at the thought.

"Ye have seen that the light of the Sun will burn ye. Prolonged exposure can kill ye. Ye can endure short exposure with massive amounts of sunscreen and heavy clothing, including gloves. A heavy hood or wide-brimmed hat and sunglasses are essential for such forays into the light."

This conjures up images of me dressed as a stereotypical spy right out of a Cold War movie, complete with trench-coat, hat, and glasses.

Or, worse yet, I can picture myself as Inspector Clouseau.

I must be grinning, because Moira pauses.

"Laddie, ye must take this quite seriously."

My grin vanishes. "Sorry."

"Even prepared as such, ye will begin to feel the Sun's heat immediately and will begin to be in pain in mere minutes. So, tint the windows of yer car and park close to any entrance. It should be enough to get ye to and from work, if ye are cautious."

"Tinted windshields are illegal. Won't the cops stop me?"

"Nae so often as ye might think, but, if they do, use Persuasion."

I start to question, but she goes on.

"Ye told me yer sister appeared to go willin'ly with Rebecca on the night she was murdered?"

I nod.

"That was Persuasion. 'Tis an act of imposing yer will on that of a mortal. Ye fix a mortal's gaze with yers and ye speak forcefully and imperiously to them. Nae loudly, mind; ye can whisper. 'Tis a matter of *yer* will against *theirs*. For all but the very strong willed, ye may command them to do anything. Even if they *are* very strong willed, ye can *distract* them, get them to doubt what they see, get them to focus on something else."

"I don't understand."

She nods with a smirk. "I will demonstrate tonight. Persuasion can be a great evil. 'Tis a sin to rob another of their free will. As ye well know."

Her look sobers. "I *chose* this existence, though I repent of it now, too late, with all my heart and damned soul, but ye, Carl, ye did nae choose it."

That thought hangs in silence between us.

I may not have chosen this "existence," as she calls it, but my *choices* led me to it. "I chose to pursue Rebecca," I say. "I chose to play along with that sick, abominable Cult. Even while I was careful to avoid sexual sin myself, I was constantly *exposed* to it, every minute I was in Michael's depraved 'Temple.'"

We met most often on Friday and Saturday nights, but you could find members of the Cult assembling at Michael's "Temple" most nights of the week. The "Temple" was an older mansion located in a wealthy neighborhood on the lower slopes of the foothills just above the state capital building. The many rooms and the main hall were lit only by candles. All of the windows were covered. The furnishings were rich and antique. "Antebellum South," I think it's called.

Couples were everywhere, mostly men with women, but sometimes women with women. People kept changing partners. There never seemed to be enough men . . . or perhaps there were too many women.

I got the impression Michael preferred it that way.

Full nudity was not common (though there were many private rooms for that and couples drifted in and out of those constantly), but many members of the Cult were in various states of partial dress. Most couples were engaged in some sort of intimate activity, from kissing, to stroking, to grinding against each other, whether standing and dancing to the constant, driving music or lounging on the numerous sofas and loveseats.

And, of course, there was the "Feeding." Everyone had small knives, supplied by the Teachers. The usual practice was to make a tiny nick in the skin of your partner on the neck or the wrist or elsewhere (it didn't matter where) and then to lick at or suck at the wound. "Feeding" was often done in concert with more sexual activity, but not always. Sometimes a couple would "Feed" off each other at the same time. Sometimes one would play the "prey" and the other the "hunter."

I always managed to pretend *to "Feed," never really tasting or ingesting anything, but I could not avoid getting "Fed" from. Not that any other Novitiate or Chosen ever took more than a little blood. Afterward, a Teacher or the Master himself would come and Feed from the wound.*

They would take more.

There was almost always at least one Teacher present . . . or the Master. Rarely, there were two of them, but never all four of them: Michael, Rebecca, Chikah, and Benjamin. Never all four, that is, unless Michael called an "assembly." At most other times, the Teacher or the Master would lounge there on one of those big thrones on the dais at the end of the main hall, watching over us with those intense, ravenous eyes. They would often be fawned over by one or more of the Novitiates or the Chosen. Mostly it was the women who fawned over Michael, but not always. For Chikah or Rebecca, it was mostly men, but not always.

Nobody fawned over Benjamin.

The Unwilling

Benjamin was the worst of all. To say he was creepy was like saying the ocean is "slightly moist." The hunger in his bright eyes mingled with the hatred and the longing that always burned there in his youthful black face. Fortunately for me, his glares were almost exclusively reserved for the women . . . and for Michael. I always got the impression, from the few times I'd seen them together, that Benjamin both loathed and loved Michael with an intensity that I couldn't fathom.

I couldn't decide what he was. Was he a dwarf or what he appeared to be: an eight or nine year-old child? I couldn't conceive of a child as one of the leaders of a cult, so I assumed he was an unusually well-proportioned dwarf, a malignant black carrion bird waiting hungrily for something to die.

Sometimes a Teacher or the Master would address the lower Circles. At such times, all would sit in rapt attention as the Teacher or the Master would speak to his or her audience. The subject matter would range from talk of their "love" for their "children" (meaning us) to matters of discipline to occasional discourses on Lilith and the Great Secret (which we would be introduced to once we were Chosen). At the time, I thought it was all total garbage, just part of the manipulation. Now the information on Lilith and the Great Secret took on new meaning. I hadn't listened very well. I had no idea at the time that it would someday be important to me . . . or that any part of it could possibly be true.

Benjamin never addressed us. I couldn't remember ever hearing him speak. If he and Michael were together, I would occasionally see him whisper into Michael's ear.

Benjamin was my first Teacher, the first to Feed from me. The other Novitiate, a woman named Mary, was playing the hunter. She had me sit on a loveseat and then she made a small slice in my neck. Her blade was sharp, so the cut didn't hurt as much as I thought it would. Then she inclined her head and sucked at my neck. She wrapped her arms around me and her hands roamed around my back and head and neck. It was so bizarre. There was a little pain, but it felt more like she was giving me a passionate "hickey." When she was done, she got up and wiped blood from her lips and acted as if she had just had the best make-out session of her life.

I saw Rebecca walking sensuously toward me to finish the Feeding, but before she reached me, Benjamin was suddenly there, on the loveseat. He fastened his lips on my throat and I felt pain . . . a piercing pain for a second, but then there was a rush of euphoria. I felt great. My whole body tingled.

Then he was done. He got up, licking his lips, and the euphoria faded. I was left breathless. Benjamin gave me a look of utter contempt, and then he slipped silently away to his throne. He sat there like a malevolent spider in his web.

Meanwhile, Rebecca was nowhere to be seen. I felt my neck and could feel no sign of the wound.

I shudder at the memory.

"Laddie, ye are nae *listenin'* again." Moira's voice wrenches me back once more to the present. "Ye have a cover story: chronic actinic dermatitis. 'Tis an adult-onset condition that makes ye hypersensitive to sunlight. 'Tis rare, but 'tis real. 'Twill serve as an excuse for the tinted windows and other measures ye must take to protect yerself from the Sun."

"Is that what I have?"

"Ach, nae! 'Tis merely a convenient lie to explain why ye must avoid the sunlight!" She looks annoyed. "Now, pay attention. The Sun will be setting and ye need to be ready."

I nod and try to focus.

"Ye can be killed . . . by the Sun, obviously. Anything but a catastrophic injury will be healed immediately . . ."

"By the Seed and the Essence?"

"By the Seed," Moira corrects. "I'll explain that later, but for now, ye must know ye can only be killed by something so devastatin' that the Seed cannae repair it in time."

"When you say 'catastrophic,' what do you mean? Gunfire? Wooden stake through the heart?"

"Gunfire, nae. Yer body will repair the damage and expel the bullets. A bullet to the brain could result in memory loss, but the brain itself will heal. A large object, such as a stake (it does nae have to be made of wood), driven into the heart, if it remains there for very long, will prevent the heart from repairing itself. Decapitation will kill ye. Ye can cut off a limb and reattach it quickly and it will heal. If ye wait more than a minute or so, the limb will begin to regenerate on its own, but 'twill take a while. Ye cannae reattach a severed head."

"No pain?"

"Nae, ye will experience *all* of the pain, but 'twill nae last for long. Ye are immune to disease and resistant to injury, but *nae* to pain. The Healing can be painful and it can be horribly itchy or both."

I can't resist a glance at my hand. "I thought it was a trick!"

"What are ye talkin' about?"

"Benjamin . . ."

Benjamin had "displeased" Michael. That was all Michael said about the offense. He called us all to an assembly to witness Benjamin's punishment and Michael's power and "love."

Benjamin entered the main hall from the door to the Hall of the Chosen where none but the Circle of the Master and the Circle of the Chosen were allowed to go. He wore a choke-chain dog collar and a leash. He was dressed in rags, but he was often dressed like that. Michael entered after him, carrying the end of the dog leash. In his other hand, he carried a sword. From where I sat with the other Novitiates and Chosen called to assemble, it looked like a Civil-War-era Confederate officer's saber. I could see "CSA" etched on the blade.

Rebecca and Chikah followed Michael and Benjamin onto the dais. Benjamin knelt and prostrated himself in the center of the dais in front of the thrones, as if he were bowing to a middle-eastern sultan. Michael stood behind him, striking a stance that looked to me as if he were posing for a military memorial statue. He held the saber in one hand so that the blade rested on his shoulder and he held the leash in his other hand. Rebecca and Chikah separately approached their thrones and curled themselves into the chairs with feline grace. Their hungry eyes fixated on Michael and Benjamin. Chikah leered at Benjamin as he knelt silently. Rebecca seemed to be inwardly laughing at some private joke. Benjamin glared at the floor, his lips pressed tightly together.

Michael placed his foot on Benjamin's neck, like an ancient conqueror declaring victory over a captive of war. The Master gazed on us and then he began to address us.

"My children," Michael drawled in that rich, southern baritone of his, "Benjamin has displeased me. He has displeased his Master." One of the Chosen, a pretty, young, dark-skinned woman, giggled out of lips that twisted up at one corner in a lurid sneer. "And what, my children, is the punishment for incurring the displeasure of your Master?"

And on cue, as we had been taught, we all cried, "He shall be Marked!"

Michael continued the ritual, "And if he incur my wrath?"

"Vengeance! Seven-fold!"

"And if he betrays the Great Secret?" His eyes flashed over us and I was reminded of Rebecca's eyes in the alley. But I had to play my part. I had to focus on why I was there: justice for Julie.

"Vengeance! Seventy and seven-fold!" I almost forgot to say the response for the betrayal of the Great Secret.

"As it was in the beginning," Michael drawled on, "coming down through all the ages of the Earth, from She who is the Mother of us all, from Lilith, daughter of Cain, Mother of Immortals, Mistress of the Great Secret, Source of the Essence, Queen of Night, High Priestess of the Son of the Morning, so shall it be until Night devours Day and the Children of Lilith shall reign supreme over the Children of Adam.

"The Law must be fulfilled."

I felt the bile rise in my throat as we assumed a kneeling position and prostrated ourselves, our arms outstretched toward him as if in passionate supplication. We had been taught this ritual, this horrible liturgy, but I'd never actually seen a Marking. Once, I asked another Novitiate about it and he told me, with an expression I could only describe as religious rapture on his face, that he had seen a Novitiate seared with a red-hot branding iron and then subsequently "healed" by the kiss of the Master. He'd heard the screams of pain, he'd smelled the burning flesh, and then he'd seen Michael lingeringly kiss the charred flesh, and soon the flesh was whole again. I expected something of the kind now. I knew it had to be some kind of illusion, but still, the rapt anticipation of the Cult members made me sick.

"The Law must be fulfilled," we cried, continuing the awful rite.

"And what says that Law?" Michael had them worked into a frenzy.

"He shall be Marked!*" I tried my best to imitate the fervor of the Cult as I struggled to keep the contents of my stomach from flying out of my mouth.*

"Then let him be Marked!*" Michael cried.*

We all began to chant, "Marked! Marked! Marked!"

Michael dragged Benjamin up from the floor with the leash until Benjamin was kneeling before him. The Master dropped the leash and took Benjamin by the hand. I looked around the dais for a branding iron, but I couldn't see it. Michael raised Benjamin's arm until it was parallel to the floor.

"Marked! Marked! Marked!" The chanting rose in volume and intensity.

Suddenly, Michael raised the saber above his head. The blade gleamed in the candlelight, but that was nothing compared to the fire in Michael's eyes. He brought it down, severing Benjamin's arm in the middle of the forearm.

I was frozen in shock.

Blood shot from Benjamin's stump, but the only sound Benjamin made was a grunt.

Michael held the severed limb above his head while our chant changed to "Make him whole! Make him whole! Make him whole!"

My breath came in ragged gasps as I stared in disbelief. In my mind, I spoke my own litany of incredulity: "This must be a trick! This must be a trick!"

The blood from Benjamin's mutilated arm slowed and stopped, and still he held what remained of his arm rigid. He said nothing, but he growled through his clenched teeth. And he stared up at his Master, pain and hatred burning in his eyes.

Michael waved the black, bloodied hand and severed forearm above his head for a moment more and then he said, "Let him be whole!" He handed the saber to

Chikah, who took it and licked the blade with obvious delight. Rebecca chuckled to herself as if this were all a good and familiar joke.

Michael grasped Benjamin firmly by the mutilated arm and joined the two pieces of the limb together and held them there as if they were two pieces of a broken ceramic statue being bonded together with Super-Glue. Benjamin's hand hung limp at the wrist, lifeless. Michael held the two parts together like that for what seemed an eternity to me, but was probably no more than ten seconds in reality. Benjamin began to wriggle the fingers of his hand. Michael released him and a cheer rose up from Michael's "children."

"I have made him whole!" *Michael cried in triumph as he drank in the worship of his followers.*

I stared openmouthed and then I remembered to cheer with the rest of them. It must be a trick, *I thought over and over again. What I'd just witnessed was impossible. It had to be fake.*

The analytical part of my mind, what was left of it, remembered the words of Sherlock Holmes: "When you eliminate the impossible, whatever remains, no matter how improbable, must be true." Or something like that.

It had to be an illusion. There was no other possibility.

"Michael cut off Benjamin's hand and then reattached it. It was supposed to be a punishment for some offense. I thought it was a trick . . . an illusion . . . just another part of Michael's sick mind games.

"But, it *wasn't* a trick, was it?" I say. "That sick bast . . . *monster* chopped off his arm and then reattached it. So that means that Benjamin is a vampire too."

"Aye, he is," Moira answers. "He's a Teacher."

"How *old* is Benjamin?"

"Benjamin is forever nine years old, but he was born over a hundred and forty years ago. He was Michael's slave when they were both mortal. Michael took him as a catamite when Benjamin was only six."

Catamite? "You mean as a . . . a . . ."

"Sexual plaything, aye."

I may be sick yet.

"Michael was a plantation and slave owner in the South during yer Civil War. Benjamin was one of his slaves. Even before he became a vampire, Michael was a beast with many carnal appetites. When Michael became a vampire, he tried to Convert the boy, but Benjamin was too young to consent. Ye know that, until he is at least eight, he *cannae* consent. 'Twill nae work."

I close my eyes and try to control my breathing, try to calm my stomach.

"Benjamin is every bit a slave now as he ever was," she continues. "He *hates* Michael and he *loves* Michael in equal amounts. He would like *nothing* more than to kill Michael, but he's *terrified* of losing him at the same time. He will never grow up."

"So that explains why he hates women. He was always glaring at them with such animosity."

"He hates what he cannae have. Oh, he *lusts* after women, but he will never be physically able to have one. He will be a little boy until he dies."

I need to focus on something else. This is sickening. "Then the brandings I heard about and the healing?"

"The Marking?"

I nod. *Don't puke, Morgan!*

"The branding was real enough. Those branded were mortal. Michael "healed" them with a kiss, did he nae?"

I nod again.

"He was using his saliva, which is strong with the Seed, to Heal them. The Master does this to demonstrate his powers, to convince his followers or worshippers, if ye will, that he is very nearly a god."

"That's why the wounds from 'Feeding' always seem to disappear," I muse.

"Aye, the Seed in our saliva heals the wounds caused by Feeding on our prey, leaving no trace."

"Moira, how do you know so much about Michael and his Cult? Were you ever a member . . ."

"Nay, but I have questioned several of his Chosen over the years and used Persuasion to make them forget about the questioning. The Chosen know more of the truth than the Novitiates do. The Novitiates are still deceived by the spectacle. Ye did nae think I would risk exposure for myself or danger to the city at large by nae keeping a watch on the Cult as best I could?"

"But Michael is a monster," I protest.

"Aye, he is that, but he's a *contained* monster who only Feeds on the willing . . . for the most part. He wishes to avoid exposure, himself. In this world of computers and instant access to information, no sane vampire wants a string of corpses drawing attention and inviting the police to search for a serial killer or group of serial killers."

I take a minute to digest this last bit and then I ask, "So Julie's murder wasn't normal?"

"Nae so much in this day and age, unless she was a failed Chosen, but Rebecca must have had her reasons."

I look up at her with a question on my lips.

"I dinnae know the reason, yet," she says.

"Jealousy, wouldn't it be?"

"Possible, but 'tis hard to say. Michael and his wives take many lovers (temporarily), but I dinnae know if jealousy over yer sister would be enough for Rebecca to risk Michael's wrath over the death of one of his pets . . . if he ever found out, that is."

"You said a vampire licks the wound to close it after Feeding."

"Aye."

"But Julie's throat was cut open and left that way. The police said it almost looked like it had been *torn* open."

"'Tis common enough," she says. "Ye rip the neck open with yer hand or yer teeth (after Feeding) and leave it that way to make it seem as if the victim was killed in a more *normal* fashion."

I mull this over for a second and then say, "What can you tell me about Rebecca . . . and Chikah, of course?"

"Rebecca is Michael's latest wife. He Converted her fifteen years ago when she was in her early twenties. So, she's very young as vampires go. She's jealous and possessive. That much ye know. She fears Chikah and rightly so.

"Chikah is Michael's *current* first wife. She's vicious and likes to *play* with her food. She was Converted over forty years ago in Japan, so she is nae Michael's Convert. She loves the Hunt, even if Michael has forbidden it . . . *especially* if he has forbidden it.

"She came to this country twenty-five years or so ago, chasing elusive prey. She followed her victim when he fled here, tracked him down and killed him *slowly*, over the course of a month, torturing him, letting him get close to death and then Healing him enough to keep him alive. When his sanity broke, she lost interest in him, and so she killed him.

"She met Michael and joined him after killing Michael's wife at the time. She took her place. I think she *tolerates* Benjamin because she enjoys watching his misery. She's extremely dangerous, and ye must nae underestimate her, despite her petite size.

"For that matter, dinnae underestimate Benjamin. What he lacks in size, he makes up for in speed and cunning. Personally, I fear him the most." She hesitates. "Frankly, he gives me the willies!"

I snort. I can *relate* to that.

I'd been watching the mansion for over a month. I would sit in my car or up in a tree and observe the house through binoculars, but the windows were always covered. The only things I could really observe were the comings and goings at the front door. I hadn't been able to make any progress toward getting in.

The recruits (you could usually identify them from the Goth-style clothing and makeup) had no other social life. When they left in the early morning hours, when it was still dark, they went home or straight to work. I trailed as many of them as I could on different occasions looking for someone to help me get into the Cult.

They were mostly very young and attractive, once you got past the makeup and the silly clothes. There were some men, but the majority of them were younger wo-men. There was one housewife, a mother of three small children. She was there several times each week. That sickened me. She left her three children sleeping at home alone while her husband worked nights. She left her kids to fend for themselves just so she could hang out with these people. For a while, I thought about approaching her.

I hadn't tried to make contact with any of the people I observed, yet. I knew I probably had one *shot at getting in. Once I made that first contact and failed, it would look suspicious if I kept approaching other members of the Cult.*

Only once, in all that time, had I caught sight of Rebecca, but I knew *it was her the instant I saw her through the open front door. There was no way I could forget that face, those eyes. I saw her for only a few seconds, but it kept me going, knowing I'd* found *her.*

I hadn't caught even a glimpse *of her since that first sighting.*

On that night, I was perched in a tree across the street, watching intently for any sign, any way in, any Cult member who looked approachable. It was cold, but not unseasonably cold for December in Utah. I was considering whether a newer recruit, a man, might be safest to contact, when the drape covering one of the win-dows was opened. This was a rare occurrence in the house. I immediately focused on that window . . . and there she was! Rebecca! *But that time, she seemed to be staring right back at me. The window was abruptly covered again.*

I kept my gaze focused there for a short time, still in hopes of seeing something else, when I suddenly became aware of the two white eyes watching me intently from above. I was so startled that I nearly fell out of the tree. I looked up and saw the eyes shining from a higher branch. At first, I couldn't make out the face. Then a wide grin filled with very white teeth appeared just below the eyes. It reminded me of

Alice's Cheshire Cat from the Disney cartoon when you could see only the eyes and the grin. Until I saw that smile, I could have sworn the eyes were . . . malevolent, but then they appeared . . . charming. Abruptly, the face became discernible. The face was so black that it had been hard to see in the darkness.

Initially, I could do nothing more than stare stupidly up at the face. After an awkward silence, I managed a shaky, "Hello." The face disappeared . . . maybe the eyes closed or the face turned away . . . and then I could see the dark form of a small person climbing down toward me, then past me, and quickly dropping to the ground. The figure motioned for me to follow and I did, climbing down, but not as gracefully. When I reached the ground, the person (I couldn't say whether male or female at that point) reached out a dark hand and took mine in its small one. It pulled me gently, but insistently, toward the house. I followed, still completely at a loss as to what I should be doing. I noticed the person leading me was limping badly. This, combined with the short stature, made me think of midgets who had an awkward gait, as I'd seen in movies or in real life. I concluded this was a midget (or is the proper term "dwarf?") leading me toward the place I had sought to enter for so long.

I tried speaking again. "Hi. I'm Carl. What's your name?" I waited for a response, but got none. There was only silence as we steadily approached the house, the house where I knew I'd find Rebecca, Julie's killer.

And suddenly she was there.

Right in front of me. Those same blue eyes boring into mine.

"I'm Rebecca. That's Benjamin. He doesn't talk much." Her voice was . . . honeyed and seductive in quality with a pronounced proper British accent. "Thank you, Benjamin. I'll take him in hand from here." Benjamin looked up at her and then glanced at me. I saw a flash of the malevolence I'd seen before in his eyes. An instant later, he lowered his gaze and released my hand and stumped on toward the house. I spared him one last glance and then returned my focus to Rebecca.

She was looking at me with an amused expression, but her smile was welcoming. This is Julie's killer. *That thought burned in my brain, but I tried to keep my face passive. I didn't want to screw up my one chance.*

"I'm Carl." I extended my hand. She took it in hers. Her hand was warm. I was shaking. I hoped she attributed that to the cold air.

I suddenly felt dizzy for a moment, but the vertigo passed quickly.

"I'm very pleased to meet you, Carl, but you're shaking!" She drew me close enough to put an arm around my waist. "Let's get you inside where it's warm." She began leading me toward the house again.

This was all happening too fast. I'd blown it!

"That's where you want to be, isn't it?"

Oh, crap, she knows, *I thought.*

"You've been watching us for some time," she said with a smile, *"haven't you, Carl?"*

I swallowed hard. I didn't know what to say.

"It's OK. You must want to join us very badly to have spent so much time watching us. Come in and meet the family."

"It was Benjamin and Rebecca who found me watching Michael's 'Temple,'" I say. "Benjamin scared the snot out of me when I saw him perched in the tree above me. He brought me to Rebecca. *She* brought me in. I thought for sure, at the time, that Rebecca was *suspicious*, but she brought me right in and introduced me to the Cult."

Moira gives a short, quiet laugh. "Laddie, did ye have a moment of vertigo, when ye met her?"

How does she know that? "Yeah, I did."

"Persuasion, laddie."

Oh, no.

"She probably asked ye everything and ye probably told her everything and then she made ye forget it all. She knew why ye were there. She knew everything."

Her expression turned thoughtful. "And yet, she still Converted ye. What *is* she up to?"

Rebecca knew everything? "How could I be so stupid?" She's known everything from the beginning.

"Lad, she probably recognized ye from the night she killed yer sister. Our senses are very keen and our memories are long."

"What does it mean?" I feel weak.

"I dinnae know, but it certainly does change things."

She looks at me with concern. "Carl, are ye feeling faint?"

"Actually, I am . . . a little."

"Well, ye need to Feed again."

I do feel terribly hungry, but . . . "Why? I just drank two quarts!"

"Aye, but ye needed that to strengthen ye after yer Conversion. Yer body has metabolized it all. Now, ye need to Feed as ye would normally."

I nod my head. It's disgusting, but I crave it. I crave *blood*. It's a horrible admission. "Please."

"Please?" She looks momentarily flummoxed. Then she realizes what I'm asking, but can't bring myself to say. "Ah, ye think I have *more*. Ye have consumed it all, laddie, my whole week's supply."

I think she can see the panic in my face. This must be what a junkie feels like when he finds out his stash is gone.

"It's all right, laddie. We will just have to go Hunting."

Now the panic is full-fledged.

"Dinnae fret, Carl. We'll just take sustenance from some of the criminal element. It'll come naturally to ye."

She rises, but I stay rooted to the sofa. I feel like my limbs weigh a ton each.

"Come along! The Sun has long set. 'Tis a fine night for Huntin'."

She cocks her head and smirks at me. Then her smile widens and she winks at me. She takes my hand. "Come, Carl. 'Tis time to learn to *fly*."

Now *that* is something I can sink my teeth into.

Yuck! "Sink my teeth into."

Did I really just think that?

Chapter 5

I'm flying! FLYING!
I'm soaring in and out of the low-flying clouds in the moonlight. Wheeling, floating, climbing, diving, rolling. I do a cloverleaf maneuver that I haven't done since Undergraduate Pilot Training at Columbus AFB in Mississippi. Not much use for *that* maneuver in the BUFF. The B-52 wasn't built for aerobatics. I start the cloverleaf by pulling straight up and letting my speed bleed off, then, when I'm fully vertical, rolling to the left ninety degrees, then pulling back until I'm inverted. Then I pull through the rest of the loop. I repeat this three more times to complete the four leaves of the cloverleaf maneuver.

It's *glorious*! I feel like a comic book superhero! I just *think* about what I want to do and it *happens*!

The air is brisk as it whips across my face. It's freezing, but exhilarating. I'm *aware* of the cold, but it doesn't seem to have any effect on me. I'm moving so fast that the wind is causing my cheeks to flap like a dog's when he sticks his head out of the window of a moving car. I have to squint my eyes to shield them at this speed. *Maybe goggles next time!* I laugh out loud at the mental image of a vampire wearing goggles and an old leather flying helmet.

My clothes are whipping around me so badly that I actually have to tighten my belt to keep my pants from flying off. I feel a quick tug at my left foot. I look at my feet. Yep, I lost a shoe!

My wings are spread out behind me, beating fiercely at the air.

The old B-52 pilot in me, the logical part of my brain, is analyzing everything about them. They *look* like they are flapping. They *sound* like they are flapping. They seem to respond to my thoughts as I maneuver through the air, feathers pointing up at the back of the left wing to decrease lift when I bank left, but I don't *feel* anything to confirm what I'm seeing with my eyes. I'm flying. *FLYING!* But the wings aren't *real*.

The rest of me couldn't care less about the fact that the wings aren't physically there.

This . . . is . . . so . . . much . . . *FUN!*

I'm pretty sure my top speed is about two hundred knots. I push it as hard as I can, but, when I can't suck enough air into my lungs, I know I'm at about that speed. That's pretty much the maximum airspeed at which you can breathe. I remember that from aerospace physiology class, but I learned it *first* from comic books as a teenager.

Really.

No kidding.

I pull up and climb straight toward the stars. If I don't *think* about the idea that my airspeed *should* bleed off as I climb, I can shoot upward as fast as I can go. Most aircraft, except for some modern jet fighters, cannot *accelerate* in a straight vertical climb and, if they can accelerate, they can only sustain it at full power for a short time. I can accelerate until I can't breathe anymore.

Like right now.

As I climb, the air rapidly thins out. It gets harder and harder to breathe. My brain becomes fuzzy. If there were more colors to see at night, they would all be going gray as my brain goes hypoxic.

I halt my climb. I stop right where I am and I just hover. I look down and try to judge the altitude. It's harder to get a sense of this at night, but I know I must be above fifteen thousand feet to be feeling so light-headed. The air pressure feels like it did on those longer cross-country hops we used to do in the T-37 jet trainers at twenty-three or twenty-five thousand feet. The Tweet (as the T-37 is affectionately known) is unpressurized, so your skin feels . . . how do I describe it? Exposed? Dry?

I remember my training session in the altitude chamber back at Columbus AFB. I was a new student pilot and we were still in our aerospace physiology training period. We all sat in the altitude chamber wearing our flight suits, helmets, and oxygen masks. We were on benches along the sides of the long horizontal cylinder of the chamber. We connected the hoses on our O_2 masks and got accustomed to breathing with the masks on.

The air was gradually sucked out of the chamber until we were simulating the air pressure at twenty-five thousand feet. We unhooked our oxygen masks and breathed the rarified air. We were given those toddler toys, the hollow plastic ball with the blue half and the red half. It had holes with different shapes on it and you were supposed to put these yellow plastic pieces into the various holes. There was a star, a circle, a square, an oval, a hexagon, a cross, and so on. Each shape would fit only in one hole. The point of the exercise was to recognize the symptoms of hypoxia early and to put our O_2 masks back on and flip the switch that would *start the flow of pure oxygen. I started putting the shapes into the holes, but I soon found that it became harder and harder to focus and get the right shapes in the right holes. The colors faded toward gray too. Once I recognized the signs, I clipped my mask back on and flipped the switch. The colors all came back and I could finish the task of putting all the pieces into the ball.*

One guy, a really tall drink of water who had gone through AFROTC at BYU with me, volunteered, as part of the training, to let us watch him go through the same exercise without going back on oxygen. An instructor stood by to put his mask back on and supply the oxygen after the demonstration. The point of that exercise was for the rest of us to be able to recognize the symptoms in someone else.

He removed his mask and started to put the pieces in the ball. At first he did OK. He got three pieces in and then he got slower and slower. Then he started to make mistakes. By the time the instructor put his mask back on and flipped the oxygen switch, the poor guy was just sitting there, staring at the ball and spinning his hands in little circles. He wasn't even holding a yellow piece.

As the oxygen started to flow, gradually, his hands stopped spinning and he picked up yellow pieces again and continued as if nothing had happened. When he was done, he said he didn't even remember losing it for a while.

We had a small laugh at his expense, but we all got the point: if you're not careful, hypoxia can sneak up on you before you know it. And in the stress of combat, you might not notice at all.

And then you'd be dead.

OK, I'm *really* feeling light-headed now. Time to get down to where I can breathe.

I realize I'm already in free fall without meaning to be, so I flip head-down and the wind howls in my ears as I speed toward the ground. I pull up hard out of the dive when the air feels better. I guess I must have stopped my initial climb somewhere above twenty-five thousand feet.

Whatever else I am, I'm vulnerable to hypoxia. Maybe it won't kill me, but I could pass out. Apparently, as I lose control, I start to fall out of the sky. I have to *think* about what I'm doing when I fly. OK, so I need to stay fifteen thousand feet or below.

Important safety tip. Thanks, Egon.

Man, I'm still a little loopy!

Where's Moira? I look around for her, but I can't see her.

Panic starts to set in.

Keep it together, Morgan! Don't panic.

It's just like in the BUFF: think first and *then* act. I remember an older Lt. Colonel flight instructor, an old BUFF pilot, telling me, "In an emergency, first and foremost, you *fly the airplane*. Then you do the BOLD FACE emergency procedures. Then you eat your lunch. Then you decide what to do next." It was great advice. Stay calm. Stay in control. Take care of the immediate danger. Then you take a breather so you don't make the situation worse by acting rashly.

First, I hover and try to get my bearings.

There are the mountains. That's east. I can see the moon reflecting off the Great Salt Lake below me. I'm *way* out over the lake. OK, that mass of lights to the southeast at the base of the mountains has to be Salt Lake City. I'll make my way back that direction. I speed off to where I can now pick out Temple Square with my Seed-enhanced vision. I've always had good eyes (always twenty/twenty or better . . . that's what it takes to fly bombers), but this is *incredible*!

I could find my way to my house, I'm sure, but I need *Moira*. I don't know what I'm doing. I really didn't pay attention to where we started from, where *her* house is. Once we got outside into the night, the instant I thought of myself as flying I was gone!

Up into the sky, Junior Birdman!

I don't have the slightest clue where her house is. I don't know her number. She doesn't know mine. I guess I could look for her at the hospital. But I'm not prepared to move about in the daylight. Does she work nights?

I feel the panic closing in again.

As I approach the city, I see something shooting toward me from below at high speed. It's Moira! Her silhouette contrasts sharply against the lights, her wings beating furiously. I slow and pull upright into a vertical position and . . .

She slams into me at full speed.

We're locked together, tumbling, falling through the air for several dizzying seconds, and then she straightens out and pulls up, yanking me by the armpits, just as you would lift a small child. She looks at me with fury in her beautiful green eyes.

Then she hauls back and punches me full in the jaw. I feel my jaw break. I don't feel the pain. *Probably shock.* It's already knitting back together. I *can* feel the *itch*.

"Dinnae do that again," she growls through her teeth. "I thought I'd *lost* ye!"

Suddenly she's hugging me close and sobbing into my shoulder, her hair brushing against my now completely healed jaw.

"I . . . thought . . . I had . . . lost . . . ye," she says between sobs. "I . . . cannae . . . lose . . . ye. " Her sobbing eases as I put my arms around her. "I have waited . . . so long. So very, very long."

"I'm sorry," I manage to say. "I didn't mean to . . . I was just . . . flying . . .'"

She grabs my face and kisses me fiercely.

I don't know what to do. I haven't kissed anyone since Sharon died. I barely *know* this woman. But I *need* her. I *trust* her.

But this is too soon.

When I don't respond, she stops. Still holding me tightly, she says, "I'm sorry, Carl. I did nae mean to . . . I've been alone so long. I have nae had *hope* in centuries. I'm so sorry . . ." Her voice trails off and she starts to cry again, softer now.

Awkwardly, I stroke her hair with one hand and return her embrace with the other arm. I clear my throat. "It's OK. You're fine. I . . . It's just . . . It's too soon."

"Too soon," she echoes softly. Her voice is like a melancholy breeze.

We hover there in the air, locked in an embrace, our wings gently flapping in unison. It's so comforting to hold her. There is something consoling in her quiet tears. Her hair *does* smell good. And she *does* feel nice. And the air is cold and she's so warm.

I could imagine falling in love with this woman. This sweet, beautiful woman that I need so very much right now. I'm *lost* without her. And I'm single, widowed now. I'm all alone . . . except for Moira.

But it's too soon.

And I barely know her.

"Moira," I say gently, "I *trust* you. I *need* you. I want to help you even though I don't know *how* to help you. But we only met today. And it's . . . too soon."

"I know. I know," she murmurs. "Forgive me?"

"No problem." Man, her hair does smell good! She's so warm.

I let go of her and take her face in one hand and dry her tears with the other. "And you're not exactly *easy* to resist, pretty lady."

She smiles at me wryly.

Dazzling.

Darn hard to resist, actually.

"Let's give it some time, Moira. Apparently we have all the time in the world to see what happens."

She nods, her eyes shining. "Aye." She winks at me. "*Laddie.*"

My stomach rumbles and I'm suddenly aware of a gnawing hunger, a thirst that is almost overwhelming.

She gives me a lopsided grin. "I *heard* that! It's time to get ye Fed, lad!"

She pulls away and takes my hand. Together we glide toward the city.

I notice that our wings intersect, just passing through each other, like impossibly solid-looking holograms.

Just an illusion. No substance at all.

Moira's hand, though, is very *real* in mine. Very soft and very warm.

Chapter 6

After the heady rush and freedom of flying, this terrible *hunger* is a brutal reminder of the price I must pay: I need human blood to survive. I'm not some superhero; I'm a *parasite*, a damned soul who must prey on the living to prolong my hellish existence.

The hunger gnaws at me until it becomes an ache. The ache becomes a burning in my gut and throat. I've never felt such a *need* in all my life.

The thought of biting a stranger, even if that stranger was a criminal, on the neck and drinking blood from him is *revolting*, but as this burning grows, I can *imagine* myself doing it. Moira says that my new instincts will make it easy.

Too easy.

"The challenge will lie in avoiding *killing* yer prey, especially if ye think they *deserve* death. 'Twould be so easy to decide that the world would be better off without them. But I know a *better* way. Follow my lead and I'll show ye what to do."

Moira has brought us to a neighborhood in northwest Salt Lake City that she says is rampant with gang violence. The Tongan Crips gang makes this area hell on earth for those who live here. Moira tells me we won't have to wait long for suitable prey to come to us.

We stand in the deep shadows at the side of a rundown auto-repair shop. It's weird to think of shadows at night, but my eyesight is so sharp that the subtle differences in the light cast by the Moon and stars really stand out. The dirty white walls of the garage are covered with incomprehensible graffiti. *At least it's incomprehensible to me.* The street-lights on this block are all out. Most likely they were shot out by the gangbangers who terrorize this neighborhood.

Since I lost one of my shoes while flying, I've kicked off the other as well. Now I stand here in my socks. I can feel the cold of the sidewalk under my feet. I'm not dressed warmly, but the cold spring air doesn't seem to bother me.

I guess that's a vampire *thing.*

It doesn't matter. I have *other* concerns to occupy my attention right now.

Moira says vampires are very hard to see in the shadows, especially if we don't want to be seen. "It's nae *invisibility*. We are creatures of darkness and the darkness swallows us, effectively hiding us from mortal eyes."

Looking right at her, standing beside me in the darkness, I can see her bright eyes, but even this close, even with my enhanced senses, I find it hard to see her face. She's wearing a long black cloak and hood. Her hands move behind her neck, over her head, and in front of her face. She must have pulled her hood up, because now even her eyes are hard to see. I *like* the cloak. I need to get one of those for myself. Very melodramatic, or at least it would be on me. On her it looks . . . well, it *suits* her. And right now, it helps her blend more completely into the shadows.

"How will we . . ." I start to speak, but she holds a finger to my lips, silencing me.

"Nae need to be so *loud*, laddie. I can hear yer slightest whisper."

I *was* whispering before, but I realize that her voice is so low that nobody . . . no *mortal*, that is . . . could hear it even *this* close. I, on the other hand, can hear her perfectly.

I try to match her volume. "How will we know if someone really *is* a violent criminal as opposed to just *looking* like one?"

"Ye will feel it. Ye will *smell* it," she replies. "Can ye nae feel it now? Can ye nae feel the approach of evil? Does it nae draw ye?"

And I *do* feel it. Something is *pulling* me. It's on the very edge of my senses, like an odor I can't quite identify.

I can smell the blood now. I can smell other things too: body odor, cologne, bad breath, sweat, oil, dirty feet, all combined with the scent of tires, grease, and metal from the garage. But above all there is the *blood*. And it smells *better* than the blood Moira gave me to drink when I first awoke in her home. I guess that's because *that* blood had chemicals in it to preserve it. This smells *sweet* and fragrant and salty, like . . . chocolate-covered pretzels.

For a fleeting moment I think of Sharon.

But Sharon's face fades and is replaced by the thought of *blood*.

My mouth begins to water and I feel my teeth . . . my *fangs* extending. I feel the pull, the *urge*, to fly out and fall upon my prey and take its miserable life! I want to *kill,* to consume the life ... The urge is *unbearable!* The pain in my gut and throat is *agony!*

Moira's hand takes mine in the dark and she says in her should-be-inaudible whisper, "Steady, laddie. Stand fast a wee bit. The prey is comin' to *us.*"

I struggle to remain still. The blood draws me. And Moira is right: I can *feel* their approach. I can feel the pull of *evil.* I can feel the evil pulsing in their veins. I want to *take* it, to *snuff* them out like a candle.

Why would I want to destroy *evil? Why is* that *part of vampirism? Why do I feel the need to* consume *the evil?*

"There are six of them," I hiss softly. I can *feel* it. I don't understand how I know, but I *know.*

"Aye."

"They mean to do ... *violence,*" I say. "They have the blood of innocents on their hands."

"Aye, laddie."

"I want to *kill* them. I want to drain the *life* out of them. Then I want to tear their bodies limb from limb!" I'm barely restraining myself. Moira's warm hand is the anchor that holds me back.

"Aye, laddie. Ye are *drawn* to evil, but ye must wait."

Wait? Wait for what? "*Why?*" I hiss, drool spilling from my mouth.

"Because ye must nae punish the guilty until ye have *proof* of their crimes."

She wants to be just. *I only want to kill, to sate my hunger, to* destroy *them.* I try to focus on her words, on her hand holding mine.

"No," I snarl softly, "that's not what I mean. Why am I drawn to *evil?* Why aren't I drawn to destroy *innocence?* Why am I drawn to *evil?*" I repeat.

"Ah, laddie. Think of the cunnin' of Lucifer who made the Covenant with Lilith so long ago."

I don't say anything. It's taking all I have to keep from flying at the prey that's coming closer.

Closer.

The scent is maddening.

"If a vampire takes the life of an *innocent,* that vampire sends the innocent to the loving arms of a merciful God. If he takes the life of a human *monster,* he sends that wicked, unrepentant soul to face the *justice* of God. We *corrupt* the innocent, but we are *driven* to take away the chance for the guilty to *repent.* We are *driven* to take them in their *sins.*

"'Tis what makes us truly evil, laddie. That's why ye must nae *kill* them."

That breaks through the crimson haze of lust and hatred and burning and pain that has blinded me.

"Scare them within an inch of their lives," she continues, "enough so that they might *repent* of their wicked ways, but dinnae *kill* them."

I can see them now.

Six men. They're approaching a small home. There are no lights inside, but I can see the glow of a TV through the window. I can hear people inside laughing at a Spanish-language TV show. I can *smell* the blood of the family in the home as well, but it doesn't smell the same. It's . . . cleaner. It doesn't *call* to me like the sweet blood of these evil men.

The six men draw weapons. With my Seed-enhanced senses, I can see two semiautomatic handguns. I can smell the gun oil and the gunpowder residue. The other men carry a variety of weapons: a baseball bat, a couple of switchblades, and a lead pipe.

"That's proof enough for me," Moira whispers and then she's gone.

In an instant she's across the street. I watch in wonder, my hunger momentarily pushed to the back of my mind, as Moira moves with uncanny speed. It's like watching an insane ballet. She's *graceful*. It looks like she's *dancing*, her cloak swirling around her. She disarms the two gunmen, tossing the guns across the street to me. I catch both easily, without thinking. I check the safeties, but she's already switched them on. I drop the weapons to the ground.

I look up from dealing with the guns just in time to see Moira gracefully duck the baseball bat. The bat then connects with Lead Pipe Guy, breaking his forearm with what sounds to me like a loud, wet crunch. He screams and drops the pipe, clutching his arm. The arm bends in ways God never intended.

In the meantime, Moira has tripped Bat Boy . . . *Bat Boy,* I snort at that one . . . landing the big man flat on his back. He hits the ground with a very satisfying *thump,* and, a split-second later, his head cracks against the street.

Knifey Boy and Knifey Jr. (might as well keep up the insane comic book naming convention) come at her from behind, their long switchblades held back at their sides ready to stab her in the kidneys. Gun Man I and Gun Man II (OK, not so creative), bereft of their weapons, but not of whatever the Tongans call machismo, taunt her from the front with foul words in both English and what I assume is Tongan. *I'll bet "fai" isn't exactly used in polite Tongan society. They say that one a lot.*

I notice for the first time how *massive* these Tongan brutes are and how petite Moira is by comparison.

I *know* what she is. I *know* she can handle herself, that she's in no danger from these animals. But my blood boils and my mouth waters afresh at the sight of this small woman facing down four huge thugs. The hunger is raging through me like a fire storm. I want to tear them to shreds with my bare hands, rip their throats out with my fangs. I want to drain the life from them.

Instantly, I'm across the street, placing myself between Moira and the cowards rushing her from behind. They are *massive*. I should be scared out of my mind and I would be, were I mortal. But I'm *beyond* caring . . . beyond fear.

I am Fear itself.

I am Terror.

I am Horror.

A feral growl rips from my throat. Knifey Jr. hesitates and then lunges at me. I snatch the switchblade out of his lunging hand with my left hand and grab his wrist and twist with my right. I crush the bones in his thick, muscular wrist and I can hear tendons snap in his shoulder as I dislocate his arm, nearly ripping it from the socket.

I could easily *have ripped it from the socket.*

The rage and the hunger spur me on.

Junior is out of commission as he falls to his knees and Knifey Boy looks at Junior, then at me, and then at Moira. He appears confused. I don't want him to be *confused*. I want him to be *scared*. I want him to be *terrified*.

I growl again, lower in my throat, not so loud this time, but more menacing all the same. I stare him in the eyes. I don't want to try to *Persuade* him. I want him to experience every *ounce* of the horror that I'm about to inflict upon him.

I'm dimly aware of Moira's encounter with the two men behind me, but all of my focus is on Knifey Boy.

"You worthless, gutless *coward*." I speak low, but distinctly. "You *parasite*. You foul, rotting pile of *filth*." His eyes grow huge in the dim light from the windows of the home he and his buddies had sought to invade. His expression is one of shock which quickly transitions to anger. I don't think he likes being called "coward" . . . or "parasite" . . . or "filth."

He opens his mouth to speak, but I cut him off as I raise my hand. "Do you see this hand, you pathetic *worm*? I'm going to crush your hand around the handle of that pathetic little knife and then I'm going suck the life out of your veins and there is nothing you can do to stop me." My voice is icy, not exactly calm, but cold as Outer Darkness.

He looks uncertain. Then he looks scared. Then he panics and takes a swipe at me with the knife. I snatch his hand and hold it in a grip of iron. Then, slowly . . . I *squeeze*. He begins to howl in pain. He begins to scream like a helpless little girl as the bones in his hand crack and splinter. I continue squeezing as I reach up to his huge neck where the muscles and veins bulge in his agony. I pull his neck toward me and I bare my teeth. Terror chases the pain from his face as he sees my fangs. He tries desperately to pull away. He beats at my back and shoulder with his good hand.

I feel the blows, but I don't care.

His blood calls to me. I can see it pulsing just under his skin.

Saliva streams from my mouth and runs down my chin as I close my lips over his straining neck. I pause for one long second with my fangs pressing lightly against his flesh as he continues to scream.

And then I bite down, piercing his jugular.

Blood . . . sweet, salty blood streams into my mouth and I gulp it down. Part of my brain registers that his impotent struggling ceases and his screams turn to moans of pleasure as my saliva enters his bloodstream. The blood tastes different from the stuff that Moira gave me to drink. Even though there are no preserving chemicals, I *do* detect something *foreign*, probably the remnants of alcohol or drugs in his system, but Moira told me that such things won't affect me at all, especially in the blood of my prey.

This is *nectar*.

I want to take it all. I want to drain his life, to destroy him . . . to rid the world of him.

It's his hand, the hand that was beating at my back moments before, that brings me out of my feeding madness. His hand has taken a firm grip on my shoulder and is holding on to me tightly, but not in anger. It feels like . . . *passion*? He's feeling the Seed-induced euphoria that comes over a vampire's victim.

And he wants *more*.

I think I may be sick. I'm drinking the blood of this monster and he *wants* me to take it!

I break it off, instinctively giving his wound a lick to seal it so he doesn't bleed to death. I pull free of his grip easily and release his mangled hand. The knife drops to the ground. He follows it as he collapses to the street.

He's still moaning.

Did I take too much? Have I killed him? No, I can hear his heart beating strongly enough. He probably had a bit more blood than most people in that massive frame of his.

My breathing is coming in ragged gasps as I look around at the carnage strewn about me in the street. My prey is lying on the pavement in front of me, caressing his healed neck wound with his good hand, the misshapen hand lying useless before him. Knifey Jr. is still kneeling beside me, sobbing like a little child, clutching his mangled wrist to his stomach. I can see Lead Pipe cradling his broken arm to his chest like a mother holding a baby. Bat Boy is out cold.

And suddenly I remember Moira. I spin around to see what's become of her.

She's Feeding.

She releases her hold on Gun Man I (or is that II?), who sinks to his knees next to the other Gun Man who lies moaning, like Knifey Boy behind me. Those two look unhurt, otherwise.

She turns to me, licking the blood from her luscious red lips. She's not even breathing heavy.

Moira quickly takes in the destruction left in my wake and says with a wry smirk, "Well, laddie, ye did nae do so badly for yer first Feedin'. They'll live, but they will nae be *leg breakers* again. *Next* time, ye'll control the rage better." She pauses for a moment and then smiles sadly. "Ye did far better than *I* did my first time."

She cocks her head as if listening. "Only one?"

I nod, comprehending. She can hear the stronger heartbeats of those from whom I *didn't* Feed.

"Take some from two more. Ye dinnae need to take much, but 'twill make the Persuasion stronger. I'll take the one with the cracked noggin. The Seed'll help repair the damage to his skull."

As she descends upon him like some black bird, both beautiful and terrible, she adds, "And be *quick*, laddie. The police are on their way."

She's right: I can hear the sirens, even though they're impossibly far away.

I do as she directs. My *need* is gone, but I take a few gulps each from Junior and Lead Pipe. With my rage spent, the thought of what I'm doing is repulsive, but the taste is still sweet.

My hunger is completely sated now.

The moans of pleasure coming from my prey are sickening.

Moira watches me, apparently waiting for me to finish. I look up from Lead Pipe, and she says, "Now, laddie, we have to cover our tracks and, at the same time, we're going to rid the streets of these vermin." I look at her quizzically, but she winks at me. "I told ye I know a better way.

"Now, watch, my bonny wee bairn. I'll show ye what must be done with *one* of them. Then ye must follow my lead with the others."

Moira turns to the Gun Man I. She takes him firmly by the shoulders and stares into his eyes. "Listen to me carefully," she says, her voice one of firm command . . . not loud, but *intense*. "Ye're a *bad* man. Ye'll wait here in the street for the police. When they arrive, ye'll turn yerself over to them and confess all the evil ye have ever done. Ye'll confess every detail. Ye'll answer all their questions. Ye'll repeat yer confession as often as they ask. Ye'll hold nothin' back. And ye'll *ne'er* hurt another living soul. If ye do, I'll return and I'll haunt yer dreams every night for the rest of yer squandered life. Ye'll ne'er speak a word to another livin' soul about me or my . . . companion. Do ye understand?"

"Yes!" he answers immediately. He looks at her with naked longing as if he would do anything in this world to please her. I'm dumbfounded. This was Persuasion, of course, but I never realized the sheer *power* of it. Listening to her voice, *I* want to obey her!

She breaks her stare with the first man and turns to the second gunman lying on the pavement. Over her shoulder she says to me, "Quickly, Carl. We have nae but minutes."

I shake my head to clear it and to try to focus on the task assigned to me.

I turn quickly to Knifey Boy. The nickname I gave him is stupid, but it helps me keep the vermin straight in my mind. My hands tremble as I turn his face so I can stare into his eyes. He looks at me with sick longing. *Speak authoritatively*, was what she said.

"Listen to me," I say with all the authority I can imbue into my voice. "You're an *evil* man. You've done terrible things in your life. The police are coming. When they get here, you'll go to them and surrender. You'll confess every crime. *Every one.* You'll cooperate with them completely. You'll confess everything."

Crap! I already said that!

I'm wasting time!

"You'll answer all their questions. You'll give them dates and names and evidence for everything. You'll never hurt anyone ever again." This reminds me of the hokey "Jedi mind trick" from the movies, but it *feels* like it's working! He stares back at me in rapt attention. My kids (*Lucy! April! Joseph!*) *never* paid this much attention when I gave *them* a serious talking-to. I falter for a second at that memory, but then I push on in a low, commanding voice. "If you ever hurt anyone again, I'll come back and drain the life from you. Do you understand?" He nods quickly, never taking his eyes from mine. "Oh, yeah ... Don't ever speak of me or my partner to *anyone!*" He nods again.

I release him. He still stares after me. I turn to Knifey Jr. I try Persuasion with him. It goes a little smoother this time, and I can tell that it works just as easily as it did the first time.

I turn to Lead Pipe and repeat the Persuasion. No problem here, either. This is *too* easy. It's far too easy for me to rob a man of his free will. As Moira said, it's a great evil. I'm putting these men (*wicked* men, true, but *men* all the same) into a prison in their own minds.

Moira is just finishing with Bat Boy. She had to rouse him before she could Persuade him.

"Does it ever wear off?" I ask.

"Nae as *ye* mean it," she says sadly, rising to her feet and turning to look at me. "Oh, it does nae change *who* they are. They'll still be wicked, evil men unless they *want* to change, but it'll bind them until they confess repeatedly to the police. It should be enough to put them away for the rest of their lives. It may even get them the execution they so richly deserve. And they'll live in both terror and longin' for us for the rest of their days. That terror may be enough to prevent them from hurting others."

She looks up at me. She must see the sorrow in my eyes.

"Carl-laddie, ye have merely facilitated their arrest and, maybe, just maybe, given them a chance to repent. Ye did nae take a life and ye prevented a great evil tonight. *Ye saved lives.*"

"I robbed these men of their agency. I'm *forcing* them to do something they didn't *choose* to do."

"True enough, laddie, for the moment, but, tell me, Carl: How are ye any different from the police officer who'll arrest them and put them in jail?"

I don't know what to say to that.

"What ye have done, laddie, is put them in a position where they'll pay for their crimes. That's all. Ye could've *executed* them for their crimes, but ye did nae. Ye held *back.*"

"They'd planned to murder and cripple innocents in that house, and we prevented it."

The sirens are getting very close.

"We must go, laddie." She takes me by the hand. "Let the police handle it from here."

She pulls me along, and soon we're running back to the utter darkness of our original hiding place at the side of the garage. Once more in the night shadows, we press our backs against the wall. Moira, by holding my hand firmly against the wall, silently communicates to me that we're going to wait and observe.

Moments later, two police cruisers race into view, stopping abruptly, just short of the fallen gangbangers. Four officers emerge from the vehicles, cautiously, hands on their holstered weapons. The six massive Tongans all lurch to their feet. The officers draw their weapons and point them at the huge men. The Tongans, putting their hands above their heads (at least the ones at the ends of arms that still work), approach the police. Six deep Tongan voices begin babbling at the officers, confessing to a huge list of crimes: murder, rape, assault, drug dealing, burglary, theft, arson, vandalism, littering . . . *Littering?* I stifle a giggle, but I'm instantly sobered by the realization of how many lives these men have destroyed. I feel sorrow for their victims and the families of those victims. I also feel some pity for the *monsters,* themselves.

Before long, the officers have them all handcuffed and sitting on the curb. *Why don't they just take them away?* Other cars arrive, unmarked cars with internal flashers and sirens. Plainclothes policemen (detectives, I guess) emerge and, after consulting with the officers, start to question the thugs.

It's at this point that Moira pulls me away from our vantage point and off into the night. We walk in stealthy silence for a minute until we find a deserted spot. She nods at me, and her wings appear to unfold behind her. Soon we're airborne again.

"Aren't they going to take them away?" I ask as we fly to I-don't-know-or-care-where.

"Oh, aye, they will, but they need probable cause to *arrest* them. The baddies confessed to violent crimes, so the patrol officers restrained them for the safety of everyone involved and called in the detectives. The detectives will take their confessions and that'll give them probable cause. They'll be arrested and their injuries will be treated. And they'll be off the street forever. Maybe they'll find God in prison. 'Tis nae likely, but 'tis possible."

"I crushed one man's hand," I say bitterly, "and I nearly ripped another's arm off."

"And yet, ye did nae *kill* any of them. Ye did well. Next time ye'll do better."

That is a depressing thought: there *will* be a next time.

Her hand finds mine as we fly and she squeezes it gently.

"You said that you rarely Hunt," I say quietly.

She turns her head and looks at me. "Aye, laddie. I rarely do. I can obtain enough blood at work for the pair of us under normal circumstances. Tonight was a *necessity*. Ye took enough tonight, so ye should nae need to Feed for a *week*."

That raises my spirits a little. Or maybe it's just the warmth of her hand in mine or her enchanting green eyes.

"Dawn is comin' soon and we need to prepare."

"For what?"

"I dinnae know about *ye*, but *I* have to prepare for work."

Work!

"I haven't been to work since *Thursday*," I say. "I need to get to work *today*." Getting to and from work will present a lot of challenges. The enormity of tackling what should be such a simple task overwhelms me. "I have no idea how I'm going to pull that off. Maybe I can just go straight there, right now and wait for dawn. I don't know what else to do." My face twists in a grimace. "I'm kinda *new* at this, ya know?"

She winks at me.

Man! She's *gorgeous!*

"I'll get ye through it," she says. "But ye cannae go to work like *that.*"

"What d'you mean?"

"Laddie, ye need *shoes*, for one thing. And how will ye get home?"

"Wait for dark, I suppose. I don't know!"

"Dinnae worry, laddie. Moira knows what t'do. And 'twill be a lot more fun doin' it *together.*"

She gives my hand another squeeze and lets go.

"Race ye home!"

And, with that, she's off like a shot, speeding away. I pursue as fast as I can, but she has one critical advantage: I don't know where she lives.

Chapter 7

*I*t's a good thing I kept the van.

After Sharon and the kids (*Lucy and April and Joseph*) were killed, I *had* thought about getting rid of it. Now, it's a lifesaver.

Literally.

I can see the flashers through the ultra-tinted rear window, even with my sunglasses on. *Four days in a row* I've made it to and from work without a problem and *now* I'm getting pulled over? I *don't* need this. I wasn't even *speeding*. I don't want to call any more attention to myself than my dark windows would.

Like it or not, I've got to pull over.

I'm driving, as is my habit, in the left lane (not the sacred carpool or "High Occupancy Vehicle" lane that requires only two people in a car for it to be "highly occupied"), so I carefully change lanes until I can pull off to the right of I-15. I make sure I leave enough room on the right side of the vehicle (the side away from the Sun). The Davis County sheriff vehicle follows me and pulls up behind my van.

The deputy takes his time getting out of his SUV, and I use that time to quickly double-check my protection. Gloves pulled tight. Sleeves pulled down. I tug at the sleeves of the oilskin duster that I always wear now when I have to venture out in daylight. The sleeves cover my arms and hands almost to the knuckles. I adjust my broad-brimmed hat that I purchased at a costume shop. It reminds me of an old parson's hat. It's not a fashion statement; it's a necessity. The sun-glasses will have to go, though, if I need to use Persuasion on him. So I put them in the glove box and remove the doctor's statement (written for me by Dr. Moira) explaining my "chronic actinic dermatitis."

I can hear him getting out of his vehicle. I hastily check my other precautions. The newly installed shades on all the tinted windows past the front seats are in place, ready to be pulled down. I can't see the two new heavy tarps stowed under the middle seat, but I can smell them. My refuge is ready in the back. I need a place to hide from the Sun in an emergency, such as if my van were to break down.

I hear the deputy's footsteps on the pavement of the road shoulder with its smattering of pebbles. He's in no hurry. I can also hear the safety strap on his sidearm holster being unsnapped. He's ready for trouble. Now he's tapping at the window ... the right window, the window away from the lethal sunlight.

Well, at least that *much is going my way.*

I press the switch and roll down the right window. The deputy leans down so he can see me clearly through the opening, while keeping a safe distance. He does *not* have a friendly face. His nametag says, "HADLEY." He has dirty-blonde hair that's gelled into a short, crisp flattop. He isn't wearing sunglasses. *Good.* Persuasion is easier if I can see his eyes. They look hard and stern.

"Yes, officer?" I ask innocently. "I wasn't speeding."

"Your windows are illegally tinted, sir." Yep, his voice matches his face: not friendly at all. And his blood smells *too* good. Am I dealing with a crooked cop? Or just a wicked man who happens to be a cop? I'm not even hungry. Moira brought home blood for both of us just last night. He must be *tainted* for his blood to draw me so.

Time to use my cover story.

"Officer, I have a medical waiver. I have a severe sunlight allergy. I've got a doctor's statement right here."

He seems to be considering it. There really isn't such a thing as a medical waiver, but maybe he doesn't know that.

Maybe he doesn't care.

"Your windows are illegally tinted, sir," he repeats. "The *reason* doesn't matter. You can't operate this vehicle on my highway," he says with a slight smirk. He's enjoying this. "Now get out of the vehicle."

"I can't do that, officer. I can't be exposed to the Sun. I have a severe Sun allergy." This is not going well.

"Step out of the vehicle, sir!" His hand goes to his weapon.

OK. This has gone far enough.

I can still see his eyes, so I stare right into them and say, with all the Persuasion I can manage, "Calm down, Deputy Hadley. I'm not a threat. I have an allergy to sunlight. You have to let me go on my way."

He stares back at me and for a moment I'm not sure if it's going to work. Suddenly I *feel* it, like a key turning a deadbolt. He nods and says in a firm voice, as if it were all *his* idea, "Everything seems to be in order. Go ahead, sir. Be careful."

And with that, he turns and walks confidently back to his vehicle. I can hear his footsteps receding, crunching on the gravel. I can also hear the sound of his holster safety strap snapping closed.

I breathe a huge sigh of relief. I quickly roll up the window and, checking the oncoming traffic, start to pull forward and merge back onto the freeway.

Moira warned me that Persuasion doesn't always work, especially if someone is very strong willed. But even if it doesn't work, you can usually plant a suggestion that might distract him. Of course, my inexperience and lack of confidence doesn't help. There's also the fact that I really, really, *really* hate taking away someone's free will, even for a moment.

Safely merged back onto the freeway, I glance in my mirror and see that Deputy Hadley is still sitting in his vehicle which hasn't moved yet.

OK, I dodged that bullet.

The rest of the drive is uneventful. I pull into the parking garage and find a spot at the back of the lowest level and shut off the engine. I go over my protection once again and double-check the tube of heavy-duty sunscreen in my coat pocket. I grab my laptop bag and get out of the van and lock it. I carefully scan my path ahead, looking for stray beams of sunlight so I can navigate as best I can between them. This building was built to house medical offices and, indeed, there *are* several doctor offices (including my doctor, not that I *need* a doctor anymore), but the videogame studio I work for occupies the top two floors. There's a small patch of openness about three feet long at the exit of the garage before I get to the safety of the entrance ramp that leads to the building's first floor. However, this time of day, there's no direct sunlight in that patch. I step through it quickly all the same and hurry up the long, covered wheelchair ramp.

Once inside, I opt for the elevator, because, in the morning, the Sun is on this side of the building and shines through windows in the stairwell. Still, when the elevator opens on the second floor, I instinctively cringe back into the elevator car away from the morning light that's shining so brightly through the second-floor lobby windows. An elderly gentleman and his sweet wife, both with the halting, arthritic steps of great age, hobble into the car with me. They look at me with some concern. I must look a sight, dressed as I am on a spring morning. I look like the proverbial Cold War—era spy, with my duster and sunglasses. The broad-brimmed hat doesn't quite fit that image, perhaps.

I smile and ask, "What floor?"

"Three, please," the man replies, giving me a twitchy smile that tells me I've done little to allay his fears. They *do* have reason to fear me. They probably can't put a *name* to their fear, but I make them uneasy: I'm a *monster*. Their blood smells pure, not like Deputy Hadley's. The old lady's wrinkled hand finds her husband's and they try to look away, at the floor, the walls, the buttons, the elevator display showing what floor we're on, *anywhere* but at me.

It's a short ride for them, just one floor, but it takes far too long. The automated female voice announces, "Third floor," and the couple hastily shuffles out.

Arriving on the top floor, I exit the elevator and hurry out of the lobby which is awash in sunlight. Hugging the bank of elevator doors, the deadly rays touch only my shoes. I'm in no danger as long as I don't linger, I know, but the memory of my burning flesh urges me out of the light as quickly as I can manage with dignity.

Once I reach the office entrance, I wave my wallet with the passkey card across the sensor and hear the lock click open. I open the door and take the shadiest route to my cubicle. Luckily, my team sits away from the windows and my teammates prefer to keep even the artificial light to a minimum. I stuff the gloves into the coat pockets, put the sunglasses into another pocket, remove my duster and hat, and hang them on the end of my cube wall.

"Morning, Carl," Steve Martin (no relation to the comedian) says from the adjoining cube, still with his back to me. Steve, the UI artist on the team, is intent as usual, on the latest screen layout that he's designing.

"Good morning, Mr. Martin, sir," I reply. "Good morning, Mr. Wallace," I say to the engineer in the next cube, without really seeing him. He answers with some noncommittal response, as if he hasn't decided about the relative good-bad rating of the morning.

I use their last names when I first greet them, but I'll use their first names throughout the day. I'm not sure why I do this. Just habit, I suppose, maybe from my days in the military. Or perhaps the few years during my youth that I spent in the South where manners ranged from the redneck to the courtly.

I remember one of my professors at BYU thought I was being arrogant when I called him "sir," especially in light of the fact that I was wearing an AFROTC cadet uniform and he was of a somewhat liberal bent (a rarity at the Mormon school, even for English professors). I didn't understand his hostile reaction to my question about an assignment. When people become rude, I tend to become more polite. It's a defense mechanism, I suppose, but, in this instance, it seemed to irritate him all the more. His attitude boggled my mind.

The next time I had to talk to him, on a different day, he started the conversation with, "Were you raised in the South, Morgan?" When I replied that I'd spent several years there in my youth, he said, "That explains it. You're just being po-lite, aren't you?"

"Yes, sir," I replied cautiously, even more on my guard than I was when the conversation started.

"You know, son, I thought you were just some arrogant military jerk before, but I think we got off to a bad start, and it's my fault." He smiled.

I gave him a lopsided grin and replied, "I'll try not to take that the wrong way, sir. You got one out of three right, though." He looked at me puzzled, so I felt com-pelled to explain my stupid joke: "The 'military' part, sir. Maybe the 'jerk' part too."

Or maybe I just do it to *bug* them. We all get along great and make a good team. We even go to the temple over lunch on Thursdays, some-times.

Well, we used to. I had to beg off yesterday. There's no way I can enter the temple anymore. Moira says that she has only ever been able to *touch* the exterior wall of a temple . . . and that only once. She's never been able to even set foot in the lobby of one. My "skin condition" serves as a convenient excuse. I stay indoors during the entire workday now. Why go anywhere during the day? It's not like I need to go out to *lunch*.

The day is long. I didn't get much Sleep last night, not that it's particularly easy to Sleep at night, but I was at Moira's home.

I flew to her place for "dinner." That's what she called it. She even served it in wine glasses by candlelight. We sipped the blood slowly and talked, mostly about trivial stuff, like how I was adjusting or various tidbits of advice on living as a vam-pire. After we finished it all, we talked some more, mostly about Rebecca and how we might get justice for Julie. We decided it was useless to try to confront Rebecca in the presence of the Cult or the Teachers; she'd be too well protected, and we wouldn't stand a chance. Without actually saying it out loud, it was understood that we would have to kill her. There was no prison that could hold her and no mortal court would sentence her to one.

"What about the others?" I asked. "Aren't they every bit as evil as Rebecca?"

"Oh, aye! Even more so. Rebecca is the mildest of that lot. But, laddie, would ye take their lives without proof?"

I was astonished. "They're vampires! Isn't that proof enough?"

The irony of my question struck me at about the same time that Moira said with a sad smile, "As are ye, laddie. As are ye."

"I haven't taken a life! That makes me different! They're murderers many times over!"

She bowed her head. "I've taken lives." Her voice is quiet. "I have slain seventy-two men. Will ye kill me, as well?"

"You told me that they deserved to die, that they were guilty," I protested.

"That they were, lad. Forty-six of them were guilty as the Man o' Sin himself and I dispatched them all. I had absolute proof of their guilt: for, ye see, I was there. Aye, I was there. The other twenty-six? I judged and convicted and sentenced them to death. I was their executioner. They were convicted based on the witness of one man and that testimony was taken from him against his will. Were they guilty? Aye, I believe they were. Did they deserve death? I'm nae so sure. I slew them for vengeance and I've paid a terrible price for my revenge."

She was quiet for a long time. She just sat there at the table with her head bowed. After a while she rose and, taking me by the hand, led me outside onto her back lawn.

She let go of my hand and she lay down on the grass. She put her hands behind her head and gazed up at the stars, but said nothing more. After a while, I lay down beside her and put my hands behind my head. I waited like that for what seemed like a very long time. At last she spoke, never taking her eyes off the stars:

"My Donald and I were to be married. Oh, I was so happy! I was young and in love and I was to be a bride. But Bonnie Prince Charley came, and all the young men of the village marched away with him . . . including my Donald. Many of the ald men too. My father would have gone with them, but he was too ald. Donald and I said our good-byes in the gloamin' and he kissed me . . . and then he was gone.

"Several weeks later, word came to our village that the Scots had been crushed at Culloden. Bonnie Prince Charley had fled, and, of the prisoners taken by the English, half had been executed and half had been freed to return home.

"My Donald was among those executed.

"I mourned. I wished that we could have been married and that I could have given him a child. But, nae, he was gone and nary a wee bit of him remained, save in my memory.

"I had nae long to mourn, though. Within a week of the news from Culloden, there came a detachment of Redcoats. They burned the farm. They slaughtered the sheep and the goats and the cattle.

"They raped me.

"There were forty-six of them. They left me bleedin' and, they thought, dyin' beside our smolderin' cottage, my father and my mother burned alive inside.

"I thought I was dead. I wished I was dead, but I did nae die.

"'Twould have been better had I died.

"But, nae, I crawled into the ruins of a burned-out barn, and, slowly, my strength returned. I lived on charred gobbets of meat from a goat that had burned to death in the barn, unable to escape the flames. As I lay there, in my rags, gnawing bits of charred flesh from the bones, I dreamed of revenge.

"I had a plan, ye see.

"I knew of the Ancient One who haunted the kirkyard. When, at last, I had the strength to leave my hiding place, I sought her out. I begged her to help me seek vengeance for my Donald, for my family, for my virtue, for myself.

"I dinnae know why she did nae kill me, but the stories said she only preyed on men. She took me and she taught me and she prepared me. I swore the Oath, I partook of the Ritual, I had the Ordination, and, before I collapsed into the Sleep, I begged her to make my Offerin' any one of the forty-six soldiers in the nearby English garrison.

"When I Awoke after three days, there he was. I knew him. I knew his face. 'Twas seared into my memory.

"I drained him.

"I reveled in the blood, in my revenge, and, filled though my belly was, I hungered for more.

"I killed them all, every man jack in that garrison. I drained them and I gloried in their blood. One each night. Just one, so their terror would be the greater. They dispatched couriers to beg for relief or reassignment, but I killed those men on the road. They ne'er delivered the pleas for succor.

"One of the couriers, a lad barely shavin', recognized me. He thought I was a ghost come to haunt him for his crimes. He sobbed and he cried like a wee bairn. He begged me to forgive him, but I would have none of it. He pleaded with me, tellin' me that he had nae ever been with a woman before or since and that he only raped me because he feared the ridicule of his comrades. I terrorized him for an hour or more before I drank from his neck and then, while he yet lived, I ripped off his privates with my bare hand and let him bleed out between his legs.

"When there were but a dozen of them left, they abandoned their post. But I followed them and slaughtered them all . . . one by one. I saved the captain for last. He did nae rape me, but he stood by and watched as his men had me one by one and left me for dead. As he swore to me on his knees to do anythin' if I would spare his life, I demanded of him where I could find the men who had executed the hielanders taken prisoner at Culloden. He told me where the soldiers were likely to

be garrisoned. He begged me to spare him so he could return to his wife and baby daughter. Wife and baby girl? I was so disgusted with this monster who claimed love for the women in his life and yet condoned rape and murder that I did nae drink his blood. I simply ripped his foul head from his shoulders.

"I was so consumed with rage that I flew that night to the location he gave me. I found the commander of that garrison and, by Persuasion, I learned the name of every man who participated in the executions. The Scots had been hung as traitors, because they chose to follow the son of the rightful King of Scotland and England, rather than that Hanoverian Usurper George.

"I killed him, for he had ordered the executions. I killed all the men who'd taken part, twenty-seven in all . . . all save one.

"'Twas on Christmas Eve in the Year of Our Lord 1747 that I tracked down the sergeant who had commanded the squad that hanged my Donald from the gibbet. I remember it well. The snow was deep and blowin' and the wind was howlin' when I broke down his door. In a trice, I held him by the throat, suspended against the wall of his small home, while his wife, with a bairn in her arms, and his wee son watched in horror. He pleaded for me to spare his wife and children. I told him I'd show him and them as much mercy as he'd shown Donald MacDonald when he hanged him for a traitor. He choked and gagged as he said that he'd nae but served his king and his country, he'd done naught but his duty. His wee son grabbed at my knees and pleaded with me nae to kill his father.

"I ignored the lad.

"And then he bit me.

"The wee lad bit me on the back of the leg. I dropped his father and wheeled round. I raised the brave, yet terrified, screamin' child into the air. I think I was about to dash the boy's brains out when the father pleaded with me to take his life, but to spare his child.

"I stopped myself. What had I become? A monster that would kill an innocent child for the sins of the father? And what of the father? Had he nae served his king and country as my Donald served his prince? Were they so very different?

"I placed the lad back on the ground and fled into the storm and the night.

"From that day to this, I have nae taken another human life. In abject loathin' of what I had become, I went to a priest of the Kirk, but he told me I was damned, that there was nae hope for redemption for the likes of me in this life or in the life to come.

"After that, I struggled to survive. I could nae die, but I hungered for blood and I became weak from the lack of it. I tried to Feed off animals, but received nae nourishment. Only human blood would suffice. I tried to simply abstain and let myself die, but after months of languishing in agony, I finally decided to go on livin'.

"I would haunt the hospitals and the homes of the dyin' and drain the blood from the newly dead. On occasion, like the night ye first Awoke, I would chance upon a murderer or some other villain in the act of committin' violence and I would stop the crime and take some blood for my trouble. But I have nae taken another life.

"I've tried to atone for my sins, but I cannae replace the lives I've taken. I cannae purge the demon inside of me.

"I've traveled the world seekin' redemption. I became a midwife to help bring souls into this world, since I cannae have children of my own."

I looked up at this, but she continued without seeing me, her gaze still fixed on the stars, "Male vampires may impregnate a mortal woman who could then bear a mortal child, but female vampires cannae carry a baby to term. The Seed attacks the bairn as it would any foreign object and expels it from the body.

"I'm denied even that comfort."

She looked over at me then and took my hand. It was so warm. I wanted to comfort her, but she seemed as if she no longer needed it. She turned her gaze back up to the sky, but she left her hand in mine.

"I studied medicine. I've been a doctor many times. Sometimes I'm a nurse. I've studied my condition and sought a cure, but I have nae found any. I know the Seed is similar to a virus. I've tried to kill it in one way or another, but the only way I've found that works is to remove it from the body. Denied the Essence, it dies quickly. 'Tis the demon that sustains it.

"So, I've used my knowledge to save lives. But, that cannae compensate for my crimes.

"Yet, 'tis all I can do."

She gave me a sad, tight-lipped smile.

"So, I ask ye again, laddie: Will ye kill me as well? Do I nae deserve to die?"

I really couldn't think of anything to say that wouldn't sound unbelievably trite. Instead, I just squeezed her hand.

She turned her face back to the stars. "Ye saw Rebecca kill yer sister. Ye have nae seen Michael, Chikah, or Benjamin's murders. If ye are going to be judge, jury, and executioner, ye better have proof."

We lay on the grass, hand-in-hand, watching the stars in silence for a long time.

The meetings are *brutal.* Today is the biweekly planning day when we set our goals and tasks for the next two weeks. I call it, "Meeting Hell." I struggle to stay awake. I *always* struggle to stay awake during Meeting Hell, but, after so little Sleep yesterday, I'm really fighting it now. If I fall asleep, I may not wake up till nightfall. Vampiric Sleep is almost like being in a coma, especially during the day. It's very regenerative, but it takes a lot to wake us, or so Moira has told me. The smell of prey could do it, if we're hungry, but I'm not. Even surrounded by all these sources of food (my co-workers), that wouldn't rouse me. Only sunset would.

I can imagine my co-workers trying to rouse me if I *did* fall asleep. After shaking and slapping failed to wake me, they might call an ambulance. I might be taken out and exposed to sunlight. *That* would rouse me. It would also cause quite a stir when I burst into flames.

It sounds like we might be wrapping up.

Finally!

As soon as the first person rises to go, I'm out of the conference room like a shot. I go to my desk and try to get a head start on Monday's tasks.

One by one, my teammates leave for home. The one advantage to Meeting Hell is that we get to leave early (pretty much as soon as the planning is done), but I linger till the traffic dies down. I don't want to get stuck in traffic and risk exposure to the Sun any more than I have to.

Also, there's nobody to go home to.

As it is, I'm rarely the *last* one to leave the office, but I'm close to it.

Around seven o'clock, I get to a stopping place in my coding, pack up my laptop, and prepare myself to venture out into the light. First, I apply a generous coating of sunscreen on my face, neck, and arms. Next I put on the long duster, the sunglasses, gloves, and hat. I turn the collar up on the coat, grab my bag, and take the safest route to the elevators. With the Sun on the opposite side of the building, this is far easier in the late afternoon. I make it into the parking lot without any direct exposure. The lowering Sun penetrates deeper into the garage now than it did in the morning, but I parked in a dark corner at the back. So, I take the longer way around to my parking spot, but I'm able to stay in the shadows.

Moira's story last night has stirred up a tempest of confusing emotions. I *understand* her motivations. No, that's not quite right. I haven't gone through what she went through. I've suffered loss (*Sharon! Lucy! April! Joseph!*), but I haven't been gang-raped and left for dead. So, I can understand on *one* level, but I can't *begin* to comprehend the trauma on the other.

However, I get what led her to become a vampire: it was hatred, a desire for vengeance, and a sense of utter *powerlessness*. I've never hated anyone like that, not even Rebecca, but I can understand why *Moira* felt that way. She knew of no other way to fight back. She got her vengeance, but at such a cost!

On the other hand, it's comforting to know she trusts me enough to share her pain. I had wanted to comfort her last night, but she didn't need comfort so much as she needed *understanding*. I think she's at peace with what she is. Or she *was* at peace. She told me that my coming into her life has stirred feelings that she abandoned long ago. She has *hope* now, but I have no idea how to help her. I'm just as trapped as she is, in spite of the fact that . . .

I hear his heartbeat and his breathing before I smell his blood, before I smell the sweet *corruption*. I *know* that smell. He's very close. I must have really been deep in thought not to notice it until now.

I freeze.

He's behind me.

"Deputy Hadley?"

I turn around slowly, so I don't see the nightstick before it connects with my head. The pain seems to register too slowly. My vision goes gray, and I'm falling. So slow. I crumple to the concrete, and blackness takes me.

It's dark and I'm crammed into a small space. I can see the *hint* of sunlight here and there. I smell oil, gasoline, and dirt. And there's a sensation of movement.

I'm in the trunk of a car and it's still daylight. The car is traveling down a road. From the way it stops and turns, we're still in town.

I took a nightstick to the head, but I couldn't have been out for long. It was enough to get stuffed into a trunk, though.

But my head doesn't hurt at all, thanks to the Seed.

My wrists and ankles are bound with what feels and smells like duct tape. I tear out of the tape as if it was tissue paper.

OK, Morgan. You're in trouble.

Think. Assess.

The Sun won't set for at least an hour or more. My protection? My hat's gone. So are my sunglasses. I still have the duster and gloves. So my head is completely unprotected except for the sunscreen on my face and neck. That won't stop my hair and scalp from bursting into flame. I check my pockets. The tube of sunscreen's still there. I could smear it on my scalp, I suppose.

We could stop at any time, and I could be exposed to the Sun's deadly rays, so I pull the tube out and squeeze a ton of the sunscreen into my hand. I smear it over my head, applying extra to my face, neck, and ears. I work it deep into my ears. That feels disgusting!

I might have limited protection for my head, but I'd have to keep my eyes shut. I'd be blind. I *could* force my way out of the trunk, but I don't know where I am or how far away shelter might be, so that probably isn't a safe course of action . . . at least not until dark.

Assess. Think.

I check my pockets. My cell phone is gone. So, no calling for help. *Besides, who would I call?* Moira is as trapped, wherever she is, as I am. My home teacher? My elders quorum president? My bishop? I almost laugh at the thought, in spite of my predicament. Even if I *had* my phone, *they* wouldn't know what to do. I couldn't even tell them where I am.

I have my keys. I have my wallet.

In the confined quarters of the trunk, I can't move much, but I feel around with my hands and feet. I find the role of duct tape, some rope, a shovel, some plastic garbage bags, and not much else.

What's going on here? Is Hadley some kind of serial killer? He knows what he needs in order to dispose of a body. Either he's done this before or he's studied or worked on serial killer cases. What made him target *me?*

I can feel his evil blood drawing me. I can smell it stronger than all the smells of the musty trunk. This is one *seriously* bad man. I'm not hungry and I *still* want to kill him.

We're on the freeway now. He'll want to head out of town a ways, I'd imagine, so maybe I have some time. Will I have enough time to wait for sunset?

Assess. Think.

Sunlight is the big danger. I doubt Hadley would have anything else that could do me serious harm. A knife, maybe, but, unless he puts it into my heart, and I'm unable to pull it out quickly, I'll be in no danger. I'll be *pissed*, though, if he shoots a hole in my duster. It's the only long coat I have and it was *expensive!* Of course, if he shoots me in the head, Moira says I could lose memory, knowledge. That would be a lot worse than a hole in my coat.

I guess all I can do is wait.

We drive for what seems like a long time. I occupy my mind with engineering problems to stay awake. Falling asleep could be a problem if he stops before sunset. I'm not really scared. But I *am* angry. I'm getting more angry by the minute. I can't afford to lose my focus here. I could be in *real* trouble at any moment.

Stay calm, Morgan.

Back to the engineering problems.

We've been traveling on a country road for a while, when I can see the hint of sunlight fade away. I can *feel* the coming of night. I sense the extra boost of strength and energy which comes with the setting of the Sun flow through me.

I'll give it a few more minutes to be sure, but then, at last, it'll be time to deal with Deputy Hadley.

We're stopping now. *Good timing.*

Maybe it would be best to burst out of the trunk and surprise him. Is the Sun really down, though? Maybe I should wait as long as possible. He'll be expecting me to be bound and helpless. I can't maneuver enough to get new duct tape on, but it wouldn't hurt to hide my wrists and ankles and make it *look* like I'm still bound up. I put my arms behind me and hide my ankles as best I can.

He's getting out of the car. Whatever happens, I have to focus on *not* killing him. Whatever he is, whatever he's done, the *police* can deal with him. *I* don't need to kill him. Scratch that: I *do* need to kill him very badly. I *want* to. His blood *calls* me to me. My fangs are already extended and my mouth is watering at the thought of tasting his blood.

Focus, Morgan! You are not *a killer!*

Rebecca is one thing. Mortal justice can't touch her, but you are *not* going to execute this man! *Focus!*

I gain enough control to retract my fangs. But I can still feel the incredible pull of his blood.

Hadley is taking his time. He has no reason to hurry. He thinks I'm no threat.

I hear him insert the key into the lock. It turns.

The light is dazzling! *It's too soon!* I shut my eyes in panic.

No, wait.

This is just twilight and it's only *bright* in comparison to the darkness of the trunk.

I open my eyes and there he is. His face is a mask of rage.

"What . . . did . . . you . . . *do* to me?" he growls.

What is he talking about? Persuasion? That must be it. He wants to know how I got away from him this morning.

Here comes the nightstick.

He hits me hard across the chest. Pain blossoms in my chest. I hear ribs crack. The pain is bad for a moment, but is erased quickly by the Seed. It sucks to get hit, but as long as he stays away from my head, I can handle this all night . . . if necessary.

"Answer me, damn you!" He hits me again. "What"—a*nother* blow —"did"—*another* —"you"—*another* —"do"—*another* —"to"—*another* — "me?"—*an extra hard one.*

OK. This has been fun. I've had enough. Moving with the speed of a striking snake, I snatch the nightstick out of his hand before he can hit me again. I rise up out of the trunk and shove him to the ground.

He's so startled that he hits the dirt and lies there stunned. I leap to the ground and stand over him before he thinks to reach for the gun at his hip. He draws his weapon, but I bend down and rip the gun from his grasp. With one hand, I crush the barrel and hold the mangled weapon in Hadley's face for a moment before hurling it away in contempt.

He stares at me, raw, naked fear on his face. I notice for the first time that he's not wearing his uniform. A very quick glance behind me confirms that the car is *not* a patrol vehicle. By the time I turn back to him, he has regained some of his composure, if none of his dignity: he's still flat on his back.

"What are you?" he gasps.

"You picked the wrong guy to mess with, Deputy." I pause for a heartbeat and then bend down quickly and grasp him by the shoulders. I lift him high over my head.

For a moment he just stares at me. Then he cries out, his eyes widening, "What the hell are you?"

"Hell?" I muse out loud. "You have *no* idea." My voice is still deadly calm in spite of the fury raging inside me.

He struggles to free his arms and, failing that, he tries to beat at my arms with his fists, but he can only pat weakly at them. He kicks at me and connects with my stomach.

That just stokes my rage.

"Stop that," I say in a low voice, full of implied menace. I use no Persuasion . . . not yet. "You're annoying me, Deputy. And you *really* don't want to piss me off." *You wouldn't like me when I'm angry.*

He stops struggling.

Still holding him aloft effortlessly, I fight to hold my rage, my *need* for his blood, in check. All I want to do is *kill* him.

"Tell me, Hadley, why is it that your blood calls to me for vengeance? What have you done that is so *evil*, other than assaulting and abducting me?"

He says nothing, but stares at me with an expression of shock on his face.

"TELL ME!" I roar at him. The rage is building. I don't know how much longer I can control it.

"Go to hell!" he says, but there's no conviction in his voice.

I drop him, but, as he falls, I take a firm hold on his ankle and fly into the air, my wings beating insubstantially behind me. He screams like a little girl as we climb into the sky.

I climb rapidly to what I judge is about three thousand feet, careful to stay out of the light of the Sun, and I stop abruptly. This elicits another scream from Hadley. He stares at the darkening ground half a mile below us.

"*Tell* me," I say in a quiet voice that belies the fury boiling inside me.

He starts to whimper. I give him a little shake.

"*Tell* me." It's almost a whisper, but I'm sure he can hear me.

"I'm a bad man." He's crying now.

"Tell me something I don't know."

"My step-daughter. I'm . . . sleeping with her," he sobs.

The rage is now warring with my urge to vomit.

"You mean you're *raping* her."

"Yes."

"How old is she?" I'm struggling to hold my voice steady.

"She's six."

I let go of him.

He plummets, screaming toward the earth.

For a few seconds I struggle with the rage that makes me want to let him fall to his death, but with the scent of his evil blood gone, I take a deep, calming breath to clear my head and then I dive after him. As I close on him, I slow to match his speed. He's still flailing about, tumbling through the air, screaming. I snatch his ankle and arrest his fall.

His screams don't miss a beat.

I start to climb back up into the darkening sky. I shake him by the ankle to get him to shut up.

When we get back up to about a mile in the air, I shake him again. He cries out. "Please! *Please*! Don't drop me! I'm sorry! I'm so sorry!"

I *want* to. Oh, how I want to drop him! With a great effort, I make sure my voice will be calm. "Tell me why I should let you live, Deputy Hadley."

He whimpers.

"Tell me why I should let a monster like you live."

"I'm sorry!" he sobs.

"That's not a reason. You've destroyed a child's life. Sorry won't fix that."

He sobs something I can't make out. Not that I really care what he has to say, but there's something else I want to know. "What were you going to do with me?" I ask.

No response except a whimper.

"TELL ME!" I roar at him. The rage is starting to get the better of me. I want to rip his leg off and then let him and his leg fall separately to the earth. I imagine the blood spurting from the ruin of his hip.

I imagine draining him here in the air and then dropping his lifeless carcass.

Get control, Morgan.

"Tell me," I repeat coldly. "*Now.*"

"Rough you up."

"I don't believe you."

"Kill you. Maybe. I don't know."

"*Sure*, you don't know. Why kill me?"

"I had to know what you did to me this morning."

"Why?"

"Because . . . *nobody* tells me what to do . . . especially when I wear the badge." How ironic: this pathetic monster, this child rapist, this *control* freak isn't in control of anything anymore.

I try to keep my rage at bay, my blood pounding in my ears, *his* blood screaming for me to take it. "So, you were going to kill me because you're a control freak and I got the better of you?"

"I'm sorry."

"Have you killed before?"

He whimpers. "No."

"I don't believe you," I say, my voice like death, and I shake him again.

"Yes!"

"Who?"

No answer from him, except whimpering.

"WHO?" I roar at him.

"Drug dealers . . . pimps . . . human garbage."

"And people who you stop on the highway?"

"No! Just people who get in my face. *Please don't kill me!*"

How I want to!

Get control, Morgan!

What am I going to do with him, though? I don't want to Persuade him. I don't want to take his free will. But, if I let him go, I don't think I can trust him to turn himself in. If he goes home again to that little girl . . . even one more time . . .

No, it's time to use the "mental handcuffs." But not here . . . not up in the air.

We descend to the earth near his car, its trunk still hanging open like the maw of some dark beast, a beast Hadley fed me to.

When I'm a few feet from the ground, I drop Hadley. He falls in a heap and lies there, racked with heaving sobs.

"Get up." I'm not in a position to look him in the eye, but my voice is commanding. He slowly gets to his hands and knees. Then he hesitates.

I can see it.

He's planning something.

He gets one leg up, his foot on the ground and then he suddenly grabs for something at his ankle. Another gun. In all my anger, I missed that he had a second gun. If I'd grabbed the other ankle just once . . .

The first shot takes me square in the chest. I feel an incredible explosion in my chest, but there's no pain. He follows with seven more shots, all hitting me in or near the heart. I'm knocked onto my back.

And then the pain hits. There is *so much pain* that I can't quite sort it out. There's *agony* in my chest. I think my heart has stopped. I can't breathe.

And then I can feel it. My heart and lungs and chest repairing themselves, and the pain is gone, replaced by the awful itching sensation of tissue and flesh rebuilding.

I roar in anger as I arch my back and vault to my feet in a move that would make Jackie Chan envious.

Hadley is still on one knee in front of me.

I fix him with my burning eyes. He's staring at me in mute horror. I look down.

Crap! He's ruined my coat!

"Now you've done it, Hadley," I growl between gritted teeth . . . gritted teeth with fangs now prominent. "You've made me angry."

I snatch the empty gun away from him and bend it in half. I fling it away. I yank him to his feet so he's staring me in the face. I rear my head back and give him a good look at my fangs. His scream starts low and rises to a soprano high pitch. I plant my fangs in his neck and feel the hot sweet blood of a murderer and child rapist pour down my throat. His screams morph into moans of pleasure.

I take two quarts from him. I wasn't hungry, but I could have drained him there. With a supreme effort of will, I pull my lips from his throat, lick the wound to seal it, and thrust him to the ground with a snarl.

I stand there, my breathing ragged, fighting the urge to rip his head from his neck. He lies on the ground, panting and caressing his neck. He looks up at me with unmistakable *longing* in his eyes. It makes me sick.

Really sick.

I fall to my knees, bend over, and vomit Hadley's blood onto the ground. When I stop retching, I turn my face back to him. He's still lying there. He's reaching one hand toward me, his expression pleading.

I rise unsteadily to my feet. I stare him in the eye and command, "You will get up and drive to the sheriff's office. You will confess everything, every murder, every rape, but you will never mention me. You will beg them to lock you up. You will never go near a child again so long as you live. You will never mention me to anyone in any way. If you do not obey me, I will kill you. I will . . ." (Moira's story comes to mind) ". . . rip off your worthless . . . genitals . . . with my bare hands and throw them to the dogs to eat. I'll let you bleed out from your crotch. Do you understand?"

"Yes."

"Then go."

He gets shakily to his feet and staggers toward the car.

Crap.

He's in no shape to drive. I'm going to have to keep on handling this filth myself.

"Stop," I command. He stops. I rise into the air and scoop him up with my hands under his armpits and up we go into the night sky.

I start heading west and it takes me a second to get my bearings. Those lights over there are the Bountiful Temple. I head toward that.

Where do I find a police station or sheriff's office? I have no idea where to take him.

I could call 911. My phone! "Hadley, where's my phone?"

"In my car." His voice is weak, his pulse rapid, but steady.

With a sigh, I turn around and head back to his car.

Once there, I have Hadley retrieve my cell phone. I ask him if he has a phone of his own. He answers that he does and I command him to call nine-one-one and report his crimes to them. I leave him sitting next to his car with instructions to wait for the police.

I hover in the starlit air high above as I wait for the flashers of approaching police cars. I remain there long enough to listen with my Seed-enhanced ears as Hadley tells his confession. When I see him handcuffed, I turn around and head toward Bountiful and my car.

On the way back, I phone Moira and tell her about my night. She's sympathetic, but reminds me that I've left blood and tissue samples (meaning my *own* tissue) at the scene. "I suppose 'twill add corroboration to Hadley's story, laddie, the part about him being a murderer, at least," she says, "but 'twill also leave the sheriff with a wee bit of a mystery, since Hadley will nae tell him about ye."

"What should I do?"

"Nary a thing, laddie. I think ye have done well enough. Anyway, it's too late to go back now."

So I tell her I'm heading home for the night and I'll call her tomorrow. "I need to Sleep. I'll probably Sleep all through the day tomorrow."

"I'll bring ye 'dinner' tomorrow night, Carl. Yer place, an hour after sunset?"

"Sure." I land just outside the parking garage. "Tomorrow night."

"Sweet dreams, Carl-laddie."

I have a fleeting mental image of Moira tucking me in and giving me a kiss on the forehead. She's dressed like my mother in a house-dress. That image shifts and she's kissing me good-night as she lies beside me in bed wearing something that I never saw my mother wear.

It's gonna be a long drive home.

I pull the van into the garage and close the door with the remote. I grab my laptop bag and get out of the van. I head into the house. Once inside, I set down the bag and take off my coat. It's shredded, front and back. The bullets must have gone right through me. My shirt and . . . what's underneath it are ruined too.

My hair's still greasy with sunscreen. I need a shower. I lost my hat and sunglasses. I need to find something else to use as protection from the Sun.

OK. No Sleep yet. I'll shower first and then I need to go shopping. I HATE shopping for clothes.

I'm most angry about the duster. I'm going to have a hard time replacing that. And where am I going to get a hat with a wide-enough brim tonight? The costume shop is in West Valley City and I'm sure it's closed by now.

Ah, no! I know *exactly* what I'm going to have to do and I *don't* like it.

Not one bit.

I look really *stupid*.

I look like an *idiot* in a Stetson.

I had to go to a western apparel store. I barely made it there before closing. I was able to get a duster, and that's good . . . but a *cowboy* hat? I'll have to make do.

Moira is going to laugh herself *silly*.

At least I had *one* good idea out of all this: A hoodie. I got one at the big discount store and I got it extra-large so I can pull the hood down low. That'll be my backup. I got new sunglasses too, while I was there.

I am *really* beat now as I pull the van into the garage for the second time tonight. I'm just *dragging*.

A knuckle-dragging vampire. I picture a gorilla with fangs and an opera cape.

And a stupid Stetson hat.

As exhausted as I am, as soon as I enter the house, I'm instantly alert. *Someone* is here in my house. I can hear the breathing. I can hear the heartbeat. I can smell the blood. It doesn't smell right. I can't put my finger on what's bothering me about the scent, but I feel as though I should recognize it.

Focus, Morgan.

Upstairs. In the living room.

Whoever they are, there are *two* of them. I can hear two distinct heartbeats, two people breathing.

I creep up the stairs, and there they are, sitting on the couch. Or rather *one* is sitting. The shorter one is standing.

And I recognize them.

Even with the lights off, I would know those eyes.

It's Rebecca.

And beside her is Benjamin, glaring at me.

Chapter 8

Benjamin has a short sword in his right hand. It's pointed at my heart. His right foot is slightly forward and pointed at me as well. His left foot is turned outward. His left hand is back. This is a classic fencer's stance. He looks for all the world like he's *protecting* Rebecca: a child-sized bodyguard with inhuman strength, speed, and cunning. I need to be very careful with Benjamin. His eyes shine from the blackness of his perpetual scowl.

Hatred burns in those eyes.

Hatred for what? For me? For the whole world?

Rebecca looks completely relaxed as she sits languidly on my couch, her feet drawn up under her. Golden hair cascades gently over her shoulder. She looks . . . *seductive.*

It's not going to do her any good with me. I know this woman is a *viper.*

And she knows everything.

"Get out of my house." My voice is a low growl.

Impossibly, Benjamin's scowl deepens even more, and I hear a low hiss escape through his clenched teeth and tight lips.

How very much like a snake *this* one is too.

No, not a snake: a spider.

Rebecca's hand caresses his cheek. "It's all right, love." Her British accent is soothing in its tone. Only the slightest movement of Benjamin's head pressing against her hand betrays his notice of her. His *eyes* remain fixed on me.

His sword never wavers.

"Dear Carl," she says, her eyes turning to me. "Is that any way to speak to your *mother?*"

"Get out of my house," I repeat more slowly and forcefully.

"*Really,* Carl. Such *terrible* manners. A mother deserves *better* from her *son.*"

"*Mother?*" I snarl. "What makes you my *mother?* Because you *Converted* me? Because you *damned* me for all eternity?"

She gives me a saccharine-sweet smile and bats her long lashes from eyes wearing too much makeup. "When you didn't come home after you Awoke and ran away from the Temple with your Offering, I got *worried*, you naughty boy."

"*Get out of my house!*" I want to rip that smile from her face. *Let's see how pretty she looks while her jaw is growing back.* But I don't dare take her on with Benjamin here. I'm not sure I could take her by myself at this point anyway.

"Was she *sweet?* Hmm? Your Offering?"

"I wouldn't know," I snarl. "I never tasted her."

Her eyes widen in shock. Even Benjamin drops his perpetual scowl for a moment; his sword lowers slightly.

"I took her to the hospital," I say. "She's fine."

"You . . . never . . ." Rebecca has not regained a shred of her composure.

I decide to press my advantage while it lasts, but I can't take her on at the moment. I'll try a psychological attack, make her even more uncertain of who I am and what I'll do.

"No," I continue, my voice rising, "I haven't *killed* anyone, in spite of you. Now, *get out!*"

"How have you survived?" She's sits straight up, placing her feet on the floor. "You look well Fed."

"Oh, I've Fed, but I haven't killed. And if you leave *now*, I won't kill *tonight*."

That got her attention. "I'll leave," she says as she reclines with casualness that seems forced to me, drawing her feet under her again, "but not until you hear me what I have to say."

"You have nothing to say that I want to hear."

"You don't even want to know why I killed your sister."

OK, Rebecca. Now you have my attention.

I realize that she knows everything about why I tried to infiltrate the Cult. She used Persuasion to get it from me on the night she brought me in. But the two of us have never spoken of it.

At least . . . not that I remember.

This is surreal. My sister's killer wants to *confess?* She wants to *explain?* What is she? A comic book villainess who has to pontificate about her crimes?

"Go on," I reply curtly.

She smiles a feline grin, like a cat that plays with a mouse before she kills it. She knows she has my attention. I'm the mouse.

"Would you believe me if I told you it was *self-defense?*" she asks.

I snort in derision.

"I thought not," she replies while casually picking lint off her black clothing. She seems almost bored. She knows she has me . . . for the moment . . . and she's going to milk my attention for all its worth. "But it's true. I killed Julie to *protect* myself."

"Oh, I'm sure she was a *huge* threat to you." I make no attempt to hide my sarcasm. "You, Michael, and Chikah have numerous sexual partners. There's no way you'd be so jealous of Michael taking another lover that you'd have to kill her."

"Yes, we do have our little diversions, but, sadly, *you* were never among mine. Not that I didn't *try.*"

She *did* try. Many times.

"I even tried to Persuade you, but to no avail."

"What? When? How . . ."

". . . did you *escape?*" she asks coyly. "Persuasion doesn't work if you're exceptionally strong willed. And on this *particular* point, you are *very* strong willed, I'm sorry to say."

I never considered that Persuasion could be used to seduce me.

Please, Father, let it be true! Let me never have fallen in that *way!*

"For a while, I thought you were just not into women, even a woman as *irresistible* as me," she says, languidly running her fingers through her golden hair. "But, no, you told me all about your dear departed Sharon and your lovely children and your religious *restrictions.* You told me all of it under the influence of Persuasion."

Hearing Sharon's name from her foul lips makes me growl. "Leave my wife and children out of this!" I hiss.

"But, I digress," she says, ignoring my anger. "Where were we? Oh, yes! Why did I kill your sister? Julie? That *was* her name, wasn't it?"

She pauses for a response, giving me a look of false innocence. I just lock my jaw and wait.

Unperturbed, she continues, "*Pathetic* little thing. Forever moving from one batterer to another. You always rescued her when she'd had enough of whoever the abuser-of-the-month was, as I recall. And then she found *Michael.* I never heard *how* she found her way to us, but there she was one night in that pitiful getup that the chattel wear in our humble little Cult. Soon she was fawning over Michael. I'm not sure why he picked her out from the rest of them, unless he was drawn to her *need* to be abused. Michael can be so *sadistic*, can't he, Benjamin, love?" She caresses his cheek again, and this time he leans into the caress unabashedly, even though his eyes never leave me.

What is going on with her and Benjamin? I thought Benjamin was Michael's . . . toy. Is "love" just a British endearment such as you hear on TV or in movies sometimes? Or does it mean *more* in this case? Physically, he's just a little boy, but inside he's a twisted, corrupt *old* soul.

"I thought nothing of it at the time," she continues, "but, of course, I watched her. When Michael took her as a lover, I watched closer. When he elevated her to Chosen, I knew I had to move. I couldn't allow her to live."

"Why?" I snap. "Why would you care if Michael had another wife? You're already his second. You chose to be a second wife willingly, didn't you?"

"Carl," she says, pursing her lips in annoyance, "I know you're not *stupid*, so why are you being so dense?"

She's baiting me. *Just hear what she has to say and get them out of here. You can't fight them alone.*

"I joined Michael because I was in *love* (or at least I *thought* I was) and because he promised eternal life. He embodied *everything* I wanted: strength, immortality, security. You see, I was much like Julie when he found me. I never wanted to be *vulnerable* again. I never wanted *any* man to have power over me again. So Michael seduced me, made me what I am, but, don't you see, Carl? He has poor Benjamin and me under his total control. He can do anything he wants! And the way he abuses poor Benjamin!" She caresses his cheek again, and he closes his eyes in naked pleasure at her touch. "Chikah stands with Michael. All she loves is the Hunt. Michael, of course, forbids it, but that makes it all the more desirable to her. So she finds ways around Michael's prohibition. She has what she wants: a ready supply of food, a city to Hunt in, available and willing playthings, and the safety the Cult ensures.

"Benjamin and I are *powerless*. Michael can do as he pleases, and we have no choice but to obey, to go along."

"So leave him."

She laughs. It is a mirthless laugh. Soulless.

"Where would we go? We need to Feed. We need protection during the day. And we need money. Can't get by without money in this world! All these things the Cult supplies."

"OK. I get it." My voice drips with sarcasm. "You're *powerless.* You can't leave him. Blah, blah, blah! You *are* like Julie! You're *pathetic!*"

She exhales loudly in exaggerated exasperation and gives me a little pout. "Oh, Carl! Grow up, will you? I killed Julie because I couldn't let her become a *vampire.* I couldn't let her stand with Chikah against me."

"Against you? How?"

"Because, my dear, silly, errant boy, I mean to kill Michael and replace him as Master. What is it the young people say?" She makes a face of mock stupidity. "Duh!

"Carl," she continues, patronizingly, "didn't you ever wonder why there are several Chosen, but only four Teachers? Haven't you ever wondered why there aren't more Children than we four?"

Actually, now that she mentions it, it is *strange.*

"Because," Rebecca continues, "I can't let Michael get any *stronger.* If he did, I'd never be able to *kill* him."

"Let me get this straight," I say incredulously. "You killed Julie . . . so you could kill Michael?"

"And Chikah. Carl, don't be *stupid!* That's *exactly* what I'm saying. Julie would have served Michael without question. She would have added to his power. She would have *died* for Michael. Benjamin and I cannot stand against Michael and Chikah, let alone against Michael, Chikah, and an immortal Julie!"

"You and Benjamin? You're planning some kind of coup?"

"Yes! Precisely! Can't you see? Michael is *evil!*"

I can't believe I'm hearing this! "Evil? So are you, lady!"

She actually looks shocked! *Why? Because I called her "evil"?*

"You murdered my sister!" I cry incredulously.

"I killed to survive! You do the same!"

"I haven't killed."

She smiles at me smugly. "You didn't kill your Offering, so you say . . . ," she starts, but I interrupt her.

"I *didn't* kill that girl."

"Pity," she sighs. "She smelled so sweet. What a waste. But you must have Fed . . ."

"I've found . . . other ways . . . to Feed . . . without killing." I'm not sure how much they know about Moira or even if they know she exists. If they don't know about her, I want to keep it that way.

"Not *animal* blood!" she protests. "That doesn't work! I've . . . tried." Her eyes drop from mine.

That's a shock. *Why would she try animal blood? She had to know it wouldn't work.*

"Animal blood? Of course not. I am what you made me, but I will not *murder* to survive." *Let her puzzle it out.*

"Why would you . . . Why did you . . . Convert?"

"I didn't 'Convert.'"

"Yes, you did! You're a Child of Lilith! You're not mortal anymore. You're one of us! You're a vampire!"

"Oh, I'm a vampire. You made me one. You damned me to eternal hell, but I'm *not* one of you. I'll *never* be like you. I won't *murder* to survive."

"Why would you choose . . .?"

"I DIDN'T CHOOSE!" I roar at her. "You *stole* my choice! I'm damned, and I *never* wanted this . . . this *eternity* of darkness! I never wanted this foul, wretched . . . existence. You murdered Julie and then you *stole* my *life*! I'm damned for all eternity, and I'll never see Sharon or Lucy or April or Joseph again! You stole *everything* from me! I have nothing left!"

How I hate her! I realize with a start that I hate her more for what she did to me than for what she did to Julie.

She's actually cowering! She's gasping as if there's not enough oxygen in the room. She looks at me again. "How can that be? You spoke the Oath, you tasted . . . you *chose*!"

A bitter laugh escapes me. "I thought it was a sick game. Just a perverted fantasy you and Michael and the others used to get those poor wretched people to worship you. It never occurred to me any of it was *real*."

"You didn't *choose*?" She's actually *trembling*! Benjamin looks frightened too.

What is going on?

"No, I didn't," I say bitterly. "You made me an unwilling vampire. I understand I'm the first."

"That's impossible!" She *is* frightened! "I didn't Persuade you! It doesn't work anyway. You have to be *willing*!"

"Well, just call me the 'Unwilling'! There: add that to the list of words we vampires capitalize," I add with a nasty chuckle.

She flinches.

They both do.

"You *voluntarily* said the Oath and tasted my blood and received the Essence."

"Yeah, you're right," I sneer. "I did it willingly enough because I thought it was *garbage*. How do you British say it? 'Rubbish!' I thought it was no more real than all the tripe about 'Lilith and the Covenant and the Great Secret.' But I guess that's all real as well, isn't it? I never believed any of it. But, you know what, *'mommy?'* Believing or not, willing or not, I am what you made me. Now I have nothing left to live for except to get justice for Julie." *And for myself? No, not for me. I hate her for what she did to me, but if I make this about* me, *then it becomes vengeance and not justice.*

"Now, get out of my house!" I yell.

"No, Carl." She has regained some of her composure, but the attempt at seduction is completely abandoned. "I'm not leaving until you hear me out. You are still my 'son,' and I . . . need your help."

"Lady, I'm not your 'son.' Now get out! Both of you."

"You have to *help* us," she begins to plead. "Ever since he lost Julie, Michael's been suspicious. He assumed Benjamin killed her. That's why Michael punished him." Benjamin glances down at his arm. There's no mark there, but I'm *sure* there are scars in his mind that will never heal. "Michael's preparing to Convert *all four* of the remaining Chosen at once so he won't risk losing any more of them. If he does, he and Chikah will be invincible."

"That's *your* problem, Rebecca. You chose this life. Deal with it."

"The Cult can't sustain so many vampires. The young ones will have to Hunt among the mortal population. And they won't have *your* compunction about killing. They're all Chikah's disciples and look forward to the Hunt with anticipation. They're all *eager* to Convert."

No! No! NO! I can't be considering this! She murdered Julie! She damned me! I can't help her! She's evil! She's . . .

She's right.

"When?" I ask through clenched teeth.

"When what?"

"When are they to be Converted?"

Her face splits with a grin. "That's what I love about military men: pragmatic and decisive! On the night of the full moon. That gives us just a few weeks to come up with a plan."

How did I come to this? I'm actually going to have to *help* these two monsters. Rebecca's right. She has me; I *must* help her. I'm making an unholy alliance with the devil. Churchill and Roosevelt with Stalin. Who was worse? Hitler or Stalin? In the long run, it was Stalin, but Hitler was the *immediate* threat.

What will Moira think? Will she join me? I don't think I could bear to *lose* her now. She is . . . *dear* to me.

"I'll help you," I say.

Her shoulders sag in obvious relief. She really had a lot riding on this tonight.

"But first, some questions," I say.

"All right, Carl. Ask your questions. No secrets between us, love."

"Oh, make no mistake, Rebecca," I say menacingly. "There is no *love* between us. I *will* help you, but this is a *truce* only."

She nods. Benjamin glares and resumes his fencer's stance with the sword pointed at my heart.

First things first.

I turn to look at Benjamin. He's small, but I know he's *fast*, even for one of us. "Benjamin, put that thing away."

He glares at me with such intense hatred it's almost a physical presence in the room.

And he doesn't move.

"It's all right, Benjamin, love," Rebecca coos to him. "We're all friends here."

I glance at her and growl.

"Well, maybe not *friends* exactly, but *allies*," she corrects. "We don't *threaten* our allies."

He doesn't move a muscle.

She reaches up and places her hand on his shoulder. He seems to melt. All the tension flows out of him like water down a drain. He lowers the sword and thrusts it into the leather scabbard at his hip. He looks much more relaxed, but he stays where he is, still protecting her.

"Come here, Benjamin, love." She extends her arms, and in a flash he's in her lap, his arms around her neck, clinging to her like a little boy clinging to his long-lost mother, his head nestled on her breast. He still watches me out of the corner of his eye. Her arms fold around him, but her eyes come back to mine.

I swallow hard. This is so far from where this all started. In my heart, I'm in turmoil. I could never have imagined in my wildest dreams I'd be allying myself with this ... *creature*. Everything has changed. Time to take a deep breath and focus on what needs to be done. As my old flying instructor, Lt. Col. Daggett, used to say, "There is nothing so worthless as altitude above you or runway behind you." In other words, no use focusing on what you don't have, on the past; focus on what you have to do right now.

"Why did you induct me into the Cult and Convert me when you knew I was there to destroy you?"

"Well, Carl, lo ... Well, in the *first* place, I *love* a challenge. In the second place, I needed an ally, and most of our Novitiates are wretched sheep who just want to *belong* somewhere. When I first 'interviewed' you ... all right, *Persuaded* you (and the Persuasion almost didn't work on you and probably *wouldn't* have if I hadn't taken you completely unawares, by the by), I discovered that you were a *military* man with an analytical mind. I'm no strategist. I'm just a girl Michael seduced. You were strong and resourceful and logical as a mortal. As a vampire, all of that would be enhanced. Michael has Chikah, the Chosen, and all of the Novitiates to protect him. I needed someone to help me find a way past all of that. And, as things *progressed* and you resisted all my attempts to seduce you, I was convinced you'd be a strong ally who, once convinced to join me, would see this through to the end."

I nod. I think she's actually telling me the truth as she sees it. And I *do* get the necessity of joining with her ... for now.

"OK," I continue. "Next question: why is Benjamin with *you*? I thought he was devoted to Michael, as sick as that may be."

Benjamin growls at this, but his hold on Rebecca tightens.

Rebecca smiles at me, a wicked smile full of dark and forbidden knowledge. "Benjamin and I have ... an *understanding*." She runs her fingers through his thick-curled hair. "Michael has forbidden him to touch a woman, not even to *Feed*. With his apparent age, no woman would have him, and the taboos are so *ingrained* in this culture that even Persuasion wouldn't convince a woman to be with him. Not that Benjamin *uses* Persuasion; he doesn't *speak* except to whisper to Michael. Until Michael is gone, I've promised to be the mother he never had. Once Michael is *deposed*, Benjamin will be my consort. We'll ... work it out when the time comes, won't we, love?" She kisses his forehead, but her eyes never leave mine, and she gives me a slow, carnal wink.

Stalin or Hitler?

Focus, Morgan. Focus on what needs to be done right now. I can hear the voice of Col. Daggett: *Worry about the flamed-out engine after you pull the aircraft out of the spin. Fly the plane. Fly the plane.*

"Why not just have Benjamin put that sword into Michael's heart?" I ask.

Rebecca purses her lips in consternation, but doesn't break the rhythm of her caressing the head of the child-monster in her lap. "Benjamin can't do that. He can't be the one to kill Michael. He just can't bring himself to do it." Her expression is sufficient to communicate to me that she's spared no effort to get Benjamin to do this very thing and she's had no success. "Besides, Michael doesn't *allow* weapons anywhere near him unless they are in his *personal* possession. And Chikah's never far away. There is no Child of Lilith more dangerous than Chikah . . . except for Lilith herself, of course." Rebecca flinches when she says the name this time.

She's afraid of Lilith? I'm just beginning to accept the idea that the story of Lilith and the Covenant and the Great Secret is more than a myth. Why would Rebecca be afraid of a vampire from six thousand years ago? Moira told me, in one of our talks about vampirism, that there are very few truly old vampires. Surely Lilith was dust long ago!

"How did you find my house?"

She gives me that look of mock stupidity again.

"Persuasion, of course," I supply my own answer. "From my first 'interview.'"

She nods to confirm my conclusion.

"How can I contact you to discuss the plan? I'm not going anywhere near the Cult. And I don't want any of *them* anywhere near *my home*. Do you hear me?"

"Agreed. As for where to meet, only Benjamin and I know of this place. Meeting here might be safest."

The image of the three of us sitting around my dining room table discussing battle plans is repugnant, but I can see the sense in what she says.

"Agreed," I say, "but under one condition: you will *never* enter here again without my permission, without me being here first."

"Agreed."

"How *did* you get in?"

"Benjamin entered through your upstairs bathroom window."

"Never again," I say to the little horror in her lap. "Are we clear?"

Benjamin nods.

Rebecca kisses his forehead again without taking her eyes from mine. "I'll call you in a week if we can get away."

I look at her quizzically.

"We cannot get away from Michael all that often. He's very . . . possessive . . . very controlling."

Benjamin squeezes her tight again. Looking at him like this, I realize with a start that I *pity* him. He never had a chance. Michael is a demon, and his corruption of Benjamin started at such an early age, even before Michael's Conversion. But, whether he's a victim or not, I need to be very wary of Benjamin.

"Carl," Rebecca asks tentatively. "How *have* you survived?"

I will not betray Moira to these fiends. "The details of my private life are my own now. It's enough for you to know that I won't kill."

"But Michael and Chikah must die."

"I understand. That's different. This is war. I've killed in war."

She smiles. "Yes, you have."

"Yes, I have. Now, get out."

She winks at me. "Call me!"

"I don't have your number."

"That's all right. I have yours. Besides, I can't have you calling at the wrong time. Michael or Chikah might overhear."

"Get out. Dawn is coming."

She extends a hand for me to help her up from the sofa.

"Get out," I growl, pointedly ignoring her gesture.

She smirks at me, but she withdraws the hand. She lifts herself and Benjamin from the sofa and gently sets him down on his feet. She takes him by the hand. He puts his free hand on the hilt of his short sword. He gives me a glance of unadulterated hatred, and then they are gone through the front door.

I lock it behind them. I go right to the upstairs bathroom and lock the window. I spare a glance at the toilet that I'll never need to use again. I note the hard water discoloration in the bowl and think I should clean it.

Tomorrow night.

I'm so tired. I need to Sleep.

But not yet. I need to talk to Moira.
I pray that it won't be for the last time.
I can't imagine life without her now.

Chapter 9

Are ye completely *daft?*" Moira shouts over the phone.

Ouch! I should have turned the volume *way* down. It's not like I wouldn't be able to hear a *whisper* over the phone with my Seed-enhanced hearing.

"Moira, please hear me out," I'm trying to keep my voice calm. *I need Moira.*

"Ye've made a deal wi' the Divil! Ye dinnae ken that she's the Divil?" Her brogue is markedly more pronounced, probably because she's angry.

"She's not the Devil, Moira."

"Oh, aye! Tha' she is! Lucifer himself! Or close enough to it!"

"Stalin," I say simply.

She stops mid-rant. "What did ye say?"

I take a deep breath. At least she might *listen* now. I have to make my point quickly and succinctly. "Rebecca is Stalin. Michael is Hitler."

She's silent, except for her rapid breathing. She's digesting my analogy, I hope. I so wish I could have done this in person, but dawn is coming very soon.

I hear her take a deep breath. "They were both horrid, wicked men," she says in a calm voice. This is much more like the Moira I know who seems at peace with who she is. "They both murdered millions."

"Yes, they did, but we allied ourselves with Stalin to stop Hitler."

"Aye, that we did, laddie. And 'Uncle Joe' turned out to be far, far worse than 'Uncle Adolf.'"

"Yeah, that was true in the long run. Stalin lived a lot longer and killed and destroyed far more people than Hitler did, but Hitler was the more immediate threat."

"Aye, ye could easily say that. But how does that apply to Michael? What makes him so much more dangerous right now that ye would ally yerself with the woman who murdered yer sister?"

There is so much I want to tell her. I want to tell her how conflicted I am that I've had to make this profane alliance with Julie's killer. *Killer?* Why *killer* and not *murderer?* I'll have to analyze that later. I need to keep control of this conversation. *I need Moira!*

"Michael is going to Convert his four remaining Chosen on the full moon. Four new vampires, Moira. And four new Offerings."

There is silence for a moment and then she says, "Why? Why would he do that?" She sounds shocked.

"Because he doesn't want to lose any more of his Chosen. Apparently, Rebecca has been killing them as they approach Conversion to prevent Michael from gaining loyal soldiers."

"The Cult cannae sustain that many vampires at once," she says slowly. "They'll Hunt among the mortals. And there would be the deaths of four innocents when they Awaken."

"That's what convinced me. I have to stop Michael *first*. *Then* I can worry about Rebecca."

"Aye, I can see that. So, she's plannin' on killin' Michael? Ye do know that is the only way to stop him, do ye nae?"

Good. I think she might be onboard now.

"Yeah, Michael and Chikah both. Rebecca's planning a coup. She wants to be the Master."

"Chikah is far more deadly," she says matter-of-factly. "She'll have to be taken out first."

"I believe it."

"What about Benjamin? What does she plan to do with him?"

"He's with Rebecca. She's . . . *using* him."

"Oh, that poor, twisted, ruined creature! How did she get him to betray Michael?"

"Can't you guess?"

There's a pause, then a gasp, and then, "Nae!"

"Yep," I reply soberly. "Only, I'm not so sure how deep his betrayal goes."

"What d'ye mean?"

"Rebecca has already tried to get him to assassinate Michael, but he refused or was unable to carry through. I'm sure his feelings toward Michael are very . . . complicated."

"Aye, I can believe they are."

"With that said, Benjamin seems utterly devoted to Rebecca. She's only providing 'motherly' affection for now with the promise of more

... *carnal* affection once Michael and Chikah are dead and Rebecca is the new Master. Master? Mistress?"

"Master," she replies. "There have been few female Masters. Lilith prefers it that way."

"Seriously? Lilith? You speak of her in the present tense."

"Oh, Aye. She's still alive. She reigns from Kansas City."

"Kansas City?" *Kansas City? Why on Earth?* "How . . . *Really?*"

"Every Master must answer to her. They're all her consorts."

"Consorts? That's what Rebecca said Benjamin would be. But 'consorts'? The word implies that if there are *female* Masters, then they would be her . . ."

"I said she *prefers* male consorts, nae that there is nae the occasional female one."

"Gross."

"Nae more 'gross' than Michael who has a young catamite along with his 'wives.'"

Good point. "But, Lilith must be . . ."

"Nigh six millennia old. Aye. The daughter of Cain. More wicked, more powerful, stronger, and more seductive than any of her Children. And she's protected by the Covenant. No vampire can gainsay her and none of us can slay her. We're *incapable* of it. The Oath binds us and makes us unable to commit any act of direct disobedience. So we avoid her when we can. Even the Masters avoid her, unless they're summoned. Never havin' been a member of any Cult keeps me safe, unless I were to meet her in person."

"Have you ever actually seen her?"

"Nae, and I never want to. Pray that ye never cross her path. With your unique . . . history, ye would nae survive the encounter. She would bend ye to her will and force ye to break every taboo ye ever had. She would relish yer corruption."

"OK. Enough on *that* pleasant subject."

"Do ye have a plan already?"

And just like that . . . I know that Moira is with me.

My throat is suddenly tight and my eyes moist with tears. No, not just moist. Tears are spilling down my cheeks.

"Carl?" Moira inquires. "Laddie? Are ye there?"

Until this moment, I didn't comprehend how *much* Moira's support means to me. I was prepared to do what I must to prevent Michael from bringing four new vampires into the world, no matter the cost, but to *know* that she'll stand with me, that she won't *leave* me, that I won't be *alone* is a relief beyond measure, beyond words.

"Carl!" Her voice is frantic. "Speak to me!"

I try to speak, but I can't get anything out. Not a sound. I try to clear my throat, but there's nothing.

"I'm comin', laddie!"

I hear a clattering sound. Did she drop the phone?

And then there's only silence.

Eventually, I hear the chime of a dropped call.

Moira is coming here.

But so is the dawn.

My front door faces south. I run to the door and open it. I look with horror at the lightening sky. It's over thirty miles from Moira's home to mine. My mind races through the calculations. Her top speed, or at least the top speed at which she can breathe, is about two hundred knots. That's about nine minutes. I don't think she has that long. Maybe five or six minutes at the most.

Father in Heaven, please *let her arrive safely. Don't let her die because I couldn't control my emotions. Don't let this wonderful woman die. I . . . I need her.*

All too soon I see the fingers of deadly light lancing down from behind the mountains, reaching to the street in front of me. I'm sheltered from the light by the exterior wall of the garage. I scan the southern sky desperately looking for Moira, my angel of mercy who saved me, who took me in when I had nowhere else to go, who mentored me. I search the sky, but I see nothing.

There! Low, almost level with the houses and trees! Her wings beating furiously, she is a trail of smoke. She looks like one of Saddam's surface-to-air missiles homing on my B-52 over Iraq. The SAMs missed because we jammed them, made it hard for them to 'see' their target: our aircraft.

Please, Father, don't let her miss her target!

I brace myself for the impact.

She hits me at full speed. We go tumbling through my door and into the living room. She ends up on top of me, and I'm furiously patting at the smoldering remains of her clothing with my hands.

I have to act quickly. If she sets the carpet or the walls on fire we'll both die. I push her off me and scoop her into my arms. She's limp, unresponsive. There are two embers on the carpet, but I stamp them out quickly.

I'm up the stairs with Moira in my arms. I race to the bathroom and the tub. I hold her limp form upright against me as I turn on the water. I stand there in the tub, holding her up under the shower's stream. In moments, she is cooled. I listen for her heart and her breathing. Both are picking up in tempo. The obvious burns are already healed. I'm sure her hair was on fire, but now I see no sign of it. The Seed must provide some protection for her hair too.

Her eyes flutter open. It takes her a moment or two to focus, but then her eyes latch onto mine.

And then she's kissing me. Passionately. Fiercely. Her arms are around me tightly.

And I'm kissing her back. Passionately. Fiercely. My arms are crushing her to me.

It's not that I don't think about Sharon. I've thought a lot about Sharon lately. I *love* Sharon. I will *always* love Sharon. I chose her to be my eternal companion, but Sharon has gone where I can no longer follow. I know that God will take care of her, ensure that she's happy, but I've *lost* her forever.

Moira is here. And I *need* her.

It comes with the sudden force of a revelation, as if the heavens have opened: it's *OK* to love Moira. And I do ... I *love* her ... so dearly.

With that realization, the ferocity and passion are gone, replaced by tenderness. Moira's intensity changes to match mine.

And there we stand, tenderly kissing as the water washes over us like a cleansing spring rain.

Slowly I become aware that the water is getting cold. I'm also now aware that there isn't much left of Moira's clothing. I think it *used* to be a nightshirt. And I'm suddenly *intensely* aware of the curves of her body, the softness of it pressed against me with so little separating us. *OK, Morgan, close your eyes and take control before this goes too far.* Not that I don't *want* to go further. I do. Badly. But, whatever I am, no matter how far I've fallen, I will *not* cross that line. I will *not* betray myself or Moira or my memory of Sharon in that way.

I grasp her shoulders firmly and, kissing her one last time, lingering over her soft lips, I gently push her away. Our breathing is labored. We stand there like that, under the cold water, my forehead resting on top of her head.

I reach behind her and turn off the water. Leaving my eyes closed, I reach out and grab a towel. I wrap this around her shoulders.

"I'll find you something to wear."

Months ago, I packed up Sharon's clothes and donated them to Deseret Industries. I did the same with Lucy's and April's and Joseph's clothes. I think Sharon would have wanted them to go to someone in need. So, all I can offer Moira is something of mine. I find her some sweat pants and a sweat shirt. They're too big for her, but still they look so *appealing* on her. I'm sure *I* never looked so good in them.

I stand at the edge of the living room watching her. She's brushing her wet hair, apparently lost in thought, sitting on the same sofa where Rebecca had been not all that long ago. She has her legs drawn up under her. The pose is similar to the way Rebecca sat there, but the contrast between the two women couldn't be starker. Both are physically very beautiful women, but, whereas Rebecca is *sensuous*, Moira is *wholesome* . . . if one can say that about a vampire. Whereas Rebecca is *brazen*, Moira is *demure*. Whereas Rebecca is greedy and grasping, Moira is generous and giving. Whereas Rebecca is driven by fear, Moira is driven by compassion. Whereas Rebecca has spent her life seeking self-gratification and indulgence, Moira has spent her life seeking redemption and in service to others.

And I'm in love with her.

It's as if all the emptiness, all the loss, all the loneliness, all the pain are gone. I'm not alone anymore. If I'm damned to spend the rest of my existence here, I'd be content to spend it with Moira. I love Moira and I know she has feelings for me, but I'm not sure if what *she* feels is the same as what *I* feel. I asked her to give me time. We've known each other less than a week, after all. Maybe now it's *my* turn to give *her* time.

She looks over at me and gives me a dazzling smile. My heart pounds as I smile back at her.

"I'm sorry . . . ," I begin to say, but my voice breaks. "I'm sorry I put you in danger."

Her eyes sparkle.

They're moist?

"Carl, my dearie," she says as a tear runs down her cheek, "surely ye must ken, I . . . would do anythin' . . . I cannae bear the thought . . . I thought . . ." Her voice trails off and the tears flow freely.

I realize that my vision is blurred too.

She puts down the brush and extends both hands to me. I move forward and kneel in front of her, taking her hands.

"I was just so relieved when I realized that you would"—I choke—"*stand* with me. I just couldn't speak."

Her smile looks sad. "Ah. Ye *need* me."

"Yes, Moira, I *do* need you." *More than you know.*

"Ye're goin' to need me when you go up against Michael."

"Uh, that's . . . *not* what I meant." *Am I reading her right? She seems disappointed. Does that mean what I think it means? What I hope it means?* "Of course, I need your help, but what I was trying to say was . . ." Her beautiful eyes lock with mine. I swallow hard. "I was afraid you . . . I was afraid that I . . . I *have* to do this. I *have* to stop Michael, but I was afraid that I would . . . lose *you* in the process."

"Never," she says with fresh tears in her bewitching green eyes, a huge grin brightening her face, brightening the whole room.

She pulls me close and kisses me tenderly. She pulls back a little, looks me in the eye, and says breathily, "Have ye had enough time, laddie?"

I blink stupidly for a second, and then I understand *exactly* what she has asked. I grin and nod.

Very deliberately I say, "Aye, *lassie*. I have." It's my best imitation of her brogue.

"And?" she asks, still holding me inches from her face.

"Moira MacDonald," I say, and pull back until I'm kneeling in front of her and take her hands again in mine, "I don't know how long this life, this *existence* will last, but I cannot imagine . . . I don't *want* to imagine spending it without you. I realize that we've only known each other for . . . What? Six days? And I know . . . I *know* in my head it isn't enough, but in my heart . . . in my *heart* I know I *love* you, Moira MacDonald. I hope you feel the same." *Oh, man! I hope that didn't come across as lame as it sounded to me!*

Suddenly, her expression is very serious. "Mr. Morgan, was that some sort of awkwardly worded proposal? Because, if it was, 'twas *terrible*! The *worst* I ever heard. I mean, ye did nae even mention *marriage*." She winks.

Speaking quickly before I lose the moment, I say, "Moira MacDonald, will you *marry* me?"

She purses her lips and looks thoughtful. "Where?" she asks in a soft voice.

That is not *the response I was hoping for.* "Where?"

"Marry ye *where?* At City Hall? In a church? Where?"

I understand what she's asking now. "I don't know. I'm sure I could get my bishop to marry us."

"Carl, I want a *temple* marriage."

I'm stunned. I can't say anything for a second, but then I manage, "How's that *possible?*"

"Carl, until I met ye, I would nae have dared to *dream.* But, ye have changed everythin' I ever believed about my . . . condition . . . about *our* condition. I have *hope* now. I have hope that someday I . . . *we* will find a . . . a path to redemption. I'm willing to wait until we can do this the *right* way. Are *ye* . . . willing to wait for *me?*"

"If it takes a thousand years . . . and it might . . . I will."

She throws her arms around my neck and kisses me again. I love her all the more because she wants to wait, as impossible as it seems, for an eternal marriage.

After a moment, though, I gently push us apart. "We have a problem, my dear, sweet Moira," I say, breathing hard.

"And what is that, my dear, sweet Carl?" she asks, equally breathless.

"If we don't cool it, and quickly, one of us is going to have to leave," I say with a wicked grin, "and there is nowhere either of us can go until nightfall! You're driving me *crazy*, lady!"

She returns the grin and adds a wink. "All right, laddie. What do ye suggest we do?"

"Well, I suggest we get some Sleep. We're both exhausted. You can have the bedroom. I'll take the couch."

"Ye're quite the gentleman, laddie. Walk me to my room?"

We're sitting at my dining room table. As she promised, Moira has provided "dinner." After we awoke at nightfall, she flew home in the darkness, cleaned up, and retrieved some bags of blood, before returning here. I like how her idea of dressing up is a simple, tasteful, modest dress, not something . . . slinky. I've put on a suit. It's not like we could go out to a restaurant. So, I have supplied candles and goblets on china saucers with placemats and cloth napkins. I've put some Celtic music on the stereo. Moira seems to appreciate it. *I wonder if she likes bagpipes.* I ask her.

"Oh, aye, it stirs the blood, a good pipe and drum band does, but 'tis nae suitable for a romantic dinner. Besides, it makes me think of Donald and I dinnae want to think of him tonight. Tonight is about *us*. I know someday we'll have to talk about Sharon, especially in light of the fact that, if we somehow succeed in marrying in the temple, I'll become yer *second* wife. I suppose I'll look forward to meeting her and yer children someday. But tonight I want to talk about us."

"Deal," I say. *She said a mouthful.* "Moira, what makes you so certain we can find a way to . . . cure vampirism?"

She considers this for a minute, and then she locks eyes with me. Those incredible green eyes . . . they take my breath away. When she looks at me like that, it's hard to think of anything else. I could spend all night just gazing into those eyes.

"Carl," she says, "last year, on Christmas Eve, I stood on the grounds of the Salt Lake Temple. I go there often. I like to listen to the concerts and look at the lights at that time of year. But mostly I go to the temple and try to touch the outer wall . . . just *touch* the outer wall, mind ye. Any mortal may do so, even if they are nae allowed to enter. The wickedest mortal alive can touch the *walls*.

"Earlier that evening I'd rescued a young woman from would-be rapists. Ye can easily imagine that I did nae treat them with much kindness. After they supplied me with sustenance and I'd sent them seeking the nearest policeman to turn themselves in, I attended to their intended victim. She turned out to be a lost, wayward girl who'd abandoned her Mormon beliefs and was living a very hard life. Her boyfriend abandoned her and she'd done much of which she was deeply ashamed. She saw no way back. She hated herself for what she'd become. She'd bought into the *lie* that she was worthless, that she had nae hope for anything better.

"I convinced her to go home to her parents, that they would *welcome* her back. When she agreed, I took her home to her family. 'Twas a very nice Christmas present for her and for her parents. 'Twas a very *satisfying* evening for me."

"Moira," I interrupt, "I don't understand how this relates to *us*."

"Trust me, laddie," she says with a wink. "I'm gettin' there.

"After delivering her to her parents, I returned to the temple grounds. 'Twas after hours. The gates were shut, so I flew down inside the walls of Temple Square. I stood, as I have so many times before, trying to touch the walls.

"As always, I extended my hand and reached toward the wall. And, push though I might with all my strength, I could nae touch it. Something always stops me just short of the wall. An inch, maybe, is all I lack. I can feel nae *barrier*; I just cannae touch it."

She pauses and pours us both more blood. She takes a sip and seems intent on the scarlet liquid in her glass.

"I turned to go," she continues after a bit, "and I did something I have nae done in centuries, nae since before my Conversion: I *tripped*. I dinnae ken what I tripped on. But I tripped and stumbled and caught myself before I could fall. I looked up and saw what I'd caught ahold of with my hand to steady myself. 'Twas the wall of the temple. I was *touchin'* the wall of the temple. I was so surprised that I flew home, my head and my heart filled with a mixture of wonder and a wee bit of hope.

"I've been back many times since and I have nae ever been able to repeat it. I cannae touch it, but I *did* once. I dinnae know what it means, except that it means I once touched something truly *sacred*."

She sees the puzzlement in my eyes. "Laddie, do ye nae see? I've walked the halls of cathedrals and other places of worship equally sacred to their believers all around the world, but I have ne'er been able to so much as *touch* one of the temples before or since. 'Twas the primary reason why I moved to Utah, once I'd determined that there was somethin' *different* about the temples. I know there's somethin' here that's more powerful than the Essence. And I could only touch it when I was nae *tryin'* to touch it. So, the block has to be within *me*. And it *can* be overcome!

"And then *ye* came into my life, defyin' everythin' I've ever accepted about the Seed and the Essence. *Ye*, who have ne'er murdered. *Ye*, who did nothin' to deserve yer damnation. And yet, ye *are* a vampire. By all I know, that should be *impossible*. Every other vampire since Lilith first made the Covenant has *chosen* to be a vampire. It cannae be *forced* upon them. But *ye* did nae choose. Something our kind has always accepted as absolute truth is *false*. I dinnae know what the key is yet, but I know it must be here if we can only see it.

"We can *beat* this thing, laddie! We can be *purified, purged* of the Essence. And then we can marry. We can have *children*. Oh, how I do want *babies* of my own! We can grow *old* together. And someday, after a *brief* separation, we will meet again, and we will be together for all of eternity. And I will be yers forever. And ye will be mine forever . . . or at least mine and Sharon's."

I look at her in wonder and unabashed admiration. "Moira, you are the most selfless person I have ever met."

She gives me a wink. "Well, laddie, I've had *centuries* to practice. Heaven knows I made enough mistakes along the way. But, dinnae worry, laddie. Ye'll be just as good at it in a century or two!"

Chapter 10

I'm pretty certain the Cult is nae aware of me," Moira says.

Perfect. I don't want to reveal her existence to my unholy allies. I want to *protect* Moira, but I'll need her as my secret weapon. And, besides, there's no *way* she'd let me leave her out of the fight.

The last thing I want to do, though, is act in haste. We have two weeks in which to act. I have some ideas for tactics that I hope will be decisive in battle.

Battle.

That's *exactly* what it'll be. Will it be just *one* battle in a larger *war*? I'm not sure, but I think so. Even if we succeed, and Rebecca and Benjamin are all that's left of the Circle of the Master, those two will continue to corrupt lives. Rebecca will eventually create new vampires and each one will result in an Offering. Yes, I'm going to have to deal with Rebecca and Benjamin eventually, but *first* I need to stop Michael and Chikah.

A hurried call from Rebecca to my cell sets up a meeting for tomorrow night. Thursday night is typically a slow night for the Cult. Most of the Novitiates are there on the weekends, but Thursday seems to be the day when all but a handful of them are taking care of their regular lives so they can spend the weekend in vampiric indulgences.

"How do you know so much about the inner workings of the Cult if you've never been inside one?" I ask Moira. We're sitting on a blanket under the stars in my backyard, sipping our "dinner." "A picnic under the stars," she called it.

"I have a source among the Chosen," she says. "Nae a *willing* one. He does nae know that he's being Persuaded to give me information. He calls me every week or so to keep me informed, and then he forgets the phone call. I have a couple of Novitiates who do the same.

"I first became aware of the Cult a few decades ago when Michael, Angelica, and Benjamin had already been operating in Salt Lake City for years. I was working as a nurse at LDS Hospital when I noticed a number of anemia cases that screamed 'vampire' to me."

"Who's Angelica?" I interrupt.

"Angelica was Michael's first wife. *She* Converted *him*. 'Twas Chikah that killed Angelica to take her place.

"It took a great while, but I was eventually able to trace things back to Michael, by Persuading victims and then Novitiates and then Chosen. By that time, the Cult was well established."

"How long have there been vampire Cults?"

"As I understand it, for thousands of years. 'Tis how Lilith keeps control. Renegades, like me and ye and the Ancient One who Converted me, give her no direct control."

"Rebecca told me that she killed Julie to keep Michael from gaining power. I'd think, with the number of Chosen, that there would be more Cults, more vampires."

"Oh, aye, ye'd think so, but very *few* Chosen are Converted. Rebecca is nae unique. The killing of Chosen before they can swell the ranks of the Master's loyal disciples is quite common. And there are so few truly *old* vampires. We have the tendency to kill one another, but even more of us simply give up and kill ourselves."

"Why is that?"

"Can ye imagine an endless existence more boring than constantly seeking fulfillment in Feeding and sexual gratification? After a few decades, most tire of it. Oh, they try for a long while to find meaning in increasingly perverse sexual activities or in the corruption and domination of others, as Michael has. Or they try to fill the emptiness with the Hunt as Chikah has. But eventually they fall into severe depression and end their existence, usually by deliberately exposing themselves to the Sun."

I shudder at the thought. The memory of Moira in flames as she flew to my aid, the smell of her singed flesh, her burnt hair, is too fresh.

"And yet, *you* are . . . still here . . . ," I say and my voice breaks, "with me." I can't seem to find the words to express my gratitude that Moira is still alive.

"I've spent my life trying to atone for my sins, laddie. I cannae do it. I cannae atone. Nae for all that I do, 'twill nae be sufficient. But, as long as I can save a life, deliver a baby, or do some good, I think it's worth . . . going on. And having found *love* after all this time . . ."

"Have I told you lately how much I love you, Moira?"

"Nae for at least two minutes, dearie," she replies with a grin.

"I love you, Moira MacDonald."

"I *know*, laddie," she says in mock seriousness. "And I love ye, but now we must talk *strategy*. And that brings me to the subject of yer gift."

"My gift? What gift?"

"Well, I'm glad that ye are so unobservant as to miss the fact that my bag was extra full tonight, but I will say it does nae bode well for ye as a commander in battle." She winks.

She rises and begins to gather the blanket and now-empty goblets. "Well, Mr. Morgan, if ye would be so kind as to follow me . . ."

"I'd follow you anywhere, pretty lady. I enjoy the view."

"Brother Morgan!" she cries in mock horror. "What would yer bishop say?"

"I imagine he'd say or at least *think* the same. He'd glance and then whistle a hymn. He's *married*, not dead! Besides, I'm widowed. I can *look* as long as I don't *touch*."

I take the blanket from her arm and I *do* follow her and I *do* enjoy the view.

From her bag in the dining room, she pulls out something long. Whatever it is, it barely fit in there. I should have noticed that she brought was longer than usual, as Moira pointed out. The item is wrapped in cloth . . . oilcloth, from the scent. She places it in my hands and the weight is more than I expected.

"Go ahead," she prompts.

I unwrap the oilcloth windings and see the gleam of gold and silver. No, not gold and silver: brass and steel. It's a *sword*. I can tell that it's old. It has an ornately wrought brass basket over the hilt. The blade is broad and double-edged with grooves running nearly the entire length. There's a red tassel attached to the end of the pommel.

"Wow." I suppose I should say something more than that, but it's all I can manage.

"It belonged to my Donald. I made the tassel myself and affixed it there before he went off to war. I took it back from one of the soldiers who'd taken it for a trophy. He was one of the squad who hung Donald. I want ye to have it. I'd be honored if ye would wield it in the battle to come. May it bring ye more luck than it did him."

I notice the smell of salt before I see her tears. I place the sword gently, reverently on the table and take her in my arms, and I just hold her and let her weep quietly, her head on my shoulder. In a minute or so, she looks up at me with those shining emerald eyes, moist with tears. "I love ye, Carl."

"Thank you, my love."

"Dinnae die."

I chuckle and say, "I'll do my best."

She kisses me quickly and then pulls away. "There's more." She wipes away her tears.

Turning back to the bag, she retrieves something else wrapped in oilcloth. "'Twas my father's."

I unwrap this and see that it's a long, wide knife. A dirk.

"It's been in my family for generations. I had to carve a new handle for it. The original was burned in the fire that destroyed our home in the Hielands. It's called a 'dirk.'"

"I know what a dirk is. It's bigger than any dirk our Special Forces carry."

"The other is called a 'claymore.' It means, 'great sword,' although the original swords with that name were much larger."

"Is this the best weapon to fight a vampire with?"

She chuckles. "There are four principal ways to kill one of us: sunlight, fire, beheading, and impaling the heart long enough."

"How long is that?"

"Oh, I would imagine a minute or two would do it. I've ne'er slain a vampire myself. A sword or a spear (or a stake) would do nicely. And a sword has the advantage that it can inflict crippling damage. Ye can cut off an arm or a hand. Ye can also cut off a head. I dinnae suppose ye know how to use a broadsword and dirk?"

"I took a couple of fencing classes in college."

"That's a start. I doubt Michael knows as much. Though he lived through yer Civil War, he mostly posed as a doctor to give himself access to the dead and dying. Still this is nae a wee fencing foil. 'Twould be best if ye had some training."

"Who's going to teach me how to fight with a broadsword?"

"A swordmaster, of course, laddie."

"A swordmaster?"

She curtsies. "I studied under the famous Captain Sinclair a couple of centuries ago. I'm quite capable. We'll begin tomorrow after the meeting with Rebecca. I'll nae have time to instruct ye properly, but we'll build on what ye know."

"What will *you* use since you gave me these?" I indicate the claymore and dirk.

"I have a 'hanger,'" she replies. "'Tis a type of saber that I took from one of the soldiers that I killed. But we'll nae be using these for training. I have practice blades made of oak. I dinnae want to cut ye should ye fail to block a thrust. 'Twould stain my skirt!" She gives a playful wink.

I'm about to respond to that, when I hear a car pull up outside the house. Moira hears it too (of course) and we both freeze and listen. Shortly, there's the sound of a car door and footsteps. Someone's coming to the house: just one person, a man, by the sound of the tread. I'm not expecting anyone tonight. It's not like I've had any visitors lately. *Why would anyone come this late in the evening?*

There's the doorbell. Motioning Moira to stay back and out of sight, I go to the door and look through the peephole. It's a man in a suit. A *rumpled* suit. His tie is loosened. His left hand is balled up in a fist at his side. He's holding up a police badge with his right as if he expects me to check him out before opening the door. *Which is . . . exactly what I just did.*

"Police," I whisper so low that only Moira could hear me.

I open the door cautiously.

"Carl Morgan?" the cop asks, still holding his badge in plain sight. My nose is assaulted by smell of the man. Sweat and something else I can't quite place. He smells . . . *bad.* Not *evil,* just . . . *sickening.*

"That's right," I reply. "Can I help you, officer?"

He flips the cover closed on his badge and pockets it. "Detective, actually. Detective Johnson with the Davis County Sheriff's Department."

"Can I help you, Detective?"

"Mr. Morgan, can I ask you a few questions? May I come in?" He spares a glance at me, but is trying to look past me into the house.

"Care to tell me, Detective, why you're calling so late at night?"

"You're a hard guy to get ahold of, Mr. Morgan."

"No, I'm not, Detective. You can find me at work any weekday."

"I don't want to disturb you at work, sir."

"OK. So, why are you disturbing me at"—I look at the clock— "10:30 at night?"

"Might I come in, sir?"

"I'm busy, Detective. Call for an appointment." There's nothing evil about this man, but he rubs me the wrong way. And he *stinks*.

"It's about Deputy Roger Hadley."

I blink once at the name. I'm sure the detective caught it. I don't think being evasive will help me after *that* blunder.

"Please, Mr. Morgan," Johnson presses. "May I come in?"

I open the door and step back to admit him. He enters as if he owns the place. He walks over to the sofa and says, "Mind if I sit down?" Without waiting for a reply, he sits. I close the door with mounting irritation. I cross over to the loveseat and sit there.

"How can I help you, Detective?" I glance up to see Moira standing in the family room, just out of sight of Detective Johnson. She stays where she is, listening, breathing so quietly that no mortal would detect her presence.

Johnson pulls a notebook and pen out of his suit coat with his right hand. The left hand is still closed, not in a fist, I realize, but *covering* something. He opens the notebook one-handed and says, "I'm investigating a serial murder case, Mr. Morgan, and I have a few questions."

"Am I a suspect, Detective?"

"No, sir," he replies in a deceptively calm, almost bored-sounding voice, as if we were discussing the weather rather than multiple homicides. His thundering heartbeat belies his outer calm. "We have our man. Terrible business. He was one of our own deputies. He's confessed to multiple murders and . . . other crimes. He's given us enough physical evidence to corroborate his story."

"So, how can *I* be of help to you, Detective?" *Why is he here? How did he connect me to Hadley?*

"Well, Mr. Morgan, it's funny, you know, because Hadley confessed to enough murders to get himself executed, more than once, which would still be better than he deserves, but he won't say a word about what appears to have been his *final* victim. We have enough evidence to indicate that he murdered someone last Friday night, but we can't get anything out of him about it. Not a word."

"What does that have to do with *me*, Detective?" *I don't like where this is going at all.*

"Well, sir, I have reason to believe that you were involved."

"You said I wasn't a suspect."

"No, you're the *victim*."

That makes me pause. It takes me a second to collect my wits, but I come back with, "As you can see, Detective, I'm very much alive."

"That you are, sir, but near as I can tell, you were shot and killed last Friday."

"OK, Detective, I don't . . ."

"Would you mind removing your shirt, sir?"

"My shirt?" *Is he going where I think he's going with this?*

"Yes, sir."

"Why?"

"Would you please remove your shirt, sir?" He's tapping the pen nervously against his notebook where He has written down exactly nothing.

"Why on earth would I do that?"

"Because, sir, we found blood and tissue samples at the scene of Hadley's arrest. The DNA matches a hit from the Department of Defense DNA database. It matches *your* DNA. You served in the Air Force during the first Gulf War. So it's either you or a very close male relative. I checked: your only son is dead and you have no close living relatives. So, either it's you who was shot multiple times in the chest on Friday or your twin brother was."

"I don't have a twin brother."

"Exactly." There is sweat rolling down his temples.

"Why do you say I was shot in the chest?"

"Because a small, but significant part of the tissue recovered was from a human heart."

OK, Morgan, try a different tack: cooperation. "OK. Let me clear this up for you, Detective." I stand up and remove my shirt. "See, not a scar on me except for . . ." *Where's the scar I got from the bird strike? It's gone!* I never noticed it's absence before.

We were flying a low-level training mission over eastern Montana when we took a golden eagle right through the nose of the B-52. The instrument panel exploded toward us. The AC (aircraft commander) was covered in blood, feathers, and bird guts. His side of the cockpit was destroyed. He was unconscious. The wind howled like a banshee through the hole in the nose. I had to declare an emergency, initiate a climb, and take the aircraft into Minot AFB in North Dakota for an emergency landing. It was a long hour from the bird strike to the landing. I had the gunner and the EW (electronic warfare officer) unstrap the AC and administer first aid. The air was screaming into the cockpit, and the controls didn't feel quite right. The aircraft didn't feel right.

We were unpressurized with that huge, gaping hole in the nose, so I had to stay below fifteen thousand feet, especially for the sake of the crew members who were out of their seats and off oxygen. Once I leveled off at thirteen thousand feet, I ran through some flight-control tests and determined that the aircraft was still flyable. When the aircraft takes physical damage like that, a pilot ends up flying an airplane configuration that nobody has ever flown before. As Col. Daggett told me, "You suddenly become a test pilot, so test out the airplane. See how she handles. But do it from a safe altitude."

I got a vector from the navigators and turned directly toward Minot. I called Center ATC (Air Traffic Control) to get emergency clearance for a direct route.

When we got closer to Minot, I lowered the landing gear and practiced a landing approach at thirteen thousand feet to make sure the landing gear would come down (it did) and that the airplane was still flyable with the gear down.

The approach and landing was mostly uneventful, except I squeaked the aircraft onto the runway, landing too softly. (This meant that the tail was dangerously low.) I taxied off the runway, and we were met by emergency vehicles and the AC was attended to. He spent a couple of weeks in the hospital at "beautiful" Minot AFB having his wounds tended to, but otherwise, he was fine.

At the time, though, still sitting in the cockpit when the shock wore off, I realized I had a large chunk of glass from one of the shattered instruments sticking out of my ribs. Minot AFB hospital stitched me up, but I had a decent scar to remember the whole episode by.

"Not a single scar." *I guess the Seed has taken that from me too. Ah, well.* "Can I put my shirt back on now?"

"Yes, sir. Thank you."

I put my shirt back on and tuck it in.

"Anything else, Detective?" I ask, remaining on my feet, willing him to get the hint and leave.

"*Do* you have a brother, Mr. Morgan? An illegitimate son, perhaps, or a son from another marriage?"

OK, now I'm pissed.

"I have no brother," I say with a snarl. "My *son* died last year, thank you very much. I've only been married once and I've never been unfaithful and, yes, Detective, I was a *virgin* when I got married. Now, is there anything else?"

"How do you explain . . . ," he begins, but I cut him off.

"I *don't* explain. That's *your* job," I say curtly.

"As I was saying," he presses on, seemingly unfazed, but with sweat now pouring down his face, "how do you explain a large quantity of Hadley's blood at the scene with not a mark on him and him white as a sheet? The doc said he'd suffered significant blood loss, but there wasn't a cut or puncture on him and only *your* blood on his clothing. Oh, and, by the way, how do you explain his blood at the scene being mixed with *stomach* acid?"

Moira said this might present them with a mystery. I just didn't expect them to tie it back to me.

"From the footprints," Johnson presses on, "it looks like there were two people there. One was obviously Hadley. What shoe size do you wear, Mr. Morgan? Would I be right if I said ten-and-a-half or eleven?"

That's my size.

"Why do the footprints disappear in one location and reappear ten feet away with nothing in between?"

What can I say? How can I possibly answer this?

"Mr. Morgan, can you explain to me how a nine millimeter semi-automatic handgun gets crushed? We found two at the scene."

Nothing. I have nothing I can say.

"Oh, and one last bizarre little detail: The trunk of Hadley's car fairly reeks of *sunscreen*. What does that all add up to, Mr. Morgan?"

Moira strides angrily into the room, her green eyes blazing at Johnson. She fixes him with her stare. "Ye will leave this house, Detective," she commands, her voice cold with Persuasion. "Ye will forg . . ."

"What are you doing?" cries the obviously terrified man.

Uh, oh. It isn't working.

"Ye will leave this house!"

"No!" he cries and attempts to scramble backward up the back of the sofa.

He brings his left hand up and produces something from inside his fist. It's a silver cross. He brandishes it at Moira and then at me by turns.

"*I know what you are!*" his voice is rising to an unnatural pitch.

Moira looks at the crucifix in alarm for a moment and then she breathes a huge sigh of relief.

"And, what, pray tell, are we supposed to be?" she asks calmly. She's in total command of the situation now.

"The Undead! Vampires!" he cries, holding the cross out at her. His hand trembles.

"I see," she replies, nodding her head thoughtfully. She holds out her hand. "May I?"

Johnson hesitates. He begins to hand the cross over to her, pulls back, and then drops it into her hand and recoils quickly. Maybe he expects her hand to sizzle and burn at the touch.

Moira turns the silver cross over and then twirls it in her fingers. "Is that also why ye came here reekin' of garlic, Detective Johnson?"

Garlic! That's the smell!

I recognize it now. Almost *all* mortal food smells bad to me now, which is good, since I can't eat it anymore.

Johnson stares at her in wonder.

Moira hands the cross to me. She turns back to Johnson.

He's poised up on the back of the sofa looking from one to the other of us. He actually looks comical, or he *would* if the situation were not so . . . *delicate.*

I hand the cross back to him. He takes it warily and stares at it.

He came here with a cross in his hand and stinking of garlic. He *knew* that I'm a vampire. *What does he think now? Why would he come here if he thought I was a vampire?*

"So, you think I'm a vampire, Detective?" I ask him, trying to sound amazed.

He opens his mouth a few times, but says nothing.

"You can climb down now," I say. He doesn't move. I extend my hand to help him down from the back of the sofa. He stares at my hand and then gingerly takes it. At first, he flinches as he touches my hand, but he leaves it there and lets me gently but firmly help him down. I pull him completely off the couch and onto his feet on the floor in front of it.

"What is it, Detective?" I ask. "Were you expecting my hand to be cold?"

He looks at me and I can see it in his eyes. I've hit the mark. He's off-balance, uncertain what to do next. *Good. Let's keep it that way.*

"Detective, may I introduce my fiancé, Moira MacDonald?" I say, moving to Moira's side and putting my arm around her waist. She places her left hand over mine and squeezes it warmly.

She extends her right hand to the confused officer. Johnson takes it. Moira gives him a friendly handshake. She gives him a dazzling smile too. He takes his first good look at her face and gasps. She *does* seem to have that effect on people: she's *very* beautiful. And when she smiles ... Well, no red-blooded man can resist her smile.

"I'm sorry we got off to a bad start, Detective," she says sweetly. "I feel terrible. What can I do to make it up to ye?"

He looks at her. "Uh, I . . . feel like such an *idiot*."

Good!

"So, tell me, Detective," Moira says. "I'm a wee bit curious. Why on earth would ye venture into the den of a man ye suspected was a vampire during the *night*? Why nae confront him during the daylight hours?"

He gives her a sheepish half grin. "Does seem pretty *stupid*, doesn't it? I mean, it was obvious that you can move around during the day. Hadley made a traffic stop on your van during daylight and you went to work that day."

"Why not get a warrant and search my home looking for a coffin or something like that?" I suggest.

"I can't . . . get a warrant for this," he says with a grimace, turning his attention to me. So different from the way he looked at Moira . . . not that I blame him. "At this point, we have enough to go on with what Hadley confessed to and the evidence he supplied, so the Sherriff wants to let the rest go until and *if* we get a missing-person report. So, no warrant.

"Also, there was a similar case in Salt Lake of six gangbangers confessing to violent crimes. They were in pretty bad shape physically. Beaten pretty badly. There was no evidence of blood loss at the scene, but they were all pale. And they couldn't shut up about their crimes. There was also a similar incident in December of three perps confessing to a Metro Police officer."

"So, why, Detective, would ye go to the lair of a suspected vampire?" Moira asks again.

Why is Johnson being so open with her, telling her all this? It's not Persuasion. Apparently that didn't work on him. He must be very "strong willed," as she puts it. She said you could "distract" someone who couldn't be Persuaded. Is that what she's doing?

"Because," Johnson answers, "this 'vampire,' if there is such a thing, behaves more like a vigilante than a monster."

I blink at him. "You came here hoping to find . . . what? An ally? A crime fighter?"

"We had no clue about Hadley. *I* had no clue. I worked with the man before I made detective. We were *friends*. We had barbeques together. My kids played with his daughter. That poor kid." He shakes his head.

"What poor kid?" I ask, knowing the answer.

"I really shouldn't say," he answers. *He shouldn't be saying any of this. Is this Moira's doing?*

"So, why are ye here?" Moira prods. "Why seek out this 'vampire vigilante,' as ye say?"

"Hadley was right under my nose," he says. "I never saw it coming, but *somebody* got him to confess. Somebody got the gangbangers and the other three perps to confess. There have been a few similar cases over the years. I wanted to . . . know how it was done. One of Roger's . . . I mean Hadley's victims . . . was my kid brother. It was years ago. Roger tortured him and killed him. Buried him alive. I never knew. I never knew what happened to him."

His eyes are moist and Moira pulls away from me to go to him and give him a hug. He hesitates, but then returns it. She pats his back, as if she's comforting a crying child. He *is* crying now, sobbing into her shoulder. She's making cooing, soothing noises in his ear. I just watch in mute fascination.

Eventually, he quiets down. She slowly releases him and looks up into his eyes.

"I'm so sorry for yer loss," she says softly.

He nods mutely.

"But we can do nae more for ye here. Be content that yer brother's murderer is caught."

"I better go. I'm sorry to bother you folks."

Without another word, he turns and leaves.

I listen intently as he walks to his car. Once his car starts and drives away, I turn to Moira and ask, "How did you do that?"

"Ach, 'twas just a variation on Persuasion. As I told ye, if ye cannae Persuade someone, ye can distract them. Mortals *trust* us, if we want them to. We could be such good liars, if we choose, and mortals would believe virtually *anything* we say, will tell us virtually *anything* we want. All the better to deceive them, lull them, make them our easy prey. As if we *needed* any more advantage over them! If we cannae command them, we can get them to do what we want through other means. Flies to honey."

"Johnson brought up something that's been bothering me."

"And what's that, laddie?"

"I weighed myself this morning. I've gained a total of twenty pounds since my . . . Conversion."

"Are ye saying that I'm fattening ye up with all my good cooking?" She grins.

"Funny," I say flatly. "No, I mean, when we're Converted, our muscles become denser and so do our bones, right?"

"Aye," she says slowly. "That's true. It makes us stronger, sturdier."

"Is twenty pounds enough to account for me being able to crush a gun in my bare hands?"

Moira stares at me, her mouth open. She glances away, thinking, and her mouth snaps closed. She shakes her head slowly.

"How was I able to crush a gun in my bare hands? For that matter, even if I'm *strong* enough to do it, how is it that I didn't break bones in my hands? Surely, my bones aren't stronger than *steel*. I've seen a sword cut through Benjamin's arm, so our bones *can't* be stronger than steel. How is it possible?"

"Laddie, I dinnae know. Now that ye say it, it makes nae sense. I have nae ever thought about it like that."

"Moira, on the night that I first flew, when you . . . punched me . . ."

"Aye," she says, looking up at me with her head tilted downward, "I'm sorry about that."

"Don't apologize. Anyway, that's not the point. When you punched me, you broke my jaw. Did you break your hand?"

She shakes her head slowly. "Nae, Carl, I did nae break a bone." Her head snaps up, looking me full in the face. "What does it mean?"

I don't have an answer, but it has to mean *something*.

Chapter 11

Hey, Carl, are you in some sort of trouble?" My co-worker, Steve, is standing at the entrance to my cubicle.

I tear my attention away from the bug I've been trying to track down and spin my chair around to look at him quizzically. "Why?" I ask. "What's going on?"

"There's some police detective here asking questions about you."

"Really? What's he asking about?"

"He wants to know about your sunlight . . . allergy . . . *thing*, about how you spend your nights. Hey, are you engaged?"

What a change of subject! "Yeah. I am."

"Congratulations! I don't suppose I know her, do I?"

It has to be Johnson. I guess he hasn't given up. Nobody else knows I'm engaged, because Moira and I haven't told anybody. Steve and I don't interact much outside of work, so we have no mutual acquaintances. The only way he could possibly know is if Johnson told him.

"No, I don't think so. She's my . . . doctor."

"I thought your doctor was here in the building . . . and a *guy*." He folds his arms and shakes his head. "Anything I should know about?"

I grimace and shake my head.

He grins. "Maybe you should bring her by sometime."

"Uh, I changed doctors because of my . . . condition."

"Wow! That was fast! It's only been a couple of weeks, right?"

Oh, boy. This could get awkward. It's not like I can really *explain* anything.

"Yeah," I say. "We haven't known each other long, but we really hit it off, you know? We have a lot in common." *Man! That sounds lame!* "Look, Steve, is the detective still here?"

"Yeah, he's talking to Phil in the Game Room."

"Listen, I'll fill you in more about Moira, my fiancée, but . . . later. I want to go see what this is all about."

"Sure," he replies.

I head off toward the Game Room, keeping out of the light from the windows. There's been talk, lately, of moving the studio to another building and that might prove really awkward if there's more sun.

The Game Room is a small room with a huge flat-panel TV, five-speaker surround sound, and every game console on the market (plus a few that aren't anymore) where designers, artists, and engineers go to do research on other games. Sometimes it's used to just play video games for fun over lunch or after work, but the vast majority of the time, it's serious research. Phil, my manager, is in there talking to Detective Johnson. I can see them through the frosted-glass wall.

OK, so he hasn't given up. If he's asking about my "skin condition," he's still pursuing the vampire angle. What I don't understand is *why*. He referred to us, Moira and me, as acting like vigilantes. Is he looking for a partner in crime fighting? Does he think of us as vampire superheroes? That's the stuff of movies and comic books. I'm not a hero. I'm just a guy with incredibly bad luck.

Except for Moira.

Johnson glances up and sees me. A grimace flashes across his face and then is gone. He returns his attention to Phil. *Does he suspect I can hear them?* I can. I can hear them both quite clearly.

". . . not since his sister died," Phil is saying. "He took a couple of days off then. This is a guy who never takes a sick day. Never has, as far as I know, except for one day about a month ago. Even that wasn't a sick day; he just had stuff to take care of."

"And that's when the sun allergy started?" Johnson asks.

Bingo.

"Around there, sure," answers Phil. "Doesn't stop him. Heck, during the winter months, some of these guys get here before the sun comes up and leave after it goes down. They probably don't *see* the sun except on weekends. They're like bats, ya know?" Phil chuckles.

Johnson gives a mirthless chuckle back. "How does he get along with his co-workers?"

"Fine, I guess. I haven't gotten any complaints."

"Does he have friends here at work?"

"I think so. You talked to one of them already. There are guys he goes to lunch with sometimes."

"Lately?"

"I have no idea. Probably not so much now that the sun is a problem."

"Have you ever seen him *eat*?"

"What?" Phil looks surprised.

"Food. Have you seen him eat food?"

"Why in the heck would you ask that?"

Johnson says nothing.

Phil shrugs. "Sure. The guy loves doughnuts. He's always trying to enforce the donut policy we have for coming late to a meeting. You know: if you're late, you have to bring doughnuts to the next meeting?"

"Recently?"

"I think so, although most people show up to meetings on time *because* of him. It's all in good fun. Sometimes he brings doughnuts just *because*. He always brings way too many, so people will stop by his cube throughout the day to get one . . . or two."

"He brought doughnuts . . . recently?"

"Yeah, yesterday or the day before." Phil looks at him curiously. "These are really weird questions, you know?" Phil hesitates for a moment, clearly uncomfortable. "Is Carl in some sort of trouble?"

"This is just routine, sir. It's part of an ongoing investigation, and Mr. Morgan is *not* a suspect, I can assure you."

"Good," Phil responds, clearly not totally convinced.

"Thank you, Mr. Horowitz. You've been very helpful." Johnson rises to his feet.

"Sure," says Phil, also rising. "Anytime." He shakes hands with the detective and comes out of the Game Room. He's visibly startled when he sees me for the first time. He raises his eyebrows and subtly glances in the direction of the detective.

I give him a small nod and a wink with a little smile that I hope doesn't look as fake as it feels. I turn my attention to the detective.

Johnson is trying to leave the Game Room, trying to ignore me. I block the doorway and he stops abruptly.

"I thought you said I wasn't a suspect," I say, his face inches from mine, although he doesn't look at me.

Johnson says nothing and tries to slip past me, but I'm not giving an inch.

"Are you trying to get me fired, Detective?" I ask.

"Just following up," he says after a moment, looking me in the eye for the first time.

"Right," I say slowly. "Just 'following up' on an unauthorized investigation."

He stares back at me, unflinching.

"I'll tell you what, Detective," I continue. "I'll call the Sheriff's Office and tell them *all* about it. Maybe they'll give you a *commendation* for going *above* and *beyond* the call of duty."

"That won't be necessary, Mr. Morgan."

"I thought not," I reply. "Now, I'd appreciate it if you'd leave me alone."

"Excuse me. I have to get back to the office."

"Pursuing the big, bad 'vampire' on your *lunch* hour, Detective?"

He tries to push past me again, and this time I let him . . . after a moment.

I watch him leave the studio and then I head back to my cubicle, carefully staying in the shadows.

I'm almost there when Phil catches my attention and motions me toward his office. I nod and step in. There's some sunlight coming through the windows, so I stand near the door. Phil shuts the blinds and then motions me to close the door and take a chair. Once we're both seated, he says, "Mind filling me in?"

"The guy thinks I'm a vampire," I say flatly.

Phil blinks and then snorts out a laugh. "No kidding?"

I shake my head. "Honest." I raise my right hand, three fingers pointed at the ceiling, with my thumb holding my pinky down. "Scout's honor."

"Huh." He stares past me, looking toward the Game Room. Then he shrugs. "Takes all kinds." He rolls his eyes. "Thanks." He gives a nervous laugh. "You're not, right? A vampire, that is?"

I hesitate just a moment for dramatic effect and then . . .

"Boo!" I say, and he jumps a little. We both laugh. "Can I get back to work, boss?"

"Yeah, sure." He grins. "Stay out of the sun, will ya?" He makes a ghostly "woo-ooh" sound and smiles.

"Sure thing, boss," I say as I get up. He waits until I'm gone and then opens his blinds.

Once I'm back in my cube, I sit down, check my messages, notice that there's nothing pressing, and turn around to talk to Steve.

He turns his chair to face mine.

"So," he begins, "tell me about her."

"Her name is Moira."

"Yeah, you mentioned that. Is that . . . what . . . Greek?"

"Scottish, actually."

"You got a picture?"

"As a matter of fact, I do."

It was the first night after I made the lamest *marriage proposal in the history of the world. Moira insisted we have a photo done together right away at a department store portrait studio. She paid for a rush job, and we got the pictures back the next evening. She had laughed when I asked if we (meaning vampires) could be photographed or seen in a mirror.*

"Well, now. 'Twould be a wee bit difficult to get a driver's license with an empty photo, do ye nae think? That's just a silly myth started in Eastern Europe. Before my time."

"At the risk of being a complete jerk, how old are *you, pretty lady?"*

"I told ye, I'm well into my third century."

"You know what I mean!"

"How old would ye *say I am, laddie?" she asked with a wicked grin.*

"Not going to go there! Uh-uh! I'm not *completely* crazy. *Or* daft, *as you would say."*

"Nae fair, laddie! If I have to reveal my biological age, ye have to guess *first."*

I was doomed *and I knew it. I couldn't win. In Korea, when a woman asked me to guess her age (and they did . . . a lot), my best bet was to add a few years, because women there prize maturity. Here? No matter what I said, I was in deep kim-chi.*

Then I grinned. I have it, *I thought. "Timeless" I reply at last with a grin.*

"Oh, ye are a slippery *one, ye are!" she cried.*

"Well?" I pressed.

"I'm seventeen."

My jaw dropped. "No way!"

She put on a mock pout. "Do I look so ald to yer eyes?"

"I would have said midtwenties."

She smiled at me brightly and gave her luscious auburn hair a toss. "We matured earlier back then, in the Hielands. I would have been considered an ald maid at eighteen."

"I'm old enough to be your father." *Just barely. Technically.*

"Aye, laddie, ye are." She winked. She brought up her hands and began counting on her fingers. "And I'm old enough to be yer great-great-great-great-great-great-great-great-great-great-great-grandmother!"

"Wow."

"I promise ye, laddie, never to make a big deal about the difference in our ages and yer lack of maturity, if ye won't!"

I kissed her. "Maybe someday you'll stop calling me 'laddie.'"

Her grin was beyond wicked. It was downright evil. "Maybe . . . laddie!"

"She's *hot*," Steve says. "Too bad you had to ruin the photo by being in it."

"Yeah. She *is* hot."

Steve hands the photo back to me. "So, where'd you two meet? At the doctor's office?"

I put the photo back into my wallet. "We met at the hospital, when my condition first . . . showed up. She works there."

"So, you two just hit it off, huh? I mean . . . it seems really . . . fast."

"Well, for one thing, she has the same condition as me, actually. And there's the fact that she lost her fiancé long ago." *Really long ago.* "And I . . . lost Sharon."

"So, is that *it*? *That's* what brought you together?"

"No," I protest, "we have common interests, common goals."

"OK," he replies slowly. He's hesitating, nervous. "Is she LDS?"

Ah, I get it. "You know, I'm not absolutely sure. I know she *believes* in the Church, but I'm not sure she's been baptized."

His face twists in concern. "Dude . . ."

"Don't worry. She wants a temple marriage."

Now his jaw drops in disbelief. "And she's not a member?"

"It was *her* idea . . . and I said I'm not *sure* if she's a member or not. I know she *wants* to be if she's not."

"Don't you think that little baptism detail is something you might want to find out about?" It looks like he really wants to ask more, but he's holding back. He's uncomfortable getting this personal, I guess. It's not like he and I talk *outside* of work.

"I'll ask her tonight," Like *that's* the big obstacle . . . but I can't tell him about the real problems . . . little things like demonic possession and eternal damnation.

"If she's not baptized, you might want to get that taken care of and get the clock started ticking."

He's referring to the year we would have to wait after a baptism before a temple marriage. He has no idea we could be waiting for *centuries*.

Or forever.

"In the meantime, dude, you better be careful. A year is a long time to wait."

"Tell me about it! But she's *worth* it."

"How can you know after two weeks? I mean, dude, that's really *fast*." He leans closer and whispers, "But she *is* smokin' hot!" He turns back to his computer.

And I've seen the smoke *to prove it, brother.*

And that sets me wondering (and not for the first time): Does Moira love *me*, or the "hope" I represent to her? For that matter, do I love Moira simply because I *need* her, because she and I are thrown together by Lilith's hellish Covenant, because we're all each other have? I sit there staring at my computer screen, not thinking at all about the bug I'm supposed to be fixing, just thinking of beautiful emerald eyes in an exquisite face framed by waves of luxuriant red hair.

I pull out the picture of the two of us together, and I put it next to the frame I have on my desk with Sharon's picture. These are two beautiful women, both uniquely lovely in their own way.

Sharon and I fell in love when I returned to BYU after my mission in South Korea. At first she was polite, but uninterested. I was smitten with her, though. So I courted her and, eventually, I won her over. It took nearly six months to get to the point where I dared ask her to marry me.

My mother sent me her very own engagement ring for me to propose. I put the ring on the collar of a plush stuffed dog. I gave the dog to Sharon and left the room. I waited for her to see the ring. At first (after she discovered the ring), she turned me down. It took another month for her to accept my proposal. We were married two months later in the Provo Temple.

We were so happy together. In time, our love overflowed into the life of a child: my Lucy, a beautiful, perfect baby girl. Three years later came April, my precious little April. Two years later came Joseph, my darling little boy. We tried again afterward, but it seemed that three were all the Lord was going to give us.

But three months before they were all killed, we learned that Sharon was expecting again. I never knew if the baby was a boy or a girl.

Is Moira right? Is there hope that someday we'll overcome this . . . curse . . . and someday I'll be reunited with Sharon and Lucy and April and Joseph?

Please, Father, let it be so.

For now, though, there is only Moira.

I look at the picture of Moira and me. Next to me with my ordinary brown hair, she looks far too gorgeous to be with the likes of Carl

Morgan. Of course, I always felt the same way about Sharon. When I met Sharon, she was still a very young woman, younger than I was. When I met Moira she was both far older than I am *and* much younger. And there is no question that I *need* her. I literally cannot survive without her right now, but that isn't all there is . . . my need for her and her physical beauty. There's a sweetness and a wholesomeness to Moira. She's a vampire, cursed with the Seed and the Essence, damned to this Earth, confined to the night, and driven to consume human blood, just as I am, but I've never known a *purer* soul.

I've seen Moira, fangs extended, take on monstrous thugs twice her size. I've seen her drinking blood from human prey. I've heard her story about how she was raped and, the horrible vengeance she took. I know she's *capable* of great violence, but she's spent *centuries* healing the sick and delivering babies, though she can have none of her own. She's spent *lifetimes* seeking for redemption without the slightest hope of finding any, yet she still keeps seeking and serving. She's the kindest, gentlest, and purest soul I think I've ever met. How could any single (or widowed) man *not* fall madly in love with a woman like that?

I hope she sees something in *me* that's worth loving. But, even if she *did* fall for me because of her impossible hope, I'll take it, because it's a start and it'll grow. It already *has* grown.

Maybe I'm damned, but I'm *blessed* as well.

Chapter 12

Rebecca knocks at my front door an hour or so after sunset. When I open the door, I find her standing there alone. No Benjamin. Not that I mind: Benjamin is just too *creepy*.

Rebecca's wearing a black midlength evening dress that looks almost *modest* until she walks in and I can see that it's slit up both sides to midthigh. *I'll bet she thinks she looks seductive.* Compared to Moira or Sharon she just looks . . . pathetic. Actually, all by herself, she looks *cheap*. Does she still hope to seduce me?

Dream on, lady.

"Where's your 'consort'?" I ask.

"Oh, Michael wanted him tonight." She waves her hand dismissively.

I literally gag. If I had Fed recently, I'd be losing my lunch right now.

Benjamin is being used by *everyone*. He's being used by Michael in unspeakable ways. Rebecca is using him to destroy Michael so she can gain power.

I motion her in through the door, close it, and lead her to the dining room table. I've laid out paper and pencils and erasers. I have sketches drawn from my memory of Michael's "Temple." I wasn't privy to most of the layout. I'm counting on Rebecca to fill in the missing details.

As she walks past me, she draws her fingers slowly along my arm. Her touch makes my skin crawl, but I don't flinch. I don't want her to think she has some advantage over me. It needs to be clear that *I* am in control, that *I* am in command. *She* needs *me* right now, and I need to keep it that way.

I motion for her to sit. She actually stands there waiting for me to pull out her chair for her. "Just sit," I say. She hesitates for a moment, opens her mouth to say something, and then . . . sits.

"Carl," she begins, but I cut her off.

"Give me a full layout of the mansion: every detail you can give me, including furniture." I point at my sketches. "Show me every window, how it opens, the lighting, the plumbing, everything you know."

"Carl, listen . . . ," she starts again.

"Rebecca, we have a truce, a *temporary* alliance, no more. If you want this truce to work, avoid pissing me off with your *pathetic* attempts at seduction or any pretense that we will ever be anything more than uneasy allies. You murdered my sister."

She opens her mouth to speak, but I stare at her with a glower, and it stops the words in her throat.

I motion to the sketches. She sighs and turns to the paper.

She begins to fill in the details. As the layout of the house takes shape, I start to ask questions.

"What's this behind the dais?" I ask, noting some odd lines behind the oval of the raised platform with its four thrones. "That," I say, pointing at a line, "is the door you Teachers use to enter the Great Hall. But what's this?" I ask, pointing to another line next to it.

"Oh," she says in her clipped British accent, "am I now permitted to speak?"

"Just stick to business," I say curtly.

"Yes, sir!" she says in mock seriousness, giving me a mock salute. "It's a secret door."

"Like a secret passage?"

"A passage. Precisely. It's behind the tapestry. It leads to Michael's Observation Lounge. It's a room where he keeps all his monitors."

"Monitors?"

"TVs."

"Security monitors?"

"Well, I suppose you could use them for that, but, no. They're for watching the various bedrooms." She gives me a leer, but the lecherous grin fades when she sees the revulsion on my face.

She goes back to sketching.

"Are they capable of watching anyplace else in the house?" I ask.

"I don't think there are cameras in other parts of the house, except for the Great Hall. And the front and back doors. At least, I haven't seen any other labels on the buttons you can use to select your view."

"So you can monitor the front door, the back door, the Great Hall, and the bedrooms. Not much security in that. And the main door behind the dais leads to the Hall of the Chosen, right?"

"Yes, and beyond the Hall of the Chosen are the stairs leading to the Sanctuary."

"Yeah, I remember." My voice is ice. "Where do Michael and the rest of you Sleep?"

She smirks at me. "Of course. You never graced my bedroom or Chikah's . . . or Michael's."

"Where?" I prompt through gritted teeth.

"Beyond the Sanctuary," she replies. She sketches them out. The rooms branch off a corridor hidden behind a tapestry that hangs in the Sanctuary. Michael's room is at the end of the corridor. Chikah's room is on the right and Rebecca's room is on the left.

"Where's Benjamin's room?"

"He has a cubby off Michael's room," she says, not taking her attention away from the sketch of the basement as she continues to draw.

"Cubby?" I ask.

"A cubby is . . . well, a closet, really."

"So Benjamin sleeps in a closet . . . when Michael doesn't . . . want him?"

"Oh, yes," Rebecca replies with some obvious relish. "Michael literally chains the little bugger up in there, not that the chains could really hold Benjamin if he wanted to escape. He has a filthy straw mattress. I'm not even sure where Michael obtains a *straw* mattress these days, but I know for a fact that it gets replaced every few years when the smell becomes too horrid."

It's impossible not to feel some pity for Benjamin, the poor twisted creature.

She cocks her head and looks at me. "Michael makes him *watch*, you know."

"What?"

"He commands Benjamin to watch from a hole in his cubby when Michael has Chikah or me or someone else in there."

I groan audibly. *That poor boy!*

Boy? Sometimes it's hard to wrap my mind around the fact that Benjamin is *not* a child. He's a vile monster. Short in stature, but filled with a very *old* hatred . . . toward women, toward men, toward all mortals really . . . even toward Michael. I'm not sure he has anything left but hate and unfulfilled desire . . . and fear.

"Tell me, Rebecca," I start to say.

She looks up at me and bats her eyelashes. "Yes, Carl?"

"Do you feel anything at all for Benjamin?"

She shrugs and returns to sketching. "Disgust. Loathing. Pity, I suppose. Disgust, mainly." She sounds bored.

"What do you plan on doing with him once Michael is gone?"

"Do you mean, 'Am I going to sleep with him'?" She doesn't look up. "I suppose so. I'm going to *need* him for a while, at least. I can't rule the Cult alone."

I'm not sure why, but I'm a little relieved to hear that she's not going to simply dispose of Benjamin. At least not right away. I have to ask myself: *is Benjamin responsible for any of his actions?* I really don't know the answer to that. One thing I *do* know is that my revulsion for this woman could not be more intense.

Rebecca sighs. "Eventually, I'll have to get a new consort or two, men capable of satisfying my needs. I mean, mortals are so . . . fragile and weak."

OK. Enough of that.

I point out the doors to the mansion. "Here and here are the only doors. There are windows. What other exits are there?"

She shrugs again. "Michael says there's a tunnel leading from his room, an escape route, but he hasn't shown it to me."

"Does Michael ever leave the mansion?"

"Once every year or so, he'll go to a movie."

"You're kidding," I say incredulously.

"He *loves* movies, especially a really good *vampire* flick or a rerelease of some classic of the silver screen. There's something about seeing a classic in a theater full of people, and it just isn't the same watching it on the telly."

"Any chance he'll be going to the movies soon?"

"I haven't heard of anything that would catch his interest."

OK. We have to attack inside the mansion.

"Michael is always surrounded by Novitiates and Chosen at night," I say. "How is he protected when he Sleeps during the day?" I ask.

She stops sketching and looks at me with a quizzical expression. "*You* stood guard. You should know."

"Actually, I never did. I was Chosen for so short a time."

"Yes, you were. Such a short time. Maybe I was too hasty. No, I think not. Anyway, there's nothing to do about it now. There is one Chosen and one Teacher on guard from sunrise to sunset. The Chosen stands in the Hall of the Chosen and the Teacher in the Sanctuary. Michael never stands guard for the rest of us."

"How are they armed?"

"Benjamin has his sword. I prefer a pair of long hunting knives. Chikah carries her sword. It's Japanese, of course."

"A katana?"

"I have no idea what that means. Is that a Japanese sword? Is this a military thing, that you know your weapons?" Her smile is probably meant to be charming or perhaps flattering.

I have no intention of telling her about my lack of knowledge on the subject. I just know the katana from TV and movies. "And Michael has his saber," I say, mostly to myself.

"Yes. He told me he used it to fight Yankees in your American Civil War. I think that's a lie, personally. I know he was a vampire long before the war, so he wouldn't be cavorting around a battlefield in the daylight."

"Does he know how to use it?"

"Not as I have seen. He's used it to punish Benjamin."

So have I. I shudder at the memory of Benjamin's severed arm.

"How about Chikah? Does she know how to use her sword?"

"Oh, yes. She's quite proficient. She was in the Japanese mafia before she was Converted. She was an assassin."

Perfect. Just what I need. A Yakuza-trained assassin. No, that's impossible. Yakuza are covered from neck to wrist to ankles in tattoos. Or would the Seed eliminate tattoos as something foreign to the body? Probably. Yakuza training would make her extremely dangerous.

"Will Benjamin act against her?"

"Oh, yes. He loathes Chikah and she despises him."

"And the Chosen? How are they armed?"

"They have . . . What would you call them? Machine guns?" she says uncertainly.

"You mean automatic weapons?"

She nods tentatively.

"Such as a soldier would carry? Like an M-16 or AK-47 or Uzi or something like that?"

She shrugs her shoulders.

"Draw one for me." I motion at the paper.

She turns back to the table, takes a fresh piece of paper, and draws what looks like an AK-47. It's possible to get those in the US, but they're illegal or horrendously expensive if they're fully automatic.

"Rebecca, have you ever seen one of these rifles fired?"

She nods.

"Do they fire single shots or do they fire a burst of bullets?" I ask. I need to know if they're semiautomatic or fully automatic.

"I told you. They're machine guns." She waits a second and adds, "A *burst*," then sticks out her tongue at me.

How I would love to clamp her jaws shut on that tongue and make her bite it off! *Keep control, Morgan! Focus on what has to be done.* Besides, if she bites her tongue off, you'll have to wait for it to grow back to get any more intel out of her.

If they have automatic weapons, even the speed granted by the Seed will not help us all that much in those close quarters. A stray bullet could slow us down enough for the shooter to zero in and *really* slow us down. A bullet to the head could be disastrous. The gunfire would attract the Teacher standing guard in the Sanctuary. There's not enough room in the Sanctuary to use superior numbers to our advantage. The sounds of combat might even arouse a Sleeping vampire. So the daylight assault is out. We'll have to go with Plan B.

"Have you considered," she begins, "attacking on the night of the Ritual when the Chosen are asleep during their Conversion? They would be ours for the killing."

"I will not kill the Chosen unless I'm forced to. We have to do this before the Ritual."

"Why not?" She sounds indignant. "During the early stages of the Conversion they are still . . . consumable!"

"We have to kill Chikah and Michael. I will not slaughter mortals. If you're not in agreement on this, consider the truce broken. Are we clear?" I'm really angry, I realize. My hatred for this woman, for Julie's murderer, is boiling to the surface. I thought I had it under control, but, at least for the moment, I don't.

Her face hardens and she nods.

"Say it!" I demand.

"We're *clear*. No mortal casualties."

"Good," I say as I struggle to control my rage. I take a few deep breaths.

Now for the sixty-four-thousand-dollar-question. "Do you think you and Benjamin *together* could take on Chikah?"

"Not in a *fair* fight," she replies.

"Do you think you could hold your own alone against Chikah long enough for Benjamin to put his sword through her heart from behind, if he could sneak up on her?"

A grin slowly forms on her face. "I *knew* you were worth the risk! Yes, I think I could, if Benjamin were fast and silent."

"OK, then. I have the beginnings of a plan, but first I need some assurances from you."

She rises from her chair with a sensuous, feline grace and places her hands on my shoulders. "And what assurance, pray tell, could I possibly give you that you'd accept?"

"The kind of assurance that you'll give to me when you know I *will* kill you without hesitation should you break your word to me."

She purses her lips, and her eyes harden. She drops her hands. She turns and heads into the living room. "What assurances?" she asks icily as she sits on the sofa.

I follow her into the room, but remain standing.

"First, no mortal casualties."

"I've already agreed to that," she says with a hint of impatience.

"What do you do with Chosen who aren't Converted?" I ask.

"They're consumed, or if we're *especially* fond of them, we Persuade them to forget the Cult."

"That's what I want you to do: Persuade them to forget the Cult."

She starts to object, but I hold up a hand, stopping her. "You said they were disciples of Chikah. They're not going to follow you loyally if we eliminate their favorite Teacher."

"That would be such a *waste!*" she counters.

"You wouldn't be able to trust them."

"I meant their blood. Losing their *blood* would be such a waste."

"No mortal casualties, remember?"

She pouts. *Pouts!* Is her pout supposed to be *cute?* It's *not* cute; it's childish. She has the whole Cult to Feed on. And she *pouts* over not being able to Feed off the Chosen?

"All right, you can have your precious mortals . . . this time."

"Fine. I want both you and Benjamin here to go over the plans next week. We'll need to practice some maneuvers, I think, so plan on a few hours."

"Why not tell me your plans now?"

"I have something I need to check out first, but I have one question for you."

"And that is?" She raises a curious eyebrow.

"Why do we have wings?"

"So we can fly," she says without hesitation.

"They don't move the air. They have no substance. They provide no lift, no thrust, and no drag, for that matter. They have nothing at all to do with flying. They look pretty and they make noise. That's all."

"I never thought about it. Honestly! What does this have to do with anything?" She looks exasperated. "You're supposed to be planning a battle! We have more important things to think about!"

"Actually," I say slowly, "it may be all important to our battle plan." I want to ask her about how I can bend steel without breaking the bones in my hand as well, but I don't want her to realize how little I comprehend about the way vampirism works. I need her to think of me as being in command. I really don't want her to think she has the upper hand in this alliance, not ever, not for a single second.

She looks pensive for a moment. Without looking directly at me, she asks, "How have you survived without killing? How are you Feeding?"

"What made you try to survive on animal blood?" I counter.

A look of shock and then panic flits across her face. That slip was something she didn't want me or *anybody* to know! Rebecca opens her mouth to speak and then clamps it shut. She purses her lips in consideration. "I tried to leave Michael after a few years with him. He lied to me about so much. I thought that perhaps . . . he'd lied about that . . . maybe. I tried . . . to stop . . ."

"You were a Penitent?"

"No!" Her face is wrinkled in disgust as if she smells something putrid. "Never! What do you think I am?"

A murderer. That's what you are. I say nothing.

"I'm no mewling religious *fanatic* trying to toady up to God for forgiveness, not when I'm a virtual *goddess* of the night!" she snarls. Then she sighs. "I just wanted to be *free.* If I had started killing to survive, the bodies would pile up and the mortals would be looking for a serial killer, and I might be exposed. No, I just wanted to be . . . free of *Michael.* I wanted to be my own woman."

I consider this for a moment. I actually feel a little sorry for her. A little. She was seduced and corrupted by Michael only to have to compete with Chikah and *Benjamin* for his attention. He promised her power, but only so long as she was bound to him. And, in her mind, she has nowhere to go. In some ways, she's as trapped as Benjamin is. And killing Michael and Chikah is the only way out that she sees. She needs the Cult to survive. Which means she'll have to create more Chosen and thus more vampires.

I'll deal with that after we remove the threat of Michael. And Chikah.

"One more question," I say.

"There seems to be no end to your questions. I think you just *enjoy* having me around."

I'm not going to give her the satisfaction of a response. "Did Michael know about my Conversion?"

She sits up rigidly. It looks like I hit a nerve. "Yes and no."

"What do you mean?"

"He approved your elevation to Chosen," she begins in a guarded tone, "but he didn't approve your Conversion. I undertook that myself while he was . . . away."

"Michael was *away*?" I ask incredulously.

"Lilith summoned him. He took Chikah with him."

Moira talked about this. All Masters must answer to Lilith. That explains quite a bit. That explains why I was Converted so soon.

"How," I ask, "did you explain my disappearance to Michael?"

"I led him to believe that Benjamin killed you. Michael cut off Benjamin's thumb for that one." She grins evilly and adds, "Made him grow it back."

It's all I can do to control my urge to rip her head from her neck.

"Call me soon," I say, keeping my voice steady with supreme effort. "We need to meet again right away. Now, get out."

She rises. "You never answered my question."

"Nope," I show her the door.

The scowl twisting her face is priceless.

Chapter 13

I want to call Moira. I want to call her right now, but I need to check some things out first. I have a *theory*, or at least the *beginnings* of a theory.

I return to the dining room table, and I gently sweep aside the drawings of the mansion. I take a fresh piece of paper and pull a pen from my pocket.

Rats! It's a pen from work. I must have stuck it in my pocket by mistake. I'll have to remember to take that back on Monday.

I look around for another pen. There's none to be found. I sigh and pick up the pencil. *It still stinks of Rebecca.*

When I need to examine a problem logically, sometimes it helps for me to list things on paper. So I begin:

Problems:

Wings

Can't touch temple

Too strong

These three things are really bothering me. I can feel in my gut that they're important. Something tells me they may be *extremely* important. I'm not sure why, except they just don't add up. And, when things make no sense to me, they *nag* at me.

That's why I'm in this situation, because I couldn't let the mystery of Julie's murder rest. Then I couldn't let her killer go unpunished. Now I'm a vampire, damned for eternity. Now I'm trapped into helping Julie's killer . . . at least for now.

Next to *Wings* I write:

Immaterial, make noise, don't move the air.

Next to *Can't touch temple* I write:

Moira can't touch unless she's not thinking about it.

Moira can't touch it. *Can I?* Why is it that she can only touch it when she isn't thinking about it? Is it some kind of *mental* block? Is *she* preventing herself from touching it? Is it all in her head?

I add:

Can I touch it?

Maybe I'll make a quick field trip to the Ogden Temple and find out.

In a little bit.

And then there's the matter of strength. Next to *Too strong* I add:

Moira punched me, broke my jaw, but not her hand. I bent a Glock in half without hurting my hands. Not enough increase in bone and muscle density to account for increased strength.

I stare at the list and let my thoughts and questions crystallize. I wonder how much I can lift. Are there limits to my strength? Can I lift a car? Probably not, but there's one way to find out.

I get up from the table and go into the garage. The van and my old car, the one I can't drive during the day anymore, sit side-by-side. I ignore the car. If I'm going to test this, I might as well test it with the van.

First, I open the door of the van and set the parking brake. Next I close the door and go to the front of the van. I bend down and get both hands under the front bumper.

Hold on a second, Morgan. Even if you can *lift up a van, if you lift it by the bumper, you'll rip the bumper off.*

OK. That isn't such a good idea. Now what?

I could lift it (or *try* to lift it) at the jack point. Or for that matter, why not just try to lift the *side* of the vehicle?

Much better.

I move around to the side of the van, squat down (*lift with your knees!*), and grab the chassis with both hands. Then I lift.

Or *try* to.

Oh, I can lift it up a *little* way, but the tires never leave the floor.

I set it back down. I guess I can't lift a car. I didn't think I could.

Or can I?

I bent a Glock in half. I was angry when I did it. I wasn't really *thinking* about it at the time. I just did it. Maybe it's all in the attitude. Maybe I couldn't lift it because I didn't *think* I could.

I try again and this time I imagine myself lifting the car. I really put all my strength into it and . . .

I nearly tip the van over!

Whoa!

I have to steady it and set it down gently, one hand lifting and one hand steadying the van on its side.

I was holding it up with one hand!

Can I lift it with just one hand? I lift it again . . . with just one hand. In fact, it wasn't really all that hard.

How about one finger?

The van lifts right up with just one finger under it.

I *should* have ripped my finger off doing that. There's no way that one finger, no matter how strong I am, can lift a minivan. I look at the flesh of my finger. Not even marked. I could have been lifting daisies.

He should be pushin' up daisies instead of pressin' 'em down!

Focus, Morgan! This is serious.

What does it mean? How did I do that? Telekinesis? Can I lift things with my mind? Like Luke lifting his spaceship out of the swamp?

I take one step back and try to visualize the minivan rising off the floor. I stare at it and put all my will into it.

Nothing.

I try again, willing myself to *believe* I can lift it.

Nothing.

OK. It's not telekinesis.

I reach down with one hand and lift it up again. I won't say it's effortless, but it isn't terribly difficult.

If I touch it, I can lift it. If I don't, I can't.

I move back to the front bumper. I squat down and cautiously try to lift it with one hand, being careful to pull the bumper up no more than a few inches. The bumper and the van come up together . . . and the bumper shows no signs of stress. I pull a little harder. The front of the van comes up off the floor and the bumper holds fast.

That shouldn't be possible. If the weight of the front of the van is all resting on the bumper, the bumper should collapse.

I pull my fingers away one at a time until I'm holding the car up by the bumper with just one finger.

If the weight of the van were all resting on top of my finger, the bumper should be dented in around my finger. But it's not.

I take hold of the bumper with one hand and put the other underneath the front of the van and lift.

The entire van comes off the floor.

Carefully, I set the vehicle down.

I just lifted the entire van off the floor from the front. It wasn't balanced. I lifted it because I *thought* I could.

I think I've read about this somewhere . . . *this* or something like it.

I rush back into the house and plop myself down in front of the computer. I turn on the monitor, open up the Internet browser, and go to a search page.

It takes me less than a minute to come up with:

Tactile Telekinesis – The ability to use telekinesis only through physical contact, usually with the hands.

I don't have superhuman strength. I'm a tactile telekinetic. The power is really coming from my mind. Well . . . from my *Seed-enhanced* mind, actually.

Is that how I can defy gravity and fly?

I stand up and walk to the center of the room. I imagine myself floating in the air.

And, of course, I'm floating in the air, my wings stretched out behind me. I drop back to the floor and my wings fold up and disappear.

Can I do it without the wings?

I concentrate on lifting myself off the floor.

And instantly I'm floating in the air. No wings.

Still floating, I move to the back door, out of it, and into the backyard. After glancing around and listening for any possible observers (to make sure nobody is going to see me), I shoot into the sky.

I'm flying! No wings. It's just me.

It works.

No wings.

And no flapping sound. I'm *silent*, except for the rush of air past my body.

I do a barrel roll in celebration.

I feel so free!

Did I have wings just because I *believed* I did, because Moira *told* me that vampires have wings? I think of myself as having wings and, suddenly, they're there, flapping behind me. I can hear them flapping at the air. I think of myself *without* wings . . . and they're gone.

I wheel about in the air and, spying the lit-up Ogden Temple to the north, I zoom toward it.

I haven't tried to go near a temple since my Conversion. I haven't tried to go near a temple because I *believed* I couldn't touch one . . . because I'm damned, cursed, unholy, possessed by the Essence.

But that makes no sense! *Satan* stood with Jesus on the roof of the Temple in Jerusalem! If Lucifer himself can stand on the roof of the Temple, surely I can.

As I approach the temple, with its golden spire and statue of the angel Moroni, I scan about for people who might notice me flying.

I see a few who might.

So I hover high above the temple under the canopy of stars as I wait for my chance.

After a minute or two, I see an opening, so I dive for the spire at the center of the temple roof. I pull up hard next to the gold statue at the pinnacle.

What if I'm wrong? What if this doesn't work?

Don't hesitate. Just do it!

I reach out a hand and touch the golden angel's shoulder.

I'm touching it!

I feel an almost *electric* thrill run through my whole body.

I let go and descend to the roof. And land on it. *I'm standing on the roof of the temple!* Just to be sure, I take off my shoes and socks and touch the roof with my bare feet.

Suddenly, my strength fails me. I sink to my knees and my tears flow freely.

Sharon! Moira was right! *There* is *hope! It may take a* thousand *years, but I will* find my way back to you!

I remain that way for several minutes, weeping on the roof of the temple under the stars of heaven.

Eventually, the cold night air registers on my conscious mind; so I put my socks and shoes back on.

OK. Now I'm going to call Moira.

I call Moira as I fly toward home. It's all I can do to conceal my excitement. After filling her in about my meeting with Rebecca, I ask her to meet me at my house. She tells me she's bringing dinner.

Good. We'll need the extra energy.

I watch for her from my backyard until I see her descend, her wings beating ineffectually, but noisily at the air. She looks . . . angelic. She's wearing a mid-length solid-red velvet dress. She's dressed up for dinner.

So, I guess it's a good thing I put on a white shirt and tie, even if it wasn't for dinner. I dressed up for her *surprise* later.

I'm trying so hard to keep my facial expression under control. I think I need to do this carefully or it *might* not actually work. I have nearly three centuries worth of incorrect traditions and an entire belief system to overcome.

Immediately after she lands, she's in my arms and kissing me passionately. Her lips are so soft, so sweet. For a moment it drives all other thoughts from my mind.

Eventually I slowly, reluctantly break off the kiss and pull back from our embrace. She grins up at me. "Ye're hiding something, laddie."

Crap! "Is it that obvious?"

"Aye." She nods, an expression of mock severity on her lovely face.

"Well, I have some good news, but let's eat first. I was *hoping* to surprise you." I take her hand and lead her back to the house.

Once inside, she opens her bag and sets out the placemats, cloth napkins, and goblets. And four pint bags of blood with the tubes still attached. Usually she brings only two. She opens one of the bags, and as she begins to pour the blood into the goblets, she says, "Carl, would ye be a dearie and get the candles out of my bag and light them?"

As I'm pulling out the candlesticks and candles, I ask, "Are we celebrating?"

She stops and puts her fists on her hips. "Carl Morgan, ye are an insensitive lout!" She looks genuinely *angry*. Only the twinkle in her green eyes makes me think maybe she's not. *It is a twinkle and not a flash . . . I hope.* "Are we celebratin'?" she mocks, her brogue as thick as I've ever heard it, as she shimmies her whole body left and right. "I'm nae so sure I want to marry a man who cannae remember his own one-week engagement anniversary!"

I don't know what to say. I can't tell if she's really angry or not.

"Close yer mouth, laddie." She still looks angry. "Ye look ridiculous." She winks.

I snap my mouth closed. I didn't realize I was staring at her with it open.

"Ye do know I'm teasing?" she says with a lopsided grin.

"I do *now*," I say with relief. I puff out my cheeks with a big, "Whew!"

"It's OK, laddie, ye are a *man*, after all. In all my years, I've learned men are as stupid as can be when it comes to such things." She leans in and kisses me lightly on the nose. She motions me to sit.

Instead I move over behind her chair and pull it out for her. *Take that, Rebecca!*

She cocks her head, gives me a dazzling smile, and nods at me. Then she assumes her seat like a high-born lady. Pretty good for a Highland lassie!

Once I sit, I say, "I think you'll forgive me after dinner when I give you your surprise."

"We'll see."

"Do you trust me?" I ask her as we stand in the backyard under the stars. Moira asked *me* that once. Now I need *her* to trust *me*.

"Aye, Carl. I do." She says, her eyes shining.

"Then take my hands."

She puts her hands in mine and looks me in the eye.

"Now," I say, "close your eyes and keep them closed."

She closes them. I feel a small pang of regret since I can no longer look into her bewitching eyes. *If this works, though, it'll be worth it.*

We lift off the ground and soar into the night sky. Her wings are out and flapping. I don't want to spoil the big surprise so I have my wings out as well.

Moira keeps her eyes closed. She says not a word as she lets me guide her until we're hovering high above our destination.

Once again, I have to wait for an opportunity for us to descend unobserved. Once I find an opening, we descend quickly and land. Our wings fold up and disappear. To tell the truth, I was a little worried it wouldn't work, but here we are. What if there had been a difference between Moira and me? What if she had been still barred from touching the temple? But here we are. Together.

"Can I open my eyes now?" she asks with an eager grin, like a child anticipating Christmas morning.

I shush her and then whisper, "Not yet." Then I add, "Soon." I take her arm by the wrist and pull her hand out until it touches the bottom tier of the multi-leveled white spire in front of us. I breathe an audible sigh of relief when she touches it easily.

The Unwilling

When her hand is resting firmly on the spire and I'm standing beside her, I fix my gaze on her face and whisper, "Now! Open your eyes!" I want to savor every instant of her reaction.

Her eyes open, and for a second she looks confused. She doesn't know where she is. Her eyes follow the spire upward until she sees the golden statue of the angel above us. She gasps and recoils, but I hold her hand against the spire.

She glances around herself in a panic and then, abruptly, she ceases her efforts to pull back. Slowly a smile splits her face from ear to ear. *I guess I can let go now.* I release her wrist. She pulls back, but like someone testing the temperature of a pan on a hot stove, she tentatively reaches out and touches the spire lightly again and then rests her hand against it.

Her face turns to me, and I'm again reminded of a child on Christmas morning. Her joy is that *pure*. She lets go of the spire and throws her arms around me and kisses me fiercely and then tenderly. She looks up into my eyes. Tears are spilling down her cheeks. I realize my tears are flowing freely too.

"How is this possible?" she asks in wonder.

I must be grinning like an idiot. "I think it always was ... possible," I say. "Moira, you sensed that the temples were holy, right?"

She nods. "Aye, I could feel it."

"Well, you thought that you were *unholy*, so you couldn't *let* yourself touch the wall of the temple."

She looks doubtful.

"I don't understand it fully," I say, "but I think it's all related."

"What's all related?"

"Your inability to touch the temple, our impossible strength, our ability to fly, our wings. All of it. I think it's all related."

"I dinnae understand."

"Well, let me show you what else I learned tonight," I say as I gently pull free from her embrace.

I take a step back, pause, and rise a couple of feet into the air. She stares at me for a second without comprehension, and then suddenly the shock is plain on her face. She gasps.

"Where are yer wings, Carl?" she cries in astonishment.

"Wings? Why on Earth would we need wings to fly?"

"I ... I dinnae ... But we've *always* had wings!"

"You mean, like these?" I imagine myself with wings and they suddenly appear.

"How did ye do that?"

"The same way I can do this," I say, and I make the wings disappear.

She gasps again.

"Moira, imagine yourself flying up to join me *without wings*."

"But that's nae possible. We have wings. We have *always* had wings!"

"Why?"

"Because we *do*," she says feebly.

"Look at me, Moira. I'm flying without wings. You can too. We have wings because we were *told* we have wings."

She shakes her head.

"Just try it, Moira. Please. Trust me. Trust your own eyes."

She nods her head slowly, and then she lifts off the roof of the temple to take my hand. Her wings flicker in and out as she stares into my eyes. Her breathing is rapid, but she slowly brings it under control and, as she does, her wings vanish completely.

"I still dinnae understand. How is this possible? What makes us fly?"

"Actually, I have a theory, but I think it may be easier and *safer* if I demonstrate it at home," I tell her. *I don't want to be lifting cars with my finger on a public street.*

"If ye say so. But, before ye do that, laddie, will ye do something for me? I mean, ye have given me such *hope* tonight, but I want just a wee bit more."

"Anything, pretty lady," I say with a grin.

"Do ye have yer temple recommend with ye?"

I wasn't expecting that. I don't know what I *was* expecting, but that was definitely *not* it. "Yeah, sure."

"I want ye to walk with me into the temple entrance. I'll wait in the waitin' room, but ye show yer recommend and go into the temple. I want to see ye do it with my own eyes."

Wow. "OK. I'll give it a shot." *It's a good thing I'm wearing a tie.*

Together we float, wingless, to a spot behind the temple. We walk hand-in-hand around to the entrance. We're both trembling in nervous apprehension. Before we get to the outer door, I stop and pull out my wallet and pick out the little white and gold document encased in its clear plastic sleeve, the document I never expected to have occasion to use again. My temple recommend: the document that certifies I'm worthy to enter the temple.

I stare at it. Am *I worthy to enter?* I have to interview with my bishop and a member of the stake presidency every two years to certify that I'm worthy. My recommend hasn't expired. I know I'm a vampire, but what sin have I committed that would bar me from the temple? I'm not sure. I'm not sure I've done *anything* worthy of *damnation*. I was just in the wrong place, hanging out with the wrong people. I said some words I thought were meaningless. I participated in a ritual I thought was bogus. I did all this to catch Julie's killer. I haven't killed. I've consumed human blood. That's it. *So what have I done that's worthy of damnation?*

Nothing. Except for the blood.

I take a deep cleansing breath, and then I start forward again. Moira is at my side. I realize that she stood there waiting patiently with me as I debated in my head.

OK. This is it.

There are glass doors at the entrance to the temple. They open onto an outer foyer. From there, people who do not possess a temple recommend can turn right and go into the waiting room, where they can wait for those who are inside the temple. Temple recommend holders can proceed through another glass door to the recommend desk, where a temple worker will check the validity of the recommend and admit the bearer into the temple proper.

Moira and I walk up to one of the automatic outer doors. The door swings open.

I step forward and cross into the outer foyer of the temple. And Moira is beside me. *Inside.* Inside the outer foyer. Tears are streaming down her face. Down mine too. She releases my hand and turns to the right and enters the waiting room. She sits demurely on one of the chairs, and her smile is rapturous. I give her a little nod and continue in.

My visit is quick. I show my recommend and am admitted into the temple proper. Once inside, I stand there for a minute, letting it all sink in. *I'm here.* I'm still immortal. I'm still a vampire, but I'm not barred from the temple.

After a minute, I turn around and walk back to the outer foyer. Moira looks at me expectantly and I give her a small nod and a smile.

She arises from her chair and walks slowly to join me. She takes my hand, and we walk unhurriedly out of the temple.

Once outside, we walk leisurely around the grounds for a long time, not saying a word. We remain that way, walking under the canopy of heaven, our joy too profound for speech.

And then we sense the approach of evil.

Chapter 14

I can feel the all-but-irresistible attraction of the blood of someone truly evil. Moira has suddenly gone rigid beside me. Of course, she can feel it too. The corrupt sweetness of the evil blood calls to me. My fangs extend, and saliva runs from my snarling lips in streams.

There are four of them. I can feel them approaching.

Moira squeezes my hand and gives it a slight tug upward. No other communication is necessary. We leap into the air and fly up to the temple roof so we can get a better vantage point.

Neither of us has wings.

From our vantage point on the roof, we can see a nondescript car pulling into the temple parking garage. At this hour, the last of the temple workers should be leaving the temple for the night. Anybody arriving *now* probably has no legitimate business here. The malevolence is inside that car.

I can hear voices from the car. It's an expletive-laden tirade against the Mormons and their precious temple. Whoever is in that car, they're intent on violence.

I want to swoop down right now and rip the roof off the car and lift the occupants screaming into the air, to drain their worthless lives. The vampiric rage threatens to take control, to drive me to kill. I can feel Moira trembling beside me as she controls *her* rage, *her* lust for blood.

We have to wait for proof. Hopefully we'll have proof enough before there's any violence.

Soon I can hear the sound of four car doors opening and shutting again inside the parking garage. In a few moments I can see four figures carrying baseball bats and plastic bags filled with . . . yes, I can smell it . . . spray paint.

This is the big evil? They're going to vandalize the temple? I mean, that's . . . bad. *Very* bad. But not enough to pull me so forcefully.

The four men divide into pairs and take positions on either side of the temple entrance. The entrance is well lit, but there are shadows at either side. I hear two sets of shuffling feet inside moving toward the door. The footsteps must belong to temple workers who are leaving for the night.

And these men plan to hurt them or to kill them to gain access to the temple. They're not wearing masks, so that means they do *not* plan to leave witnesses.

Now the burning rage inside me has all the justification it needs.

Moira releases my hand, and we leap into the air and land on either side of the white-haired couple just now emerging from the temple. We're standing between them and their would-be attackers. The evil men have just come out of the shadows with their baseball bats raised high. I immediately drop to a feral crouch and growl at the two men on my side. Behind me, I can hear the old woman faint dead away. As she falls, I hear the unmistakable sound of a bone breaking and flesh ripping and I can smell the old woman's *blood.*

Blood!

"Edna!" the old man cries.

I glance behind me and quickly take in the sight of the old lady fallen to the ground, her right leg twisted in a compound fracture. The jagged bone sticks out of the torn skin, and her blood flows. The aged bones must have broken when she fell.

Her husband falls to his knees and spreads himself over her. *He's trying to protect her with his own body!* He gropes feebly at the ruin of her leg, trying desperately to staunch the flow of blood.

Blood!

The scent of her blood makes it hard to concentrate. It isn't the sweet corruption like that of the four thugs, but it's . . . almost overwhelming in its *availability.*

The attackers hesitate for just a moment and then rush at us as one. They each hold bats in both hands. The weapons are raised over their heads.

With my left hand I snatch the bat out of the first creep's hands and swing it around to strike the bat of the second man. When my appropriated weapon makes contact with his bat, the creep's weapon explodes with a loud crack like a thunderclap. His hands drop the remaining splinters of his bat, and he screams. It looks like the force of the blow shattered all the bones in both his hands. The first man, the one whose bat I took, stands looking at me in shock. I take a handful of his hair in my hand and bend his neck to one side. He takes a good look at my fangs and my blazing eyes, and he screams like his friend with the mangled hands.

I plunge my fangs into his neck. I must have nicked the jugular because the sweet blood gushes into my mouth. I gulp down a quart or so and lick his neck to seal the wound. My saliva does its job, and the bleeding stops. I drop him to the ground.

I quickly Feed off the second man and turn to Moira and the elderly couple.

Moira's assailants are flat on the ground. Both men have both arms broken. They're screaming and cursing at Moira. She hasn't Fed from either of them. If she had, they'd be moaning for more.

No, Moira's attention is on the old woman, on her leg. Moira's *Feeding* from her leg? She left the evil-doers and is Feeding from the sweet old lady?

No. Wait. The old woman's leg. It's *straight!* Moira is *healing* her injury with her saliva, with the Seed! The *control* she must be exerting to not take *any* of the woman's blood is *unbelievable!* I can see that Moira is trembling, no, *shaking* with the effort. She must have set the bone with her bare hands. Now she's holding the wound open with her fingers as she lets streams of saliva drool into it. Slowly, she allows the wound to close, pulling her fingers out one by one, until at the last she licks it and the torn flesh seals without a mark.

The husband is cradling his wife's head in his lap. He's saying soothing things to her, but his eyes are wide with terror.

Moira lifts her head from the healed leg. She looks at me. Her face is ashen. "Carl," she says, with a tremor in her voice, "I've done all I can. She's in shock and she's lost a lot o' blood. She needs to get to hospital immediately. I'll take care of this lot, but I need ye to fly her to McKay-Dee emergency room. Her blood type is A-positive. Can ye remember that?"

I nod. I guess Moira can identify blood types by taste or smell.

She says through gritted teeth, her fangs prominent, "I dinnae trust myself to do it. I'm nae . . . in *control.* I must . . . *Feed.* Can ye do it, laddie?"

"Sure." I turn quickly to the old gentleman. "Sir, can you drive and meet your wife at the hospital?" He nods mutely, his jaw agape.

I gently scoop up the old woman in my arms and cradle her against my chest. I elevate her legs and lower her head to treat her for shock.

Her husband clambers painfully to his feet.

I zoom into the air with the old woman in my arms.

I can hear the old man gasp as he sees me fly. A moment later I hear his voice fading fast below me. "Edna! I love you!" His desperate cry is mingled with the screams and curses of the two men that Moira disabled.

One foul voice cuts off abruptly.

I guess Moira is finally Feeding.

I fly with the old woman, Edna, as fast as I dare. I would go faster, but I worry that she won't be able to breathe. I worry about the wind chill too. If she's in shock, the cold could kill her. I can hear her heart beating under the noise of the airstream. It's weak, unsteady. I shift around so I'm flying backward to shield her from the airstream as much as I can. This makes navigation difficult. I constantly have to turn to get my bearings. I have a general idea of where the hospital is from the ground, but locating it from the air at night is much more difficult.

I know I'm probably in the general area, but it's not like there's a big lit-up sign on the roof that says, "HOSPITAL." *Or is there?* Yes! That "H" is for the helipad near the emergency room! There's the hospital!

I dive for the entrance and land a few feet shy of it. Then I rush Edna into the emergency room.

It's twenty or so minutes later when Edna's husband enters the emergency room at a run. I can tell it's causing him great pain to move that fast. He sees me and runs straight to me and grabs me by the shoulders.

"Where's Edna? Is she . . ." He can't bring himself to ask if she's all right. "*Where's my Edna?*"

"The doctors are with her now," I assure him. "They gave her a transfusion. A-positive. They're keeping her warm, treating her for shock, but otherwise she's OK. Her heart is beating steadier now. She's feeling just fine."

"Have you talked to the doctors?" he asks. "Where is she?"

I've actually been eavesdropping on the doctors and nurses from here. I've discovered that, if I concentrate, I can single out the conversations I want to focus on from the babble and the noise of the ER. So I've been following her progress. But I can't tell him how I know this. The Seed that got into her bloodstream has made her feel wonderful. I can't tell him that either.

"What's your name, sir?" I ask

"Fred Spencer," he replies. He looks puzzled. "But you know that, don't you?"

What? How the heck would I have known his name?

"She's back this way," I say and lead him through the doors to the corridor where the treatment rooms are located.

A nurse (or orderly?) tries to stop me, but I simply say, "This is *Edna's* husband." She nods and turns to lead the way.

"Fred," I say, tilting my head in the nurse's direction, "go ahead with this nice young lady."

The nurse gives me another nod and extends a hand to Fred.

Fred gives me a look that I can't quite read. It's part gratitude, part awe, part . . . something else. "Thank you." He takes the nurse's hand and hurries off.

I hear cries of joy when that sweet couple is reunited moments later. That brings a smile to my face.

I'm still grinning like an idiot when I catch sight of Moira standing outside the door. She motions to me to join her.

Once outside, she kisses me quickly, then turns and takes my arm and leads me farther away from the hospital.

"How is she?" Moira asks.

"I overheard the doctors and nurses as they treated her. She should be fine. What *you* did was amazing!"

"We have a problem," she whispers so low that only a vampire could hear.

"What's wrong?" I whisper back.

"I took care of those vermin back at the temple. The police have them in hand."

"So what's the problem?" I ask, puzzled. She should be *pleased* with the way things turned out.

"I caught up with Edna's husband as he drove here. I listened to him in his car as I flew above him. He was praying frantically all the way."

"Makes sense to me." I still don't see what she's driving at.

"He thanked God for sending His *angels* to save the two of them."

"Angels?" I say, perplexed.

And then it dawns on me. "Oh, you mean *us*."

"Aye, laddie," she replies grimly. "Us."

Fred saw us fly. He saw us take down armed thugs. He saw Moira heal Edna. "Angels" seems like a logical enough conclusion.

But we don't need the extra attention. And we *certainly* don't need to give Detective Johnson anything else to go on.

"I will nae use Persuasion on that sweet man and his Edna," she says with a fierce conviction.

"Fred," I say absently as the immensity of the problem falls on me. "His name is Fred Spencer."

"Fred, then. Aye. Carl, what are we goin' to do?"

I don't know what to say. I agree with Moira. Using Persuasion or "mental handcuffs" on Fred and Edna would be *wrong* on so many levels. It would be unforgivable to force them to forget.

But what if it weren't *forced?*

"Moira," I begin. "What if we told them the truth?"

"Are ye *daft?*" Her voice is a hiss.

"We don't have to tell them *everything*, just enough of the truth, and then we asked them to keep our secret."

She stops and looks at me incredulously. "And tell them what?" she demands.

"I don't know. At least tell them that we're not *angels*. Just people with special . . . gifts."

"Now ye are soundin' like one of those comic books, laddie."

"Well, I've read enough comic books to at least *imagine* that there are decent people who will protect the secrets of their . . . protectors."

"I will nae become a vigilante . . . some super heroine protecting the streets of Salt Lake City . . . or Ogden. 'Twould draw too much attention."

"Yeah. For one thing, we don't need any more Detective Johnsons asking too many questions. And there would certainly be more police interest if there were a rash of roughed up, anemic hoodlums confessing their crimes."

She nods. "There has been too much of that already lately. I told ye that I rarely Hunt." She throws up her hands in exasperation. "Now ye know *why*."

We take a few more steps in silence and then she says, "Let's give the truth a go."

For several hours we walk around the hospital grounds, wandering closer to the ER from time to time and listening for Edna's progress. There's a debate going on about where all the blood went. There are some hurried tests to check for internal bleeding. After those turn up nothing, there's another debate over whether to keep Edna overnight, with Edna adamantly claiming she feels fine, hasn't felt this good in decades. Fred insists she be released. And so it goes back and forth with Fred and Edna eventually winning out.

We hear the words "miracle" and "healed" from time to time. We don't hear everything, but we don't catch any mention of "angels."

Eventually (and uncomfortably close to dawn), Fred and Edna come shuffling out of the hospital, her hand in the crook of his arm. They look so perfect together, so sweet. Someday I want that to be Moira and me: the sweet elderly couple walking hand-in-hand, growing old together.

He's so attentive, matching his stride to hers to support her better. When they get a little out of sync, he shuffles a bit to match her again. As they approach where Moira and I are standing, he catches sight of us. His broad grin exposes teeth yellowed with age.

Moira and I approach them. When we meet, I extend a hand. "Fred, Edna, I'm Carl and this is Moira." He hesitates for a moment and then takes my hand. I'm careful to be gentle as I shake his hand. Don't want to crush any brittle bones.

"You *are* angels, aren't you?"

"Sorry, Fred," I shake my head. "We're not angels."

"But I saw . . . But you healed . . . You *flew*. You *saved* us."

"I'm just glad we were there to help," I say. "But now we need *your* help."

"What?" he says. "What can we *possibly* to do help *you*?"

"Please don't tell anyone about what you saw. I really . . . can't . . . Well, I'd *rather* not explain what you saw. But, please trust me when I say that it would be very *bad* for us if word were to get out about what happened tonight."

"We value our privacy, ye see," Moira adds, "and there would be a lot of questions we could nae give answers to."

"But, what you did was a *miracle*," Fred says earnestly.

"Not exactly," I say.

"God sent you to save us," says Edna, her eyes moist with tears.

"Nae, 'twas nae heaven," says Moira sadly. "What ye saw was nae divine."

"Let's just say that we have special . . . gifts," I add.

"Well, then God gave you these gifts." Fred's tone is decisive.

"Would 'twere so," says Moira with a wistful smile.

"Will you keep our secret?" I ask.

They look at each other for a moment and then turn their heads back to us. Fred says, "Yes, we will, but I will thank God all my days that you gave me my Edna back." His tears course down his wrinkled face.

"Thank you," I say.

Edna gasps. "Oh, my!" She turns her face to Fred. "You told that nurse about the 'angels'! Oh, dear." She turns back to us. "I hope that doesn't ruin things for you!"

"That's right!" her husband exclaims. "I did. I told the nurse who took me back to see Edna. I told her everything." He starts talking very fast. "I said you came down from the sky and gave those hood-lums what for and then you saved Edna and me, healed her leg, and then you *flew* her to the hospital." After this torrent of words he stands speechless for a moment, and then he says, "I'm so sorry! I had no idea."

Moira smiles sadly. "Well, there's nothing for it now."

"I'll tell anybody else who asks that we don't know *what* we saw," says Fred. "And, from what you told me, that's true enough."

Moira sighs. "We'll just have to hope that'll be the end of it".

I hope that *will* be the end of it.

But my gut tells me different.

Chapter 15

Tactile telekinesis?" Moira's standing in my garage, watching me. I'm holding my van, obviously overbalanced, up off the floor.

"Yep. I tried just lifting it with my mind, but that didn't work," I reply. "I can only lift it when I touch it. And the object I'm lifting takes no damage, doesn't deform where I touch it." I set the van back down.

"Do you remember tonight," I continue, "when I shattered the second creep's bat *and* his hands with one blow from my bat?"

"Actually, laddie, I was so busy dealing with my own 'creeps,' and then Edna, I did nae pay attention to what ye were about."

"You were incredible, fixing her leg like that. I can't imagine the control you were maintaining to do it." I point toward the door leading back into the house.

"I very nearly failed," she says. "I could feel my control slippin'. I could feel the bloodlust, directed at the 'creeps,' as ye so aptly call them, but I had tasted *Edna's* blood. The urge to Feed from *her* was gettin' the better of me. I needed ye to take her away for *my* sake as much as for hers."

"Wow. That makes what you did all the more amazing."

She leads me into the living room and we sit on the loveseat, turning to face each other. I take her hand in mine. "Can you heal *anything* that way?"

"Ye mean, like cancer?"

I nod.

"Ach, nae," she says with a rueful shake of her head. "Such healin' would require the Seed to spread throughout the patient's body and remain so for a bit. Without the Essence to sustain it, the Seed dies quickly. Mostly, I can repair minor damage. I could nae do what I did tonight without ye there to take the patient away. I fear I would *kill* more often than I would heal, were I to try that on my own."

"And you can taste the difference between blood types?"

"Aye. That and more: I can taste infections, impurities, drugs. I can tell if the blood is HIV-positive or if the prey has a cold. I have sometimes tasted a patient's blood sample to diagnose an illness. I've been at this for a long time, laddie. To be honest, I dinnae care for the taste of the preservatives we put in blood to store it, but I've learned to tolerate them. Your palate will become more refined in time."

Moira smiles. "Now, laddie," she says in an obvious change of subject, "ye were going to explain to me about the bat."

"Oh, yeah," I say with a sheepish grin. "My bat pulverized the creep's bat *and* his hands, but didn't take any damage itself. I think this is part of the tactile telekinesis. It's like when you punched me and broke my jaw, but didn't hurt yourself. The power comes from your mind. The Chinese call it *'chi.'* I think a Kung-Fu master practices a small amount of tactile telekinesis when he strikes a target; the power of his mind is focused on his own hand at the point of impact. So he breaks boards or cinder blocks without hurting himself. My guess is that the Seed enhances this. OK, it enhances it *exponentially.*

"It's what makes us *fly*, I think. We lift ourselves through the air because we imagine ourselves flying. When we stop thinking about flying, we free fall."

"Aye, I think ye may be onto something," she says and then looks puzzled. "How is it that *ye* figured this out when nae other vampire has in *six millennia?*"

"I'm pretty sure Rebecca didn't teach me everything she was supposed to. Also, I think that, because I never *believed* any of it, I never took it at face value. I dismissed it for the most part. It's like the wings. You accepted without question that vampires have wings, so you projected wings just like your Teacher had. I did the same, but only because I saw you do it. The wings never made sense to me." I pause in thought.

"What is it, laddie?"

"I wonder why it was important for us to have wings."

She looks at me quizzically.

"I mean," I continue, "somebody had to come up with the idea and perpetuate it."

She thinks for a moment. "I'm fairly sure it goes all the way back to Lilith. She's depicted in early Mesopotamian art as having feathered wings. Later artists portrayed her with bat-like wings, but she's *often* portrayed as having wings. And, I find it interesting that Lilith and her wings in art predate angels being depicted with wings."

"That's fascinating. I think it may have something to do with our ability to fade into shadows too. If we can project the image, even the *sound,* of wings, why not *darkness* to hide us?"

"Now that ye say it, it does make sense." She nods. "There are legends of vampires impersonating the dead to deceive mortals. There are also stories of the female succubus and the male incubus who seduce mortals, sometimes by impersonating a wife or a husband. Maybe those were simply vampires who were more adept at projecting an image . . . or using Persuasion."

"And maybe," I add, "it was just a case of, 'No, really, honey. I thought she was *you*! She looked just *like* you! I *swear!*'"

"That's nae funny, laddie," Moira says in a serious tone. She tries hard to maintain a solemn expression for a moment, and then barely suppresses a very unladylike snort of laughter.

"Speaking of being faithful to yer spouse," she says when she gets her mirth under control, "in light of what happened tonight, I think it's time I talked to my bishop about a recommend for marriage."

"Your *bishop*?" I ask, stunned. "I had no idea you had one!"

"Ye're doing it again, laddie," She indicates my open mouth.

I snap it shut.

"Aye, my bishop," she adds with a raised eyebrow. "Why would I want a temple marriage if I was nae a Mormon?"

"I . . . I j-j-just *assumed* . . ."

"Aye, I suppose 'tis understandable," she mercifully interrupts my hopeless stammering. "But, I've been a member longer than ye have been alive, *laddie.*"

You could stick my finger in an empty light socket and throw the switch and I wouldn't be more shocked.

"What?" I say. "How?"

"Same way as anyone else," she replies to my poorly articulated question. "I was baptized nearly half a century ago. My bishop knows all about me."

"He *knows*? I haven't told my bishop anything."

"Aye, he knows. He and many of his predecessors have been trying to get me to go to the temple and receive my endowments for nigh on twenty years. I've taken the Temple Prep class a dozen times. I stopped going a couple of years ago because I could never touch the temple wall.

"Besides, it meant that I had to keep getting a substitute for my Primary class on Sundays."

"You . . ." I swallow. "You teach Primary?"

"Aye, I had to get a substitute for my Sunbeams when I was tending to ye after yer Awakening."

"You . . . teach . . . *Sunbeams?*" Moira teaches three-year-olds on Sundays?

"What? Do ye suppose that I'm nae a good teacher? Because, I will have ye know, *Brother* Morgan, my bairns love me!"

"Bairns?"

"Babies! Wee ones! *Kids!*" she says with annoyance. "And ye with a good Scottish name like Morgan to nae know what 'bairns' are! Ye are such a wee bairn yerself, laddie!" She winks at me and gives me a dazzling smile.

"But you're a *vampire!*" I cry.

"So are ye!" she replies. "Actually, I held off getting baptized for decades after I came here. I believed I was unworthy. Eventually a determined pair of young elders and a persistent bishop convinced me I should try."

She looks at me for comment, but I can't come up with anything to say. So she continues, "My bishop knew all about my history, what I am. He told me that I'd killed men in times of war and, though I killed in vengeance and swore oaths and made covenants with evil, my repentance in the centuries that followed had been absolute. He said the Atonement of Christ was great enough to cleanse the truly repentant. He said baptism would cleanse me of my past sins. And I wanted so much to believe him.

"To be certain, he wrote to the First Presidency. I dinnae know how much he *explained* to them, but the President of the Church at the time gave clearance for me to be baptized. I have nae ever seen the letter, but the bishop told me that it 'cleared me to receive all the blessings of the restored gospel.' That letter has been passed down from bishop to bishop ever since."

She pauses for a moment. All I can manage is, "Wow."

"Wow, indeed," she continues. "On the day of my baptism, I was certain I would burst into flames right there in the Tabernacle baptismal font. (Aye, they used to do baptisms there.) But it did nae happen. My bishop thought that perhaps my baptism would overcome my inability to enter the temple, but it did nae make any difference. He even gave me a blessing saying that I would be able to enter the temple, but that changed nothing. I still could nae so much as touch a temple wall. And I remained a vampire, a Child of Lilith.

"But from that day to this, I've served where I can. Each succeeding bishop knows of my condition, and all have encouraged me to prepare for the day when I'd nae longer be barred from the temple."

She stares meaningfully into my eyes. "And it appears that day has *finally* come."

She leans toward me and kisses me long and tenderly.

"So," she says when she finally breaks the kiss and leans her forehead against mine, "I'll call and set up an appointment to talk to my bishop so I can finally get that temple recommend he's wanted to give me for so very long."

Sitting up straight and pulling away from me, she adds, "And ye need to speak to yer bishop as well. We'll both need recommends for marriage."

Crap! "How am I going to explain this whole *vampirism* thing to my bishop? *And* my stake president? You know that we need interviews with both, right?"

"I'll have my bishop call yer bishop and yer stake president. He's familiar with our condition. How's that?"

"I . . . suppose. I really have no idea how he's going to take it. But if you're going to do that, have your bishop call today."

"I'll try to do that in a few hours. The Sun will be rising soon. We both need Sleep. I need to be getting home. We have a busy night tomorrow." She stands up and heads to the dining room to fetch her bag.

I follow her. "That's right. I need to pick up some things in preparation for the battle with Michael and Chikah."

"And I need to give ye some more training with the broadsword and dirk tomorrow." She winks at me. "Ye still have much to learn."

"And we need to go over the battle plan."

She pauses at the back door, turns to give me a kiss good-bye, then throws her arms around me and kisses me passionately.

I hold her tightly. I never want to let go of her.

But soon . . . too soon, she pulls back and says, "How is Wednesday night for ye? Unless we can get it arranged for Tuesday?"

"For training and planning? I thought we were doing that tomorrow night."

"No, laddie." She shakes her head. "For our *wedding*. Ye're nae planning on backing out on me now, are ye?"

"Wow. That's . . . really quick."

"Ye have nae family to invite. Nor do I. I'm sure our bishops will want to be the witnesses. And," she adds jabbing a finger into my chest with each word for emphasis, "there is nae possibility that we're going into battle *without* being sealed in the temple . . . now that it's possible. I'll nae risk losing ye without being sealed to ye for time and eternity. So Wednesday or Tuesday night, if I can arrange it?"

Her logic makes sense, but . . . so *quick*. So soon. And we *are* going into battle . . . and if I should lose her . . .

She mistakes my pause for second thoughts. I can see it in her eyes. Before she can say anything, I say, "Absolutely. Yes! We may have to delay the honeymoon until after the battle . . ."

She smiles wickedly. "Tuesday it shall be then! If the temple were open on Monday, I'd arrange it then! I'm nae delayin' my weddin' night until after any wretched battle! I swear I'll find a temple with an opening for a weddin' if I have to go outside of the *state*!"

"Hey, pretty lady," I say with a wide grin, "I like you this way."

"What way?"

"You can be patient as a statue, but once you've made up your mind, you don't waste any time."

"Waste time? Are ye daft? I've been waitin' for my weddin' night for *two and half centuries*! Who'd have thought *I* would be the *impetuous* one?"

"It's just like . . . Wow! I'm getting married in a few days to a woman I've known for less than three weeks! OK. It's just coming at me really fast, but I guess I'm ready for it. Are you sure *you* are?" I see her nod, but I have to ask a question that I really don't *want* to ask. "Moira, do you really *love* me that much or am I just the only . . . the only vampire available?"

"Carl Morgan," she says sternly, "ye would nae believe how many marriage proposals I've had over the centuries, especially after moving to Utah."

"Actually," I interrupt, "I *would* believe it. I don't see how any single (or widowed) man could resist you."

She smirks, but continues, "As I was saying, I've been proposed to by many men over the centuries, among them many good men. I've even *considered* some of those proposals, but I've only been in *love* twice in all my long, long life. I ken what love is. And I love *ye*, Carl Morgan, with all my heart. More than I loved Donald by far. But what about ye? Am I the only eligible 'vampire in town'?"

"Well," I say, trying to sound serious, "there *is* Rebecca. And Chikah."

She punches me in the shoulder. Not too hard, but hard enough.

"Ow!" I say. "I was *kidding*, you know?"

She looks at me coldly. "Did I *break* anythin'?"

"Not *this* time," I say, rubbing my shoulder.

"Good," she says.

"Moira, I know what love is too. I love Sharon. I will *always* love her. For all eternity. Nothing will change that. I love you too. I'm hopelessly, *irreversibly* in love with you. I *need* you, but it's more than that. You gave me the hope . . . *more* than just hope . . . that I'll see Sharon and Lucy and April and Joseph again. I'd love you for that alone. But I love you . . . *you*, Moira MacDonald, with all my heart."

She kisses me once. "More than ye love Sharon?"

My eyes go wide.

How the heck am I supposed to answer that?

"I'm just kidding ye, lad." She gives me a wink and a stunning smile. She kisses me long and hard and then she's gone into the brightening sky.

Chapter 16

My opportunities to Sleep during a work week are very limited. Saturday is my one day to Sleep, so after a week with little or no rest, the rising of the Sun on Saturday finds me exhausted. But I can't Sleep now. I have to wait until I can call Bishop Edwards. And he probably won't be up for *hours*.

I spend the time going over and over different attack plans, weighing different options. My primary objective is to avoid 'civilian' casualties and still achieve victory. This may be a war, but there has to be a way to do this *and* avoid killing mortals. Even if I don't kill any mortals myself, I have no doubt that Michael and Chikah wouldn't hesitate to use human shields. I'm certain that Rebecca or Benjamin wouldn't balk at putting a blade through a mortal to get to Chikah.

Next Sunday is the night of the full moon. I need to have this plan finalized before my next meeting with Rebecca and Benjamin.

My cell phone vibrates in my pocket. I pull it out and check the caller ID. *Speak of the devil and she will appear.* It's Rebecca. And she's calling during the day. She must be standing guard duty.

I flip the phone open.

"Go ahead," I say curtly.

There's silence on the other end for a moment. "Oh, you're awake! I expected you to be Sleeping. I was just going to leave a voice mail."

"OK," I say. "When are we meeting? Remember that it needs to be *both* of you this time."

"I think we can get away tonight."

"Good. Come with your weapons."

"All righty."

"Make it as soon after sunset as possible."

"As soon as we can get away."

"I have some questions."

"What's that, love?"

Her tone disgusts me. "Don't start with me, I'm warning you."

"Sorry." Amazingly, she sounds *chastened*.

"The Ritual begins next Sunday night?"

"That's right."

"When?"

"At midnight."

"OK. What happens to the Novices when the Ritual begins?"

"A Teacher watches over them. In this case, it would be me."

"What about Chikah?"

"Since the Chosen to be elevated are all her disciples, she'll be there with Michael in the Sanctuary."

"So, with all the Chosen in the Sanctuary with Michael and Chikah, you and Benjamin will be the only ones watching the outer doors?"

"That's correct, lov . . . That's right."

"Michael and Chikah will be unarmed?"

"No. Since no Chosen will be left to stand guard in the Hall of the Chosen, they'll *both* be armed."

I was hoping to catch a break. Ah, well . . ." All right. Tonight after sunset."

"Yes, after sunset."

I hang up.

I arrange the sketches of the mansion in front of me on the table. I have some time to kill before I can call the bishop. It's only about seven in the morning. I should wait till ten or so before I try to call.

I still have no idea what I'm going to say to him.

Hey, Bishop! Guess what? I'm a vampire! See? Here are my fangs! Did you cut yourself shaving this morning, because you smell just like breakfast! By the way, I want to get married in the temple. It's OK, because she's a vampire too! I know it's only been six months since Sharon and Lucy and April and Joseph were killed, but, hey, it's time to move on, you know! Oh, and don't worry about the rush job on the marriage. I know what it looks like, but she's not pregnant. Trust me! We've been good! OK, there was that time we took this long shower together, but I was completely clothed and she was, well, wearing little bits of something over her underwear! And, yes, I know she slept over one day, but we slept in separate rooms! Honest! No appearance of evil there! No, sir! But it's OK because she can't get pregnant! She's a great gal! You'll like her! She teaches Sunbeams! Oh, and don't worry about her age! She may be only seventeen, but she's also older than the United States of America! So, waddaya say, Bish . . .

My phone rings, cutting off my manic mental babbling. I don't recognize the number right off the bat, but it looks familiar.

I answer it with, "Carl Morgan."

"Carl, it's Bishop Edwards," says the familiar voice.

"Hi, Bishop," I reply. I'm not *ready* for this.

"Carl, I just received the most *bizarre* phone call from a Bishop Adams in Salt Lake."

I bet you have, Bishop.

"Can you meet me at my office? I know it's early, but . . ."

"What time, Bishop?" I ask.

"I need to make a couple of phone calls first. I . . . Carl, is any of this . . . stuff . . . Is any of it *real?* Do you even know what I'm talking about?" He doesn't want to say it, to give it a name.

"Yeah, Bishop. I do. And, yeah. It's *all* real. I'm still getting used to it myself."

"Give me an hour. I've got to get dressed and then I'll make those calls. Bishop Adams was very insistent." He pauses for a long time. I know he's still there because I can hear his breathing. "Carl, you better bring your temple recommend."

That sounds ominous. "Sure, Bishop. See you in an hour."

The bishop hangs up and I sit motionless at the table, the battle plan forgotten. *He wants me to bring my temple recommend. He's going to ask me to surrender it.*

This is simply too much for him to deal with. I just ventured into the temple for the first time since my unwilling Conversion and now I'm going to lose my temple recommend. Not that I blame Bishop Edwards; it's simply too much. I had hoped that Moira's bishop (Bishop Adams was it?) would've been able to convince him, but it just wasn't enough. To go from the wild hope that Moira and I could be sealed to *losing* my access to the temple entirely when I'd barely gotten it back is overwhelming. A minute ago, I had hope that I would see Sharon and Lucy and April and Joseph again . . . and now I've lost them all over again.

Grief floods through me. I'm drowning.

I fold my arms and lower my head onto them and sob for a while. Eventually I kneel down beside my chair and pour my heart out to God.

Eventually, I pick myself up and make my preparations to go to the church to meet the bishop. Mechanically, I apply generous doses of sunscreen. I put on my new duster, gloves, sunglasses, and the ridiculous Stetson hat. Then I go out to the garage, get in the van, shut the door, and push the button to open the garage door. I start the engine, but I just sit there for a few minutes. *I don't know how to face this.* Moira has been there to help me face the worst of my . . . challenges since becoming a vampire. I'll have to face this without her. After that I'll have to tell her that where *she* can now go, I no longer can. Maybe her bishop is wrong. Maybe neither of us can possibly *ever* be worthy. We're tainted, cursed, damned. There's no hope for us. This hell is all we'll ever know until our lives are taken from us.

I pull the van out of the garage and begin the short drive to the church. As I drive, I nearly break down and give in to despair again. I can't face this. I don't know how. The gospel always gave me hope, courage. Now I have *no* hope.

I have never felt so alone.

When I arrive at the church, there's already a car in the parking lot. I don't really know what the bishop drives, but I assume it's his. I park as close to the entrance as I can. I double-check my protection and prepare to make a dash for the door. "Dash" isn't the right word. I'll have to walk fast, but running is more likely to expose flesh to the deadly Sun.

I open the van door and get out as quickly as I can. I slam it closed and speedily make my way to the shelter of the church. As I look up, I see Bishop Edwards holding the door open, furiously motioning me inside. I hurry inside, and reach the safety of the shadows. The darkness of the unlit hall envelopes me like a burial shroud. It matches the bleakness that fills my heavy heart.

A few short hours ago I had hope. Now I have nothing.

Bishop Edwards locks the church door behind us. I'm standing in front of his office entrance. It's open. The lights are on and there is muted sunlight coming in through the frosted glass of the office's single window. The window faces east toward the morning Sun. The patch of sunlight rests right on the chair that sits in front of the bishop's desk, the chair that I would be expected to sit in.

"After you," he prompts.

I hesitate, my eyes riveted on the chair. The light is subdued enough that I could sit there for a while with my protection, but the way the chair is framed in sunlight . . . It seems to be saying, "Damned, cursed, forsaken, hopeless."

Bishop Edwards, noting my hesitation, says, "What is it?" He looks at me and then follows my gaze. "Oh, my," he says in sudden understanding. "Oh, Carl, I'm *sorry*."

He pushes gently past me and moves the chair to the corner of his desk, out of the light. He motions me in. Still, I pause for a moment, but then I enter the office. He sits behind his desk and says, "Close the door, will you?"

I close it and turn to face my bishop. I take my seat. Out of the sunlight. Out of the light. Into the darkness.

Eternal darkness.

"Carl," he says hesitantly, "I don't know where to begin. You're really a . . . a . . ."

". . . vampire," I finish for him. "Yeah."

"I had no idea . . . Who would have believed . . . ? You haven't . . . killed anyone?"

"No, Bishop. I haven't."

"But you drink blood, right?"

"Yeah. I *have* to. I can't survive without it."

"So, do you kill, like . . . animals?"

"No, Bishop. It has to be *human* blood."

"So . . . if you aren't killing people, how are you getting it?"

"Moira, my fiancé, works at LDS Hospital. She brings home expired or tainted blood. That's what I drink . . . mostly. I've taken some from murderers and rapists who are . . . in the act of committing violence, but I didn't kill them. I did *hurt* some of them pretty bad."

"Really?"

"Yeah, we can sense evil in people. When I encounter someone truly evil, a . . . *rage* comes over me and an awful hunger and I feel compelled to kill them violently. So far . . . I've kept it under control enough to keep from killing. Moira has controlled it for over two and a half centuries."

"What about the . . . innocent?" he asks.

"It isn't the same. The innocent are just . . . food. *You*, for example, smell *delicious*. It's like walking past a bakery and smelling fresh-baked bread or smelling a turkey roasting in the oven on Thanksgiving. It smells *really* good, but you don't feel *compelled* to rob the bakery or eat the turkey raw. You can *resist*. Unless you're literally *starving*. Then it would be harder. I've never felt compelled to Feed off the innocent."

He nods. "I see."

"When I was . . . Converted . . . turned into a vampire, I was given a young woman with her throat cut open enough to create a slow stream of blood. She was what vampires call an 'Offering.' I was supposed to kill her. She was innocent. I *didn't* kill her. I took her to the hospital. She smelled so tempting, but I resisted.

"The guilty, the truly evil, however . . . Moira says that vampires *corrupt* the innocent, but we're *driven* to send the guilty to the justice of God."

"So, have you *corrupted* the innocent?"

"Not so far . . . Bishop, why are you taking this so *calmly?*"

"Calmly?" He chuckles nervously. "I'm not calm. I'm freaked out of my mind, actually." I can hear his heart thundering, the blood pulsing in his veins. "I suppose I should be *terrified,*" he says. "This is all so strange . . . It's hard to believe I'm sitting here talking to a vampire, something out of a horror movie, something I thought was fantasy, a ghost story . . . here . . . in my office, much less interviewing one for a temple marriage!"

"*Inter . . . Interviewing?*" I stammer. *Did he just say what I think he said?* "Temple marriage? I thought . . . when you told me to bring my recommend . . . that you were going to *confiscate* it."

He grins sheepishly. *He's embarrassed!*

"Don't think it didn't cross my mind," he says. "I frankly didn't know *what* to do! That Bishop Adams who called me? He confused the *heck* out of me. I didn't know *what* to believe. The stuff he told me . . ."

"You mean . . . ," I interrupt him. *I can hardly believe what I'm hearing!* "I can marry Moira . . . in the *temple?*"

"Well, we need to have the interview first, but unless something comes up in the interview, I would say, 'Yes, of course.'"

In a heartbeat, I'm out of my seat and around his desk and lifting him up in a hug. I hear him struggling for breath. I release him gently. "Did I break anything?" I ask in a panic.

He pats at his chest with both hands. "I think I'm bruised a bit, but nothing broken," he pants.

"Bishop, I'm so sorry! It's just that . . . I'm so happy! I thought I was *damned*! Cursed! Barred from the temple! At least until last night. I visited the temple for the first time since my Conversion. I was ecstatic! And then, this morning, when you told me to bring my recommend, I . . . lost all hope."

"Carl," he says as he settles back into his chair, still rubbing his chest gingerly, "The reason I asked you to bring your recommend is because I have to get some information off your *existing* recommend in order to issue a recommend for sealing. I know I *could* look it up on the computer, but I barely remember my password and I've never used that thing. Besides," he adds a bit sheepishly, "I'm a bit flustered with all of this today." He motions me back to my chair.

I take the seat gratefully. I can't contain my joy. Tears are streaming down my face. "I thought I'd lost everything, Bishop. When this . . . *happened* to me . . . when I became a vampire . . . I thought I'd lost Sharon and Lucy and April and Joseph for all eternity. I thought I was *damned*. And for what? What did I do that . . . that deserved *this*?"

I continue, "I investigated . . . I went undercover to find evidence to convict Julie's killer. I just wanted to bring Rebecca (she's the vampire who killed Julie) to justice. I didn't *know* that she was a vampire. I didn't *believe* in vampires. I had to pretend to join their Cult. I had to pretend to buy into their . . . *bull* (well, I *thought* it was bull at the time) to get close to Rebecca. I had to pretend to go along with it all."

He says nothing.

"I was surrounded with sex all the time, Bishop. I kept myself pure from it. I didn't *indulge*. And it would have been so *easy*. You can't surround yourself with that stuff and *not* be affected by it. But I didn't *do* anything. And Rebecca tried to Persuade me into her bed. Persuasion is like . . . super hypnotism or something. But I resisted even that!"

When he says nothing, I press on. "Before I knew it, Rebecca was 'elevating' me to Chosen. That's what they call the mortals that they're grooming to become vampires, not just to be used as food or as sex partners. Then, before I'd even had all the instruction you're supposed to get, I was saying some stupid words and going through a Ritual. I wasn't even listening. I thought it was all bogus. Just mind games."

I shake my head. "But it turned out to be real! Without understanding it, I was Converted. That's what they call it. I was a vampire and I didn't even believe such things existed! And then I had this terrible hunger. And the girl I was supposed to kill. And I saved her, but then I collapsed at the hospital because I needed to Feed and I hadn't Fed. Then Moira found me. And it all was just out of my control. And I've tried to be good! I haven't killed anybody. I've wanted to, but I stopped myself."

I realize that I'm babbling. He's looking at me openmouthed. I take a deep breath. "Sorry, Bishop. I must not be making a lot of sense."

"Not a lot," he says slowly, "but let me see if I got some of it right." He looks at me expectantly and I nod. "When the police couldn't find your sister's killer, you located her yourself."

I nod.

"You said something about a *cult?*"

"The vampires organize a Cult of mortals. The Cult members don't even realize that vampires are real. They think it's some sort of game. The Cult provides the vampires with a ready food supply and sex partners."

"And they don't . . . *kill* their . . . cult members?"

"You really don't need to take that much blood in one Feeding to survive. The vampires take small amounts from many different acolytes."

He shudders.

"I know," I say. "It's pretty gruesome stuff."

"So," he continues, "you . . . What? Infiltrated this cult?"

"Yeah."

"To get the goods on . . . Rebecca?"

"That's right."

"And you avoided sexual sin?"

"Yeah, I did."

"OK. But you drank blood?"

"No, I *didn't*. There was ritual bloodletting and others 'fed' from me, but I didn't actually ingest blood. Not until the night that Rebecca Converted me."

"Tell me what that was like."

I'd rather not, but he has the right to ask. "It really happened so fast. The forms of the rituals the Cult uses were just not important to me. I simply went through the motions. Rebecca had me kneel at a stone altar. I remember it was made of piled stones. She made me place both hands on the altar and repeat some oaths. I don't remember everything, but I had to swear 'fealty' to Lilith."

"Who's Lilith?"

"Lilith is the daughter of Cain." Bishop Edwards is visibly shaken when I say this. It *is* a lot to take in, I guess, but why is he reacting so strongly about Lilith? He didn't even know who she was until a moment ago.

"Cain?" he asks. "*The* Cain?"

"Yeah. *The* Cain, the son of Adam and Eve. I'd say she must be Cain's daughter from *before* he was cursed. She doesn't seem to bear the same curse as her father."

"You said 'is'?"

"'Is' what?"

"You said that Lilith *is* the daughter of Cain," he prompts.

"Yeah. She's apparently still alive and kicking."

He looks stunned. "She's . . . What? Six thousand years old?"

"Give or take a century, yeah. She lives in Kansas City, I'm told."

"Kansas City? Unbelievable! The 'daughter of Cain'?"

"Bishop, is it any more *unbelievable* than you having a *vampire* in your office?"

"Good point. It's just that . . . Well, never mind that for now. Go on."

"So, I had to swear to serve Lilith. To keep the Great Secret."

"What's that?"

"Actually, I don't know. I guess I would've found out if I'd stayed, but I didn't. The Chosen are supposed to know, but Rebecca never got around to teaching me.

"Anyway, then she laid her hands on my head, like an ordination, and said something about 'filling me with the Essence'."

"'The Essence'?" he interrupts.

"Yeah. It's what they call the *demonic* component of vampirism."

"You mean, like you're *possessed?*"

"Yeah, that's what it's *supposed* to be. But . . . Bishop, I don't *feel* possessed. I mean, except for the rage and the compulsion to kill the guilty and the lust for blood . . . I just don't *feel* . . . evil. Ya know, I feel like *myself.* I mean, everybody has stuff, urges they have to control. I have to consume blood, but I've managed to keep the other aspects . . . you know, the rage, the killing, the bloodlust . . . in check. So, if I'm *possessed*, it's not like what you read about in the scriptures.

"And *Moira!* Bishop, there's nothing *demonic* about her! She's so pure in heart. Does that sound like demonic possession to you?"

"Not in any sense that I know. Carl, you said that the . . . Essence?" He looks to me.

I nod in confirmation.

"You said that the Essence is the *demonic* component. What other components *are* there?"

"The Seed. It's the . . . um . . . *biological* component of being a vampire. Moira says it's like a virus, but it can't survive without the Essence. It's the Essence that keeps it going. But it's the *Seed* that gives us our vampiric . . . *powers* . . . for lack of a better word."

"So, how did you become . . . *infected?*"

"Well, that's where it gets really hazy. I know that Rebecca Fed off me . . . You know . . . drank some of my blood?"

He looks sick, but he nods.

"When a vampire Feeds off you, some of the Seed gets into your bloodstream and it makes you feel . . . euphoric." The images of my prey begging for me to Feed some more from them flash through my mind, making me queasy. "The criminals I've Fed from . . . They *begged* me to take more of their blood."

I swallow hard and continue. "So anyway . . . once she bit me, I wasn't exactly able to think straight anymore. She took out an ancient-looking obsidian knife and slit her wrist and put it to my mouth. I tried not to ingest any, but I must have. Anyway, I remember that, after I had my mouth to her wrist, I felt the rush of euphoria overwhelm me, and that's all I remember. At least that's all I remember until I Awoke three days later and was presented with my Offering (the girl I was supposed to kill), her throat bleeding. I remember knocking Rebecca to the floor and fleeing the so-called Sanctuary with the girl and running with her all the way to the hospital.

"The next thing I remember is waking up on Moira's couch. She gave me blood to drink. She knew I was a vampire, but, I guess, because I saved the girl, she thought I was what vampires call a 'Penitent,' a *repentant* vampire. So she helped me. *She's* a Penitent. She says she's never met another one . . . another Penitent, that is. Anyway, she mentored me, helped me adjust, taught me how to survive. She brings me blood to consume."

"And you fell in love?" He smiles.

I'm grateful for the change of subject. "Yeah, we did. It's been a whirlwind courtship, but we're very much in love."

"Normally, Carl, I'd be concerned about a romance this . . . quick."

I start to say something, but he puts up a hand.

"Carl, I think it's my turn to . . . reveal some things to *you* that you probably aren't aware of." He smiles.

I just look at him curiously. "What?" I'm intrigued.

"Let me tell you about *my* morning," he says. "I got a phone call at about six this morning. It's Saturday. It's not like a bishop doesn't get calls at all hours of the day and night, but I wasn't thrilled to get the call on my one day to sleep in . . . a little."

"Sorry."

"Well," he says, rubbing his hands together, "I'm not! This is all uncanny, but it's . . . well, it's *fascinating*, that's what it is! You learn something new every day! This is really . . . *out* there, but . . . well . . . On with my story!"

He gestures excitedly. "It's this Bishop Adams on the phone. He's so excited! Positively sounds like he's jumping up and down on the other end of the line. He tells me some bizarre story about me having a *vampire* in my ward! He says he knows all about it because he has one in *his* ward! Not a *bad* vampire, he says, but a *good* one. Now, this was so weird that I would've hung up on him thinking it was just a crank call. I *would've* hung up on him, that is, if I wasn't so groggy. Then he mentions *your* name and *that* woke me up. It suddenly clicked in my head, with your sun allergy and all, that he, this Bishop Adams, knows something about you. He tells me you're a vampire and you were made a vampire against your will. He emphasizes the word, *'unwilling.'* He starts babbling about a letter from the First Presidency. A letter from *fifty years ago*! The letter is about this woman in his ward and how she's to be given all the blessings of the gospel in spite of the fact that she's a vampire. He says she wants to get married in the temple and I need to give *you* a recommend for marriage because you're her fiancé and it's all so wonderful, because they've been trying to get her to the temple for over half a century."

He shakes his head, but he's grinning like an idiot. "I'm pretty confused at that point, let me tell you, so I ask him to slow down. He did. He explained it in a little more detail and then he reads me the letter. It's incredible stuff! He offers to fax it over to me. I tell him I don't have a fax machine. So I tell him to scan it and email it to me.

"Even after reading it, I *still* can't believe it! I mean, even if it *were* true, if you're consuming human blood, that's prohibited way back in Genesis! Drinking blood is forbidden, I mean, much less *human* blood. So I called the bishops' hotline."

"'Bishops' hotline'?"

"It's a number we can call twenty-four/seven if we have difficult questions or situations. They can get us legal advice, spiritual advice . . .

even connect us with an Apostle if it's warranted. Well, I called. When I asked about the letter, the operator was silent for so long I thought he'd hung up on me. He had me reread portions of the letter and told me to hold on the line.

"The next thing I know, I'm being transferred to a member of the Quorum of the Twelve! They woke him up! I was told to repeat to him everything I told the operator.

"When I was done, he told me to follow the instructions in the letter *to the letter*. He seemed to know exactly what I was talking about. He didn't offer any more information than that. He just asked for my assurance that I'd follow the instructions in the letter. Well, I gave him my assurance, and he thanked me. He said I'd receive my own copy of the letter in the mail shortly. He asked me to report back to him 'as things progressed.'"

"So what's in the letter?"

"Well, it says that you and your Moira are to be extended all the blessings of the gospel. It also mentions a *prophecy*."

"A prophecy?" I'm stunned.

"Yes, Carl. A *prophecy* made by the Prophet over fifty years ago. About you . . . and Moira."

I'm speechless. I open my mouth to speak, but I can't think of anything to say.

Bishop Edwards nods. "Incredible, isn't it?"

I nod. I swallow hard, and then I finally find my voice, but it's shaky. "Moira said nothing about a prophecy."

"That's because *she doesn't know*! The letter expressly states that the prophecy is only to be made known to *you*."

My jaw drops again. "It mentions me by name?"

"No, not by name. Just by description. It says, 'a worthy elder, the *unwilling* son of *Lilith*.' Has there ever been an 'unwilling son of Lilith?' I assume that means an unwilling vampire."

"No," I say quietly. "According to both Moira and Rebecca, I'm the *first*. I'm the only Unwilling vampire in history."

"Then it sounds like you. Here it is, Carl." He reads from a sheet of paper on his desk. I hadn't noticed it before.

"*Thus sayeth the Lord: Mine handmaid Moira MacDonald shall marry in mine holy house. She shall be sealed to a worthy elder, the unwilling son of Lilith. And, if they are valiant in my service, it shall come to pass in the fullness of time that they shall be the sword of my vengeance to slay the daughter of Cain, and death shall fall upon all her children. In that day, mine handmaid Moira MacDonald and her husband, my servant, shall both die, but they shall see their Redeemer's face in the resurrection of the just."*

He looks up at me. "I didn't notice that part before. It says you're going to *die* when you 'slay the daughter of Cain.'"

I swallow hard again. If *we're valiant, we're going to* die *when we kill Lilith. We are going to kill Lilith and then we will die.* "And then we will see our 'Redeemer's face in the resurrection of the just,'" I say out loud.

"It sounds like you're being called on a mission and you're being told that you won't return alive."

I nod, but then it dawns on me what the prophecy *really* says. I rise to my feet. "But, it says that we'll see our Redeemer's face! Bishop! That means that we'll be saved! We'll both be redeemed! I'll see Sharon and Lucy and April and Joseph again!"

Another realization dawns on me. I sit down again. "It also means . . . that Moira will never have her *babies.*"

"'Her babies'?"

"She wants to have children of her own."

"Once you get married . . . ," he starts to say.

"No, Bishop. Female vampires can't have children. I can *father* children, but the Seed, the part that makes us immortal, immune to disease, and helps us heal incredibly fast . . . the Seed rejects anything *foreign* to the body . . . like a *baby.*

"Moira has spent more than two hundred years delivering babies, and now she'll never have one of her own."

"Not in this life," he says.

"'Not in this life,'" I echo.

"You know, Carl, there are a lot of good, worthy couples who can't have children in this life."

"I know. I know. And I can't even tell her about it, right?"

"That's not what it says," he counters, taking the letter in his hand again and looking at it. "It says that the prophecy is only to be revealed to Moira MacDonald's fiancé when he asks to be married to her in the temple. It was only to be withheld *until that time.* It sounds like you can tell her yourself."

"It also says, 'in the fullness of time,' right? When it talks about us killing Lilith? Before we have to die?"

He looks down at it. "Yes. It sounds like you could have a long life together before that happens."

I give a little laugh. "In vampire terms, Bishop, that could be a *very* long time."

"Well, you came here to get a recommend. Let's get that taken care of. Then I need to call the stake president and tell *him* all about this. He's been out of town this week and got in late last night. It looks like I'll have to wake *him* up." He actually looks gleeful at the thought! He sees the look on my face. "Hey, if Bishop Adams can wake *me* up and I can wake up an *Apostle* on account of this, I can wake up President Harkin!"

Chapter 17

It's eleven in the morning by the time I'm finished with my interview with the stake president. I had to repeat to President Harkin most of what I told the bishop. His reactions were similar to the bishop's, but Bishop Edwards was able to prepare President Harkin before I got there. I guess the fact that President Harkin *knows* and *trusts* Bishop Edwards helped him to accept things more easily. He did delve a little bit more on some difficult subjects.

*"Brother Morgan," he said, "this doesn't sound like demonic possession in any sense that I understand. What's more, you don't feel evil to me. You certainly have challenges that most people don't have to deal with, that most people couldn't ima-*gine *dealing with, but* everyone *has challenges."*

He shook his head. "My first impression was that we should cast this out, try to heal you, but that doesn't feel right either. I get the impression that this is something that you're called *to go through, especially in light of the prophecy. Apparently, you're going to have to kill other vampires. How do you feel about that?"*

"How do I feel, *President? It's not the first time I've had to kill someone, but that was war."*

"You know the Lord doesn't hold soldiers accountable for the lives they must take in times of war, so long as they act honorably."

I nodded.

"Brother Morgan, these people . . . these vampires *. . . are* predators, *preying on the innocent and the guilty. It doesn't sound like you can just call the police. It sounds to me like* you *are being called to stop them."*

"But, President," I protested, "I can't possibly take them all on. Moira and I . . . we're just two people."

"Teancum was just one man. He stopped two very wicked men. He lost his life in the process, but he turned the tide of the war. From this prophecy, it sounds as if you will *kill this Lilith and that will end this war. The Lord told Nephi to kill Laban so that generations of his descendants would have a chance at exaltation. Don't underestimate your worth, Carl."*

"I can't fight them all, President."

"I don't think you're being asked to, Carl. Just follow the promptings of the Spirit. That's what Nephi did."

"I'll do my best." There wasn't a lot of conviction in my voice.

"The Lord will make up the difference."

"OK, President."

"Now, Brother Morgan," he continued, obviously changing the subject, *"about the consumption of blood. Have you tried simply* abstaining?*"*

"No, President, I haven't, but Moira *has. If we don't Feed, we'll lapse into a coma and eventually the Seed will consume the body. It's a slow and incredibly painful death, drawn out over decades. If we don't Feed, we die. It's not an addiction. It's the only nourishment we can absorb. I can't even consume more than the minutest amounts of the water and the bread in the sacrament."*

"'Man shall not live by bread alone . . .'" he quoted, *"but the Lord also says not to 'run faster than you have strength.' Ultimately, I have to go by the instructions we've received from Church Headquarters. So, even if I don't understand how to deal with the blood, it says that you are to receive 'all the blessings of the gospel.' There are no restrictions."*

So I have my recommend. I'm cleared to marry Moira! We're getting married on Tuesday (or Wednesday at the latest). We're getting married! In the temple!

I still have to break the news to Moira about the prophecy, about how she won't be able to have children. Not in this life. I have to tell her about how we're going to have to kill Lilith and then we're both going to die. Someday. I plan on putting off that part as long as I can. When the time is right, the Lord will set it up.

As bad as dealing with Michael and Rebecca will be, Lilith will be in a class all by herself. If Michael is Hitler and Rebecca is Stalin, who is Lilith? I can think of no one in history to compare her to. Caligula? No, Caligula did far less damage. Lilith is . . . Lilith. She's one step shy of Lucifer himself.

I'm going to call Moira. If she's Sleeping, the phone won't wake her. If she's awake . . .

Once I'm safely inside the house, I dial her number on my cell. She answers on the first ring.

"Hello, husband-to-be," she says happily. "I've got my recommend. My bishop and stake president were both so *excited* that they came right to my home to do my interviews this morning. How are ye doing with yers?"

"I have my recommend too, but I found out something that you need to know." I'm trying to keep my voice buoyant, to focus on the positive, but I'm not entirely successful.

"What's wrong, laddie?"

"I really need to tell you this in person."

"Is it somethin' that'll keep us frae marryin' in the temple?" Her brogue is thick. That means she's upset or worried.

"No, if you'll still have me, we'll be married in the temple as soon as we can find an opening."

"If I'll still have ye?" she says, joy replacing trepidation in her voice, "Ye cannae *escape* me! I'll hunt ye down!" She laughs. It lifts my heart to hear her laugh. "And it *will* be Tuesday. There are openings on Tuesday night all over the area. Nae a very popular night for a wedding, 'twould seem."

"I can't imagine a better night."

"What temple would ye prefer?"

"Uh-uh. I've *had* a temple wedding. This one is *yours* to choose. You've waited a lot longer than I have."

"Oh, aye! Rub it in, will ye? Pointin' out my age, are ye?"

I can imagine her eyes twinkling as she says this.

"That's right, pretty lady. But, seriously, *you* choose. You must have a preference."

"Ogden," she says immediately.

"Really?"

"After last night, I would choose Ogden, the first temple I was ever able to set foot in."

"That sounds perfect to me." I sigh. "Moira, I do have something important I need to tell you. Can I come over? I can drive right down."

"Aye, my love. Come to see me. But come quick. We're both in need of Sleep. We have a very busy night ahead of us. I'll call and make the reservations at the Ogden Temple while ye're on the road."

The better part of an hour later, Moira opens her door, keeping to the shadows, to let me in. I hurry through and into the welcoming dark. She shuts the door behind me. I remove my sunglasses and gloves and put them in the pockets of my coat.

She turns to me and pulls off my ridiculous hat. She flings it away and throws her arms around my neck and plants a huge kiss on my lips. I return the kiss tenderly. *I love this woman.* I've known her such a short time, and still I *ache* for her when we're apart. Now we're together, and I ache for her in a different way. Suddenly Tuesday seems like an eternity away.

And I still have to tell her about the prophecy.

So, I gently release her and take her by the hand and lead her over to the sofa. She helps me off with my coat.

She sits and pulls me down on the sofa beside her. She takes both of my hands in hers and looks deep into my eyes. I'm having a hard time focusing on what I have to do.

"You know that letter your bishop received from the First Presidency half a century ago?" I say.

"Aye." She smiles.

"Well, it contains a prophecy."

She starts a little at the word and looks confused. "A prophecy?"

"Yes, Moira, a prophecy written by the President of the Church about *you.*"

Her eyes go wide. "Me?"

"Yes. It mentions you by *name.*"

"*Me?*" she says again, obviously stunned.

"Yes, *you. And* me."

"*You?*"

"Yeah. Not by name, but it's me, all right."

"What does it say?" Her voice is a whisper.

I close my eyes and try to recall the words. The image of the letter appears in my mind. I've never had a photographic memory, but apparently the Seed has enhanced my ability to recall. I can *see* the words in my head:

"Thus sayeth the Lord: Mine handmaid Moira MacDonald shall marry in mine holy house. She shall be sealed to a worthy elder, the unwilling son of Lilith. And, if they are valiant in my service, it shall come to pass in the fullness of time that they shall be the sword of my vengeance to slay the daughter of Cain, and death shall fall upon all her children. In that day, mine handmaid Moira MacDonald and her husband, my servant, shall both die, but they shall see their Redeemer's face in the resurrection of the just."

I can feel her trembling as I say the words. When I open my eyes, tears have left streaks down her face. I fold her into my arms, and she sobs quietly on my shoulder. I stroke her auburn hair with one hand and hold her gently with the other.

I hear her swallow hard and then, in a choked voice, she says, "Nae bairns."

No babies.

"Not in this life," I say quietly.

Her sobbing starts up again. I hold her for a long time. Slowly her sobbing eases. Without pulling away, she says into my shoulder, "I'm willin' to sacrifice *my* life to rid the world of . . . of . . . our kind. I'm nae willin' to sacrifice *yers*."

"I'll stand with you," I say quietly, but firmly. "In life or death. If you'll still have me, we'll face this together."

"Still have ye?" She grips me more tightly. "Ye are more precious to me than ever." She's quiet for a few seconds and then says, "It said we'll be sealed and we'll see the Savior's face."

"That's right," I confirm.

"Then that will be enough for me. Will it be enough for ye?" She pulls away and looks me in the eyes, peering into the depths of my soul.

"I'm more blessed than any man deserves," I say with a small smile. "It's *more* than enough. Besides, it says, 'in the fullness of time.' That means we may have a long and happy life together before we have to face . . . the end of this life and the beginning of the next."

She leans in and kisses me gently, sweetly.

How could any man ask for more than this?

She breaks the kiss and hugs me again. She asks, "Where shall we go for our honeymoon? We'll only have a few days. We'll have to be back when?"

"We attack Sunday night. We'll need to return by Sunday. Probably Saturday. Where do *you* want to go?"

She pulls away again and her eyes light up, sparkling like two emeralds. "Ye know where I have nae ever been?"

"You've seen more of the world than I have."

"Aye, laddie, but I've done it *alone*. Some places ye just cannae go alone."

"OK. Name it. Where?"

She gives me a huge grin. "Disneyland."

I snort. "You're kidding!"

She does *not* look amused.

"No problem!" I say quickly. "Disneyland is great!"

The grin returns to her face, but there's some trepidation too.

"It's just . . . ," I start. *Wow! This is going to be awkward.* "Well . . . that's where I . . . honeymooned with *Sharon.*"

She nods slowly. "Ah, I see."

"It's not a problem, really."

"Will it be difficult for ye?"

"No, it would be . . . *nice.* After all, it was you who gave Sharon and Lucy and April and Joseph back to me."

And then she gives me her dazzling smile. I can't help but smile back.

"Then Disneyland it shall be, laddie!" She kisses me quickly. "Dinnae worry about a thing. I'll arrange it all. Ye just worry about yer battle plan . . . and arranging yer time off from work."

"Moira, there's no time to plan a big wedding."

"Laddie, the only part that matters to me is the part inside the temple. What I meant was that I'll arrange the *honeymoon.* Our appointment at the temple is set. We'll need to be there at 3:30 in the afternoon for my endowment. That'll get us out of the temple after sunset. I'm afraid we cannae *avoid* a reception. Bishop Adams has already notified the Relief Society president. I begged him nae to do it, but he said that I have many friends in the ward and stake who'll want to be there. So they're hurriedly putting on a reception. It'll be at yer stake center, which is close enough to the Ogden Temple. The Relief Society president has already scheduled the cultural hall. We have nae time for formal invitations, but if ye wish for someone to be there, ye might want to notify them right away. I also reserved the largest sealing room in the Ogden temple. I will nae ask ye to wear a tuxedo to the reception. Do ye have a nice suit?"

She pauses for a second. "Ye look like a deer in headlights, laddie. Am I going too fast?"

"Yeah," I say breathlessly. "Kind of. It's just that minutes ago you were . . . *grieving.* Now, you're in full-fledged wedding-planning mode!"

"Aye. There's nae anything for it. I cannae change the prophecy. I may nae have the opportunity to bear children, but I can still get married in the temple to a man I love more than life itself! 'Tis enough. So I'll do what I've done for centuries: do what I can do and let the rest be." Her expression is wistful.

Once again, I'm amazed at the wisdom and maturity of this woman who looks like she's barely old enough to be out of college. *And, biologically, she's younger than that!*

"The answer is yes."

"What?"

"I have a nice suit."

And just like that her smile is back.

Soon, too soon, I'm on my drive home. *Home.* Not for much longer. We decided it made more sense to make our home in Moira's house when we get married. Hers is paid for. Mine isn't. Hers is larger. It's also a lot closer to work for both of us. And it'd be a little weird making a home together in the home I shared with Sharon so recently.

I need to get home and get some Sleep before facing Rebecca and Benjamin. I'm getting sleepy now, so I turn on the radio. After flipping through a few music stations and finding nothing to hold my interest, I push the preset button for the local talk radio station. Just in time for the news too.

"An accused serial killer has escaped from the Davis County Jail in Farmington," the announcer says. Any trace of weariness in me vanishes in an instant. "Former Davis County Sheriff's Deputy Roger Hadley, who reportedly confessed to at least seventeen murders and sexual assault on a child, escaped from jail last night. Jail officials are baffled, but security tapes clearly show Hadley walking out the front door of the jail as jail personnel watched. When questioned about the incident, none of the guards, including those shown on tape, have any recollection about the escape.

"Witnesses place Hadley at the scene of the gruesome murder of a Layton mother and her three children just hours after Hadley's escape. Thirty-one-year-old Linda Johnson, eleven-year-old Rachel, eight-year-old Michael, and five-year-old Tamara were found dead in their home this morning by a neighbor. Davis County Sheriff's Detective Daniel Johnson, husband of Linda and father of Rachel, Michael, and Tamara, is also missing.

"Hadley is still at large at this time. A statewide manhunt is in effect. If you have any information as to Hadley's or Johnson's whereabouts, please contact the Davis County Sheriff's office or your local police.

"In other news, congressional hearings are moving ahead into . . ."

I turn off the radio and call Moira. The phone rings enough times that I'm afraid she's gone to Sleep, but eventually she answers.

"Great timing, laddie. I just made reservations for us at the Grand Californian Hotel at Disneyland, and I booked the last flight for Orange County on Tuesday night. We'll nae be able to spend more than an hour at the reception, but . . ."

"Hadley escaped from jail," I interrupt her. "He apparently murdered Detective Johnson's entire family and Johnson himself is missing. I just heard it on the news."

"Ach, nae!" she exclaims. "When?"

"Last night."

"And Johnson is missin'? That poor man!"

I do feel sorry for him. He was a pain in the butt, but he didn't deserve this.

"Did nae Hadley kill his brother, as well?" she asks.

"That's what he said."

"That poor, poor man. That poor woman and those poor, poor children."

The children! "Moira, when I Persuaded Hadley, I specifically commanded him to never go near another child. How could he . . . break through that?"

"Persuasion is nae absolute. Ye cannae change who someone is on the inside. It held long enough to get him incarcerated . . ."

I groan.

"Laddie," she says, "it's nae yer fault! Ye did all ye could!"

"I'm not blaming myself," I say. *Not really.*

"He may be coming after ye, Carl," she says gravely.

I hadn't thought about that. "You might be right."

"I think you'll be safe enough at night, when ye are awake, but I suggest ye do nae Sleep at home, not until Hadley's caught. Laddie, why dinnae ye turn around and come back here? Ye can Sleep on my couch and fly home right after sunset. I'll drive yer van to yer house after Rebecca and Benjamin are gone."

"Sounds like a plan. See you in a bit. What would I do without you, Moira?"

"Starve. Get murdered in yer Sleep," she says in a flat tone.

"I don't know about that," I say, deadpan, "I could have started a Cult of my own. Think about it: all of those nubile young women . . . in Goth makeup . . . Never mind."

"Watch yerself, laddie!"

"No, seriously! I can't stand that Goth crap!"

"One more word, laddie, and ye can take yer chances at home!" She laughs. "I'll see ye soon, my love."

"Spending the *day* at your house . . . unchaperoned . . . People will talk!"

Chapter 18

How are you *doing* that?" Rebecca's voice is filled with shock. I'm hovering in my living room. Benjamin is staring mutely, openmouthed. "Where are your wings?" Rebecca cries.

"You mean *these?*" I say and then I make the wings appear. I can hear them flapping furiously behind me. Rebecca and Benjamin gasp loudly. They gasp again when I make the wings vanish. Only this time the gasps sound louder in the absence of the sound of beating wings.

"We don't . . . have . . . wings," I say, emphasizing each word. "They're just an illusion, a mental projection." *A deception.*

"I know they're immaterial," Rebecca argues. "*Everyone* knows that! But they're part of who we *are*. They're a symbol of our *power*."

A symbol of our power? That's an interesting choice of words.

"They're *noisy*, is what they are," I counter. "Not very useful when you're trying to be stealthy." She looks completely flummoxed. "Think about it." I settle back to the floor. "You could sneak up on Chikah from behind with only the sound of your heart and breathing to alert her. This is crucial to our attack."

I can tell from her expression that she isn't buying it. Benjamin just stares at me as if he's never seen me before.

"We are *gods!*" she hisses. "The wings are a manifestation of our *power!*"

"We're *not* gods," I say evenly. "We're *demons*."

She stamps her foot in frustration.

I ignore her little tantrum.

"And the wings are nothing more than a mental projection," I continue. "You just have to visualize yourself flying without them. It'll take a little concentration at first, but soon you'll be flying without them and it'll take no effort at all."

She stares daggers at me. If looks could kill, I'd be a dismembered corpse.

"Try it," I say. "Just imagine yourself hovering without wings."

Still she stares.

I look beside me and Benjamin is hovering, his wings flickering in and out of sight. I nod at him. "That's it, Benjamin! Keep trying! You're almost there!"

He closes his eyes and then . . . just like that . . . the wings are gone.

"Good job!" I say. Benjamin's being able to fly silently is absolutely essential to my plan. Rebecca . . . not so much.

Benjamin's face lights up in the first genuine grin I've ever seen on his face.

I turn to Rebecca. She's still seething. If anything, Benjamin's success has further enraged her.

"Give it a try," I say, turning to her. Benjamin begins to flit about the house. He reminds me of a hummingbird as he hovers and flits from one place to another. Other than his heartbeat, he barely makes a sound. He's holding his breath sometimes! *He's practicing stealth.* The look of joy on his face is profound. *Has he never* succeeded *at anything before? Has he never been* allowed *to succeed?*

Rebecca lifts off the floor, her wings beating and as noisy as ever.

"Concentrate," I encourage.

She closes her eyes and screws up her face in a look of intense effort. Beads of sweat begin to form on her face. She starts to tremble.

Still her wings beat loudly and insubstantially.

At last, she gives a scream of rage and frustration and drops to the floor. Her wings fold up behind her and disappear.

"Keep trying," I say. "You'll get it."

"*Bugger off!*" she hisses at me through clenched teeth. Her normal clipped and proper-sounding British accent is gone, replaced with a common-sounding guttural Cockney.

Is her accent a fake? It's still British, but . . .

She turns her fury on Benjamin. "Get back in here, you foul lit'l black *worm!*"

Benjamin quickly flies into the room again. His face is fallen. His perpetual scowl returns as if it had never left. He doesn't go to her side, but he's still hovering . . . wingless.

She glares venomously at him and then turns back to me.

"Try again," I say evenly.

"I can't!" she snarls.

"Yes, you can," I say. "Just relax and try again."

She closes her eyes, and her face becomes calm. At least, it *looks* calm outwardly. Her heartbeat is still rapid. She rises off the floor with her wings beating feverishly. They stay fully visible. There isn't even a flicker.

In fact, for a moment, I think I can almost smell *the feathers.*

I watch as she tries several more times without the slightest indicator of success. With each failure, her muttered curses become more and more foul.

I finally call a halt to her efforts. "It's OK. *Benjamin* is the one who has to fly silently."

"Figures the lit'l bugger could do it," she mutters. "Neither of you are *true* vampires."

What? Not true *vampires?*

"What do you mean?" I ask.

"Neither of you has killed." Her voice drips scorn.

"What?"

"Benjamin hasn't killed. *Ever.*" Her contempt is palpable.

You could knock me over with a mentally projected feather. "What about *his* Offering?"

"He never had one. Michael never gave him one. Benjamin only gets Michael's scraps."

I look over at Benjamin. His eyes meet mine with an inscrutable look. Could this child-monster . . . this abomination be *innocent?* Could he possibly be no more than the victim of unspeakable abuse? There's no question as to whether he's twisted, horribly tainted by all the sick cruelty he's suffered all his long life. But *innocent?* Is that *possible?* Is he . . . like me? Just someone who was in the wrong place at the wrong time with the wrong people? Certainly he *would* have killed if Michael had *allowed* him to. But he wouldn't have been *driven* to kill if it weren't for Michael. He'd have lived and died an innocent, at least as much an innocent as any of us are. He'd have had a chance. With Michael, he never had a chance.

Moira has killed and *she* was able to rid herself of the wings. So Rebecca cannot be quite right. But maybe the wings are an indicator of . . . corruption? No. I don't think that's it.

I look at Benjamin with new eyes. I've felt some pity for him in the past. Now, it's something more. I feel the need to . . . *help* him. I'm not sure how to do that. I can start, though, by reaching out, by trying to gain his trust.

I give him an approving look. "Ben! My man!" *OK, that sounds really dumb.* He arches an eyebrow at me curiously. Without looking away from him, I say to Rebecca, "No, Rebecca, I don't think you understand. *Ben* is the strong one. He can make the wings go away because he's *stronger* than you."

"*Rubbish!*"

"I know *personally* how strong the urge, the *need* to kill is. Even if Michael *has* forbidden him to kill, it takes a *strong man* to control his appetites."

"*Rubbish! Rubbish! Rubbish!*" She's nearly hysterical.

I do believe I've hit a nerve.

The effect on Benjamin is just the opposite. He looks shocked, yes, but he looks . . . pleased.

"Ben, I've seen the horrific punishments Michael has inflicted on you . . . at least some of it for things you *didn't* do." I make a quick glance at Rebecca. "You never cried. You never cried out. You just kept yourself . . . in *control.* That means you have *incredible* strength of will."

I see a grin spread across Benjamin's face. He looks almost . . . *proud* of himself. I give him a nod of respect, and the grin opens to a wide smile.

Rebecca, in contrast, is red-faced, positively *livid* with rage.

"NO!" she screams at me. "'E's MINE! My child! My *consort*! You just want him for *yourself*!"

"Don't be ridiculous," I say dismissively. "Ben"—*he* likes *that name* —"belongs to nobody but himself. And, besides, I'm not . . . aroused by *boys*."

She utters an inarticulate scream.

"But," I go on, "you're forgetting what we're doing here. We're *supposed* to be planning how to destroy Michael and Chikah . . . how to *liberate* both of you. So, what do you say we get on with the task at hand?"

She stamps one foot and then the other like a child who isn't getting her way. She trembles for a few moments as she struggles to bring her rage into check. I see her mask of control and seduction slide into place belying the thundering of her heart.

"Let's get on with it then." Her clipped, proper accent is firmly back in place.

"OK," I say, noting that Benjamin's grin softens, but never quite goes away. And he keeps hovering in the air, wingless. "Here's the plan . . ."

The Unwilling

Over the course of the next hour or so we practice the maneuvers and contingencies for Rebecca and Benjamin's part of the plan. I'm not going to tell them the *whole* plan, but I don't want them to know how much I'm keeping back from them.

Neither of them has any experience in combat with vampires or mortals, although Rebecca has Hunted mortals. *Julie's killer has Hunted.* Benjamin, however, takes to this like he was born for it. I rarely have to repeat an instruction to him. He gets his maneuvers right on the first or second try. He's intelligent and observant. *And cunning*, I have to remind myself. I've made some small progress in gaining his trust, but I have to remember who and what he is. I'm not going to undo a century and a half of corruption and conditioning in the course of a couple of hours.

"Remember," I say, "if the initial attack fails, you don't have to *kill* Chikah to disable her. I know she'll heal fast, but if you hamstring her or cut off a foot or hand, you *will* slow her down. That sword of hers is meant to be wielded two-handed. I doubt she has practiced much with one hand. There are two of you. Come at her from two sides.

"Above all, it's *critical* that you take her out and prevent her from returning to help Michael. That's *your* job. Let me take care of Michael and the Chosen."

At every opportunity, I call Benjamin "Ben." It makes him grin.

It makes Rebecca scowl.

We use the flat of our blades as we practice so that we don't inflict too much damage on the blades or on each other. Once, Rebecca slices my shoulder open. I'm pretty sure it was no accident. Rebecca smiles apologetically. *Yeah, right.* Now I have vampire blood on my carpet. It's a good thing I moved all the furniture out of the living room.

Eventually, I determine that this is as good as the three of us are going to get. I hope it's enough. I call a halt and give Rebecca and Ben some final instructions.

"I don't expect to hear from you until Sunday night, but call me if there're any complications that come up," I say.

Rebecca nods at me. I motion the two of them toward the back door. They sheath their weapons and head in that direction. I follow them.

Rebecca reaches for Benjamin's hand. He takes hers, but then abruptly pulls away. He flies straight at me. His sword is still sheathed, so I don't follow my first instinct to prepare for an attack. He hovers at my side, leans toward my ear and moves his lips.

His whisper is so soft that even with my Seed-enhanced hearing I have to strain to make out the words. I don't believe there's any chance Rebecca can overhear. "I like 'Ben.'" His whispered voice has an accent that suggests Southern gentility. I had expected the accent of a black slave as portrayed in countless movies about that dark era in American history.

I nod in acknowledgement, a slight grin on my face.

He whispers once more into my ear before returning to Rebecca to take her hand. They exit out the back door and lift into the air, Rebecca with her wings and Benjamin . . . *clean*. His last whispered words, nearly inaudible, linger in my ear.

"She's lying to you."

Chapter 19

Of course she's lying to ye," says Moira as we sit at my dining room table, sipping our dinner. I called her as soon as I got over the shock of hearing Benjamin speak. Well, whisper anyway. The only person I've ever seen him speak to is Michael. Even with him, it was only a whisper in the ear. Even when he was cuddling up to Rebecca, I never saw him speak. I bet that drove Rebecca crazy to have Benjamin speak to me when he hasn't spoken to her.

After I called Moira, she drove my van up and brought her "hanger" so we could continue my training after dinner.

"I know she's lying," I say, "but I don't know what Benjamin's trying to do. Is he trying to play both sides? For that matter, is he still working for Michael? Is he a spy? My gut says no, but he's a tricky little ... monster. I don't know *what* to call him! Long ago, he was a little boy, a slave, corrupted by his evil master. Now, I don't know what he is or how to deal with him."

"I know what ye mean, laddie. Benjamin is an enigma. He's so twisted that I'm not sure *he* knows who he is or what he wants. After ye kill Michael, he's just as likely to turn on ye in his grief as he is to thank ye for freeing him. I think he hates Michael as much as he loves him. Watch yer step with that one, laddie."

"You should have seen his face when he was able to do something that Rebecca couldn't do. Or when I called him, 'Ben.'"

"He liked that, did he?"

I nod.

"Ye know, laddie, ye may be the first positive male role model he's ever had in his long, unnatural life."

"You talk about him as if he were a child, Moira. He's *not* a child. He never had a *chance* to be a child."

"Aye, I know," she says sadly, "but he is nae, and ne'er *will* be, an adult. He's something ... other."

What a profoundly sad thought. Never an adult. Unable to be a child. No place at all in this world. I need to change the subject. This makes my head hurt and (I have to admit) my *heart* ache.

"What do you suppose . . . Ben . . . was referring to when he told me she was lying?" I ask.

"Ach, it could be anything. Her intention to break yer treaty as soon as Michael and Chikah are nae more. That much for sure, I'd think."

"Agreed."

We finish our blood.

"So, what's on the training schedule for tonight?" I ask. We both stand up and retrieve our weapons from the living room, which is still cleared of furniture from my earlier training with Rebecca and Benj . . . Ben. *I need to call him "Ben."*

"Combat at close quarters," she says. "Ye've learned all ye are going to in such a short time about airborne and earthbound sword-play in an open environment. So, close quarters it is!"

As my battle plan has evolved, it has become increasingly apparent that the fight with Michael will take place in the confined space of the Sanctuary.

Moira has taught me to hold the dirk pointing downward with the blunt edge of the blade forward. This allows me to use the dirk as a parrying weapon to block my opponent's attacks. The claymore is primarily a cut-and-thrust broadsword, designed to slash first and thrust second.

Try as I might, Moira is much faster with her single weapon, her "hanger," than I am with my two. Michael's saber will be faster and lighter than my broadsword, so the dirk gives me an advantage. Also, the balance of the claymore allows me to maneuver it quickly, despite its greater weight.

As I found out with the bat I used when we took on those thugs in front of the Ogden Temple, the weight and power and resilience of any weapon I use is greatly enhanced by the tactile-telekinesis we unconsciously employ. What that means in combat is Michael's lighter saber will probably be just as durable and strong as my broadsword. Moira and I still use the flats of our blades in training, because we don't want to run the risk of blunting the edges or causing accidental injury.

In aerial combat, or even on the ground in a larger space, I can swing the sword in a wider arc. In my living room, just as it would be in Michael's Sanctuary, the movements have to be smaller, more precise, with more emphasis on thrusting than on slashing.

I'm breathing hard and desperately trying to hold my ground as I fend off Moira's blows. She looks as if she's performing a dance rather than engaging in combat with deadly weapons. Her breathing and heart rate are calm.

Occasionally, she tells me she's going to give me an opening and I should be prepared to take advantage of it. When she makes an intentional mistake, sometimes I see it and make the appropriate attack and sometimes I miss it entirely or react too late, and, before I know it, she has turned an error into a disarming stroke, and I find the dirk or the broadsword wrenched from my hands.

Eventually, she calls a halt and backs away. I lower my weapons and stand there struggling to catch my breath.

"Ye're doing very well, laddie," she says, showing not the least sign of exertion. "As I've told ye before, I dinnae think Michael knows how to fight all that well. As a Southern gentleman, he may have been trained somewhat in fencing or épée, but that'll do him little good in actual life-and-death fighting. I've prepared ye to be able to deal with that level of training on Michael's part. Now, let me demonstrate the type of saber use that was prevalent in the Civil War."

She steps back and cries, "En garde!"

I barely get my weapons up before she roars and charges at me with saber held high, her lovely face twisted in a berserker rage. I'm barely able to fend off her blow. She continues her attack with wide, rapid slashes from either side. After the initial shock of her first attack, this slashing is easier to defend against. I'm actually able to parry her blade away with my dirk and bring my claymore around for a hack at her midsection (with the flat of my blade).

As soon as I land the blow, I back off.

She doesn't. She presses her attack. In a moment, she has her blade at my neck.

"Show nae mercy, laddie." She gives me a grim nod. "*He'll* show ye none. Dinnae stop until ye have decapitated him or left a sword in his heart."

"Right," I say, chagrined.

She smiles her incredible smile at me. "That's enough of that for tonight." She sets her weapon aside.

"What was the yelling attack at the beginning?" I ask, setting my own weapons on the kitchen table and starting to move the furniture back into the room. I glance at the large wet spot on the carpet where I had to clean up my blood earlier. During practice, Rebecca sliced my shoulder open. I say a quick silent prayer of thanks for stain-resistant carpet. I can still smell the blood under the odor of orange-scented cleaner. The cleaner smells bad. The blood, even vampire blood, smells good. *Great! Being in this room is going to make me hungry. It's a good thing I'll be selling this place soon.*

"Oh, I dinnae know what they call it now," she says as she helps me move furniture, "but in my youth 'twas known as the 'Hieland Charge.' The Scots used to take a position on higher ground. Then they would lift their kilts, showing their privates and jeer at the enemy to show they were unafraid. Then they'd raise their swords high and rush downhill upon the enemy with a great bloodcurdling scream. The point is to unnerve and frighten the enemy and overwhelm them with the ferocity of the initial attack. As ye saw, it can unnerve ye."

"Yep. At least Michael won't be lifting his kilt at me!"

"Pray he does nae. 'Twould unnerve ye completely!"

"More likely it would make me puke!"

"It didn't come up tonight in my meeting with Rebecca and Ben," I say as we sit on the sofa, "but, in our previous meetings, both times I've brought up the fact that I'm an Unwilling vampire, Rebecca seemed to be really upset, frightened, even."

"Aye, ye've told me as much."

"Why would she be so freaked out about it? Would it be because she has no hold on me?"

"She knew she had nae hold on ye when ye bolted from the Sanctuary with yer Offering and then did nae return."

"So why?"

"Could it be," she muses, "that, with ye nae under her control, Michael might find out about ye? She kept yer Conversion a secret, did she nae?"

"Yeah, she did, but that doesn't *feel* right either." I stop to think for a moment. "Moira, what's the Great Secret?"

She looks at me curiously for a moment. "Did she nae tell ye?"

"No, I wasn't Chosen long enough. I didn't receive all my instruction, I suppose."

She nods. "The Great Secret has two parts. The first is simply that ye may live forever by becoming a Child of Lilith and drinking the blood of mortals."

"You're kidding, right? That's it?"

She nods.

"Some big secret," I say.

"Ye dinnae understand. The secret lies in the joining yerself to the Family of Lilith, in becoming her Child, in taking the secret Oaths. Ye are charged that ye dinnae ever reveal the Oaths to mortals. Remember that the Great Secret Satan taught to Cain was that he could murder to gain his brother's flocks. For all Cain's evil, the thought had nae entered into the heart of man, the idea that he could murder another human being for gain."

"OK. That makes sense, when you put it into that context. But you said the Great Secret has two parts."

"Oh, aye." She nods. "There is the Curse."

"You mean, like being a vampire?"

"Nae, in the older sense of the word."

"I don't understand."

"A Curse is a prophecy of doom."

"You have my attention, pretty lady. Tell me about the Curse."

"'Tis very old. It dates back to Father Adam."

"You mean Adam . . . as in Adam and Eve?"

"Aye, the grandfather of Lilith, the father of us all. As the story goes, when Adam was very old, 'stooped with age,' he gathered all of his descendants to a last great council."

"All of them?"

"Do ye mean, was Lilith there?"

I nod.

"Nae, she was nae there. The council was held during the day, and neither Lilith nor any of her Children could be there, but one of her Unconverted disciples was there. He would be what we call a 'Chosen' today. He was there, and that's how we have the tale, or so the story goes.

"At the great council, Adam blessed his descendants, and he prophesied about his family (the entire human race) from that day until the end of Time. The only part of the prophecy that has survived in living memory is the Curse. The disciple reported it to Lilith, and it's been passed down since the Dawn of Time. It's been translated into many tongues, but I learned it in Latin from the Ancient One who Converted me. She made me memorize it, because I knew nae Latin at the time. But here it is:

"*Et erit in novissimis diebus . . .*"

I have no idea what she's saying.

"Ye dinnae speak Latin, do ye?" she asks when she sees my look of utter incomprehension.

"Nope."

"What they teach or dinnae teach ye young people these days!" She gives me a smirk and then a wink. "Nae matter, laddie, ye poor uneducated bairn. Let me try to render it in English." She closes her eyes and translates:

"*Et erit* . . . And it shall come to pass . . . *in novissimis diebus* . . . in the last days . . . *cum invitit et contriti* . . . when forced and contrite . . . *in domum Domini* . . . in the house of the Lord . . . *in vertice montium* . . . in the top of the mountains . . . *coniungant* . . . shall join . . . *mater noctis praecibitabit* . . . the mother of night shall fall . . . *et mors pueris eius incurret* . . . and death shall come upon her children.*"

I feel a chill run up my spine. "Say that again."

She repeats it, this time without interruption, "And it shall come to pass in the last days, when forced and contrite shall join in the house of the Lord in the top of the mountains, the mother of night shall fall and death shall come upon her children." She stares at me.

"Do you know what that means?" I say, my voice filled with awe.

"Aye. It speaks of the death of Lilith and her Children. She's 'the mother of night.' I told ye 'twas a pronouncement of doom."

"Yeah, that much is obvious," I say, my thoughts racing. "The 'last days' are right now."

"Aye."

"Moira, 'forced' could easily be rendered 'unwilling' couldn't it?"

Her green eyes go wide as comprehension dawns on her. "Oh, Carl!"

I nod.

"And 'contrite,'" she says, "could be 'penitent!' There are nae articles in Latin . . . nae 'the' or 'a' or 'an'!"

"'The Unwilling' . . . ," I say, pointing at myself.

"And 'the Penitent' . . . ," she says, pointing at herself.

"Shall 'join in the house of the Lord,'" we say together.

"'In the top of the mountains,'" I finish. "Moira, it's just like that passage in Isaiah; the Ute word for this region, 'Utah,' means . . ."

"'The top of the mountains,'" she finishes.

"That sounds eerily similar to the prophecy from fifty years ago," I whisper.

Her hand trembles in mine. Mine is quivering just as violently.

We sit like that for a very long time, neither of us saying a word about the *other* part of the prophecy, the part about our deaths.

"That's it," I say finally. "That's what Rebecca was so upset about. An Unwilling vampire is the harbinger of doom." *And with* their *doom comes* our *death too.*

Chapter 20

Mercifully, it's *not* a beautiful Sunday morning. It's overcast, and it looks like rain. Those lovely clouds will make church a whole lot easier. I never appreciated cloudy days before my Conversion. Now I *love* them. The darker, the better!

Since this will be my last Sunday in my current ward, Moira has gotten a substitute for her Sunbeams and is going to attend my meetings with me. Our meeting schedules overlap enough that attending both sets of meetings is not an option.

Moira flew home last night and then returned to my house with her Sunday clothes and scriptures. We plan to return to her home (*our* home in just two days) via the van so we can Sleep (with her in the bedroom and me on the couch, of course) the rest of the day, safe from any possible attack by Hadley.

According to the local news, Hadley is still at large and has not been sighted since he was spotted at the Johnson home where Detective Johnson's family was murdered. Johnson is still missing as well.

Because of Hadley, I'll never again be able to Sleep in the bed that Sharon and I shared.

Church is going to be interesting. How tongues are going to wag in Relief Society today! I can hear them now in my head:

Sister Morgan only six months in her grave and he's remarrying? And so quickly! You know something has to be wrong there!

It's so overcast when we pull up at church that we don't even have to wear our protective clothing. We carry our sunglasses, hats, coats, and gloves, but we're able to take our time walking into the church building.

Moira gives me a kiss and heads into Relief Society. I don't envy her position. She's definitely going to be under close scrutiny. Sharon was well loved in this ward.

I stand outside the Relief Society room for a moment and am gratified to hear a collective gasp coming from the many ladies in there as they get their first glimpse of Moira. She has that effect on people anyway, but it's probably magnified by the anticipation of meeting the woman who's so quickly and so suddenly marrying Sharon's husband.

As the day progresses, Moira wins *everyone* over. People seem to just fall in love with her. She told me previously that the Relief Society here was already busy planning a reception on Tuesday night for us. God bless them. They're really rising to the occasion.

I wonder what will happen when I move into *her* ward. I mean, Moira is . . . *Moira.* Everyone seems to love her. How will *I* measure up to *their* expectations of the man "who finally won her over?" They've known her for a very long time.

A very long time . . . How has she been able to pull that off?

I get a shock when the opening hymn begins in sacrament meeting. Suddenly I hear this incredible female voice. It's Moira singing joyfully next to me. I look at her with surprise. I had no idea she could sing. I mean, she can *really* sing. Her voice is strong and clear and beautiful. Just like Moira. I feel like a bullfrog next to her. I can hardly sing at all. The frog and the beautiful princess. Her voice turns heads just as her looks do.

"Moira," I whisper so low that no mortal could overhear as we sit in the meeting listening to the visiting high (dry) councilman drone on, "how do you get away with . . . with living in the same ward, the same house, for decades . . . without showing any signs of age? Aren't there any older people in your ward who knew you when *they* were young?"

She smiles and whispers back, "'Tis nae so hard as ye would think. Most people move out of the ward before they realize that I dinnae age. There are a few that've known me since they were children. I taught some of them in Sunday School or Primary. Only a very few have asked about my age. I simply tell them I'm far older than I appear to be. That seems to satisfy them. I suspect 'tis because mortals *want* to trust us. 'Tis nae Persuasion, but 'tis akin to it. I'm nae intentionally lying to them, but *most* mortals accept what we say at face value. A few have expressed their misgivings, concerns, or fears to the bishops over the years. I dinnae know what the bishop has told them exactly, but they seem to accept it."

That sounds a little too easy to me. I wonder just what the bishops have told people.

"It's much harder at work," she continues. "I have to switch hospitals every few decades. I keep a low profile. I have a friend at the Social Security Office who got me a new Social Security number a few years back when I started to collect retirement benefits. It's a deception, but a necessary one in this day and . . ."

She trails off as our attention becomes riveted to what the high councilman, who is an emergency-room doctor at McKay-Dee Hospital, is saying:

". . . angels protecting the house of the Lord. Some of you may have read the story in this morning's paper. Vandals tried to break into the Ogden Temple and assaulted two temple workers in the process. According to the story in the paper, two angels descended from the sky. They stopped the vandals and healed one of the temple workers of her injuries, which were life threatening.

"This reminds me of a story about the Logan Temple when an angry mob . . ."

I feel a chill go up my spine. I suddenly notice that Bishop Edwards, seated up on the stand, is looking at me with an intense gaze. When he realizes that he has caught my attention, his eyebrows rise questioningly and he nods in my direction. *How does he know? I didn't tell him about that.* I nod back at him with a grimace on my face. He smiles knowingly at me and gives an almost imperceptible wink to Moira.

The high councilman works in the hospital. Did he attend to Edna? Maybe, maybe not, but he probably heard the story at work. It's starting to spread. *This can't be good.*

Moira and I exchange a quick glance. She's got to be thinking the same thing that I am.

The "angel" story could provide more fuel for the fire to Detective Johnson . . . if he makes the connection . . . if he's still alive.

That poor guy.

After the normal Sunday meetings are over, there are a number of people who come up to offer their congratulations. The fact that the bishop announced our wedding and reception over the pulpit probably didn't add significantly to the number; apparently the news has spread like a wildfire in dry prairie grass. Actually, it's an *absurd* number of people who come up to talk to us. There must be almost every adult member of the ward here. There are a lot of teenagers too, especially from the ranks of the young men.

They probably just want a closer look at Moira.

As we stand there amiably chatting with people near the chapel doors, the unbearably sweet odor of evil blood suddenly rivets my attention. I can feel Moira abruptly stiffen at my side, her hand clenching mine in an iron grip. She stops mid word in the conversation she's having with a pimply faced priest who's drooling over her.

My head snaps in the direction of the corruption. My mouth fills with drool, and I have to swallow hard to keep it from spilling out of my mouth. I seal my lips shut to cover my fangs, which are now fully extended.

My gaze lands on a blonde woman in a flower-print dress. There's a moment of shock as I recognize Sister Pascoe, who lives in a neighboring ward. She's holding the wrist of her young son. The toddler has one of his mother's fingers gripped tightly in his tiny hand. The moment of shock passes as the attraction of her corruption grips me like a fishhook catching a fish. I can hear the pulse of her blood as it races through her arteries, veins, and capillaries. I can see the throb of it under her skin. It takes all my force of will to stay rooted to the spot where I'm standing, surrounded by well-wishers, and not sink my teeth into her neck.

Sister Pascoe is unaware of my intense stare. I'm sure that Moira is staring much the same as I am. Sister Pascoe makes her way with her little boy down the hall and away from us, completely oblivious to our fixation. I stare after her until she passes out of sight.

I'm dimly aware that people are talking to me. Talking to *us*. The scent of delicious corruption still threatens to overwhelm my control. The voices around me change in tone. There's concern in some of the voices. There's fear in a few. *Shut up!* I want to say. *Let me focus! Don't you understand? I want to kill! KILL!*

Moira is gently, but insistently, shaking my hand to get my attention. I look at her and I see, reflected in her face, what's probably plain on mine: a burning in her eyes, an intensity that speaks volumes about the discipline she's employing to smother her rage and hunger.

As one, we take a deep sigh, and a mask of calm descends over our features. The scent, the hunger is still strong, but the rage is slipping away. I force my fangs to retract.

Then we see the faces of those gathered around us. There's concern. There's shock. There's fear.

But Moira smiles her bewitching smile, and I see the shock, concern, and fear melt away. If smiling were an Olympic event, Moira would take the gold medal every single time.

I see Bishop Edwards motioning me toward him, and so I make an excuse and gently pull Moira away. He points us toward his office, and we enter. He follows us in and then quickly closes the door.

We turn toward him. He's blocking the door with his body. "Carl, what just happened?" He looks a little scared. Judging by his heartbeat, more than a little. "Are we in danger?"

"You mean . . . from *us*?" I say, knowing that's *precisely* what he means.

"Yeah," he says cautiously.

"No," I say, glancing quickly at Moira and then back to him, "but *someone* is."

"What do you mean?" he asks.

"That woman," Moira says.

"Sister Pascoe," I clarify.

"Sister Pascoe," she repeats. "That woman is *evil*. I dinnae know what she's done, but she is . . . *evil*."

He sighs with relief. "And you can sense this?"

"Yeah," I say. "She *reeks* of corruption. I'm fighting the urge to go after her and kill her right now."

He looks horrified.

"Bishop," I say evenly, "I'm in control."

"We *both* are," interjects Moira.

"When you say that she's evil," he says, "what do you mean?"

"As I said, Bishop," Moira reiterates, "we cannae tell what she has done, but it has to be horrible."

"Such as?" he asks.

"Abuse, murder, violence against an innocent. Something bad that involves violence to others," I say.

"I see," he says.

"I can't tell you more," I say, "without spying on her or robbing her of her free will . . . and I don't want to do either."

"And I wouldn't ask you to," he says. "I'm not her bishop, as you know. I'll *call* her bishop and tell him he should be concerned about her. I'll tell him I have reason to believe something is horribly amiss in her life and he should watch for signs that she might be engaged in something extremely . . . wrong. Then I'll have to leave it in his hands."

"So, Bishop," I say, changing the subject, "let me get this straight: you pulled us in here because you thought we might be a danger to others?"

"Uh-huh," he says slowly.

"You shut yourself up in a room with what you thought were two out-of-control, bloodthirsty, murderous vampires?"

"I guess so." He grins sheepishly. "Pretty stupid, huh?"

"In my opinion," Moira says, "that makes ye one of the *bravest* men I've ever had the privilege to meet." She steps forward and kisses him on the cheek.

His face turns a mouthwatering shade of crimson.

Chapter 21

Y ou're getting married *tomorrow?*" Steve Martin's voice is incredulous and a little louder than I would wish. "You've got to be *kidding* me!"

"No kidding," I say, gesturing for him to tone it down. I really don't want to disturb everyone else at work. "Ogden Temple, tomorrow night, 7:00 p.m. You're invited!"

"Dude! What's the rush? I mean, you're getting married in the *temple* so I assume there's no . . ."

"No, Steve, that's not it," I assure him. "It's just that . . . well, we're not getting any younger . . ." *We're not getting any older, is more like it.* "I know that sounds lame, but, well, it's really all about timing. There's a huge . . . family crisis coming up. If we don't get married, literally right now, it might not . . . happen . . . for a long time." *Make that might never happen.* "It's better if we get married before we get . . . embroiled in this . . . crisis." I can see the look on his face. He wants to ask about the "crisis," but he's holding back. I need to give him something less cryptic.

"Basically, we have to get my mother out of a really bad situation, and we'll be in a much better position to deal with it if we're already married." *My mother! That's a good one! Well, it's close enough to the truth. Rebecca considers herself to be my "mother."*

He looks down and nods. He realizes this is about all the explanation he's going to get. And he seems to be OK with it.

"Where are you going for your honeymoon?" he asks, moving on.

Honeymoon! Crap! I still have to get the rest of the week off!

"Uh . . . we're going to Disneyland," I say quickly. "Listen, Steve, I still have to talk to Phil and get the time off!"

"Disneyland sounds fun."

"Yeah. Moira's never been," I say as I head off to find Phil.

Once I get to Phil's office, I knock on the doorframe. He turns from his monitor and, upon seeing me, smiles his congenial smile. He gets out of his chair and starts to close the blinds.

"Don't worry about it," I say. "It's pouring rain outside."

He blinks at me in confusion, so I explain, "No Sun."

"Ah," he says and motions me in. "Have a seat." He sits back down himself.

I take the indicated chair.

He smiles. "To what do I owe the pleasure?"

"I need to take the rest of the week off. Make that tomorrow through next Monday."

He blinks once and then scoots his chair over to the "time-off" calendar on the wall. This is a whiteboard on which he keeps a hand-drawn calendar with notes about team members who are planning on being out of the office. He looks at it for a second. "This isn't a great week for you to take off. Ryan and Ted are taking a couple of days each. What's up?"

"I'm getting married tomorrow."

"Really?" He turns to me, and his face splits in an ear-to-ear grin. "Congratulations!"

"Thanks."

"I'm happy for you." He turns back to the board. "Well, I guess we need to let you off for *that*." He takes out a marker and writes my name on the square for tomorrow and draws a line to the end of the week. "Through Monday, you say?"

"Yep. Thanks."

He writes my name on next Monday's square as well. He caps his Dry Erase marker and swivels his chair around to face me again. "So, tell me all about her!"

Phil isn't a member of the Church, so I can't invite him to the wedding, but I do invite him to the reception. He says he'll try to make it. I thank him again for giving me the time off, and then I head back to my cubicle.

It's nice not to have to worry about the Sun on days like today.

When I get to my cube, Steve is staring intently at his screen. When he hears me return, he says, "Hey, Carl. What was the name of the detective that was asking about you? Was it Johnson?"

"Yeah," I say cautiously. "Why?"

"I'm reading about him on the news."

"Did they find him?"

"No, it says he's missing. 'Whereabouts unknown.' It says his family was murdered and he's still missing," he reiterates.

"Yeah. I heard about that on the news."

"It says they were murdered by an escaped serial killer . . . another cop."

"Yeah."

"They found him."

"Who? Hadley?" I lean in to read over his shoulder.

The headline for the article on the local news website says:

Escaped Serial Killer's Body Found

"Yep, Hadley," Steve says. "That's his name. It says his body was found in Pioneer Park last night. He was stabbed to death. I hear that park can get pretty rough at night."

Hadley's dead. I'm stunned. Good riddance. *Johnson's still missing, though.*

"Wow," is all I can manage to say.

"Yeah, wow," Steve agrees. "It's a crazy world we live in."

Johnson's probably dead too.

"So, your fiancé's never been to Disneyland?" he asks, changing the subject.

Good. I don't want to think about Hadley or Johnson right now. *I'm getting married tomorrow!* "Nope," I say. "Never been."

"How are you going to handle Disneyland with all that sun? She has the same skin condition as you, right?"

"Yeah, she does. Disneyland is great at night."

"I suppose you can find other things to do during the day."

"Uh-huh," I say with a goofy grin, "but actually, it's supposed to be overcast or raining all week, so we won't have too many restrictions."

"You been to Disneyland before?"

"Yeah. Actually, Sharon and I honeymooned there."

"Whoa, dude! That's awkward, isn't it?"

"A little, but Moira has her heart set on it, so what can I do? It'll be OK. Actually, it's kinda nice."

"If you say so," Steve says dubiously.

"Like I said, you're invited to the wedding."

"Cool. I'll ask the wife and see if we can make it. When and where?"

"Ogden Temple at seven o'clock."

"In the morning?"

"No. I told you seven p.m. Avoiding the Sun, you know?"

"Ri-ight."

I leave work early so I can meet Moira at the Davis County Courthouse in Farmington. By the time I get there, Moira has already finished all the paperwork for our marriage license. I just need to provide my ID and signature. Once we have that document in hand, we drive separately to my house.

On the way, we talk via cell phone. I tell Moira about Hadley's death, but the news doesn't alter our plans for the evening and tomorrow.

We're getting married tomorrow! I can scarcely wrap my brain around it!

"We both need Sleep, laddie," she says as we drive, "and we cannae afford to Sleep through the day and miss our appointment at the temple tomorrow. After we're done packing things at yer place, we'll go back to my house and take turns Sleeping for a few hours each. Ye'll Sleep first."

"Fine, but how will you wake me when it's your turn for Sleep?"

"I'll get some blood from the fridge, pour a wee bit in a glass, and wave it under yer nose. When it's my turn, ye'll do the same for me. Make sure I'm awake by one o'clock! I want to look my best at the temple!"

"Lady, you'd be beautiful even if you were covered in mud!"

"Is that how our marriage is goin' to be, Mr. Morgan? With ye tellin' *lies* and *flatterin'* all the time?"

"Hey! It's the *truth*!" I protest. "I only lie about presents on birthdays, Christmas, and anniversaries!"

"Well, ye'd better save it until after the weddin', laddie, 'cause flattery will get ye everywhere! And we still have to get through another night and a day!"

We spend the rest of the evening and night packing up enough things for me so I can move into Moira's home when it becomes *our* home tomorrow. She also helps me pack a suitcase for our honeymoon.

And true to her word, she has taken care of virtually everything. Our flights and the hotel are booked. She has our theme park tickets, which she ordered online and then printed out. *Dr.* Moira MacDonald has even arranged for perishable medical supplies (refrigerated blood) to be shipped separately to the airport in Anaheim via air freight.

"Why don't we just have our luggage flown ahead to California and then fly there under our own power?" I ask.

She stops what she's doing and plants both fists on her hips. "I dinnae intend to arrive at our honeymoon suite with my hair all windblown. I want to look my *best.*"

"I've seen you with your hair 'all windblown' and it makes you look . . . wild and wanton . . . very alluring. I see nothing wrong with that on our wedding night!"

"'Tis my *only* weddin' night, Mr. I've-Been-Married-Afore-So-This-Is-All-Old-Hat-To-Me Morgan. And I fully intend to arrive at the hotel lookin' my *best.*" There's a fire burning in her emerald eyes as she pokes me in the chest, emphasizing every word. "And I will nae be gainsaid on this!"

"OK! OK! I yield, milady! I yield!"

"*And,*" she says with a wicked grin, "*if* we were to 'fly there under our own power,' as ye say, with nae chaperonin', I dinnae think we'd make it so far as the honeymoon suite."

Chapter 22

I know I've said that Moira is stunning many times before. But nothing compares to the sight of Moira in her white wedding gown. *Where did she get one on such short notice?* I remember the first time I saw Sharon in *her* wedding gown. It was like I'd never seen her before.

Both Sharon and Moira chose simple rather than elaborate, elegant rather than gaudy, and, of course, modest rather than revealing. And all in the purest white. Sharon's gown was of a more modern cut. Moira's could have been made in another century, but there is no sign of age. Her gown is . . . timeless.

The first time I saw Sharon in her wedding gown was when she met me outside the temple on the day of our marriage. Her mother had, of course, refused to come anywhere near the temple that day. She wouldn't have been able to attend the wedding, of course, but she could have waited for us in the waiting room. Sharon and I didn't elope: I had no family left to attend, and her family wanted nothing to do with us. I know Sharon was hurt, but the last thing we needed on our wedding day was her mother screaming obscenities at us.

Sharon was running just a little bit late, and I was getting worried. I scanned the temple grounds and the parking lot, searching for her. Maybe her mother had gotten to her finally. Heaven knows she tried! Maybe Sharon just decided I wasn't good enough for her. And, truth be told, no man was good enough, especially me.

As panic started to get its talons into my heart, I saw her. She seemed to glide up the walk toward me, floating on air. I'd stood in the presence of prophets and apostles, but I'd never seen an angel before. She seemed to shine, to light up the temple grounds, putting the Sun to shame.

And her smile was all for me.

Panic really gripped me then. There was no way I was good enough for this celestial creature, this glorious being of pure whiteness. Any minute, she'd realize this and turn and run away, rejoicing that she came to her senses at last.

And then she was there and she kissed me. All panic fled. She took my hand and we walked into the temple, two separate and distinct individuals, only to emerge a short time later as eternal companions, sealed together for time and all eternity.

No man could be more blessed.

As the time approaches for Moira and me to leave for the Ogden Temple, she emerges from her bedroom (soon to be *our* bedroom) clothed all in white. In the relative darkness of her living room with all the shades drawn, she's like the Moon shining on a clear night. Only the Moon has no light of its own; it merely *reflects* the light of the Sun. Moira is radiance itself. An angel of the night. My angel.

She takes my breath away.

And then she smiles and I literally stop breathing. As a final touch, she lifts a foot or so into the air and spreads her wings. The image is complete. Perfection.

Then she's in my arms and kissing me tenderly, and I remember to breathe. And I can think of nothing else except Moira.

After a minute, I pull away a little and rest my forehead against hers. "We have to stop." There's a tremor to my voice. "We have to go."

"Aye, laddie," she says breathlessly. "I can stand nae more of this. We must go *now*."

It's still overcast outside, so we grab our protective clothing, but don't bother to put it on. We don't even need to apply sunscreen if we're quick. I wonder if maybe Heavenly Father sent these clouds to make the day perfect for the wedding of two vampires. We make it to the van without any discomfort from the unseen Sun.

When we arrive at the temple, there's a tall, clean-shaven man with thinning, graying hair. He's in a blue suit and he's standing near the outer gate. When he sees my van, he starts to wave at us frantically.

"That's Bishop Adams," Moira says. "Stop for a wee bit."

The man runs up to the van and taps on my window. Before I can roll it down, he says, "Don't open the window! I know you two can hear me just fine! That *is* you in there, isn't it, Moira?"

"Aye, Bishop," she shouts joyfully.

"I figured it must be you with your windows all black like that!" he says. "You have Brother Morgan with you, right?"

"Aye, Bishop, he's here!"

"I saved you a parking spot near the entrance. I figured I could save you some exposure. It should be OK with these clouds, right?" He's grinning like the village idiot on a feast day.

He turns and runs off to the parking spot closest to the main entrance. He jumps in a car and pulls out so we can pull in.

Moira beams. "What a sweet lad he is!"

"Lad?" I say as I pull into the parking spot vacated by Bishop Adams. "He's got to be in his fifties at least!"

"As I said, he's but a *lad*!"

Just as I'm getting out of the van, the "lad" comes running up to the van carrying two umbrellas. He hurriedly opens one and places it over my head.

"I hope you'll forgive me, Brother Morgan, but we've been waiting so long for this day. We're very excited! I'm Bishop Adams, by the way." He takes me by the hand and shakes it with an enthusiasm that belongs more to a nineteen-year-old missionary than a balding bishop in his fifties.

I like him instantly.

"Call me Carl, Bishop," I say warmly. "I really appreciate the gesture, but it's so cloudy that Moira and I will have no trouble, even without the umbrellas."

He grins sheepishly and puts the umbrella away.

"But it was really nice of you to think of us and our . . . special needs," I say.

"Well, Brother Morgan, welcome to the ward! We think of ourselves as Moira's family. So you're family now too."

"Thank you, Bishop."

"Let's get a look at that lovely bride of yours!"

I hurry around the car and open the door for Moira. I help her out. Once she alights on the ground, she arranges the skirts of her gown and gives me a gorgeous smile.

It takes my breath away. Again.

And I'm not the only one affected. I hear Bishop Adams gasp behind me.

"Stop gawking at her, Jacob!" says a pleasant female voice. I turn my head to see a handsome woman, with graying (but not thinning) hair, walking toward us from the temple doors. "You make me positively green with envy. Of course, *every* woman feels a little intimidated with *Moira* around. But today, my dear," she says, turning her attention to Moira, "you are absolutely stunning! Who needs the sun to shine when Moira's around?" She embraces Moira warmly. Then she turns to embrace me. "I'm Laura Adams." She gives me a big hug.

She breaks the embrace, and I say, "I'm pleased to meet you, Sister Adams. I'm Carl."

"Oh, don't you dare call me Sister Adams in front of Moira! Makes me feel positively *ancient*! Call me Laura. Moira was my Primary teacher . . . well . . . a long, long time ago. I'm so pleased to meet the man who finally caught our Moira!"

"And I'm so pleased to be caught!" says Moira brightly.

"We'd best be moving inside, don't you think?" says the Bishop.

"Aye, we should," Moira agrees as she takes my arm.

The four of us start to move quickly toward the temple doors.

"Do you have your recommends and the marriage license?"

"I've got mine," I say, but I hear Moira gasp.

"Ach, nae!" she says, stopping suddenly with a horrified expression on her face. Then her face lights up with a wicked grin, and she laughs merrily. "Just kiddin' ye! Ye should see the looks on yer faces!" She holds up her new white temple bag. "I've got everything in here."

We all laugh, but there's relieved panic in my laughter.

Bishop Adams comes around to walk beside me as we resume our brisk pace to the temple. "Brother Morg . . . Carl, I spoke to your bishop, and he's going to be here for the sealing, but . . . do you have an escort?"

"No, Bishop, I don't."

"Might I . . . ?"

"Bishop Adams, I would be honored if you'd be my escort," I say with a grin.

"Good, because Laura is Moira's escort," he says.

"Does . . . Laura . . . know . . . about us?" I whisper to him.

He shakes his head. "She knows no more than anyone else in the ward, except for me, of course, and the former bishops. That's *private* and we don't tell anyone who doesn't absolutely need to know."

"What does she *think*?"

"That's . . . a discussion for another time," he says cryptically.

Moira squeezes my arm.

Her grip becomes very tight as we walk through the doors of the temple and proceed past the entry to the recommend desk.

And sitting there behind the desk is Fred, the temple worker we rescued! When he catches sight of Moira and me, his eyes go wide with shock, and his jaw drops, but then his ancient face splits in a wide grin.

"Welcome to the temple!" he says in a quiet, but enthusiastic voice as he reaches for my recommend with a trembling hand.

As he examines it, he says, "I'm so glad to see you again!" After he examines and validates Moira's recommend, he looks up at her. "My, but you look lovely!"

"Thank ye," says Moira, genuinely pleased.

He leans forward and says in a too-loud whisper, "I didn't tell *anyone* else!" He looks worried. "I'm sorry about the paper! The nurse probably told somebody."

I whisper back, "I believe you! These things have a way of spreading on their own."

"A reporter tried to interview Edna and me, but we didn't tell her a thing!"

"Don't worry about it," I say with a smile I don't quite feel. *I worry about it myself.*

"Getting married today?" he asks.

"That we are," says Moira.

"Well," he says conspiratorially, "Edna's at"—he glances at a sheet of paper on a clipboard—"the Family File desk. Stop by and see her. I'm sure she'll be thrilled to see you! Be careful, though! I don't want her to faint again!"

I assure Fred that we'll stop and see Edna. Then we turn to enter the temple.

As we move past the desk into the temple proper, Moira's hand leaves my arm and grips my hand so tightly that it's almost painful. She's trembling, but her face is bright, and tears of joy run down her cheeks.

No kiss that Moira and I have ever shared compares to the kiss we share across the altar when we're sealed. Moira has never looked more beautiful. And never have I been more certain of her love for me and of my love for her.

We're going to walk into hell on Sunday night, but now we're sealed together for time and all eternity. Not even death can separate us forever after this. Moira is mine and I am hers. Moira's and Sharon's. No matter what happens in the coming battle, we'll be together.

"Not even a wisp of smoke," I whisper to my new bride. We're greeting our guests at the reception in the cultural hall of the stake center.

"What?" she whispers back.

"You were worried that we'd burst into flame right in the middle of the temple, weren't you?"

She chuckles softly. "Aye, I was . . . a wee bit."

"Well, I wasn't worried," I say with a wide grin.

"Dinnae be so smug, laddie. Ye have nae had two and a half centuries to brood on it."

"That's it. Make me feel young and inexperienced!"

"Ye are but a wee bairn, and I'm robbin' the cradle!" She winks and then sighs.

"What's wrong?" I ask.

"Nae so much *what* as *who*." She's looking at the next person in line.

I look to see an enormous gray-haired woman in an awful orange dress. Her expression is so sour that she looks as if she's chewing on raw garlic. I realize this will not be just another exchange of pleasantries.

When she gets up to Moira, she looks poised for a confrontation. She smiles at Moira with an almost feral light in her eyes. "Oh, Sister MacDonald, how *lovely* you look tonight." Her voice is eager, *hungry* . . . and utterly devoid of warmth.

"Hello, Winnie." Moira's voice is pleasant, but I can feel her discomfort in the race of her pulse. "So nice to see ye tonight. Thank ye for comin'." Her brogue betrays her distress.

"Aren't you going to introduce me to your *young* man?" Winnie says.

"Winnie, this is my husband, Carl Morgan," says Moira, "Carl, this is Winnie Morrison."

I'm about to say some superficial pleasantry in reply, but the woman plows ahead.

"My," she says, staring straight at me, "you are a handsome *young* thing." Without glancing away from me, she adds, "Finally decided to settle on just *one*, have you, Moira? A little May-December romance, eh? *Young* man, did you know that our Moira has broken the hearts of many, many men over the *decades*? Why, when I was a *Beehive* and Moira was my Beehive *instructor*, all the young men were madly in love with her. Most of the older men too. My own husband, before he left me, couldn't keep his eyes off her. *All* of the bishops over the years have been bewitched by her, too, you know. They all told me that she has a *medical condition* that hides her true age. *Medical condition!* My Aunt Fanny's hind end! I say it's a lot of plastic surgery! I'll bet she's spent a *fortune* on that face. Do you have any *idea* how *old* she *really* is?"

During this whole tirade, Winnie's expression of feral glee never changes. As she waits for my response, she stares at me like a cat that has, after much effort, finally cornered a rather elusive mouse.

A lot of things go through my mind, including the urge to hurl this horrible creature across the room and bounce her off the far wall, but I manage to keep my head. I'm not going to let her or anybody else ruin this evening. So I swallow and then smile as warmly as I can. "Actually, uh, Sister Morrison is it? Actually, I know *exactly* how old Moira is, and I can tell you three things: First, I have the same *medical condition* that she does, and I'm technically old enough to be her father." Her eyes go wide as I continue, "Second, Moira's beauty comes from within. What you see on the surface is the palest reflection of what makes her truly lovely and makes *almost* everyone love her." I want to say, *Third, I'm sorry that your life sucks and that you're such a bitter old bat, so why don't you go find a belfry and hang upside down in it?* Instead I say, "Third, thank you for coming."

With that I turn to the next person in line. Out of the corner of my eye I can see Winnie staring at me, spluttering and hissing like a really annoyed cat (one whose long-pursued mouse has escaped), but I ignore her. Moira turns and gives me a peck on the cheek. So quietly that no mortal can overhear she says, "Well played, laddie!"

After a few moments of being ignored, Winnie stomps her foot twice. Then she stomps it again. And then she storms off. She knocks over two chairs in her haste to exit the cultural hall.

I shouldn't feel any satisfaction at her discomfort, because she's obviously a very unhappy person.

I really shouldn't.

"Are there any more like her?" I whisper.

"Oh, aye. There have been on occasion. Hers is a sad case. All her own doin', though. She just wants to make everyone as miserable as she is. In a way, I think her bitterness stops others from . . . *questioning* more about my age, because they dinnae want to be seen to *side* with her. Although, this is the first time I've heard what my bishops have told people over the years. I mean, 'medical condition' is accurate enough. I've actually worried that people thought I was a translated bein' like John the Beloved."

"Don't tell me you've met him!"

"Nae," she says slowly, "but I have met . . ."

"Wow! Your picture doesn't do you justice, lady!" says a familiar voice. "I'm Steve Martin. Not the famous one. Just the *talented* and *good-looking* one. I work with Carl."

"Hi, Steve," I say. "You made it!"

"Thank ye so much for coming, Steve," says Moira.

"Uh, my wife couldn't make it," he says a little sheepishly. "Not feeling well."

"I'm so sorry to hear that," Moira says. "I hope it's nae serious." She knows nothing about Steve or his wife other than the fact that he works with me, but her earnestness is unmistakable.

"Just a cold," he says. Then he leans over to me and says in a whisper that I'm sure he thinks Moira can't hear, "Good thing, too! Your gorgeous bride would intimidate any woman! And I *love* the accent!" He pulls back again and says at a more normal volume, "You are one lucky son of a gun, Carl!"

Moira stifles a giggle. "Remind me to tell ye what that expression means sometime," she whispers to me.

Just then, Bishop Edwards approaches from the side and says in a low voice, "Carl, I'm sorry. I tried to stop them, but they just won't listen." He looks really worried.

"What's up, Bishop?" I whisper back.

"It's the Relief Society. I told them *not* to make you cut and eat the first pieces of the cake. I couldn't explain *why*, of course, so I told them you just can't eat any cake. But they're insisting."

Moira breaks away from the line of guests and gives him a wink. "'Tis all right, Bishop. I know just how to handle this wee . . . *crisis*." To me she whispers, "Trust me, laddie. And follow my lead."

"I'd follow you anywhere, pretty lady."

And she's going to follow me into hell *in just a few days.*

The announcement is made, and soon Moira and I are cutting the cake. Once again, I'm amazed at what our Relief Society sisters have pulled together in such a short time. The cake isn't as fancy as some I've seen, but *somebody* has real talent.

Moira and I each take a small amount of cake in our hands. I'm not sure what she has in mind, but suddenly she whispers so only I can hear, "Dinnae ingest any." Then she adds with a wicked gleam in her emerald eyes, "En garde!"

Before I know what hit me, my mouth is covered in smashed cake and smeared frosting. *I see how she wants to play it!* She winks and pretends to try to avoid me, but soon her lovely mouth is covered in a similar fashion. Everybody laughs, and nobody notices that we didn't actually *eat* anything.

And thus the "disaster" is avoided.

Moira loves Disneyland.

And I love Moira.

And I love being with Moira at Disneyland.

She's like a little girl on the most magical Christmas morning ever. It's as if she's never had *fun* before in her life. *Well, maybe she hasn't. Maybe she hasn't* allowed *herself to have fun.*

She has to ride everything, including the Dumbo ride and every other kiddie ride. The delight on her face makes her so beautiful that I know I'd do *anything* in the world to make her happy. She laughs so easily and she carries me away with her.

She screams in all the right places. She encourages me to hold on to her tight, like she's really afraid when we ride Space Mountain. She claps her hands in delight at all the little Disney touches. She has to be photographed with every Disney character.

And Moira is simply *irresistible* in mouse ears!

The weather couldn't be more perfect: heavy overcast, bouts of pelting rain. It keeps the huge crowds away, and we're able to venture out in the daytime . . . when we *do* bother to leave the hotel room during the day.

Moira's "medical supplies" were waiting in an ice-packed box in our suite when we arrived at the hotel. So sustenance is not a problem. In the wee hours of our second night, Wednesday night, long after the park has closed, we have a romantic picnic, sipping blood, at the top of the Matterhorn. We *did* try to find a comfortable spot on the top of the castle, but couldn't find anywhere big enough. We sit there listening to the music drifting over from Downtown Disney, and we gaze at the lights of the park, and we gaze into each other's eyes.

It's not that there aren't glitches. On several occasions, we sense the blood of someone evil, but we keep ourselves well Fed on the supply of blood in our room and are *usually* able to ignore it.

There *is* one occasion where a little girl begins to cry when she sees the expressions on our faces when we smell a particularly sweet corruption. The child's crying snaps us out of our fixation on a man whose blood screams for us to take it.

So we move on and get back to having fun.

And there are the times when Moira looks longingly at babies in strollers or in their mothers' arms. Then, abruptly, she pulls me by the hand and rushes me off to ride the Indiana Jones ride or *Pirates of the Caribbean* or Splash Mountain again, laughing all the way.

Moira loves shopping in the Disney shops as well, though she buys very little. She stares long and hard at a resin miniature of Sleeping Beauty's Castle, but she cannot bring herself to buy it. "'Twould look trite next to my miniatures of the temples."

I try to figure out a way to buy it for her and surprise her with it, but that proves to be particularly difficult. We can't bear to leave each other's sight for even a moment. As vampires, neither of us need to use the bathroom anymore (since our vampire bodies produce no waste), so we don't even have moments like *that* apart. It's not as if I could do anything on the sly without Moira's overhearing me, either.

I finally wait until she's Sleeping on Friday. Almost nothing will wake her until sunset, so, before *I* go to Sleep myself, I call the concierge and make arrangements for the miniature castle to be purchased and delivered to our room just after sunset.

Moira is delighted, of course.

And I'm well rewarded for my *sneakiness*.

Saturday night finally arrives, and we have to leave for home (*our* home) and the coming battle. Moira looks pensive as we're cruising on the plane to Salt Lake City. She has my arm wrapped tightly in both of hers and is leaning her head on my shoulder.

By prior mutual agreement, neither of us mentions the looming uncertainty of tomorrow night, when we'll walk into Michael's den and face death together. However, that doesn't mean it doesn't weigh heavily on both our minds.

"I'm so happy, Carl," she says in a quiet, wistful voice.

"Me, too," I reply. *No matter what the future holds, I'm happy right now, and Moira is sealed to me.*

"Carl," she says, "promise me one thing. Will ye, laddie?"

"Anything, my love," I say, stroking her luxuriant red hair.

"If we both survive tomorrow night . . ."

I stiffen and suddenly feel as if icy claws are gripping my spine. "Yes, Moira?"

"If we survive, I want ye to promise me that . . . on our first wedding anniversary . . ." She hesitates.

"On our first anniversary . . . ," I prompt, trying hard to keep the fear from my voice.

"Aye, on our first anniversary, I want ye to . . . promise to . . . take me to Disney World. Will ye do that, laddie?"

I burst out laughing so hard and loud in relief that a baby starts crying across the aisle.

Moira is out of her seat in an instant and is begging the frazzled mother to allow her to comfort the child. Then I'm watching as Moira coos and pats and soothes the child until it calms down.

Disney World I can give her . . . if we survive.

But *not* what she wants most.

Chapter 23

The instant we enter my house, *my* old *house*, late Saturday night, we sense a presence.

We are not alone.

This had been meant as a quick trip to retrieve a package of supplies for the battle tomorrow night. The package was delivered while we were on our honeymoon. I'd left a key with a neighbor and asked him to watch for the package and put it in the living room while I was gone.

As expected, the package is sitting on the floor inside the door, but there's something else here that I wasn't expecting.

Benjamin is sitting on the sofa.

And he's staring wide-eyed at Moira.

And the full impact of this moment sinks in. *Now Benjamin knows about Moira.* That means the Cult will know. And Michael. And *Rebecca.*

I need to take command of this situation immediately.

"Ben," I say, "what are you doing here?"

The instant I call him by that name, his gaze shifts to me. He glances pointedly at Moira again, before looking me in the eye. The question in his brown eyes is plain.

"Ben," I say, "this is Moira, my wife." Glancing quickly at Moira and then back to Benjamin, I say, "Moira, this is Ben. I told you about him."

For the first time, I notice tear streaks on Benjamin's dark face. *He's been crying?* I've never seen him cry before.

"Hello, Ben," she says, extending a hand.

Benjamin ignores her hand. He stares at me.

"It's OK, Ben," I say. "She's a friend." He looks unimpressed. "She'll never lie to you."

"I will never lie to ye, Ben," she says. "I promise."

"She's going to help us get you free from Michael." *I wish he'd say something!*

"Aye," Moira says. "That's right. I dinnae want anything from ye. I just want to help ye. If ye'll let me, I'll be yer friend."

He still makes no move except to stare at her hand. He looks at me. I can tell he's trying to communicate a question to me, but I have no idea what it is. Maybe if I get close enough, he'll whisper to me as he did before.

Cautiously, I move closer to him and suddenly he flies up to hover with his lips near my ear.

"You mean . . . I can *touch* her?" he whispers.

"Touch her?" I start to say. And then understanding dawns on me. I get what he means. "Ben, I'm not your Master. As far as I'm concerned, you have no Master. You are your own man. She's offering to shake hands. It's your choice."

He stays put at my shoulder and stares at me for several seconds, and then he floats slowly over till he's hovering in front of Moira. He lowers himself to the floor. She's still offering her hand and smiling sweetly at him. Tentatively, he reaches out his hand and hesitantly touches hers. He flinches away at the touch, but when nothing happens, he takes her hand and shakes it vigorously. A huge smile splits his face.

"Friends?" Moira asks.

He nods happily.

"Ye know, Ben," she says, "I won't bite. Well, I will nae bite *ye*."

He says nothing.

"Ben," she says, "ye can talk to me."

He shakes his head. He looks . . . not *afraid* . . . but *upset*.

"It's OK," I say. "Go ahead. You can talk to her."

"REALLY?" he says looking at me. It's almost a shout. He turns his beaming face to Moira. "Hello, Moira! I'm Benjamin! I like to be called Ben, though. Will you call me Ben, please? I know you already did call me Ben, but I *like* it. Yes, I would very much like to be your friend. Will you teach me to read? Will you be my mother?"

I'm staring at Ben with my mouth hanging open. Moira is doing the same, but she recovers more quickly than I do.

"Aye, Ben," she says, recovering her smile, "I *will* call ye Ben. I *will* teach ye to read *and* write, if ye like. But I am nae so old as to be yer mother." His smile drains away. "How would ye like it if I were yer big sister?" His smile returns in full force.

"May I give you a hug, Moira?" he asks.

"Aye, laddie, ye may," she says, "but ye'll have to let go of my hand first!"

He lets go of her hand, and she opens her arms wide. He leaps into her arms, and she gives him a huge bear hug. She looks over at me and gives me a questioning look as if to say, "Now what?" I shrug. This is so utterly different from what I've ever experienced or expected of Benjamin. *Ben! I need to think of him as* Ben*! I can't afford to make the mistake of calling him Benjamin again.*

He turns his head and looks at me. "Thank you."

"For what?" I ask.

"For letting me talk. For letting me talk to *her*," he says, motioning with his head toward Moira. "For letting me *touch* her."

What is he saying? "Of course, you can talk to her," I say. "You can talk to anyone you like."

"No, I can't."

"Of course, ye can, laddie," says Moira. She's as perplexed as I am.

"Massa Michael says I can't talk to any woman or girl. Massa Michael says I can't ever touch a woman or a girl."

Massa Michael? That's the first time I've heard him use what I would consider "slave talk." Other than to whisper in my ear, this is the first time I've ever heard him *speak*. Except for the way he says, "Massa Michael," his speech sounds like any other child's his age. *(His apparent age, that is.)*

"You touched Rebecca," I point out.

"I *had* to," he says matter-of-factly.

"I don't understand," I say. "What do you mean, you *had* to?"

"She *told* me to touch her," he says. "I mean, I *wanted* to touch her. She said she'd be my mother." His expression turns sour for a moment, and I see the loathing I'm used to seeing on his face. "Massa Michael told me I have to obey the Teachers. I have to do what Massa says." His expression brightens again as he adds, "But you're my new Master now."

"I'm not your Master, Ben. You belong to nobody . . . nobody but yourself."

"*Please* be my Master, Carl." His voice is so intense. "I have to obey a Master. I *need* a Master. I won't *survive* without a Master. Without a Master, I'll have to return to Massa Michael. I can't Feed without a Master unless I want to *kill*. And *not* killing makes me different. Like you. I want to be like you. You're *nice*."

"I can't be your Master, Ben."

His little body shudders, and I see tears running down his face and onto Moira's shoulder. He starts to pull away from Moira's embrace.

"Oh, laddie, ye dinnae have to go," she says, trying to gently hold on to him. "We'll teach ye how to survive without killing."

"I have to go. I have to obey my Master. I *have* to."

"Nae, laddie. We'll find a way. Ye dinnae have to go."

He seems intent on going.

An idea comes to me. "Ben," I say, "are you hungry?"

He looks at me and nods. "I'm *always* hungry."

"Hold on," I say, and I head for the refrigerator. I hope there's something still edible in there.

I'm in luck. There are two bags of blood left over from the last time Moira was here. I retrieve one and fill a glass from it. I offer the glass to Ben.

Moira releases him, and he floats down to the ground. He takes the glass. He looks at it warily, and he sniffs it. He takes a small sip.

"It's cold and it tastes funny," he says with a worried look on his face.

"It's OK," I say. "We have to keep it cold or it goes bad. The funny taste is from the preservatives in it. It's real human blood. I promise."

He pauses for a second, and then he drains the glass. He smiles. "Is this how *good* vampires Feed?"

Good vampires? He means . . . like Moira and me?

"Aye, laddie," Moira says. "We dinnae kill mortals."

"I want to be good, but I have to obey my Master. If you won't be my Master, then, when Massa Michael dies, Rebecca will be the Master, and I'll have to obey *her*. I don't *want* her to be my Master. I don't want her anymore." He starts to cry again.

Something's not right here. I'm missing something. Either there's something he's not telling us or he's *manipulating* us. I really don't know if I can trust him, poor, twisted creature that he is. For all I know Michael or Rebecca put him up to this. One thing's for sure. I am *not* going to be anyone's Master, much less Ben's. Moira and I exchange looks. It seems to me that she's thinking along similar lines.

On the other hand, he was crying before we arrived. "Ben," I say, "why did you come here tonight?"

The Unwilling

He stands there crying for a minute, and then he seems to collect himself, but he stares at the floor rather than look at us. "I don't like Rebecca anymore," he says in a very stubborn and childlike manner. "She was never nice to me before you ran away. Then she was nice to me for a while. She called me 'love' and 'baby' and said she'd be my mother. She let me hug her. She *told* me to do it, so I could. She gave me kisses. She promised more than that after Massa Michael is dead. She means sex. I don't want sex. I *hate* sex. I'm too little to have sex with a woman. I'll never be any bigger. So I can't have it. I'm sick of wanting things I can't have, so I don't want it. I *hate* sex with Massa Michael. But he's my Master and I can't disobey him. I'm too little to start my own Cult. Nobody would follow me anyway. So I need a new Master."

Now he looks up at me, with tears streaming down his black-as-night face from his bright brown eyes. "Why can't I join *your* Cult? I just want to be a *real boy*." The way he says *real boy* is odd, as if that phrase has some special meaning.

If he's faking this, he's really good at it. Fake or not, the way he's acting tugs at my heart. I make a quick glance at Moira, and I can see that she's crying too. I kneel down to be on Ben's level. I place a hand on his shoulder.

"Ben," I say, fighting tears of my own. "We don't *have* a Cult. We're just a *family*."

Unmistakable hope fills his face. "Massa Michael says the Cult is our family. Can I join your family?"

I look at Moira. She pauses and then nods. I sense caution in that nod, but I also sense a *hunger* in Moira, a terrible need. And it dawns on me that Moira sees in Ben the hope for a *child*.

I look back at Ben. "Of course, you can."

Suddenly he's in my arms crushing me to himself with his vampiric strength. Into my shoulder he says, "Will you be my father?"

"Yes, Ben, I will," I say, "but that means Moira *has* to be your mother, not your big sister." Moira gives me a huge smile. "Is that OK?" I ask Ben.

He pulls back and looks me in the eye, and his huge white-toothed grin splits his little black face. He nods and then turns his head to Moira. She smiles back at him. "May I call you 'Mama'?" he asks.

"Aye, laddie, ye may."

"Thank you, Mama," he says, pulling away from me to stand between us. "Do you want me to suckle at your breast now?"

Moira's eyes go wide and her jaw drops.

"What?" I say, astonished.

He looks confused. "When Rebecca was being my mother, she said I had to suckle at her breast. 'That's what children do,' she said. 'That makes it *official*,' she said."

"Nae, laddie," Moira manages to choke out. "That is only for wee bairns, I mean, for *babies*. And ye are nae a baby."

He nods matter-of-factly. He turns to me. "Do I have to have sex with you, Papa?"

I gag for a moment and then say, "Never. Ever. *No!*"

"Good," he says.

"Laddie," Moira says cautiously, "at yer age, ye cannae have sex or engage in any activity that . . . is anything *like* sex . . . with *anyone. Good* fathers dinnae have sex with their children. *Good* mothers dinnae have sex with their children. Ye should only have sex when ye are married. That's it. And ye will nae ever be old enough to be married. Do ye understand?"

"Yes, Mama," he says, "I understand. It's just like on *The Family Show*. Kids don't have sex. Mama and Papa do, but the kids don't know about it. Mama and Papa don't make the kids watch."

"What are you talking about?" I ask.

"*The Family Show*. That's what *I* call it, because I can't read. I know it probably has another name. It has Mama Walton and Papa Walton. One of the boys is named Ben, like me." He smiles widely. "I like Ben. One of the Chosen who didn't make it (I think Rebecca killed him) left behind a little TV player. It's like a record player only for TV. You put little round silver records in it, and it plays TV. The only ones I have are from *The Family Show* . . ."

"*The Waltons*," I correct incredulously. This is all too much too fast. Before he wouldn't talk at all except to whisper in my ear. Now he won't shut up, and he talks about terrible things like they're nothing.

"Is that what it's called?" he says. Then he nods. "It sounds right. That's where I learned to talk like Ben Walton. Massa Michael won't let me talk except to him, and then I have to talk 'like a niggah,' he says. But I don't want to talk like that. I want to talk like Ben."

That explains the normal-sounding speech patterns, except, of course, for *Massa Michael* and *niggah*.

"I also have *Pinocchio*. It's about a puppet who wants to be a *real boy*. His father doesn't have sex with him. Pinocchio wants to be really good so he can be a *real boy*. In the end, the Blue Fairy turns him into a *real boy*." He looks at Moira. "You look like the Blue Fairy to me, Mama."

"When do you watch TV?" I ask. "I thought Michael kept you locked and chained in your 'cubby' all the time, when you aren't upstairs or with him, that is."

"He does. Massa Michael has a big chain that goes around my ankle. I pull my foot out when he's Sleeping. I have to crush my foot to make it go through the manacle, but it gets fixed after I get it out. I don't Sleep much. I like to watch . . . *The Waltons* and *Pinocchio*."

"Where do you watch your TV?" I ask.

"In Massa Michael's secret tunnel."

I hear Moira gasp.

We're driving south on the interstate. Ben is sitting in the back of the van, happily watching *The Little Mermaid* on the tiny video screen that comes down from the roof of the van. He's using the earphones. We have the volume turned way up so Moira and I can talk. Moira and I are discussing the implications of Ben's defection and of the information he's given us.

Everything has changed, to say the least.

First of all, Ben can no longer be a part of the battle with Michael and Chikah. He knows about Moira, and we can't let the enemy or even my unholy ally, Rebecca, have that information. We aren't sure we can trust him. In fact, we'd be *foolish* to trust him at this point. Even if he's telling the truth, he's too damaged, compromised, and erratic to be reliable. He's been corrupted, abused, and twisted by Michael for more than a century and a half. That's not going to be undone anytime soon, if ever. So, his active participation is out of the question.

Second, we have to find a place for him to stay. He can't stay at my old house, because Rebecca knows about it. We can't risk taking him to Moira's (our) home, because of the trust issue. At least not yet. Moira has a solution, though. She has a "safe house," an alternate home or refuge where she can go in an emergency if she's unable to go home. After some discussion at my old house, we agreed to pack up a bunch of Disney and other family-friendly DVDs, children's books, and toys (that I hadn't yet given to Deseret Industries) and take him there so he can wait out the battle in safety. We're on our way to the safe house now.

Third, Ben's failure to return to Michael's "temple" will cause an uproar there. Michael will be *furious*. Ben has left before for a few hours, but he has always returned before sunrise. And he has always been severely punished for these excursions if they're discovered. More importantly, *Rebecca* will know something is going on. She has already accused me of trying to take Ben from her. According to Ben, Rebecca started treating him like garbage again a few days ago. That's why he has been coming to my house (my old house) for the past two nights: he was hoping to find me there. That's why we're relocating him before Rebecca comes looking. We can't bring ourselves to talk about the possibility that one or both of us might not be coming back to get him.

Fourth, and most importantly, the information about the tunnel opens the possibility of a sneak attack during the *day*. This seems to be the ideal solution. There'd be only one Chosen in the mansion, reducing the possibility of mortal casualties down to one or zero.

Ben's casual revelation about the tunnel knocked the wind out of me. "Ben," I asked when I got my breath back, "how do you know where the tunnel is?"

He gave me a puzzled look. "Massa Michael makes me dispose of the bodies down there."

"Bodies?" Moira asked.

"What bodies, Ben?" I tried to keep the shock I felt out of my voice.

"The bodies of the Chosen who don't make it." His tone was casual as if he were describing something boring rather than murder. "Sometimes Chikah likes to Hunt. Massa Michael doesn't approve. He tells her not to Hunt, but he doesn't really mean it. If he really meant it, she wouldn't do it. Massa Michael doesn't want bodies left for the police to find. So, Chikah brings the prey back to the temple and plays with it and then she kills it. Then I have to put the bodies back in the cave."

"What cave?" I asked.

"The tunnel isn't all a tunnel. It's mostly a big cave. There are a lot of bottles down in there."

"Sounds like it used to be a bootlegger's place," I said.

"Yeah, Massa Michael said something like that. I don't know what it means."

"It means alcohol, laddie," Moira explained.

"So I put the bodies down there with the bottles. There are lights down there. Most of the bulbs don't work anymore, but some of the lights have sockets to plug in an electrical cord, so I plug in my TV player and I watch The Waltons and Pinocchio. It doesn't smell too bad down there if the bodies aren't fresh.

"I'm not supposed to tell anybody where the tunnel is. Not even Chikah and Rebecca. I'm not supposed to tell them that I know where it is. But I can tell you because you're my new Master."

"Ben," I started to say.

"I know," he interrupted. "You're not my Master, but you're my father now and it's kinda the same thing. If I don't obey you, I have to obey Massa Michael."

"Ben," I said, "can you do me a favor? Stop calling him 'Massa Michael.' Just call him 'Michael.'"

"What's a favor?" he asked.

"A favor is something I ask you to do, but you don't have to do if you don't want to," I explained.

"I have to do what you say, Papa." He was emphatic, simply stating a fact.

"OK, Ben," I said. "Let's make a deal: If I'm going to be your 'Papa,' you should obey me, but you should do it because you want to obey me, not because you have to obey me."

"I want to obey you and not Massa Micha . . . Michael."

I knew that wasn't exactly what I meant, but it was going to have to be enough for the moment.

"OK, then here's the deal. If I tell you to do something, you do it. If I ask you to do something, you get to choose to do it. OK? The same goes for Moira. If she tells you to do something, do it. If she asks you to do something, it's your choice. Do you understand?"

He looked perplexed. "I have a choice?"

"Aye, laddie, ye do," Moira said cheerfully.

"Will you cut off my foot or something if I choose not to do what you ask?"

"No way." I suppressed the shudder at the memory of Ben's punishment at Michael's hand. "But I would be disappointed."

"And then you'd cut off my foot?"

"No way. I won't cut off anything. That would be horrible. It's sick and wrong to do that even if it does grow back or you can reattach it. No, I would be disappointed. That's all."

"So what would you do? Not allow me to Feed for a month?"

"Nae!" cried Moira. "Maybe, we might say no TV for the rest of the night or take away a favorite toy for an hour."

"I don't like toys!" He was visibly upset. "They hurt."

"Toys dinnae hurt," Moira said without understanding.

I understood only too well. "He means the kind of 'toys' that Michael uses," I explained to her, disgusted at the very thought of what that monster had done to this boy. To Ben I said, "Real toys are for children and they are for fun, not for sex. You don't have to worry about sex anymore, OK?"

His face brightened. "OK, Papa."

"Hold on a second." A thought occurred to me. I jumped up and ran down the stairs to the basement crawlspace. After a short time, I returned.

"Ben," I said as I placed a teddy bear in his hands, "this belonged to my daughter. It's yours now."

He gazed at the toy in wonder. "REALLY? I can have this? To keep? Like the things in Geppetto's house?"

I laughed. Moira laughed her musical laugh. Then Ben laughed too. It was rough, as if he'd never laughed before. I supposed he probably hadn't.

"Yes, Ben," I said, "it's yours to keep."

He hugged the bear to his chest gently. He cradled it in his arms and rocked it like a baby. He began to sing to it. In a soft, clear child's voice, he sang a song I recognized: "When you wish upon a star . . ." It was hard to hold back the tears as I watched that ancient, abused child treating a stuffed toy with more tenderness than he'd probably known in his entire unnaturally long life.

Moira didn't hold back the tears. Quickly she was on her knees holding Ben in her arms as she sobbed unabashedly at Ben's obvious joy. That was probably the first time in his life he had known anything like happiness.

Soon I joined them. Moira and I cried and hugged Ben. Ben smiled and kissed his bear and continued to sing to it. "When your heart is in your dreams . . ."

Along the way to Moira's safe house, we had to make a stop a few blocks away from Michael's mansion so Ben could show us the exit from the tunnel. He had explored to the end of the tunnel, but he couldn't describe the aboveground location well enough for us to find it without his help. The *entrance* from the tunnel into the mansion is a hidden door in the wall of Ben's "cubby." This means that I could get into Michael's room (without alerting whoever is on guard duty) and put a sword into Michael's heart while he's Sleeping. Just like Teancum did to Amalickiah in the Book of Mormon. He sneaked into the enemy camp and put a spear through the heart of King Amalickiah. Hopefully, I won't end up like Teancum, though. He tried it again with Amalickiah's brother and successor, King Ammoron, and, although Teancum killed him, Ammoron awoke his guards, and Teancum was caught and slain while he tried to escape. Teancum was angry and he went in alone. But I'll have Moira to watch my back.

That would leave only Chikah to deal with. Depending on who's on guard duty, she might be Sleeping too. If not, Moira and I should be able to handle her together.

Rebecca would, of course, feel betrayed, but I will have *honored* our treaty. And the four Chosen will not be Converted. And we will save the lives of their Offerings.

"Let Rebecca feel betrayed," I say. "With the loss of Ben, she'll feel betrayed anyway. But she'll have what she wants. She'll be the new Master. She'll have the whole Cult to herself. She'll have more than enough of a food supply and plenty of lovers to last her for a long time. Of course, she'll immediately start working on creating new Chosen to Convert, but that will buy us time to figure out how to deal with her and finally get justice for Julie. I'll have honored my word, whether Rebecca recognizes that or not. After that, 'Hitler' will be dead, the alliance will be ended, and it will be time to deal with 'Stalin.'"

"Ye do know that she's planning some kind of betrayal, do ye nae?" Moira points out. "Ben told ye before that she was lying to ye."

"Ben," I asked as we selected DVDs to take with us to the safe house, "You told me before that Rebecca was lying to me. What was she lying about?"

"She told me she plans to enslave you as soon as Massa . . . I mean . . . Michael is dead." From the tone of his voice, he could have been talking about the weather. "She said that she's not sure it'll work with you being Unwilling. But she said that if you don't obey her, she's going to behead you."

"What makes her think I'd ever obey her?" I ask.

"She would be the new Master then. You have to obey the Master."

Good luck with that, lady, *I thought.*

"Maybe you don't have to obey her," he said. "You're different. And you have your own family, so maybe you are your own Master."

"Yes," I say, "but she doesn't know about you, my love." I reach over and squeeze Moira's hand. "It's not *Rebecca* I'm worried about, anyway. You know what I mean?"

"Aye, this may all be a trap. Ben may have been sent by Michael, even if Ben doesn't know it. This may all be a ruse to get ye into that tunnel and ambush ye."

"And *Michael* doesn't know about you, *either.*" I give her hand another squeeze.

We drive in silence for a while. I can hear the quiet sound of Sebastian's voice. He's singing "Kiss de Girl." I lean over and kiss Moira quickly on the cheek.

"'Twould break my heart," she says, "if Ben betrays us. Ye know that I've already started to fall in love with him."

"I know just how you feel," I say as I glance in the rearview mirror. Ben is hugging his teddy bear in one arm and a ball that used to belong to my Joseph in the other. His expression is one of complete rapture as he watches Ariel, Eric, and Sebastian and listens to the music.

But, if Ben betrays us, our hearts will be the *least* of our worries.

Chapter 24

Sunday afternoon is bright and sunny. It's *perfect* for our *new* battle plan. My original battle plan called for Rebecca to let me into the mansion tonight around midnight, just before the Conversion Ritual is scheduled to begin. (I would've sneaked Moira in later through a window.) Entering via Michael's secret tunnel to conduct a surprise attack during the *day* is a *much* better plan.

The exit from the tunnel is located in the root cellar (*yes, the* root *cellar*) of a small, modest, and ancient house in an otherwise wealthy neighborhood a few blocks from the mansion. The house appears to be inhabited: the lawn is mowed, the paint isn't peeling, and there are no broken windows. Ben has told me that Michael hasn't personally ventured into the tunnel in over a decade. To Michael, the tunnel is an emergency refuge or escape route. To Ben, it's a sanctuary, a place to hide his few belongings, chiefly his precious DVD player and DVDs.

Ben was in Moira's safe house happily watching "Dumbo" when Moira and I left around noon. Since it's sunny outside, Ben is effectively trapped there until sunset. That means we don't have to worry about him following us or betraying us. The house has no phone, and Ben doesn't have a cell phone, so he's completely cut off. We can put him out of our minds for a while.

We're standing outside the root cellar, our van parked nearby. We're dressed in protective clothing with our weapons concealed underneath our long coats. (I still have to wear the ridiculous Stetson over my hoodie.) We have so much sunscreen on every inch of skin that could possibly be at risk of exposure that even a *mortal* could smell the lotion a dozen feet away. Still, we don't dare risk staying outside very long.

There's no lock on the root cellar door. I find that surprising until we try to open the door and realize it's locked on the inside. Of course: this is an *exit*. It's meant to be opened only from the inside.

I'm about to break the doors open when Moira grabs my arm. She pulls her sword out and says, "Let's test yer tactile telekinesis theory. If ye are correct, I should be able to slice between the doors and cut cleanly through any lock or chain on the other side." She inserts her sword between the doors and slices downward. I can hear the sound of a heavy metal chain falling.

"Nice work," I say.

She opens the doors, revealing wooden stairs leading into the safety of darkness. We quickly move down the stairs, avoiding the remains of the chain piled there. I close the doors leaving only a sliver of sunlight. Even that small light is enough to reveal our surroundings to our Seed-enhanced vision.

We look about and quickly take in the scene. The floor is dirt. There are empty racks with shelves all around the walls. All the shelves are covered with decades of dust, but one rack has unmistakable handprints. Small handprints. Ben-sized handprints. That has to be the one which hides the entrance.

I hear a clattering above, as of someone running.

"We're about to have company," I whisper to Moira. I point to a particularly dark corner on the back wall, and she quickly moves into it. I take the other far corner, and we both fade into the blackness.

In moments, the door is thrown open, letting in a large rectangle of lethal sunlight. The direct light reaches only a few feet into the cellar. It's partially obscured by the silhouette of a man with what appears to be an AK-47 assault rifle. There's no shout or cry as the man slowly and cautiously descends the stairs. He moves the barrel of the full automatic submachine gun from side to side.

Once he reaches the floor of the cellar, he stands still, listening. I'm sure he can't see us and he can't hear us, but still he doesn't move.

"I know you're in here," he says, his voice tense, nervous. "I can *smell* you."

The sunscreen.

Even if he empties the gun into either of us, it won't kill us, but, unlike it's portrayed on television or in the movies, automatic weapon fire is very loud. It would attract unwanted attention *and* the rapid muzzle flashes would light up the whole room, exposing both of us. So anything that causes him to fire is something I'd rather avoid.

As I'm trying to figure out how to disarm him safely, how to approach him from an angle where he won't see me coming, it suddenly occurs to me: *stop thinking in two dimensions!* With that thought, I lift silently in the air, keeping just far enough away from the wall so that my coat and hat don't rustle against it. Once I reach the low ceiling, I rotate my body forward until I'm parallel to the ceiling. I move silently forward until I'm hovering in the darkness above him.

I'm about to reach down and pull the gun from his hands, when, to my horror, my hat slides off my head. I snatch it before it can hit him, but he hears the noise and looks up. Before he can even register the sight of me hovering above him, holding my ridiculous hat, Moira emerges from her corner and snatches the weapon from his hands. I drop the hat and lift him into the air, covering his mouth to stifle his scream.

And scream he does. He shrieks against my hand. He thrashes at the unseen force (me) that's holding him off the floor. I see Moira standing below me staring pointedly at his face. So I force his head down until he has to be looking right at her. Then she says commandingly, "Be still. Cease yer strugglin'." He goes limp. We both settle to the ground *after* I maneuver to avoid the patch of sunlight.

I release him, and he stands still. Moira has him firmly in her thrall.

"Go and close the doors and return to me," she says.

He turns and climbs the stairs. I get my first good look at him. He appears to be in his late twenties. There's not an evil air to him, not really an evil *smell* to him. We'd have sensed his approach much sooner if he were truly corrupt.

He goes outside and vanishes from view. Panic seizes me until I realize he can't reach the doors from inside while they're sitting open. First one door closes and then he reappears, pulling the second door behind him. He descends the stairs and stops to stand in front of Moira.

Even in the feeble light refracted from the remaining sliver of sunlight, her eyes seem to blaze with green fire.

"What's yer name?" she demands.

"Harry Sanders," comes the reply. He sounds eager to please her.

"What're ye doing here, Harry?"

"I live here. I guard this place."

"And why do ye guard this place?"

"Michael Beaumont pays me to guard this place from sunrise to sunset."

"How long have ye been guarding this place for Michael?"

"About two years."

"Do ye guard it alone?"

"I do now. Tom used to help me, but he died. He slipped on the ice this last winter, broke his neck. Since then, I've been alone. I haven't told nobody, 'cause now I get his pay too."

"Have you ever met Michael Beaumont?" I ask.

He ignores me.

"Answer his questions as ye would my own, Harry," Moira says.

"No. Tom told me about the job. Tax-free. Just guard this place sunrise to sunset. Don't ask no questions. Just take the money."

"Who pays you?" I ask.

"Michael Beaumont."

"He brings you the money?" *I thought he said he's never met Michael.*

"No, it comes in the mail every month. Cash."

"Were ye ready to kill us for coming here?" Moira asks.

"No. I never shot nobody, except in Afghanistan. It was just easy money. I never thought I'd actually have to shoot somebody. Nobody ever came here before."

Moira considers this for a moment. "Ye will leave this place, Harry. After today, ye will receive nae more money from Michael Beaumont. Go find another place to live. Find an honest job. And ye will *forget* we ever came here," Moira commands. "Do ye understand, Harry?"

"Yes, ma'am."

"Now, go. Close the doors behind ye."

He turns, climbs the stairs, opens one of the doors, and is gone, closing the door behind himself. The only reminder of his ever having been here is the assault rifle lying in the dirt.

"Well, that's that," she says.

I point toward the rack with the handprints. "Let's go."

"After ye, laddie."

The rack pulls away from the wall easily. It pivots on a hinge at one side. There's a dark void beyond, like a gateway leading to the Pit of Hell.

The rack has a handle on the other side so we can pull it closed behind us. We enter into the darkness and shut the "door" on the root cellar.

The blackness is absolute. Even with our Seed-enhanced sight, we can make out nothing. We pull penlights out of our pockets and survey our surroundings.

We're in a tunnel shored up with ancient planks of dry wood. The tunnel slopes gently down into deeper darkness. There's a string of light bulbs spaced at odd intervals. I find a switch, connected to the wires, near the entrance. Just in case someone is waiting for us in the tunnel, we aren't going to turn the lights on. Many of the bulbs are broken or discolored anyway.

It's time to ditch the protective clothing. It would only get in the way from this point on. We leave hats, gloves, hoodie, cloak, duster and sunglasses by the entrance and take our weapons and flashlights with us. Moira has her sword. I have Donald's sword and the dirk that belonged to Moira's father.

I give her a long, tender kiss. *I hope it's not our last in this life.* I recall Moira's words from one of our many discussions about the prophecy and the battle with Michael.

"If the prophecy says we're going to slay Lilith," Moira said to me, "does that nae mean that we'll both survive the battle with Michael?"

"What it says, my love," I replied gently, "is we will kill Lilith 'if we are valiant' in the Lord's service. That's a big 'if.' There are so many ways we could fall if we're not careful. Maybe one of us will give in to temptation and kill a mortal. Maybe we're not supposed to fight Michael and Chikah at all. I don't know. Nothing is certain beyond the fact that we'll both die if we do kill Lilith, but that is what we're being asked to do."

"Aye, but, if we're valiant, we will see our 'Redeemer's face in the resurrection of the just.' We'll simply have to live for that."

Live for the day when we will both die, *I thought to myself, but I didn't say so to Moira.*

We proceed down the tunnel into the Stygian blackness. The beams from the flashlights seem, even to our eyes, to penetrate only a few yards ahead.

Eventually the man-made tunnel gives way to a natural cave with a low ceiling. The string of lights continues, and although the cavern has other branches, we follow the wires. We proceed some distance in silence until the cave suddenly widens and we can no longer see the wall to our left. There's a foul odor emanating from the void. It's a stench so *vile* it makes me want to vomit, but I can't quite identify it.

Gesturing to Moira to stay where she is, I venture off toward the smell. It isn't just morbid curiosity that drives me forward. I know what I expect to find. No, I feel the need to corroborate Ben's story as much as possible. I *want* to believe him so *badly*. I walk about twenty or thirty yards, and then a sweep of my flashlight briefly illuminates something shiny on the floor. I aim the beam at the object, a broken glass bottle. I proceed a little farther until I find a wooden box. Inside are several bottles. I pull one out and see that it contains a clear liquid. This must be some of the bootlegger whiskey.

Whiskey doesn't account for the smell, though.

And there's also a low noise I can't identify.

A little farther and I find many more crates, most of them filled with bottles of booze. The stench is growing stronger the farther I go. It's getting hard to breathe. I don't know how much more of this I can take.

There!

On the floor is something small. It's a ladies high-heeled shoe. Another couple of yards and the floor of the cave slopes down dramatically, and the stench is suddenly overwhelming. I shine the beam down the incline and . . .

There's a face staring back at me out of the blackness below. No, *staring* isn't quite right. There are no eyes. Not much flesh, either.

I move closer to the corpse, and soon I'm standing at the edge of a charnel pit. There must be hundreds of bodies down here in various states of decomposition.

And then I really do see *eyes*, hundreds of pairs of tiny eyes. *Rats.* They're living off the flesh of the Cult's victims. The stench is not so much from rotting or desiccated human flesh; it's from the rats. It's the smell of decades' worth of their waste. And the noise is caused by their constant activity in and around the corpses.

The rats don't seem particularly afraid of me. Is it their sheer numbers or Ben's repeated visits to this awful place? I think of that wretched immortal child repeatedly carrying corpses to this horrible pit, and I just want to weep.

Get control, Morgan! Time to get back to the task at hand. I turn my back on the vermin and their grisly nest and head quickly toward Moira.

Slowly the stench lessens, and I feel less nauseated.

Something else to my right reflects the light of the flashlight and catches my eye. Hidden between two crates of liquor is a small, flat, metallic object. It's Ben's precious DVD player. And next to it is his small treasure of DVDs. *The Waltons: The Complete Third Season* and *Pinocchio.* I need to remember to retrieve these for him, when this horrible business is finished.

Every detail Ben gave us has checked out. Logically, I know that the most convincing lies contain all or part of the truth, but, in my heart, I believe him without reserve.

I continue back in Moira's direction.

I haven't gone far before . . .

Something's wrong.

There's too much light up ahead and it's the wrong color to be coming from Moira's flashlight.

I stop and listen, trying to filter out the distant noise of the rats. I can distinctly hear two sets of breathing: one rapid, one relaxed. There's someone else up there.

Moira's in trouble!

Focus, Morgan! Keep it together. If Moira's in trouble, you need to stay in control!

I switch off the flashlight and pocket it. I hold my sword and dirk at the ready. I lift off the ground so my footfalls won't give me away, and then I slowly move up toward the light.

As I approach the light, I realize it's coming from the sporadic bulbs in the overhead string of lights. I can make out the far wall of the cave. I don't see Moira, but I see shadows being cast from off to the left, around a bend in the wall. I can't make out much from the shadows themselves, but I know they must be coming from Moira and . . . someone else.

There's no way for me to approach unobserved, so I touch down and cautiously move past the bend in the wall and into the light.

The sight that confronts me fills me with horror.

Michael is standing in front of a wooden door that appears to be the end of the tunnel. Moira is kneeling in front of him with her head bowed, her sword on the rocky floor of the cave. Michael is holding his saber poised above her neck. *Why is she just kneeling there?*

"Carl, isn't it?" Michael says, his voice a languid Southern drawl. "I remember you. You never completed your trainin'. You ran away, naughty boy. You don't know what you gave up.

"Now," he continues, "what have you done with my nigger boy? My Benjamin? Hmm? The fact that *you* are here, in this place, and Benjamin is *not* here tells me that you have my nigger boy. Give him back to me and I *may* let this pretty little thing live. You have three seconds." His tone is calm, almost leisurely.

The Unwilling

Think fast, Morgan! Tell him the truth and he'll kill Moira and Ben. Lie to him and you may buy a few seconds. "I killed the little freak," I say. "He touched my woman." I'm not a good or experienced liar, but I need him to *believe* this lie. At least for the moment, I do.

"I see," he says. "Why are you here, invadin' my temple, with sword in hand?"

"Rebecca. She killed my sister."

"Ah, well. Your sister. Would that be Julie? Yes, I *do* see a family resemblance. I *do* sympathize. I really do sympathize. I will *deal* with Rebecca myself. As for you and your *woman*, you may leave."

What's he doing?

He withdraws his sword and offers his hand to Moira. "I'm sorry for the misunderstandin', my dear. Please, accept my most sincere apologies."

Moira rises to her feet and turns to look at him. He steps past her and bends down to retrieve her sword. Then he extends Moira's sword toward her, hilt first. She takes it from him and holds it in front of her.

Michael gestures toward me. Moira turns and walks in my direction. Her face is veiled in shadow, but her eyes are burning.

What's he up to? I stare at Michael, trying to read his face.

As soon as Moira is in reach, I extend a hand toward her. I glance at her, but I still can't see her face.

"Now, my dear," Michael says casually, "slay him."

I see Moira's sword flash, and I feel a searing pain as she thrusts it into my heart.

Chapter 25

Something is chewing on my face.

Something is chewing on my fingers.

I feel rats scurrying all over my body.

In panic, I thrash about trying to dislodge the rats from my face and hands. *Get off me!* I can't seem to find any purchase! I can't get to my feet! I can't roll over! Whatever I touch oozes or slips or crumbles from my grasp or away from my feet. The smell is overwhelming.

I can't see *anything!*

I'm in the pit with all the corpses! *I've got to get out of here!* I can't stand up!

First and foremost, fly the airplane, Col. Daggett says in my head.

Fly!

I fly up out of the pit so fast that I hit the rocky ceiling before I think to stop myself.

The impact stuns me for a moment, but I still manage to stay aloft. I keep myself pressed against the ceiling. At least here, I'm free of the rats.

Moira killed *me! She put a sword through my heart! Why? Nothing makes sense!*

I need to get to safer ground, away from the rats, away from the stench. I need to get to where I can think clearly.

Which way leads back to the tunnel? I don't know. Right now, it doesn't matter. I just need to get away from the smell. *Pick a direction!* I move in the direction toward which my head is pointing. *That's as good as any.* I grope my way along the ceiling to avoid the sharper rocks. I reach what feels like a wall. I turn and head along the edge of it.

The smell is easing. My brain is clearing a little.

What happened? Why did Moira stab me? Why was she cooperating with Michael? Has she been working with him all along?

No, I can't believe that!

The wall abruptly ends and I'm touching open ceiling again. I continue more or less in the same direction until my hand brushes against a wire. I've reached the string of lights in the main tunnel! That means the exit and the root cellar is off to my right, and the entrance and Ben's cubby is off to my left. It should be safe to land here.

I settle to the floor of the tunnel and just sit for a moment. I need to assess the situation.

The itching in my face and hands is gone. That means I must be completely healed now. I feel my chest. My shirt has a huge wet hole in it, but my chest and heart are restored.

I need weapons. But how am I going to find something in the dark? I have no idea where my flashlight is.

Think, Morgan! Use what you've got!

I can't see anything. Swords don't make noise, so I can't locate them with my ears. I could feel around blindly in the dark for hours and not find anything useful. What's left?

Smell.

The well-oiled steel has a distinct *smell*.

Block out the smell of the rats and the corpses.

There! I can smell the steel off to my left. I crawl along the floor of the cave toward the scent of the steel. Before long, my hand touches cold metal. It's the dirk. I can smell my own blood on Moira's hanger, so I locate that next. She must have abandoned it. It takes me only a minute or so to locate my own sword. I stand and gingerly make my way on foot back to the main tunnel.

I sit down and consider my situation.

I'm armed again. I'm effectively blind down here, but I know the general direction of the tunnel entrance. I know where the exit is.

Attack or retreat?

No question: attack.

Michael thinks I'm dead. *Why?* Obviously, Moira's sword wasn't in my heart long enough to actually *kill* me. *Moira* killed *me!* Michael's words come back to me in a flash:

"Carl, isn't it? I remember you. You never completed your trainin'. You ran away, naughty boy. You don't know what you gave up."

Michael thinks I'm still *mortal!* Couldn't he smell the difference? Maybe not, with the stench in this foul tunnel. I replay the whole incident in my head. If Michael thinks I'm not a vampire, then Moira's betrayal may actually have been something else. Why was she cooperating with Michael? Persuasion doesn't work on vampires.

And then I remember Ben repeating over and over that he *had to obey the Master.* He practically *begged* me to be his *Master.* He said that you *have to obey the Master.*

Is that part of being a vampire? Was there something in that Oath I repeated to Rebecca during the Ritual about obeying *the Master?* Yes, I think there was. Moira became a vampire willingly. She willingly promised to obey. She willingly swore to "submit freely to the will of Lilith or any of her Masters." That was the wording of the oath. Moira has never lived in a Cult. Maybe she didn't have any idea that she might be forced to obey the Master of a Cult.

Since Michael thinks I'm not a vampire, Moira may have been trying desperately to save my life! She dealt me a blow that would be instantly fatal to a *mortal,* but withdrew the sword soon enough to allow a *vampire* to heal.

Moira is in the clutches of that monster and she needs my help.

And I think I know how to free her.

In an instant, I'm on my feet and moving in the direction of the entrance. I thrust Moira's sword into my belt as I go. She's going to need it.

Moira, I'm coming, my love! Hold on!

Despite my fear for my beloved Moira, I don't want to alert anyone to my approach, so I still need to proceed quietly. It doesn't take me long, however, to find the entrance. It feels like a wooden door, but I can't find a handle or latch or release. There's a pair of hinges on the right side, so, the latch has to be on the left. *Found it!* I can feel a catch on the bottom edge of the lower left-hand corner. I check at the top for a corresponding catch on the upper edge of the upper corner. Yep! One there, too!

With both catches released, slowly, cautiously, I start to open the door. I don't want it to creak on its hinges. As soon as I have it open a few degrees, I can see some dim light coming from the other side. I suspect it's from Ben's peephole, the one that Michael forced him to use to observe sexual activities in the bedroom.

I listen hard for any sound of activity beyond the cubby. There's the muffled sound of someone breathing rapidly and one very rapid heartbeat. Nothing else. I'd bet anything (and I'm betting my *life*) that it's Moira.

I decide to risk opening the door a little faster. It makes no sound. I'll bet that Ben kept it well oiled for when he'd sneak out. It's open wide enough for me to enter now. I slip inside.

As I'm slowly closing the door behind myself, I look around in the dim light from the peephole. I'm standing in a closet amid what looks like the remains of a straw mattress. A *filthy* straw mattress, by the smell. It looks as if Michael took out some of his fury at Ben's failure to return on the only possession he thought the miserable boy owned. There's a heavy iron chain and manacle bolted to the floor. On the opposite wall is a simple sliding, wooden closet door with a peephole in the very center. Low enough for a child.

I finally pull the door (the one through which I entered this hell-hole) closed, but I don't latch it. I might need to retreat quickly, and I don't want to spend time messing with the latches.

I look through the peephole, and what I see makes my blood boil. Moira is lying on a huge bed, completely naked. She's immobile except for her face which is twisted in a contorting mask of abject horror. She appears to be struggling with all her might against . . . something. Is it the force of the Master's command that binds her? Moira's body has to obey, but her mind is her own?

I'm about to open the latch and enter when I hear the door to the bedroom. Someone is coming in. I can't see who it is because the view from the peephole doesn't encompass the whole of the huge, opulent bedroom.

It's Chika.

"Michael says you're the new *Benjamin*," she says in her harsh Japanese accent. "You're to take his place. I'm going to *enjoy* abusing you, you pretty little thing." She comes to the side of the bed. She has her sword.

"What were you *thinking* anyway, coming here to challenge Michael in his den with no Master to protect you? And with a *mortal* in tow? Didn't you know that you must serve a Master? If you don't, you are subject to *any* Master."

She leers at Moira. "You've never had one, a Master, that is, have you, pretty thing?"

Moira says nothing.

"Anyway, like I told you," Chikah continues, "you're to be the new Benjamin around here. Michael is going to . . . be a while. He's *really angry.*" She says this last with relish. She's enjoying Moira's distress. She leans in to whisper to Moira, but I can hear her perfectly. "He's taking out his anger on *Rebecca* right now. He'll probably spend a few hours with her and her . . . punishment, but then he'll be coming for *you*. He says he plans to treat you . . . just . . . like . . . Benjamin. I truly hope you *enjoy* that sort of thing. Actually, I hope you *don't* enjoy it."

She waves the sword in small patterns in the air.

"In the meantime, I'm going to have a little fun of my own. I promise not to cut *off* anything . . . at least nothing that won't grow back before Michael is ready for you."

Chikah leans in close to Moira and whispers, "By the way, you have permission to *scream* if you like."

Moira begins to scream. She howls. The sound is ear-piercing and heart-rending.

Chikah slices open Moira's stomach with a flick of her sword.

I burst through the closet door, sword and dirk in hand.

Chikah looks up in shock. For a second, she freezes as I charge, flying across the huge room, holding my sword like a lance.

She freezes, but the opening doesn't last long enough. She leaps aside at the last moment, and all I manage to impale is the far wall.

I wrench my blade free and whirl about to face her. She has recovered from the surprise of my attack and is standing at the foot of the bed, her sword ready, gripped in both hands.

I have to get her out of here, away from Moira.

She smiles at me and swings her blade in a pattern that lets me know I'm probably outmatched here.

She leaps at me, and I move the dirk to parry, but her thrust is only a feint. And it wasn't directed at me. Her blade slices into Moira's inner thigh. Blood sprays everywhere. She's trying to enrage me, get me to fight angry. *Never fight angry, laddie,* Moira taught me.

Suddenly, Moira stops screaming. The silence catches Chikah off guard. She glances at Moira.

It's an opening.

I fly across the room and impale Chikah through her gut. I keep on flying, carrying Chikah, impaled on my sword, through the ruined closet door. We push past the secret panel at the back and into the darkness beyond.

I try to bring the dirk around to go for her throat or her heart, but she has held on to her own sword, and I'm forced to parry. With her free hand, she shoves against me and pulls free of my sword.

In the light from the ruined entrance, I can see her well enough in the darkness. She takes a defensive stance and places both hands on the handle of her sword.

But she's still healing from the gaping wound in her gut. Now's the time to press my advantage.

I land in front of her and I attack. I feint with my broadsword and slice upward with my dirk. I catch her on the chest and she snarls in fury.

And she gives ground.

I press forward.

She's good. Probably a lot better than I am, but as long as I can inflict a cut or a thrust and keep her distracted with pain and the itch of healing, I can keep moving her backward, farther away from Moira.

She gets in a good hack at my left thigh, and I nearly go down, but I counter with another thrust into her hip.

On and on we fight. I manage to move her back a little at a time. Soon, we're in the open area of the cave. I keep trying to move her back toward the charnel pit, but this is a mistake. The open area gives her more room to maneuver her blade. She still gives ground, but I'm landing fewer and fewer blows. Soon she'll be more healed than wounded, and I will have lost all the advantage.

The light is becoming dimmer and dimmer as we move farther down the slope toward the pit.

I fail to parry one of her slashes, and her sword bites deep into my side, slicing through a couple of ribs.

She laughs, low and cruel in her throat, and she takes an advancing step toward me, her blade swinging in a killing stroke, when she *stumbles*. She stumbles on the discarded high-heeled shoe I discovered earlier. She loses her footing and falls backward.

I thrust at her with my sword as she falls, her legs going up in the air. My blade goes into her lower leg and slices clean through. Her foot and ankle fall to the floor.

She screams in rage and pain, and her wings explode into view as she takes to the air in the low-roofed cavern, righting herself in the process.

Time for a little aerial "Highland Charge."

I roar at her and take to the air myself. She sees me coming at her from the air, and her eyes go wide at the sight of me flying toward her with no wings. She brings her blade around too slowly, and I parry it with my dirk. My broadsword slices through her neck.

Her wings vanish as her headless corpse crumples to the floor. Her head falls to the ground and rolls down the slope toward the pit. As it rolls, I catch glimpses of a distinct look of horror on her face.

The Seed will probably keep her head alive for a minute or so.

I hope the last thing she sees is the rotting cadavers before the rats take her eyes.

I wheel in the air under the cavern roof and fly toward Moira.

By the time I reach her, the itching of my wounds has ceased.

She's where I left her, still lying naked on the blood-soaked bed. Her eyes follow me as I come flying to her side, but she says nothing.

Her leg is healed. *Of course it's healed!* The bleeding has stopped.

But she still can't move.

"I'm here, my love," I say as I bend down to lift her off the bed. I can get my arms under her, but I can't *lift* her. I strain, but I can't move her.

"Why can't I pick you up?" I say, panic filling my voice. *Get control, Morgan!*

This isn't working. I stop trying to lift her.

"OK. I can't lift you. Let's think about this. You've . . . been *commanded* to stay on the bed and not move, right? You're essentially 'flying' downward into the bed to keep me from lifting you up, right? Blink once for yes, twice for no."

She blinks once. Her eyes fill with tears, which stream down both sides of her head.

I kneel beside her on the bed, and I caress her face. "Listen to me, Moira," I say tenderly. "I think I know how to beat this thing.

"We had wings because we were *told* we had wings. You couldn't touch the temple because you *thought* you were unholy. You have to obey one of Lilith's Masters because you *think* you do. But it's not true. You don't have to obey Michael. Please, Moira, get up."

She doesn't move at all except that her face seems to contort in a useless anguish of effort.

"I know you swore the Oath willingly. I know you *surrendered* your right to choose, your *agency* when you did, but that was before you were baptized, before you were endowed and sealed to me. That was before you were *redeemed*. No oath you made before can bind you now. No curse can hold you. There's no possible way Lilith or even *Lucifer* himself is more powerful than *God*. The Savior overcame *death*. He paid for our sins. All we have to do is to *accept* the Atonement and follow Him. 'With God, *nothing* is impossible.'"

And, with that, she's in my arms and hugging me and kissing me and sobbing all at the same time.

"Oh, Carl," she says between wracking sobs. "I'm so sorry! So very, very sorry! 'Twas all I could think of to keep ye *alive*! He thinks ye're *mortal*!"

"I know, my love," I say softly, soothingly. "I know. And it worked. I'm here. Chikah's dead. We're going to be OK."

She pulls back suddenly and looks me in the face. "Ye . . . killed . . . Chikah?"

"Yeah, but *you* helped me. When you stopped screaming, my love, it distracted her and gave me my first opening."

She nods. "'Twas the only weapon I had," she says quietly.

I kiss her. "I know. And you saved me with it, dearest, sweetest Moira."

I kiss her again, long and tenderly. Then I pull away.

"You need to get dressed, sweetie," I say with a grin. "I love seeing you this way, but we've got *work* to do!"

"Aye," she says grimly, wiping away her tears. "One down. One to go."

Chapter 26

*S*ix *hours?*" I say in disbelief. "I was out for *six hours?*"

"Aye, laddie," Moira says, indicating my watch. "I suspect it had more to do with the shock of my 'killing' ye than it did with the actual injury. I was so very worried that I might have *succeeded* in killing ye or that ye might have abandoned me because of my 'betrayal.'"

"Never, my love," I say emphatically. "Never."

In my mind, I picture Moira lying here, unable to move or speak, waiting to be raped by Michael for *six hours*. I shudder at the thought.

"What is it, Carl?" she asks.

"I'm so sorry you had to go through that. I'm sorry you had to wait so *long*, thinking I might not be coming."

She nods and kisses me lightly, but doesn't say anything. After a moment, she says, "So what's the plan?"

We're still in Michael's bedroom. Moira is dressed again, having retrieved her clothes from the floor where they'd been discarded. I've returned her sword to her.

"I don't know," I reply. "To quote the famous Dr. Jones, 'I'm making this up as I go.'"

That elicits a little laugh. It's good to see her smile.

"Whatever we do," I say, "we have to be quick. Night's coming soon. Michael won't be trapped in the mansion after that. And mortals will start arriving."

"Chikah said that he would . . . 'be with Rebecca' for a while."

"And that means . . . ," I start to say, but something occurs to me, "That means the only one guarding the mansion right now is a single Chosen on watch in the Hall above!"

"Michael and Rebecca are occupied!" she says, clearly excited.

"If we can neutralize the Chosen . . . ," I begin.

"Then we'll have only Michael to deal with!" she finishes.

Together, we head toward the door with weapons at the ready. We hover above the floor so we can move silently. I take point as we move through the door and into the hallway.

The Unwilling

We pass Chikah's room, and then we pass Rebecca's room. Rebecca is screaming, and I hear the unmistakable sound of a whip and a horrible *squishing* sound. Even if it *is* Rebecca being tortured, it still makes me sick to think of what's going on in there.

But we need to neutralize the mortal Chosen first.

We emerge from the hallway into the Sanctuary. I've been here only once before, when I was Converted. The room's lit by a single brazier at the far end. The fuel burning in the brazier smells like vegetable oil. The smoke rises and exits through an opening in the center of the ceiling. (There's almost always smoke coming from one of the many chimneys of the mansion. I never understood why until now.) The walls look like they're roughhewn from the rock under the mansion, the same rock as the cave and the tunnel. Tapestries, covered with what appear to be runes of some type, hang at intervals on the walls. The altar in the center of the room is constructed from unhewn stones, just as the ancients made them. On the altar I can see an obsidian knife and a stone chalice. Four long tables are laid out around the room, one for each of the Chosen scheduled for Conversion tonight. This room is meant to look far more ancient than it actually is. Michael has lived in this city for decades, not centuries.

We float past the altar and out into the passage at the other end of the Sanctuary. The passage, which is wide and slopes steeply upward, leads to the Hall of the Chosen above. The passage isn't illuminated, except by light of the brazier below.

Good. The darkness will serve our needs.

With any luck, the Chosen on duty won't be particularly alert, and he or she *won't* be expecting trouble to come from *behind*, from the direction of the Sanctuary.

As we approach the door, I whisper to Moira in a quieter-than-mortal-ears-can-hear voice to tell her what I'm planning. She nods her understanding. I lower myself silently to the floor of the passage. I slip the dirk into my belt, but keep my sword in hand. Moira puts her sword into her belt. We want this to be bloodless. Or, at least, we want to avoid any *mortal* casualties.

Beyond this door lies the Hall of the Chosen. It's a long, large room, lit by candles and lined with sofas, love seats, and a few beds. There's also a gun case against one wall. It's filled with automatic weapons. I place my hand on the doorknob, take a deep, calming breath, and pull.

At this hour, the Hall is empty, except, of course, for the young woman, dressed all in black, standing a few feet in front of me, holding an AK-47. I recognize her at once as one of my fellow Chosen (from when I was a member of the Cult), but I don't remember her name. Right now, she's facing away from me. Before she can really glance back, I saunter past her. I can't see her, but I'm sure her eyes are following *me*, so I'm certain she hasn't noticed Moira.

"Hey," she says in a startled voice, "who the hell . . ."

Before she can complete her question, I hear the weapon being snatched from her hands. She cries out in surprise.

I wheel around to see her turning quickly to confront Moira, who has glided up behind her and disarmed her. That's exactly what I expected to see. What I did *not* expect is both the young woman and Moira gasp, looking at each other with mirrored looks of shock.

"Lucy!" Moira cries.

"It's *you*!" says the young woman (*Lucy?*) in apparent awe.

"Lucy!" Moira says again.

"You two *know* each other?" I ask.

"Aye," says Moira, clearly upset. "We do." To Lucy she says, pointing in my direction, "It's all right, lassie. He's with me. What're ye doing here, Lucy?"

"I'm to be *Converted* tonight!" Lucy says excitedly.

"Nae, lassie!" Moira says. "I took ye home to yer parents on Christmas Eve. 'Twas to be a *fresh start* for ye, a chance to get yer life back on track. Ye dinnae want *this*! This is nae life for *anyone*!"

"I *tried*, but my dad . . . He just never quit with the church crap. He just won't accept me the way I am! Besides, I want to be like *you*! I want to be *powerful* and *beautiful* and *free* to do whatever I want! And then no *man* will ever hurt me again!"

"Would somebody like to fill me in on what's going on?" I say in exasperation.

"Who's the *jerk*?" says Lucy, pointing back at me.

"That *man* is my *husband*," replies Moira in agitation.

"Just Persuade her and get her out of here, OK?" I say.

"I cannae Persuade her," Moira replies. "She's too strong willed. I rescued this lass from would-be rapists last year, on Christmas Eve. She's led a hard life born of very poor choices. I took her home to her parents and they took her in again. 'Twould seem she's left home once more and taken up with the Cult."

The Unwilling

To Lucy, Moira says, "Ye want power and freedom, lassie? Ye want to ne'er be hurt by a man again?" Moira's voice rises with her mounting anger. "Let me tell ye about what's happenin' to Rebecca right now! Michael is flayin' the flesh from her as we speak. If ye listen carefully, ye can hear her *screams*."

I can hear Rebecca's screams, but I'm not sure that *Lucy* can.

"So what?" replies Lucy angrily. "I *hate* Rebecca! She wouldn't give me the time of day! Too good for me! *Chikah* is my Teacher. She's the one who elevated me to Chosen! Chikah *believes* in me, like my father *never* did!"

"Chikah's dead," Moira says, her voice cold as ice.

"No!" cries the girl. "You're lying!"

"Nae, lassie. She's dead. And let me tell ye somethin'. Ye should *listen* to yer father. He *loves* ye. He *cares* about ye. Chikah *lied* to ye. She was *usin'* ye. She only wanted to see ye as *miserable* and as *wretched* as herself."

I've never seen Moira this angry. She's truly frightening.

She thunders on, "Would ye like to know how I hae spent the last *six hours*? I hae spent it stark naked, lyin' on Michael's bed, unable to move or to speak or even to *scream*, bound by Michael's bloody Master's command, helpless, waitin' to be *raped*! If nae for Carl, here, I would hae been! Ye'll only hae so much power as yer Master allows ye! Ye'll nae be *free*! Ye'll be his *slave*! That's what awaits ye . . . that and an eternity of darkness and damnation if ye dinnae repent! Go home, Lucy! And dinnae return to this awful place!"

Lucy has gone completely white, the blood drained from her face. She's paralyzed with fear.

"You'd better go," I say to the girl.

"*Now!*" says Moira, her green eyes blazing.

Lucy turns and runs. She sprints out of the Hall at full speed. I hear her fading footsteps pounding on the floorboards as she flees the mansion.

I turn to Moira. She still looks furious.

"Moira . . . ," I start to say.

"This ends *now*." Her tone is icy, filled with grim determination. "Today or tonight, but it *ends*. Alliance or nae alliance. Nae more corruption of the weak and the vulnerable. Nae more in my city." She pauses for a moment, collecting herself, and then says softly, "I thought I'd *saved* her."

"You *can't* save her," I say gently. "*Nobody* can, not even God, if she doesn't *want* to be saved." *Like Julie. And why did her name have to be "Lucy?" My sweet precious little girl!*

"'Like the sow to her wallowin' in the mire,'" she quotes bitterly.

"If anything, Moira, you've given her yet another chance."

"Aye. *If* she'll take it," she says softly. "Stupid lass."

And then we feel the rush of power that accompanies the setting of the Sun.

At the same time, Rebecca's screaming abruptly stops.

With the Chosen taken out of the equation, now I want to set a trap for Michael, and if we're going to do it, we have to act quickly. I figure we may have only *moments* to set it up.

"I have a plan," I say. "Follow me!"

I fly down the passage with my weapons ready in case we aren't quick enough to set up the snare. Moira follows with her sword drawn.

We're back in Michael's room. As it turns out, we had plenty of time. Michael has been shouting at Rebecca and only now do I hear her door slam shut. Moira is back on the bed, lying there, covered by a sheet. She has her sword in hand, but otherwise she's holding the same position as when she was bound by Michael's command.

She's the bait.

I'm waiting behind the door.

The plan is simple: Michael will enter, see Moira, and be distracted, and I'll come out from behind the door and put my dirk in his heart. Simple plans are the best. Fewer *variables*. Fewer things that can go wrong.

I can hear Michael approaching. From the heavy stomp of his footsteps, he sounds furious. If anything, his torturing of Rebecca hasn't cooled his anger; it has *stoked* it. His pounding footsteps are growing closer.

He throws open the door. "And now, my dear . . ."

I tense to strike, but then an unplanned *variable* appears.

Ben comes flying out of the ruined closet door. He sees Moira lying on the bed and then he sees Michael. He screams, "No, Massa Michael. Don't hurt Mama Moira!" He flies straight at his former Master.

Michael is knocked back into the corridor.

Ben beats furiously at Michael's face. I can hear bones breaking. But even while beating him, Ben pleads, "No, Massa Michael! I come back! I be yo' li'l niggah boy agin! I do anythin' ya wan'! I never go 'way no mo'! Jes' don't ya hurt Mama Moira!"

With a roar of shock and rage, Michael, hurls Ben against the wall. I hear a sickening *crunch* as Ben's head strikes the wall. Ben slumps to the floor. Michael draws his sword and raises it to behead the boy.

I block his stroke with my sword. Moira is beside me in an instant, her blade poised at the ready.

Michael's eyes go wide with raw terror at the sight of me. He knows he faces two armed *vampires*, not one helpless vampire and one foolish mortal.

So he turns and flies away, his wings beating furiously.

"Take care of Ben," I say, and then I'm flying after Michael.

I pursue him through the hall, through the Sanctuary, up the passage, through the Hall of the Chosen, and out into the Great Hall where the Cult is beginning to assemble. The mortals look up in awe. The Novitiates, at least, have never seen the wings. They've never seen a vampire *fly* before.

Michael doesn't slow down at all. He flies straight for the front door. He shoves aside a male Novitiate who was standing on the threshold, and then he flies out into the twilight.

I'm right behind him.

He rockets into the darkening sky, high above the city. He's able to accelerate before I can, because he was the first one out the door and into the open air. So the distance between us is nearly a hundred yards by the time I match his speed.

Michael looks back and, probably because he sees that there's only one vampire in pursuit, he wheels about and charges me with his sword. However, he hesitates and looks confused for a brief moment. *It's probably the fact that I'm flying without wings.* Once again, the image of a vampire flying wingless unnerves an opponent and gives me an opening.

I close the distance and strike at him with my broadsword.

He parries my blow.

And my opening is gone.

We fight in the air, steel against steel, high above the city, Michael, with his wings looking like an artist's depiction of Michael the Archangel, and me, with my slashed, tattered, bloodstained clothes looking more like a revenant or a zombie.

And he's good, much better than I expected.

We make several passes at each other. We thrust, slash, and parry, but neither of us lands any blows. We seem to be evenly matched.

Abruptly, he swoops away and tries to outfly me. *Good luck with that one, Bub!* Aerodynamics isn't really a factor here, but the laws of *physics* still apply. No matter how he moves, I stay on the inside of his turn or loop. As long as I'm able to match his rate of turn (and I do), I'm actually going faster, closing on him.

He can't get away.

Perfect.

So, I begin to chase him, always staying *below* him. I'm not really trying to *catch* him at this point. I just want to drive him higher and higher into the air. And higher and higher he goes, looping and turning as he tries to escape me.

Soon, I'm starting to feel a little dizzy due to the lack of oxygen in the thinning air. That means Michael must be getting hypoxic too. The glowing lights of the city are beginning to lose color. My head feels fuzzy.

So I pull my secret weapon from my pocket. This was in the package I ordered and had delivered while Moira and I were on our honeymoon, the package Moira and I went to my old house to retrieve last night, when we found Ben waiting for me. The package was from a civil aviation equipment supplier.

It's a small metal cylinder attached by a slender hose to a small, plastic, triangular-shaped mask, which is itself attached to a set of elastic straps. I slip the emergency aviation oxygen mask over my face and open the valve on the cylinder. I inhale the oxygen and, instantly, my head clears. The fuzziness is gone.

Michael continues to climb, and his loops and turns become more and more . . . lazy. It isn't hard at all to outmaneuver him.

And, in a moment, it's over. I catch up with him, and my sword, Donald MacDonald's claymore, skewers Michael Beaumont's heart. His wings vanish, and he looks at me in dazed surprise. I don't think he understands what's happening to him.

His saber falls from his limp hand. It tumbles and spins in the air below us.

I hope it doesn't hit some mortal. I risk a quick glance below, and I can see that we're high over a mostly uninhabited stretch of the hills north of the state capitol building. *Should be safe enough.*

I shove my dirk into my belt and catch Michael by the hair. Supporting his now dead weight with one hand, I keep my blade firmly planted in his foul heart.

I count off a hundred and twenty seconds in my head. I want to make sure he's gone.

Hitler's gone.

The pressure in my oxygen mask is diminishing. (It's designed to last for only a few minutes, and I've been breathing hard.) It's time to descend to where I can breathe without it.

By the time I return to the mansion, the sky is completely black except for the stars and the Moon. I have my sword in my belt and Michael's corpse slung over my shoulder like a sack of garbage as I land on the front lawn. There are about twenty Cultists gathered in a cluster, watching me. I walk right through them, and they part as they gape at Michael's carcass. A woman begins to sob. She's the housewife with three small children and a husband at home. Other women and a few of the men are crying as well. I walk through the front door and into the mansion. They follow.

I stride right up to the dais and toss Michael's body onto his throne. The corpse sits there sprawled in an unnatural pose like a broken doll, the head lolling back. His eyes are still open, but they're glazed over, and he appears to be staring at the crowd. *He looks like one of those "Living Dead" dolls.*

Just like Julie looked the night she was murdered.

Hitler's dead.

I'll have to deal with Stalin soon enough. For now though, I can cut her supply lines.

I turn to the Cultists who are pressing close enough to see, but not so close as to actually touch the dais. There's weeping and wailing (*and gnashing of teeth*). There's hand-wringing. There's shock and confusion. They look completely lost.

The three remaining Chosen (Lucy is not among them) are together in a group. One of them breaks away from the other two and starts to advance toward me. He looks scared. He also looks as if he's determined to confront me.

I laugh once: a harsh, barking sound. "What?" I say scornfully. "Are you going to *challenge* me? *Me?*" His face goes pale, and he backs away.

"And you!" I say, my voice rising. "The *rest* of you! What do you think you're doing here? You thought this was some sort of *game*? It's not a game! It's life and death and damnation! Look at your precious Master! He was a sick, perverted waste of flesh. He was a child rapist. He was a murderer many times over. He didn't *love* you! He didn't love *any* of you! He was *using* you! He was *Feeding* off you!"

To the three Chosen I say, "And *you* three! You really wanted to be like *him*? You were willing to *murder* other people so that *you* can have immortality? And for what? So you can never see the Sun again? How long do you think that would last? A century? Two? Most of his kind take their own lives after that. Endless sex and Feeding and murder get boring after a while, I'm told. You have to get more and more perverse in your endless quest for pleasure and even *that* won't satisfy you.

"And how many Chosen actually make it? Do you remember Julie Morgan? She was my sister. She's *dead*. Rebecca *killed* her. When was the last time a Chosen actually became a Teacher? Do *any* of you remember even *one*?"

The three of them stare back at me, their mouths agape. One of them shakes his head.

"So go home!" I continue, scanning the entire crowd of mortals. "Get back to your *real* lives. Go back to your husbands, your wives, your families and beg forgiveness. Go do something worth living . . ."

A scream stops me mid word.

Rebecca comes storming out from behind the dais. Her hair is wild, and her face is smeared with blood. Her clothes are in tatters. "Do you know wha' 'e *did* to me?" she screams, her Cockney undisguised. "He whipped me till there was no *flesh* on my back! Then he flayed the skin from my chest! 'E'd let me 'eal and then 'e'd do it *again*! And *again*! And *again*! If you 'ad just stuck with the *bloody* plan, *none* o' this would've 'appened. *I* would be the bloody Master and I'd 'ave my bloody consort and I'd be *free*!"

"Your consort!" I snort bitterly. "You never cared about that little boy."

Her face, already twisted in rage, now twists in a sneer of utter contempt and loathing. "That filthy lit'l black *bugger* . . . ," she begins.

"Rebecca," I say wearily, "shut up."

She stops abruptly. She opens her mouth to scream, but nothing comes out. Terror is plain in her eyes. She mouths the word, "No," over and over, but she's unable to make a sound. She stamps her foot in fury.

For a second, I don't understand what I'm seeing.

I get it! I'm *the Master now!*

Why? Because I killed Michael? Right now I don't care, so long as Rebecca stays quiet.

"Sit down and be quiet," I say to her.

She sits abruptly on the throne next to the one occupied by Michael's corpse. The look of abject horror on her face is . . . priceless.

The members of the Cult are staring alternately at her and at me. "Go home!" I say to them. "Go home and don't *ever* come back! Go to your bishop, your priest, your rabbi, your . . . whatever. But get some help!"

Some of them turn to go. Others just stand there looking lost. *Sheep without a shepherd. Sheep used to being herded by wolves.*

Moira enters from behind the dais. Ben is with her, holding her hand. He looks fine, fully recovered from the skull-cracking blow he took earlier. *Thank you, Father! They're both all right!* Moira gives me one of her dazzling smiles. Ben lets go of her hand and leaps into my arms. I hug him, and I say, "Ben, you're free! Michael's gone! He won't hurt you anymore! You're finally *free!*"

"Really?" He looks at me in wonder. Then he sees Michael's body and he stiffens.

"It's OK, Ben. He's dead."

"Did you *kill* him, Papa Carl?"

"Yeah. I did."

He starts to cry and he puts his face to my shoulder. I guess his feelings for Michael were . . . *complicated.* "Are you sad?" I ask him.

He shakes his head, but he says nothing, and he continues to cry softly.

Moira joins us. She puts one arm around me and one around Ben. She kisses me briefly but tenderly, and then she kisses Ben on the cheek.

We hug like that for a minute, and then I become aware of the Cult again. There are a number of them still here.

I put Ben down and turn to face the Cult members. Ben puts his little hand in mine. I squeeze it gently.

"Go home!" I say to the remaining mortals. "Go home and *never* come back. This Cult is *dissolved.*"

And, the instant I say it, I know I've made a terrible *mistake.*

I see a flash of movement behind me, but I react too slowly.

Rebecca pulls my dirk from my belt. I draw my sword, but it's like I'm trying to run in a nightmare. I just can't move fast enough.

With a flash of steel, I see the dirk slash, not toward me, but toward . . .

Ben's head rolls across the dais, his body collapses, his limp hand still in mine, and blood is everywhere.

I slash with my sword and take off Rebecca's arm just below the elbow. She barely has time to begin a cry of rage and pain before my next stroke takes off her head.

Moira's howl of anguish spins me around. She's kneeling on the floor, cradling Ben's bloody head in her arms. His lips move soundlessly. His eyes stare at her intently.

"Aye, laddie," she sobs, her tears falling on Ben's face, "I love ye too. Papa loves ye. Ye're going to be with God, now. Jesus will . . . make ye into . . . a *real boy.*"

I kneel by her side, and I touch Ben's cheek. His eyes glance in my direction. His lips move. *I love you, Papa Carl,* he mouths silently.

"I love you, too, Ben."

He smiles at me.

His eyes begin to glaze over. His smile goes slack.

He's gone.

Moira rocks the lifeless head back and forth. She looks like a lost little girl cradling a cherished broken doll.

She sobs, "When we did nae return by sunset, he came to help us. He came to *rescue* us."

I'm sobbing now too. I wrap my arms around her shoulders. "He had one happy day, Moira. That's more than he had in his long, miserable life. Now he's truly happy. And we'll . . . see him again . . . someday."

She sobs inconsolably. "My bairn! My poor wee bairn!"

Gradually, I become aware that the room is empty. All the Cult members have fled. We are alone with our grief in this vile place, surrounded by the corpses of dead vampires.

Chapter 27

We dispose of Michael and Rebecca in the tunnel's charnel pit. Let the rats have them.

After we retrieve our coats and other protective clothing and Ben's treasured possessions from the tunnel, we collapse the entrance and the exit to the tunnel, sealing the corpses in. It isn't hard to do. Tactile telekinesis allows our swords to cut into the rock of the tunnel. A few well-placed blows, and the roof collapses.

Moira and I bury Ben high in the mountains where no one will disturb him. We put his beloved DVDs and DVD player in the ground with him. I mark the spot with a stone. With my dirk, I carve, "Ben – Beloved Son – Real Boy." I dedicate the grave. Ben was the only child we'll ever have together and he was the only child Moira will ever have. We knew him, *really* knew him for so short a time, but it was impossible not to love him. We can't stay here with him for long right now, but we'll think of him often. We could never forget him.

We can't linger at the grave because we need to meet someone.

So here we are, sitting on the roof of the mansion waiting for him to appear. I figure he'll arrive about midnight. Maybe a little before. Maybe a little after.

The original plan I laid out with Rebecca and Ben called for me to arrive shortly before midnight, when the Conversion Ritual was to begin. So he should be arriving just after I was supposed to. Or maybe before. I wasn't supposed to know he was going to be here, of course.

About eleven o'clock, we see him approaching. His white wings make him easy to spot against the night sky.

I stand and wave to him from the roof. He spies me and swoops toward us. Alighting nearby on the roof, he draws his sword as his wings fold up and disappear. The sword looks like something from one of those Asian gift stores in the mall: shiny and ornate. It's probably made of stainless steel, which is too brittle for any serious weapon. I suppose it doesn't matter, though: it's not the strength of a vampire's *blade* that's important, but rather the strength of the *mind* that wields it.

"Hello, Detective Johnson," I say. "You can put that away. I don't want to fight you."

Johnson stays put and holds his sword at an awkward sort of ready position. He eyes me as you would a rattlesnake or a tarantula.

"You don't even know how to hold that thing properly," I say quietly. "Rebecca didn't have time to train you. I'll bet you're here primarily to intimidate me. You're supposed to convince me that I'm outnumbered so I'll submit or run away when I see you, Rebecca, and Ben"—*my voice breaks*—"Benjamin standing together."

Johnson says nothing.

"Rebecca's dead," I continue. "So is Ben . . . Benjamin."

Beside me, Moira's breathing hitches with grief.

"They're *all* dead," I say.

He lowers the sword. He bows his head and stands still for a moment.

"How . . ." He clears his throat. "How did you know?"

"I didn't put it all together until tonight after . . . well, I didn't put it all together until tonight," I respond. "Rebecca let something slip. She said something about her 'consort.' She used to call . . . Benjamin that, too . . . for a while. But, Ben . . ." *I refuse to call him 'Benjamin' again.* "But, Ben told me that Rebecca had started treating him badly again. My guess is the change would've happened about the time of *your* Conversion. She didn't need *him* anymore; she had *you*."

Since Johnson remains silent, I continue, "Rebecca executed Ben tonight. She *murdered* Ben . . . Ben, who never took a human life, who was a victim of vicious, evil monsters his entire miserable, long, long existence. She cut off his head . . . just to hurt *me*. She murdered my sister just so she could . . . maintain a balance of power in the Cult. Underneath this mansion there's a pit filled with the corpses of hundreds of the victims of the vampires in the Cult."

I point down at the mansion beneath our feet. "Why in the world would you *want* to become one of these monsters?"

Johnson's body sags, and he falls to his knees. He turns around and sits facing down the sloping roof, away from me. His sword is resting in his lap. His head is bowed. He's silent for a minute or so.

He clears his throat. "I wanted to *stop* monsters like Roger." *He means Hadley.* "I felt so *impotent*! Roger killed my brother. *You* caught him. *You* knew what he was. *You* stopped him."

"Hadley was your Offering, wasn't he?" I say.

"No." He swallows hard. "He wasn't."

I look at him in surprise.

Moira lays a hand on my arm and says softly, "Rebecca would have selected an *innocent*."

Johnson looks over his shoulder at her and he looks angry. "She was hardly an innocent. She was a *hooker*."

"And for *that* she deserved to die?" Moira demands.

Johnson opens his mouth and then shuts it. He hangs his head. "No."

"So ye became a *murderer* in order to *stop* murderers?" she demands.

"Roger killed my family." His voice is soft, but urgently pleading for understanding.

"*Rebecca* murdered your family," I say.

He looks over at me.

"Oh, I'm sure Hadley was *there*. Rebecca broke him out of jail. She wanted you to *believe* Hadley killed them, but there's no way she would waste all that blood."

He hangs his head again and starts to sob.

"As you investigated me," I say, "you found out about my association with the Cult. You sought them out. You found Rebecca. Or Rebecca found you."

He nods, still weeping.

"She seduced you with promises of power . . . of vengeance," I continue. "You convinced yourself that what you were doing was for the 'greater good,' that your intentions were noble. You became a *monster* because you thought it was the only way to *stop* monsters."

He nods again, dabbing at his eyes.

"You did kill Hadley, though, right?" I ask.

"Yeah, I did," he says softly.

"Didn't make you feel better, did it?"

He starts to speak, but stops. Then he shakes his head.

"Vengeance is a cancer on the soul," Moira says quietly.

"You're Catholic, aren't you?" I ask him.

He laughs bitterly. "Lapsed."

"Go to your priest," I say. "Or go to a Mormon bishop. Only God can help you now."

He says nothing.

"You're going to have to Feed to survive," I say, "so, if you take blood from criminals, don't kill them. Just know this: if you kill *anyone* else, I *will* hunt you down and stop you. You have my *word* on that."

He looks at me again from over his shoulder, there's fire in his eyes. "Who are *you* to judge *me?*" he says defiantly.

"I am . . . the *Unwilling*. I did not choose this . . . existence. I have killed in war. I've executed monsters that were beyond the reach of mortal justice, but I have *never* taken a mortal life to sustain my existence.

"Moira and I are going to bring down Lilith. I don't know how, but we're going to do it . . . someday."

"The Curse," he says.

"Aye," Moira replies. "'The Unwilling and the Penitent.'"

He hangs his head again. Then he lays his sword down on the roof. It slides away down the slope. He makes no move to catch it. It disappears over the edge. We hear it thud to the ground below.

He turns around and kneels. He lowers his head. "Please," he says, his voice broken, "*kill* me. I've killed since Roger. They were all . . . evil, but I *have* killed."

I stand up, and I give Moira my hand to help her to her feet. We stand together, hand-in-hand, looking down at Johnson.

"Not tonight," I say. "There's been enough death tonight.

"Stop killing," I continue. "Go to your priest or to a Mormon bishop. Pray. Lean on God. I believe you *can* find your way back. Atone for your sins as best you can. Put your trust in the Savior to take care of the rest. It's the only way you can ever find redemption."

Together, Moira and I rise off the roof and into the air. As we depart, I say, "Do it. Because, after tonight, if you kill again, I *will* hunt you down."

Chapter 28

Aftermath

The next morning, the mansion burned to the ground. Moira and I didn't hear about it until several days later. We were sitting on the sofa, sipping blood, watching the evening news. Arson investigators had determined that the fire started on the roof of the house shortly after sunrise. They also found one charred body amid the ruins. Dental records identified the body as that of Davis County Sheriff's Detective Daniel Johnson.

I was very sad to learn of his death.

"He gave in to despair." I set my empty glass on the coffee table.

"He was a Penitent," Moira replied. "And like every other Penitent in all the long history of the Children of Lilith, he took his own life."

"Every other Penitent . . . except *you*, my love."

"Aye." She put her glass down and snuggled closer to me on the couch. "I have everything to *live* for. I have everything I ever wanted."

Everything, except a child, I thought.

I kiss her on the top of her head and hold her close.

"I called Bishop Adams today," she said. "He said there would be some *obstacles*, what with nae birth record or other documentation, but he said he would help us process the petition. He called back later to say that he'd spoken to someone on the 'hotline' (whate'er that may be). He said he talked to one of the *Twelve*! And he said he was *assured* that the petition *will* be granted. We just have to wait a year."

"What petition? What are you talking about?" I asked.

"Why, to have Ben sealed to us in the temple, ye ninny! And to do his baptism, of course!"

I chuckled softly. *Trust Moira to look at things with an eternal perspective,* I thought.

"And, now," she said with a twinkle in her lovely green eyes, "I *finally* get to say the words to my *own husband* that I have said so many times to *other* men."

"And what would that be?"

She grinned wide and kissed me. "Congratulations, Mr. Morgan! 'Tis a *boy*!"

A real *boy*, I thought.

Acknowledgements

I would like to thank all those who assisted me with this work. Cindy Belt, Rachel Belt, Jacob Belt, Bryan Belt, Jeremiah Belt, and Beth Bentley provided enormous help with proofreading, critiquing, and editing. Bryan Belt assisted with medical research. Dr. Daniel Sellers provided information on sunlight allergies. Hal Romrell provided expertise on doctrine and church procedures. Dr. Eric Huntsman assisted with the Latin translation. Chris Belt and Randy Lythgoe ensured the accurate depiction of law enforcement procedures. Mable Belt, David Belt (my father, not me), and Olya Polazhynets (who was actually born and raised near Transylvania) supplied encouragement and enthusiasm. Beth and George Bentley gave this bizarre concept a chance.

To all of you, I wish to express my heartfelt gratitude.

Author's Note

This is a work of fiction. This is *not* a definitive statement on the doctrines of my faith, nor of absolute truth, nor of history. I have been working on the concept of this novel for a decade. Although I enjoy some pure fantasy, I have great trouble *writing* it. Things have to make *sense* in my head. They have to be *possible* within the realm of what I know or believe to be the truth. This is especially true if a story is set in the real world.

The doctrines of my faith figure prominently in this novel. I make no apology for writing from the premise that what I believe to be true is, in fact, *true*. If you are not of my faith, I hope you can enjoy this work with the understanding that it is set in a world where the doctrines of my faith *are* the truth. I believe them to be true. You are free to believe such a world is fantasy.

If you *are* of my faith, please understand that I believe real evil exists in the world. While I've tried not to be overly graphic in my descriptions and depictions of evil, at the same time, I believe evil must be represented for us to understand the nature of what *good* truly is. We must know the bitter to appreciate the sweet.

This story encompasses serious themes and topics, but, ultimately, I just wanted to tell a good story. I hope you enjoy it.

C. David Belt
July, 2011
http://unwillingchild.wordpress.com/2011/07/12/the-unwilling-child
unwillingchild@comcast.net

About the Author

C David Belt was born in Evanston, Wyoming. As a child, he lived and traveled extensively around the Far East. He served as an LDS missionary in South Korea and southern California (Korean-speaking). He graduated from Brigham Young University with a Bachelor of Science in Computer Science and a minor in Aerospace Studies. He served as a B-52 pilot in the US Air Force and as an Air Weapons Controller in the Washington Air National Guard. When he is not writing, he sings in the Mormon Tabernacle Choir and works as a software engineer. He collects swords (mostly Scottish), axes, spears, and other medieval weapons and armor. He and his wife have six children and live in Utah with an eclectus parrot named Mork (who likes to jump on the keyboard when David is writing).

CPSIA information can be obtained
at www.ICGtesting.com
Printed in the USA
FSOW01n0541180417
33169FS